LEGENDS OF AVERON:
THE KNIGHTS OF EVERUND

T.J. HARMONING

Illustrations by T.J. Harmoning
Book Cover by T.J. Harmoning

Imprint: Independently Published

Printed in the United States of America
Typeset: EB Garamond
First Edition, 2024

www.LegendsofAveron.com

For Lola

Thank you for reminding me
our gifts are meant to be used,
sorry I learned too late for you
to see what I did with mine.

Dark Awakening

White-tipped mountains of jagged, black stone rose sharply into the sky, piercing the veil of stars that hung upon their peaks. The southern spine of the Mountains of Eld howled with frigid winds scraping through the twisted passes of the Drakkar Gorrundt. A man hooded by a regal cloak trudged through the crooked paths of what remained of the fallen kingdom of Duscar. The gale of the wind and the crunch of snow under his embroidered cloth boots were the only sounds that broke the chilling stillness of the tomb-like gloom that hung over the ruins.

His attire was that of a lordly wizard with no worldly business traveling through the lands of Duscar, which were now little more than a graveyard. No mage had trespassed in those long-forbidden lands since the war that nearly destroyed the world. He was far from his homeland; the crimson cloak he wore bore the dawn of creation symbol of the kingdom of Everund.

The mage found himself crossing cursed ground that no soul dared disturb in over a century. The dragon-forged city loomed menacingly across the mountaintops with its high walls and cathedral-like architecture. The castle city's ornate designs survived a century of the elements but they seemed to be of little relevance to the wizard approaching the dead city.

The man clutched a strange book to his chest that was made of flesh and branded with symbols of some unknowable language. His blistered lips quivered with madness as cruel mutterings escaped from behind his tongue.

"Born of blood from dragon lent, cursed with shadow his soul be rent."

The ruins were forbidden for good reason, not just because it was a mass grave for the unburied warriors of Duscar and Magi of Aeris-Terran, but also for the danger the mountains themselves posed. The passes through the Eld Ridge Mountains were perilous, especially dressed as lightly as Lord Dilandau Ravendark of Everund was. No one of sound mind would enter those forsaken lands and Dilandau was certainly not in his right mind.

Voices whispered to him, though he could not tell where they came from. He ambled in a trance, stepping over frozen bodies of fallen soldiers and the remains of dragons buried in snow which went unnoticed. He tilted his head oddly to the side, listening to the voices while staring into the vast emptiness around him. His clouded eyes rolled uncomfortably independent of one another.

The vessel is not far. He heard the book say, followed by innumerable voices in the back of his mind speaking in unison.

'Find him!' the voices repeated the command over and over, urging Dilandau on. His ragged breathing created wisps of vapor as he mouthed along to their whispers. When they stopped his mouth hung open awkwardly, his black beard full of ice. Ravendark secured the book to his waist and groped through the mounds of snow in a desperate search for the object of his fevered mind's obsession.

Fear, more than the bitter cold, made his hands shake, but that did not stop him from clawing through the snow in search of the corpse of the Duscan sorcerer for whom the voices hungered. He felt their malevolent presences at the edges of his deranged mind, biting at him in the dark in horrifying excitement.

After several minutes of feverish digging, Dilandau happened upon the remnant of a crescent moon-shaped pavilion a short distance away from the main gates of Duscar. The roof of the small structure was burned away and the rest buried in snow, but even with his blurred sight he recognized the distinct damage inflicted by magically conjured flame. His bare hands trembled as he dug deeper through the snow, touching at last what he had come so far to find. The voices inside his mind cried out with hideous joy. He stopped clawing, then stood slowly, stepping backward, readying a spell.

His hands formed the sigils for conjuration, drawing unseen symbols through the air around him before uttering a single word which ignited the spell like a spark catching tinder. The wizard's palms glowed with the heat and radiance of the sun. Blinding light reflected off the snow and waned as the frost melted. Ravendark's spell revealed the area down to the very stones of the mountain.

Water rushed around his boots as he waved away the spell and the weariness of its effort sank in. Much of the pavilion was marred and the corpse at its center, which was chained to the floor, had been burned alive. It was evident that the damage was not caused by dragon's breath, for if it was, there would be no corpse left behind. The hellish flames that dragons spat turned bodies to ash and stone to molten glass.

Open the book. The command was sharp and threatening. Lord Ravendark was in no state to resist the compulsion as his mind was already enthralled by the power of the ancient grimoire. He lifted the book from his hip and pulled open its thick pages carved with symbols older than the mountains he stood upon. The crazed wizard held the book over the corpse, whose mouth hung open in a defiant final scream that could no longer be heard.

Dilandau did not know which spell to search for, but the pages of the book turned on their own until they rested upon a complicated ritual. He could not understand the arcanum within, nor comprehend the unfathomable dark magic on his own, so the insidious presence within the book steered him through it.

Dark magic, such as he was using, had always been forbidden. Its secrets were sought out and destroyed in order to prevent them from falling into the wrong hands. But even a dark artifact hunter trained to deal with curses and other malicious spellwork - such as Dilandau was - could not handle the power contained within the pages of this baleful tome. While under the instruction of the evil emanating from the book, Dilandau dug arcane sigils into the ground in a large circle around the remains of one of the world's most feared sorcerers.

His mind fought against its demands to no avail. The mage struggled in vain to regain control of his limbs but he could not stop them from finishing the terrible acts that they were perpetrating. Black clouds formed overhead as the mad wizard uttered the blasphemous words of a spell that would bring Ir'zane, the Paragon of Duscar, back to life after a hundred years of slumbering death.

Dilandau stood on shaky legs over the Duscan sorcerer, his body bitten through by cold and weakened by hours of labor that had all but drained his body of vital energy. He tapped into the pool of energy which was his life essence, his mana as the Magi called it. There was much less than usual due to his weariness, but without concern for his well-being he emptied his mana into the spell, which consumed it at an alarming rate.

The sun fell as the hours of day dragged on and it began turning red, a sanguine omen of ill portent. Dark magic flowed through Dilandau's body, activating the sigils along the ground while dark magic swirled around Ir'zane's dead body. The eldritch symbols glowed with a sickly green color while the clouds overhead blotted out what little light was escaping through the overcast sky. The unholy spellwork shook the mountain top as a hole in reality tore open just above Ravendark and the corpse at his feet.

Bright green energy glowed through the torn sky as winds wailed and whipped at his clothes, throwing back his hood and tussling his salt-and-pepper streaked sable hair. The vile book that Ravendark's bruised and frostbitten hands clasped shouted through his mind, *Finish it.* Dilandau could feel its furor to complete the ritual with its grip on him waning. His body was succumbing to fatigue but his will was growing stronger.

But even so it was too late, the spell had ripped a hole into the endless void beyond where Ir'zane's cursed soul was bound. Though he struggled to break through the haze and madness of the voices that assailed him, his efforts to regain control of his mind were futile. Unable to take back control, his shaky hands involuntarily drew a dagger from inside his robes with which he cut open his left palm.

He held his bleeding hand over the silently screaming corpse and let his crimson essence drip into its open mouth. Tendrils of blood magic encircled the bones of the burned remains of the Duscan, whose corpse started twitching. The possessed mage raised his arms into the air, rhythmically chanting a phrase in an incomprehensible language of infernal blasphemies which empowered the spell that he was evoking.

Green lightning crashed over the macabre scene as a concentration of evil magic surged into the decayed body of Ir'zane. With a horrific scream the corpse came back to life as the soul of the Duscan sorcerer returned to his long dead body. Ir'zane erupted in green flames which sent a shockwave of dark energy bursting outward, pushing Dilandau away from him. Huge flocks of birds took flight in the forests below and other wildlife fled from the evil emanating from the Mountains of Eld.

The old wizard stumbled backward, tripping on his robes. He lost grip on the Book of Souls and inadvertently threw it, flailing helplessly as he fell. The book landed at Ir'zane's feet as Dilandau hit the stone slope hard enough to knock the breath out of him. The storms overhead cleared slowly as the Duscan corpse stood on its own. The unholy green flames died down except two remaining embers for eyes, which burned in the empty sockets of its skull. Ir'zane raised his dead hands to his "eyes" and turned them over.

He saw dead flesh and panicked, groping about his chest to feel his exposed ribcage and the hollowness of his corpse body. Ir'zane realized that his heart was not beating, because it rested perfectly still inside his chest cavity, shriveled and gray. He had no lungs left to breathe the frigid air that whirled in the growing silence. His exposed flesh felt none of the deadly cold, as his nerves had decayed away ages ago.

Dilandau struggled to get back up since his body was weak and frostbitten. He saw with clouded eyes the result of the book's machinations, as the infamous dragon-blooded sorcerer Ir'zane stood before him. The undead sorcerer became aware of the wizard from Everund, and upon seeing the clothes he wore, Ir'zane's mind went back to the moments just before his death. He saw the Magi he once called friends, surrounding him, burning him to death with their magical fire. Ir'zane closed the gap between them, his skeletal fingers furiously wrapped around the wizard's neck, constricting his windpipe so he could not utter incantations.

With one arm Ir'zane lifted the frail wizard off the ground as he choked him. He looked Dilandau over while he held him but he did not recognize the wizard's face, nor the symbols that he wore.

"You are not Magi," he spoke in an old dialect that was, though not with breath or vocal cord but by some unnatural means of twisted magic. Ir'zane grabbed the wheezing wizard's cloak and looked long and hard at the crest it bore and was unable to identify it, despite knowing all the symbols worn by the Magi of Aeris-Terran.

The crest on Ravendark's cloak was a cross of equal-length bars with four red gems embedded within the rounded ends. It was encircled by an outer ring, which sat under each bar of the cross. Spikes from the middle pierced beyond the circle, and the entire symbol resembled a simple drawing of the sun.

Lord Ravendark gasped for air and feebly resisted, unable to free himself from the impressive strength that Ir'zane seemed to possess even in death. For a moment the Duscan sorcerer considered what to do with him, and out of the corner of his sight he saw the edge of cliffs nearby. He smirked with what remained of his mouth and walked toward the edge, carrying the weakened wizard with him. Dilandau gripped at the dead arm that held him prisoner as the cloudiness in his eyes lifted.

The power of the book over him was fading with distance from it. He gurgled, trying to speak, begging for his life, but his pleas went unheeded as Ir'zane stepped to the edge and held the wizard over it. Dilandau's natural blue color returned to his eyes, which immediately went wide with terror as he realized that a vast nothingness was below his feet.

What remained of Ir'zane's burned and decayed face twisted into a smile at the light returning to Dilandau's eyes and at seeing the pleading look in them. He spoke in his native Duscan language, a human dialect of Draconic, "Bol ulghur, magus," and with that, Ir'zane released his grip on Dilandau's throat, throwing him off the cliff's edge. The old wizard screamed as he fell down the mountainside, vanishing through clouds of mist coalescing around the peaks. Ir'zane stood for a moment, listening to the wizard's fading wails until silence fell over the ruins of his forsaken homeland. Turning away, he stared at the spot where his body was exhumed and the memory of his death came back to him once more.

He thought to himself how strange it was that a single mage stayed behind, and wondered if their army retreated or had been defeated. Or had he come back here alone? He looked around, searching the landscape for signs of more Magi, but he saw no one. He saw no threat of any kind, anywhere. Searching around the ruins he saw no sign of fellow Duscans either. Nor did he see or feel the presence of any dragons around, which marked the first time in his entire life that Ir'zane did not feel their oppressive will upon his mind. He could not feel their thoughts invading his, or the boiling rage of his blood which now rested, coagulated in dead veins. There was no sign of the war anywhere, only the aftermath of it sticking out of the snow.

Though he did not find any of his people or his enemies, he did find a book lying open in the snow not far from where he stood. It was likely the spellbook of the mage he threw off the mountainside, he figured, but he did not have to get much closer before realizing it was no book that any mage in Aeris-Terran would have been able to create. It was old and bound with skin, covered in infernal runes carved into the flesh.

The symbols were unlike anything that any scholar or mage would have known. He approached it cautiously and heard strange whispers inside his head that made him look around as though he expected to see himself suddenly surrounded by people, but again he saw nothing. His burning eyes delighted as they beheld what he assumed to be the infamous Book of Souls spoken of in myths by those who move in dark circles, guessing correctly at its origins.

All his life he searched for the kind of power contained within the book's pages. For the knowledge that was kept from him, the forbidden knowledge of life and death. The one thing he hoped to find, left behind long ago in ages past by a powerful necromancer. He readied himself to open it, for such an artifact would likely be cursed to keep the information within from being used by anyone other than its creator. Ir'zane reached his fingers into his own shadow, grabbing hold of it like it was a thick, sticky liquid, and pulled a ball of pure darkness from it which stuck between his corpse fingers.

With a flick of his wrist the ball of shadow burst into smoke, which enveloped his body in a shroud of darkness like armor. Thoroughly protected by his umbramancy, he turned his attention back to the strange book. He shielded his mind with another quick cast, this time a defensive abjuration spell that would bolster his resistance to compulsions, and only then did he approach and lift the grimoire from the snow.

Just as he suspected, the book attacked him psychically as soon as he touched it. Thousands of voices screaming in unison assaulted his mind, trying to break his sanity. The icy winds which flowed off the mountain peaks whistled as they flew through the hollow parts of his decayed body, yet he felt nothing and noticed them not, for he was fighting to push the voices from his mind. The embers of green flame which burned in the empty eye sockets of his skull flickered as he struggled to gain control over the voices.

He heard something inside all of their insane babbling, something hidden amongst the different screams of the damned. A word repeated within the chaos but he shut his mind off from it and took control of the book, successfully dominating the will of the damned that were trapped within the pages of the grimoire. All of its dark secrets were now his for the taking and his mind raced with terrible dreams of vengeance.

Ir'zane held the book in front of him, letting his shadow armor spell fade since he no longer required its protection. He walked absentmindedly through the snow towards the cathedral-like castle he once called home but he did not look up from his acquisition, too enraptured by its contents, so he walked by memory alone. He had no need to watch where he went as he passed through the dangerous terrain which anyone not native to the Dragonlands would need to be cautious as they traversed its treacherous paths so as not to fall to their death.

All Duscan children roughhoused across the peaks of the Eld Ridge Mountains, and his feet knew the rocks below the layers of snow and ice like old friends. He recalled the memories of the paths through the mountains as well as the features of his mother's face. But he was not thinking of his homeland or his mother now. His mind was focused on the Book of Souls, which he surmised brought him back from the dead by the hand of that pompous aristocrat he threw off the mountain. He wondered how such a weak wizard could wield the dark magic contained within its pages? How could he have read the archaic sigils, the arcane symbols so old and unknowable that even Ir'zane struggled to decipher.

There was no way for such a man to understand the depraved mind that crafted this collection of grim power. No, it had to be something else, someone else. It was then that the whispers which had driven Dilandau mad reached out to the Duscan sorcerer.

Open us, he heard as they entered his mind, *Look within.* The voices continued as he studied the book's cover, *we have the answers you seek.* They called out to him. He could feel the impatience behind their insistence. He placed his dead hand over the symbols carved into the surface of the book and smirked.

"You are no book at all. Inside these pages is far more than just knowledge."

The wizard was not controlling the power of the book; the weak-minded fool did not use its knowledge to return him from the dead. There were souls trapped within the pages of the book and they had a will of their own. It was that will which had driven the wizard into these hallowed grounds. It was the will of the dark tome that he be brought back to life. The book did not happen to fall into his possession at all, it had sought him out and he was eager to learn why.

Ir'zane cast several more warding spells around himself, weaving them with darkness since he learned long ago, he could cheat the cost of spellweaving by drawing on shadows as a way to extend his sorcery. Their latent power was always around, for wherever there was light, there was also darkness. He honed his power over the shadow in secret away from the prying eyes of the mage council of Aeris-Terran, for they had previously thwarted his every attempt to learn magic they deemed too dangerous for anyone to know.

They would have excommunicated him from their ranks and thrown him from the city towers if they had known that he mastered umbramancy. It was fortunate for him that he had, because it allowed him to fuel his spellcasting in death in lieu of having no living essence to draw from. His resurrection was a gift no doubt, a second chance to finish what he was not able to in life. The book of the damned contained more gifts in the spells he would tear from its pages.

Ir'zane cleared his mind and focused to prevent it from being led astray by whispers and illusions before opening the cover. The diagrams and text were foreign to him. They were written in a much older form of magical language than what he was trained to read. The sigils were difficult to decipher, but they were not entirely unreadable by him. He turned its heavy pages while the innumerable voices whispered at the back of his mind. After thumbing through several of the thick pages, he came across the ritual that must have brought him back, an elaborate soul-binding technique which could reunite a severed soul with its original body.

He read how it worked, how it wove the dead body with magic that linked it to the realm beyond. The soul was attached in such a way that if the body were damaged enough to sever that link, the soul would become detached from the body like a boat cut from its anchor, drifting back into the ethereal nothingness beyond. He turned more pages, looking through many ways of crafting dark artifacts from body parts, or ways to augment physical strength and gain new abilities through flesh carving, but he stopped when he saw another type of resurrection spell.

The book seemed to contain many methods of creating undead monstrosities, and this particular spell was designed to make revenant. Vengeful dead bound to the will of the one who raised them, they would retain their memories and intelligence from life but have no free will of their own. They would be nigh indestructible, feeling no fear or pain, and they would never tire in their pursuit for vengeance. Once cursed, it would not be easy to sever the spell that animated their fury. Ir'zane's twisted mind quickly put together a plan, and he marked the page in the book before shutting it. He took off through the snow in search of a body of one of his fallen kin, a Duscan warrior to test the spell upon.

While he searched for a suitable warrior to raise from the dead, what he found was so much better. Not far from where Ir'zane was burned to death, he found the former king of Duscar half-buried in the snow, pinned to a rock by four spears. Ir'zane stood over the final resting place of the mighty Viranas, who had no equal in combat, which according to Duscan custom made him king.

The sorcerer opened the Book of Souls to the page for revenant while gathering shadows in his other hand to power the spell. Ir'zane put his hand on Viranas' head, chanting the dark magic as it was written, and green flames fused the king's crown to his skull as he burned the curse of the revenant into it.

The fallen king's eyes glowed with unholy green fire as he roared back to life. Ir'zane took a step back as Viranas' body thrashed against the spears which pinned him, as the spell took hold it bound the king's soul to his corpse. Viranas became aware of his memories and personality returning, before pulling the spears out of his body one by one slowly freeing himself. The loyal revenant then knelt before Ir'zane, who smiled darkly before saying, "First a king. Next, an army!"

Ravendark's Fall

Dilandau Ravendark of Everund found himself tumbling through the sky as his complete awareness snapped back to him. The world was coming up to meet him rapidly as the grip the cursed book had upon his mind fully released. The cold wind bit hard into his eyes, making it nearly impossible to see as the weary wizard plummeted. Panic took his breath away and his mind raced for something to save himself from the certain death that was coming into view through the haze of his watery eyes.

The wizard tried to focus and control his breathing, but found it difficult to gain his composure as he fell. The heavy red cloak he wore twisted around his body as he tumbled, which made it hard to use his arms and hands to perform the necessary motions to create the magical portal he was attempting to cast. Dilandau drew the sigils in his mind instead, as the ground rapidly approached. He barely finished the spell in time, opening a portal just above the rocks below, mere moments before plummeting through it.

~

Far away from the Eld Ridge Mountains, on the outskirts of the southern kingdom of Therred, a young man sat on the porch railing of the Blackwood Manor. The manor itself laid at the edge of the small farming village of Dellow. He held a book open with one hand, his finger tracing the pages as he read by the orange glow of the lantern at his side, whose incandescence was like bottled daylight.

His azure eyes were like cats' eyes in the twilight, hungrily eating up the words written in his favorite bestiary of magical creatures. He ran his fingers through his fire-colored hair while his brow furled in concentration. He looked as though he were trying to piece together something, some ghost of an idea haunting his mind. Whatever it was he was trying to figure out, it did not keep his focus for long.

The last light of day was slipping away as he slumped against the exterior of the manor. The edge of the sunset kissed the horizon, and its golden rays shone over the rim of the world. The sight of it was beautiful enough to pull his attention away from the ideas that were now closing in his hand. Watching the sun turn red as it disappeared beyond his view, he wondered about the nature of the universe he lived in. His mind drifted away from the world of Averon, past the star it circled and through the limitless dark of the Infinite beyond. The size of it was overwhelming, and he felt so small compared to the vastness of it, such that for a moment it was as though he did not exist at all.

The young man's moment of blissful revelry came to a sudden halt when the front door of the manor flew open and Rowan Blackwood, Locke's uncle and Lord of Blackwood Manor, stepped through shouting his name. Locke jumped so suddenly from being startled that he dropped the book he was reading on the porch and nearly went over the railing himself. "Yavon's beard, Rowan!" he exclaimed, before catching himself from falling. Rowan scowled, his horse brush eyebrows almost covering his shrewd eyes.

"Mind your words, boy," he said in that familiar fatherly tone. "And just what are you doing out here lazing about? I asked you to have those horses in the stables before dinner."

Locke casually moved his foot to hide the book from his uncle's sight so Rowan would not know that he was reading one of the off-limits books from his private library. "And I was about to! I wasn't ready to come in just yet, and that's why I haven't done it."

Rowan crossed his arms.

"We're losing daylight! Bring them in before it gets completely dark, then come in and wash up."

Locke's boisterous uncle disappeared back inside, shutting the door firmly behind him. Locke sighed in relief and picked up the book which was splayed out on the ground. He closed it with care, and set it on the seat of the rocking chair resting which rested in the corner of the deck. He mused about how much he disliked that the sun set so early in autumn and thought about how it would only get worse as winter settled in.

He grabbed the lantern from the rail and headed down the road over to the pasture where the horses graze throughout the day. The three horses the Blackwoods owned were not far from the main gate, Rowan's black and white speckled horse huddled together with the pure black mare which belonged to Baryk, who was Locke's cousin by blood but older brother to him. Locke's colt, the all-white and wildest of their horses, was off on his own however, trotting around the pasture as he pleased.

Locke leaned over the fence, calling out, "Time to come in now! Come on then!" His calls rang out across the fields, which the horses mostly ignored. He whistled sharply and smacked the fence with his hand and called again, "Come on! Let's go!" Rowan's spotted horse trotted over and waited patiently by the gate, followed by his brother's horse, but Locke's colt neighed defiantly, shook his mane, and stamped around.

Since the other two were close, he grabbed their bridles from over the fence, placing their reins firmly in one hand before opening the gate with his other.

"Come out," he encouraged them, and before they got too far Locke shut the gate behind them, leaving his horse for the time being while he stabled the others. When Locke returned, his horse was still playing about and pretending like he did not see him come back. Locke leaned on the gate, "Come here buddy!" he called out but he received a snort and a head shake back.

He smirked and reached into a small sack hanging nearby and pulled a carrot from it and waved it in front of the horse. "Come on now, I've got a treat for you!" The colt stood still staring blankly at him and Locke said, "Oh days end! You gotta come in now! Don't you want this nice big crunchy carrot?" His horse cocked its head to the side but did not move, so Locke shrugged and took a bite out of the carrot with a big snap. "MMM!" he teased while chewing loudly.

The colt gave out a small whimper and bolted over, Locke held out the carrot and his horse happily chomped it down. Locke patted him gently on the side and rubbed his snout while he chewed his carrot, "Good boy," he said before grabbing the last bridle slung over the fence. Locke waited for the colt to finish the carrot before putting it on him. The colt bucked a little when he tried.

"I know buddy, I don't want to go in yet either, but it's gonna be alright. I'll get you some extra hay for your bedding tonight, hmmm? How does that sound?" With a whinny the colt let Locke put the bridle on him and finally, with reins in hand Locke opened the gate once more. They navigated back to the stalls by lamp light as the light from the sun was nearly gone.

He placed his hand on his horse's neck, patting him reassuringly as he slowly led him to his pen. Once the horse was tucked away in his stall, just as Locke promised, he grabbed the pitchfork and went around the side of the stable to a loose pile of hay which rested against the wall. With a hearty scoop he grabbed a big pile of it and carried over to his colt's stall, trying not to drop any of it on the way.

"Alright, see? I kept my word."

He lifted the hay over the gate and overturned the pile of dry grass, dumping it into the stall. With a couple of quick pushes of the fork, the hay was spread evenly across the floor.

"See what I do for you?" he teased as he went back to the pile to grab another forkful of hay. "So how about next time when I need you to come in, you don't give me such a hard time, huh? How about that?" he asked rhetorically, smiling while he lifted the second pile of hay over and spread it around in a nice even layer for his fussy colt to lay on. "Better now?" he asked. His horse neighed and nodded at him, stamping in approval.

Locke placed his hand on his snout, giving him another comforting rub before putting the pitchfork back. He double-checked to make sure the horses were secure, saying goodnight to each of them individually before putting out the lantern and heading back to the house.

A blinding flash of purple light appeared above Locke, drawing his attention upward. But what he saw was beyond his comprehension and the most fantastic thing he had seen in his entire life. Strange symbols which resembled a language he did not recognize appeared out of thin air. The glowing purple sigils spun together, forming a ring of blurred light while the patch of sky inside twisted and distorted the faster it spun. Within seconds of appearing, the arcane symbols tore open a portal that linked two locations together, and within the tear Locke could see massive mountains that were entirely unfamiliar to him.

Locke jumped back as a man wearing a bright red cloak fell out of the portal and flew across the sky, crashing into the Blackwood's stables. The mysterious light faded away, the portal vanishing as quickly as it had appeared. Locke was less interested in the strange magic, and was instead staring in the direction of the stables. He was transfixed on the person twisted about in their clothes who was trying to untangle themselves from their cloak as they climbed out of a large pile of hay.

Locke approached cautiously, unable to see the stranger clearly from where he was. The wizard grumbled and coughed, finally throwing his cloak behind him, before climbing out of the stables. He stumbled a little as he put weight on limbs that could barely hold himself up.

"Who are you? What are you doing here?" Locke shouted, putting his fists up to defend himself. The weary man only staggered toward him and fell. Locke caught him before he hit the ground, straining beneath the nearly dead weight of the crumpled wizard. He planted his feet, bracing himself and wrapping one of the man's arms around his shoulder. Locke lifted them both back to standing with great effort. He took a moment to catch his breath and noticed how gaunt the man's face was now that he could see it in the light from the Blackwood Manor.

No wonder he could barely stand, just by looking at him it was apparent that whatever he went through was harrowing. The wizard reached up with a shaky hand and pulled back his hood, revealing dark hair peppered with gray and white around his ears. His deep blue eyes lit up when he saw who was holding him up. Locke felt uncomfortable about the way the mage stared at him, his eyes seemed far away and Locke was not sure what he was looking at.

"Am I dreaming?" the wizard's voice was small and hoarse as he struggled out a few words.

"I think that's my line," Locke replied, bemused.

Rowan threw open the front door, "What's going on out there?" he shouted. When he saw Locke shouldering the red-cloaked mage he dropped the pot of stew he was holding. Rowan's mouth hung open in surprise, frozen in place as Locke carried their unintended guest towards the manor. Rowan uttered aloud, "Dilandau?"

The old wizard lifted his head and the two looked at each other like they knew one another.

"Uncle, give me a hand!" Locke grunted, "He can barely stand, and he's heavy." Rowan jogged down the steps, grabbing Dilandau's other arm and together they helped carry him inside. They brought him to the dining room table, helping him into a chair that he slumped into heavily.

For a moment Rowan rested against the door like he was using his weight to keep something on the other side from breaking through. When Locke got the wizard to sit up, he noticed his uncle was pale as a ghost.

"Who is he?" Locke asked.

Rowan scowled.

"Get away from him!"

Astonished by the sharpness of Rowan's tone, Locke slowly backed away from the wizard. Upon hearing the commotion, Rowan's birth son came down from upstairs. Lord Blackwood's children could not look more apart from one another. Rowan's only child by blood and the eldest, Baryk had chestnut brown hair and forest green eyes with heavy bags under them, he was also bulkier than Locke but slightly shorter.

"Father, what's going on? Who's that?" Baryk asked.

Rowan did not answer him, instead turning around to quickly fasten the locks and secure the front door with his hands trembling. Locke had never seen Rowan act this way before and it was beginning to scare him.

"That man doesn't look well. What happened to him?" Baryk asked while looking him over.

"What are you doing here?" Rowan asked the wizard, ignoring both of the boys. Dilandau rested his head in his uncut palm, his voice trembled as he spoke.

"Believe it or not Rowan, I-I didn't mean to come here."

Rowan crossed his arms.

"Then why did you? Do you know that you have put my family in danger coming here?"

"Do you know him, father?" Baryk asked.

Rowan finally took heed of his son.

"His name is Dilandau Ravendark, and I am sorry to say that I do." Locke noticed the emblem on the back of Dilandau's cloak and thought that it looked like some kind of holy symbol or the kind of thing that would make a headstone for a king.

"Is he from Everund?" Locke asked Rowan excitedly. But his uncle dodged the question.

"It doesn't matter where he came from so long as he goes back there, *now.*"

Baryk did not seem to agree with Rowan, "Father, he is in bad shape. Surely, we can give him a place to stay for the night and let him rest."

Rowan frowned at Baryk.

"Get out," he said definitively. Locke started to protest but was interrupted, "You too. Both of you, upstairs. I will deal with this situation; it doesn't concern either of you." Locke walked across the room and stood next to Baryk where they both hung around the bottom of the stairs. Rowan yelled, "Have you got cotton in your ears? I said upstairs, now!" Locke could not resist taking a final look over his shoulder at the wizard from Everund as the boys reluctantly went away. Dilandau gave him a soft smile and watched him leave until he was out of sight.

The boys got halfway up the stairs and stopped, just out of sight, continuing to listen to the conversation between Rowan and Dilandau. "You cannot stay here!" Rowan snapped. Dilandau lowered his head wearily.

"I told you that I did not intend to come here. I was trying to get away from something... something terrible. I think I've done something terrible."

Rowan sat beside Dilandau while the boys peeked in from around the stairs.

"Is that why you came here? You did something and you came here thinking you can hide away, is that it? What did you do? Did you offend the king?" Rowan asked roughly.

Dilandau covered his face with his hands, which were still shaking, "I didn't mean to... I couldn't stop it! I couldn't stop what it made me do."

Rowan saw the frostbite on the mage's fingers.

"Where were you Dilandau? Before you came here?"

The wizard looked up from his hands, seeing his fingers as if for the first time.

"It was so cold. I couldn't feel it at first, I didn't notice the pain until it let me go... then it all came back to me, every horrific moment." He felt awfully tired suddenly, wearier now then he had when the grip on his mind was released, "I'm sorry I just need a moment to think." Dilandau thought about how such a simple task had gone so wrong. For all the years he trained and all the dark artifacts he destroyed, he thought it strange that he was bested by a book of all things.

The tome was the kind of thing that you would tell a fresh recruit to scare them away from taboo subjects like necromancy. But this was not a ghost story, it was real. That book he found might be the most dangerous collection of horrendous magic ever compiled. The spell wards that dark artifact hunters like him were trained to cast upon themselves were meant to protect against standard curses, not for the overwhelming power of thousands of tortured souls. However, it was his responsibility to destroy such evils and he failed to do so.

Whatever happened to the world next was his fault. Dilandau was, after all the most esteemed member of his order and inheritor of the Ravendark legacy. He had trained most studiously to protect the world from accursed objects just like it. Having felt its power over him, and how it made him prisoner within his own mind; he was certain that none among his order could have resisted the psychic onslaught from it.

The wizard's shoulders slumped as his mind shifted away from his personal failure onto the larger repercussions. He shivered when he recalled what the book had made him do, the vile magics he was forced to perform, and what had been done with its power. He found it impossible to tell Rowan about what he had just unleashed on the world.

He alone bore the burden, and even if they could find a way to forgive him for what he did; he was not sure that he deserved it. Rowan had no idea what was really going on, accusing him of having other intentions for coming to the Blackwood Manor. Better that he thinks that and holds on to peace for a little while longer, Dilandau thought.

"Where were you Dilandau?" Rowan asked again impatiently, and this time Dilandau answered him.

"The Eld Ridge Mountains," he said.

"You were in the Mountains of Eld? You mean Duscar?" Rowan asked, surprised.

Dilandau nodded slowly.

"I was sent on a mission by the king."

Rowan scowled.

"How did you end up out here, so far away?"

Dilandau's gaze drifted away.

"I honestly don't know. I was falling. Falling down the mountain. Everything was whizzing past me and I tried to teleport home to Arrincroft. I guess there wasn't enough time to complete the spell properly. I barely managed it before I hit the mountainside. But when I went through the portal, somehow, I fell into your stables instead of my own bed."

Rowan crossed his arms again.

"Which is precisely why you can't stay here. Whatever you did halfway across the world doesn't matter to me, but magic is not allowed here! I am certain that the Hammar Guard posted outside the village saw that light show you put on and they'll be on their way to my home. Honestly, they may have already made it to the village by now. And In case you don't know, the Hammar Guard are mage hunters! They'll arrest you, me, and the boys if they catch you here. They'll execute all of us! You have to leave, now!"

Dilandau agreed and stood up on shaky legs, "You are right. I must go. I must inform the king of what has happened. I am sorry I came here, Rowan. I never meant to put any of you in danger."

Rowan showed him to the door.

"I will give you my horse, and you will ride far from here and never come back."

The wizard silently agreed and shambled out of the manor without protest. Rowan helped him to the stables and prepped his spotted horse, which proved surprisingly easier than trying to get the weakened wizard into the saddle. They acknowledged one another one last time and shared a look of regret, before Rowan walked back to the manor, while Dilandau looked on from horseback.

Locke ran out of the front doors and past Rowan, who failed to catch him as he went by.

"Locke!" Rowan shouted as the young man ran up to Dilandau.

"You're from Everund aren't you?" Locke asked, out of breath.

Dilandau nodded wordlessly.

"I've been told that my parents are from there. I know it's a long shot but if you happen to run into them can you tell them that I'm alright?" Locke pleaded.

Dilandau could not help but smile and he nodded again, "I will."

With that said, the wizard reached for a necklace under his robes and pulled out an amulet in the shape of a closed eye with arrows pointing in the four cardinal directions and handed it to Locke.

"This is an astromancer compass. It reads the stars to navigate to any location known by the device. This one has been in my family for generations. Take it, it will guide you when you feel lost."

Locke stared at it in awe.

"I don't know how to thank you for this."

Dilandau gripped the reins of Rowan's horse.

"You don't need to. Consider it payment for the horse," he said. With a flick of his wrist and a snap of the leather, Dilandau Ravendark rode off into the night.

A Broken World

Back inside the Blackwood Manor, Locke held the astromancer compass in his open palm, looking over its golden design. He lifted the metal lid of the strange magical glass eye that rested in the center. He gently tossed it in the air, catching it again in the same hand to test the weight of it.

"Put that damned thing away!" Rowan shouted. "The mage hunters are likely to pay us a visit soon and we don't need them finding that."

"Sorry Rowan," Locke put the pendant's chain around his neck and slid the compass under his shirt, concealing it from view. Baryk sat down at the table.

"Father, do you really think the Hammar will come here?"

The look on Rowan's face alone was enough to answer the question that he seemed unwilling to. Locke had never seen his uncle this grim before, not even when his wife had taken ill. He was genuinely afraid. Rowan's horse brush eyebrows twitched slightly as he glowered at Baryk.

"You know as well as I do that Gerod Hammond will do anything to stay in power. He has always feared your claim to the throne, and I have done everything I could to convince him that we would never exercise that birthright."

Rowan pulled a handkerchief from his coat pocket and wiped the nervous sweat from his forehead.

Locke leaned against the back of a chair.

"You think he's mad enough to kill Baryk?"

Rowan stuffed the handkerchief back into its pocket.

"The only thing that has kept him from doing so already is that the people support us. So long as Gerod fears open revolt against him, he won't touch us. But if they discover that we harbored a mage from Everund, and they search this place, then Hammond will have found every justification he needs to remove our threat to his power. For good." Rowan sighed heavily, "The fear he has cultivated in our people for magic is stronger than their loyalty to us. He has only to say that we are collaborating with magi to brand us as traitors. There are many who believe that his vicious rule is all that is keeping what's left of our kingdom safe. You should know, we have our share of enemies here as well."

Locke's uncle picked up a piece of bread from the table and stuffed it into his mouth. "You should eat," he said, trying to change the subject. Locke sat down in the chair he was previously leaning against and Baryk pulled another chair over. They shared among them a meager meal of cheese and bread, and a single apple sliced with Lord Blackwood's boot knife. Rowan seemed to be chewing on more than just dry bread, however.

"If the Hammar Guard does come here tonight, I don't want you two to stay. It's too dangerous. *If* they come, they will be looking for blood."

Baryk stared at his father in shock, "And where exactly would we go?"

Locke's mouth was full of food when he answered his brother's question, "To the Old King's Glory. We have friends there."

Baryk was unconvinced.

"Perhaps we should seek asylum in Everund?" he asked.

Rowan shook his head.

"No. That could spark a war. Tensions with Everund are getting worse by the day. Their prince was just here trying to bring food and medicine as a show of good faith and Gerod refused them at the door." Rowan got up, "Always put your faith in our people, Baryk. Locke is right, we have friends here. Now, you two should get some sleep, I will clean up here." He embraced them both tightly, "I believe a man has done right in his life if he can be proud of his children, and I am immensely proud of the men you have become."

Locke tried not to think about how this might be the last time he would hug his uncle as he left the dining room. The young men exchanged looks but said nothing as they solemnly made their way to their own rooms. They lingered awkwardly in the hallway before saying goodnight to one another and hoped that this night would pass uneventfully like any other. Locke fell back onto his bed carelessly, his mind reeling from the events of the day. He pulled the astromancer compass from under his shirt and looked it over. He wondered what Everund was like and if his parents were still there.

Locke looked out his window to the starry sky above and absentmindedly ran his fingers over the compass. Under the glow of the moon, he tested the strange device by thinking about true north, the eye of the compass opened and rolled to look north. He thought of Everund and the eye turned west ever so slightly, and his heart swelled as a hopeful idea grew there.

"Show me where my parents are!" he said excitedly, but much to his dismay the eye did not move, seemingly unable to find people the same way it could find direction or places.

In the coming hours Locke lay awake quietly listening to Baryk's snoring from across the hall. He spent the time daydreaming about the far-flung magical kingdom of Everund he had only read about in stories. Locke however, was not the only one still awake past twilight that night. Rowan Blackwood sat brooding at the dining room table, running his fingertip along the grain of the wood. He was casting glances to the mostly ceremonial but still deadly sharp sword resting in its scabbard, mounted against the wall. But ultimately, he decided against making a final stand, hoping Gerod might spare his boys if he surrendered instead.

Rowan's worst fears came to pass just a few hours after Ravendark left, as the sound of several armored guards on horseback approached the Blackwood Manor. Baryk bolted awake at hearing heavy horses approaching their home. Across the hall, Locke also heard his grim destiny approaching and hid the astromancer compass under his shirt. There was a moment of quiet after the horses stopped out front, a terrible lingering silence in which they did not dare to breathe.

Shortly after came a forceful knock which echoed through the silence of the manor. Lord Blackwood was as ready as he could be for the worst outcome but he found it difficult to face it all the same. Rowan swallowed hard, undoing each of the locks he had sealed just hours before, and then opened the door while glowering. There were four of the Hammar Guard standing outside on his porch, with lit torches in hand. The captain of the guard stood in the doorway staring at a gauntlet on her wrist, which had a multitude of multi-colored gems running the length of it.

"Good evening, Lord Blackwood, *terribly* sorry to bother you at this hour," she said, smiling through every word, "but we have eyewitness accounts that at sundown a teleportation circle was seen in the sky above this very house."

Rowan crossed his arms, "Is that so?"

The mage hunter stood face to face with Rowan, smirking slyly. She was a snide looking woman, with a narrow nose, who commanded respect solely from the authority of the position she was granted and by no other quality of her person.

"Gerod has been particularly patient with you Lord Blackwood, but you know our laws. You know that magic use is forbidden, as is the harboring of casters. Turn them over to me and perhaps we will treat you with leniency."

Rowan looked her dead in the eyes, "And you know as well as I do that Hammond does not show mercy." The Hammar Guard captain's devilish grin only grew wider hearing Rowan's words.

"You can see for yourself that there is no magic being performed here, otherwise that *bracelet* of yours would be glowing," Rowan pointed out. The captain had noted the lack of reaction from her magic finder as they got closer to the Blackwood Manor.

"That may be so, but we believe you gave shelter to a powerful spellcaster. One who is strong enough to conjure a portal in the sky that could be seen from afar."

Rowan shook his head.

"We've had no visitors in quite some time, until you of course. And since you have no proof of these claims, you can please see yourselves off of my property."

The Hammar Guard all laughed together.

"I don't think we'll be leaving just yet, Lord Blackwood, perhaps we could have a look around inside?" She drew her sword and pointed it directly at Rowan's throat, "Pretty please?" she added, mockingly.

"You have no cause to search my home!" Rowan shouted, casting a desperate look over his shoulder. Baryk had gotten dressed after the first knock and snuck out of his room, and was crossing the hallway as his father yelled downstairs. He tiptoed across the hall to Locke who opened his door, quietly letting him inside.

"What are we going to do?" Locke asked, trying not to panic.

"I don't know. But if they search the house, they will find all of dad's books from Everund in our library. We'll all be arrested and probably publicly executed," Baryk explained.

"We have to get out of here, now!" Locke said, looking out the window to the woods at the edge of their property.

Downstairs, Rowan backed away from the blade at his neck and back into the house, giving the mage hunters room to enter.

"Looks like you dropped something," The captain said, looking down at the pot of stew on the porch.

Rowan's voice was shaky.

"I was checking on the horses when a hornet attacked me and clumsy me; I dropped the stew."

The mage hunter shook her finger at him disapprovingly.

"We checked on your horses on the way in, Lord Blackwood. It seems you are missing one..."

Rowan interjected, "It... it must have got free from the pasture."

She continued, "... And with it a full set of riding gear from your stables as well."

Rowan pleaded, "Alright, yes! A mage showed up here earlier threatening my family but we chased him off! Please, we have done nothing wrong!"

Another guard joined from outside, interrupting them both.

"Countess! We found something during the perimeter sweep." The guard handed her a small book which the captain held to her forearm, but again none of the colored stones glowed in response. Rowan recognized it immediately, however, and his heart sank. She opened it up and started reading, her smile grew when she realized what it was.

"Despite this being a non-magical object, it is a book about magic, tsk tsk. Which as I am sure you are well aware is just as illegal." Rowan bowed his head as the mage hunter went on, "Lord Blackwood, you have been found to be in possession of illicit material with intent to sow malcontent against our glorious leader. You will face his judgment and his punishment. Take him and anyone else on the premises into our custody."

The Hammar Guard barged in and grabbed Rowan, who continued to protest loudly until they threw a cloth sack around his head, hauling him outside. The mage hunters rummaged about, ransacking the manor looking for contraband. The boys heard them aggressively searching downstairs as Locke opened his bedroom window. One of the mage hunters started stomping up the stairs, while Locke climbed out as quietly as he was able to, given the hurry he was in. Locke then helped pull Baryk through and the two of them stood on the roof of the manor, taking a minute to get their footing. They side-stepped away from the window, carefully avoiding knocking each other off the small slanted roof. The sounds of a door splintering rang out as the guard broke into Baryk's bedroom behind them.

Staring at the pile of chopped wood resting against the manor ten feet below them, Locke whispered, "You go first." Baryk nodded, dangling his legs over the edge. Slowly he lowered his body until his feet were just over the top of the pile. He let go of the roof, dropping onto the wood below which shifted underneath him, and knocked a few blocks to the ground noisily. They heard another bedroom door get kicked in as Locke hurried down next. Baryk helped him land so he wouldn't disturb the pile beneath their feet like he had.

"Over here!"

They heard someone shout, as one of the guards hung out of their open window looking in their direction, "Don't let them escape!" The boys jumped to the ground and took off running towards the woods with only a quick look behind them to see if anyone was following. Ducking for cover just beyond the edge of the forest, they watched from the trees as the ironclad Hammar Guard dragged Rowan through the front yard. Baryk clenched his fists tight and started to go after them, but Locke grabbed him.

"What are you doing?"

Baryk fought against him.

"Let me go!"

Locke would not release his brother, "If we go after him, they'll just get us too."

Baryk Blackwood, the boy who would be king, punched the dirt angrily as they tied Rowan to the back of a horse. The Countess issued orders that they could not hear, and the guards on watch nodded, turning towards the woods.

"We have to go," whispered Locke, but Baryk would not move. He watched the captain climb atop the horse which had his father draped over it like a bundle of traveling gear. With a heavy kick to the horse's side, she was off and the only guards left behind were now walking towards them. Each of them with torches in hand and their weapons drawn, it was obvious they were hunting the two of them.

"Fine. Let's go," Baryk said, defeated, as the boys disappeared deeper into the forest.

In the thick of the woods behind the Blackwood Manor, far from sight of their ransacked home and out of earshot of the guards that were searching for them, Baryk suddenly stopped again.

Locke called back to him, "Baryk come on. We shouldn't linger, they know we are out here." Locke took a few steps, trying to encourage his brother to follow him, but he would not.

"We need to go back," Baryk said and Locke turned to face him.

"We've been through this, we can't. We have to lay low until we figure out what we're gonna do."

Baryk shook his head.

"It's not right. We should go back!" he closed his fists again as he fought back his anger and hurt.

Locke placed a hand on Baryk's shoulder, looking him in the eye. "If we go back to the manor, they will arrest us too! There's no way we can take armed mage hunters."

Baryk shook with rage.

"We'll fight them! I'll kill them for this!"

Locke gripped Baryk's shoulder tighter.

"With what, brother? We don't have any weapons. You want to fight them with gardening tools? Look, I understand your anger. I feel it too! But if we go back now then it's all over... for all of us."

Baryk pushed his hand away.

"I can't just run away! I am supposed to be king someday!"

"I don't like running away from this any more than you do. But if we run, we survive. If they kill you now, then all of Therred loses hope, forever. They need their future king."

Baryk calmed some and when he spoke again it was sorrowful.

"They took it all from me; my legacy, my home, my father!"

Locke shook him gently.

"Rowan was my father too and Blackwood Manor, my home. I know you feel like you have lost everything, but you haven't. We still have each other."

Baryk let his arms fall to his sides, releasing his clenched fists. He looked into Locke's eyes, which were filled with that same sappy compassion he had since he was a child.

"Okay, brother. We'll go... for now." Without another word Baryk embraced him tightly.

"We will make this right, I promise. And don't worry, I have a plan to rescue him... I think," Locke proclaimed. The torchlight of the mage hunters was coming through the forest behind them so they started running toward the village of Dellow. It took them a while to get through the tangle of woods before they wound up, breathless, right behind the village. The mage hunters seemed to have anticipated their arrival as guards were posted up on the singular road that wound its way through the tiny village.

"What should we do?" Locke asked, leaning against a fence at the edge of the village.

"The Old King's Glory is still open. We go inside, and we're sure to see some regulars there, maybe one of them could find us somewhere to lay low," Baryk said.

"They might be good to have around if a fight breaks out as well. I've broken up enough brawls with most of them to know they can hold their own," Locke said, climbing the fence.

Baryk reached out.

"Be as quiet as you can. Stay in the shadows, and avoid the torchlight until we get around to the front." Locke nodded, climbing down the other side, followed by Baryk pulling himself over. The two of them then snuck across the field, doing as Baryk suggested, staying in the shadows and running from the cover of one building to the next. The guards stayed to the road which allowed the boys to sneak around the back undetected, but they still had to get inside the tavern without being seen. Unfortunately, it seemed to be a slow night inside the tavern, as there was no music playing or lively conversation to mask their movements.

Baryk hugged the wall, heading towards the front where torches cast orange light into the street. Locke followed him, carefully watching the patrol routes of the Hammar Guard like hawks, searching for an opening to make a mad dash for the door. Locke saw Baryk readying himself to make a run for it through the brightly lit entrance, but he also saw a torch snuffer hanging from the corner lantern. He grabbed Baryk to stop him, who looked back at him with surprise. Locke put his finger to his lips, while reaching to grab the snuffer, risking his arm being in the light for a moment.

His efforts thankfully went unnoticed as he pulled it down and carefully used it to put out the torch light. They waited to see if the guards noticed the light going out, but when they did not react, the boys made their move. Baryk used the cover of darkness to sneak around to the front door. Locke set the snuffer down in the grass and caught up to him. Even hidden by the cover of night they needed to be careful not to draw attention to themselves. Locke stood to the side, letting Baryk go ahead, while staying back to watch for the guards.

Locke nearly forgot about the bell hanging on the door which would ring whenever it was opened. He reached out and stopped the door with his foot just before it rang. Baryk looked up at it warily, before carefully squeezing his way through the door, struggling a bit to get through the narrower gap. By the time Locke made it inside too, they had drawn the attention of the barkeep and most of the patrons in the Old King's Glory. Locke carefully shut the door behind him and Baryk lifted a finger to his lips to hush everyone hoping they would not make a fuss over their sudden appearance.

The sounds of chairs sliding across the floor ripped through the silence and the boys cringed as the patrons stood to face them. The barkeep Grimmald bellowed out, "By the Light! Baryk! Locke! You're alive!" The patrons set down their drinks or food and gathered around the pair. Everyone was pleasantly surprised to see them alive, because they had heard about the mage hunters ransacking the Blackwood Manor.

"You escaped!" someone called out.

"How'd you, do it?" asked another.

"You all need to be quiet!" Baryk said in a sharp but hushed tone, "there are guards posted outside, and they are looking for us!" They quieted down but their enthusiasm did not diminish. Their relief and excitement showed over their rosy faces. The small gathering embraced them both, taking turns giving them vigorous handshakes, and reassuring pats on the back.

"We have been so worried about you since we saw the Hammar head off towards your place. We feared the worst when we saw them haul Rowan away. We thought we lost both of you," Grimmald said while holding back tears, his lips quivering behind his shaggy beard.

"Not yet, my friend," Baryk said. "Gerod isn't going to bury the Blackwoods that easily. I promised you all that I would restore Therred to its former splendor and I won't rest until I see it done."

They all grabbed their drinks and raised them in the air, shouting together, "To the old king's glory!" They took a long drink and Locke smiled with admiration and pride at Baryk, as he so often did. Locke always imagined having a real king on the throne and as a child he dreamt of the life he could have had inside the walls of a grand castle. In his heart of hearts, he still hoped for it, but after everything that happened tonight, he was afraid that dream might be dead forever. Being branded as traitors and on the run would make it impossible to fight Gerod head on. They would not be able to unite the people of Therred against the iron tyrant.

"What are you two going to do?" the barkeep asked, to which Baryk slapped Locke on the back and said, "Well, our boy here has a plan to get Rowan back. So that's what we're gonna do, get him back. Isn't that right brother?" Locke smiled sheepishly. The barkeep looked incredulously at him.

"How could you possibly save Lord Blackwood? They'll be taking him to the capital, and no one has ever escaped from one of Gerod's prisons."

"No one's ever been crazy enough to break in either," Locke said. He knew it was impossible, but he was worried he could not have convinced Baryk to come this far if he had not proposed at least the idea. "See... the plan is... we sneak inside Hammangard, and then once inside the capital, we break into Gerod's castle. There we will find where Rowan is being kept, and then we... you know, get him out." Baryk stared stupidly at Locke for a moment, thinking there had to be more to it, but as Locke sat there waiting for them to react, Baryk almost screamed.

"That's not a plan! That's barely an idea!" Baryk covered his mouth with the palm of his hand to quiet himself, "That's really all you've got?"

Locke shrugged and nodded.

A voice as warm and sweet as ginger snaps interjected, "I can get you both inside the city." The voice belonged to a kind old woman at the back.

"Is that right, lady Roselyn?" Baryk asked.

"Mhm, you see, I have a permit to sell within the capital. I was going to bring some unsold merchandise there in a few days to offload it, because trade has been low this season and I wanted to-"

She paused for a moment then continued with a change of words, "I *needed* to make some extra profits."

Locke scowled, "You mean from the execution?"

The woman looked pained.

"They draw large crowds; it was nothing personal. I am terribly sorry about what happened to Rowan. Please let me make it up to you! Take my wares into the city instead, you can make it through the gates with these permits."

Baryk and Locke looked at each other and Locke said, "It's a good plan."

Baryk looked annoyed.

"It's our only plan."

Roselyn smiled, reassuring them. "I can get you out of Dellow as well, and you can stay at my farmhouse for the night. It's safe there, you can rest a bit and take off in the morning."

Locke and Baryk decided to go along with Roselyn, but truthfully, they really had no other option. The boys were both too exhausted to search for something else and time was of the essence. With a few short goodbyes and a couple more hugs from Grimmald the barkeep, they were off. They snuck out one by one when the guards were not watching the tavern door.

The lady Roselyn left her horse tied up outside and the three of them went on foot. Avoiding the road, the three of them walked through the thickets along the edge of the forest and crossed the fields that led away from the village. The warm light of the torches from Dellow faded away as they trekked, and their comfort was replaced by the chill of night air.

They were shivering by the time they reached the edge of her property and were happy for the hearth when they got inside the farmhouse. Her home was not as large or pristine as the Blackwood Manor, having only one floor and peeling paint on the exterior. It looked rough on the outside but it was cozy on the inside, and that is what mattered. The stone fireplace was lit and a small fire was burning low. It was so inviting that they sat in front of it to warm up after their long and tiresome walk. Roselyn put wood on the fire, stoked the embers and warmed her hands by the flames.

"You boys hungry?" she asked and Locke's stomach growled. Roselyn laughed as his cheeks glowed a soft red. "I guess so!" she giggled, and grabbed a few wooden bowls before scooping some hot oatmeal into them. She added a splash of cream and a drip of honey, topping it off with some fresh berries she picked earlier that morning. After eating their small but satisfying meal, Locke and Baryk discussed their plan once more.

The boys went over every detail, making sure they were clear on what to do come sunup tomorrow. They knew things would get crazy inside Hammangard and it would be impossible to predict what would happen after they made it through the gates. There was only so far, they could go with their planning, and they knew they were leaving much of it to chance. Feeling they could do no more to prepare for what lay ahead, Locke and Baryk climbed into a wooden framed bed and covered up with hand woven blankets. Several restless hours plagued them both with dread, but eventually the weariness of the day took them and they drifted off to sleep.

An Unexpected Discovery

Locke arose that morning a lot less certain about their plan to rescue Rowan than he was the night before. Despite the icy fear coursing through his veins, he smiled and greeted Roselyn warmly. Baryk was already up and finished with his breakfast, but Locke was too nervous to eat. They helped the lady load and secure the wares to her cart, which they would be taking to the iron heart of their broken kingdom.

"If either of you manage to make it out of there alive you will be heroes, with or without Rowan," she said, trying to encourage them.

"That's a big if," Locke said defeatedly.

"We should go," Baryk said, covering the back of the cart with a tarp. Roselyn gave Baryk her permits and a solemn send off, wishing beyond hope for their safe return.

They traveled in silence all morning and throughout the afternoon as well. Their minds were heavy with the dread of what was to come, and it was nearly poetic the way their mood darkened with the setting of the sun. It was night when the boys finally reached the city of Hammangard, the name by which it was known since the reformation following the Great Wyrm War. All the splendor the city and castle once held had long since decayed. Its high iron plated walls, which were still blackened by dragon's fire and rusted from a century of weathering, towered over them as they approached the east side gate.

The iron coating the city walls was the product of dwarven smithing, which made them immune to magic but not to rain. The city looked ill with rust, like it was suffering as its people were. Where once there was music and laughter to accompany the hammering and sawing, now only the sounds of work greeted those who came to Hammangard. The capital of Therred once was a bustling hub of trade for the Great Kingdoms in years long past, but the splendor of the old kingdom ended under the iron fist of Gerod Hammond.

Locke wondered to himself if Gerod's fear of an uprising might be enough to spare their lives if they were caught. He smirked, which Baryk noticed and commented, "Do not think this one of our games, little brother." Locke's smile faded from his face. Baryk looked as grim as his father before he was taken from them.

"We risk more than just *our* lives this night, so be on your guard."

An armored horse and rider approached them, clad in iron chainmail and the brutish soldier in the saddle snarled at them.

"What business do you have here at this hour, you filth?" the oaf spat at them through the slits in the facemask of his iron helmet. Locke's and Baryk's faces reflected the disgust they felt at being addressed in such a rude manner, but Baryk greeted the guard warmly in return.

"Good evening, sir, I beg your pardon. We are merchants from Dellow. We heard that Lord Blackwood is to be executed tomorrow."

"And what of it?" the guard sneered.

Baryk continued without changing tone.

"Such events usually draw a crowd, as you know, which means more trade for us."

The soldier looked over his shoulder to another standing guard by the gate, who shook his head incredulously and laughed in return.

"Times have been hard on many of the eastern farms and Dellow's market is shrinking," Baryk continued, "The public execution of such a prominent figure will draw a lot of customers from all corners of our great kingdom."

The guard looked back at Baryk and dismounted his horse.

"Get off the cart," he said.

The boys looked at each other confused for a moment, and the guard shouted at them, "Now! Both of you, off!" Locke clenched his fists angrily but complied nonetheless, both of them climbed out the cart as they were ordered. The oafish soldier tore back the cloth tarp which was covering the goods in the back of the cart and started searching through their things.

"We hope to sell off some of our goods in the capital since the local markets have-" Baryk began, but the soldier threw up his hand, motioning him to be quiet. the soldier ran his hands along the side of the cart searching for hidden compartments or weapons. He looked beneath the cart as well to make sure they were not hiding anything under there either.

When the soldier was satisfied the cart was clear, he turned his attention back to the boys, grabbing Locke roughly. If Baryk had a sword he would have drawn it, unfortunately in addition to being unarmed, their cover required compliance; so, he only scowled. Locke was quickly searched for weapons and released when there were none found on him. Baryk was searched next, and the brute was even rougher with him then he had been with Locke. When the soldier finished searching him, he shoved Baryk into the cart.

"Get back in your cart and proceed through the arch. There you will wait until instructed further."

The boys took a few moments to rearrange the displaced goods, before covering them again while the guard got back on his horse. They got back into the cart as Baryk gently snapped the reins moving the horses forward slowly.

The grinning soldier on the gate motioned to archers overlooking from the ramparts who then trained their bows on Baryk and Locke. The east gate was opened and they drove the cart into a chamber between the outer and inner gates, where they were barred from going further. Behind them they saw a large arch set with different colored stones in the same pattern as those on the mage hunters' bracers. Thankfully, none of the stones lit up as they passed through it.

"Looks like you're all clear," the snickering soldier jeered.

He and the oaf entered the chamber with the cart while the east gate slammed shut behind them, trapping the boys inside.

"What is the meaning of this?" Baryk asked as the Therredan soldiers closed in, drawing their swords on the two of them.

"We know who you are, Baryk Blackwood!" the laughing soldier taunted. "You were right earlier when you said, 'times have been hard lately,' but not just for you farmers," he said.

"So, you're going to turn us in," Locke retorted.

The brutish soldier laughed this time.

"For what? A pat on the back?"

The boys looked confused, and the other soldier grinned.

"We are only going to turn you in if you don't cooperate. Give us all of your money or by this time tomorrow I'll be watching the two of you jerk at the end of a rope."

Of all the things Locke thought could go wrong, getting robbed by the guards was not one of them. Not wanting to provoke a fight they emptied their pockets of all the money they had with them into the open hands of the Therredan soldiers.

"Good boys, now that you paid up, you are free to go about your *business*," the overly amused soldier hissed. The inner gate opened, creaking loudly as it lurched upward. The soldiers walked away from them, laughing and counting their gold coins. They paid the boys no further attention. Neither Locke nor Baryk said a word as they passed through the iron walls and entered the capital for the first time since they were children.

The inner gates sealed shut behind them and they wondered how much further they would realistically get. The soldiers patrolling inside the city seemed to busy themselves with harassing random citizens, making idle threats with smug looks on their faces. The people of Therred living inside the capital wandered around aimlessly with bowed heads and sullen expressions. Well, this place has as much cheer as a damn graveyard, Locke thought.

In the dim torch light, they could see that the buildings were rundown and falling apart, and the muddy roads had likewise not been maintained. The road itself was full of ruts and was difficult for the horse to pull the cart through. They eventually parked the cart behind a small leatherworker shop and began looking for a way into the castle. Baryk was trying to get a headcount of the guards posted outside when he noticed a side entrance to the castle which had only a single guard posted.

"There! We get in there. That passageway must lead into the castle's food stores and the kitchen, it's nearly unguarded."

Locke agreed.

"How are we gonna get inside though? We can't just walk up and say, how are ya?"

Baryk thought for a moment before replying.

"No. No, we can't. The castle is surrounded by soldiers and the interior is crawling with the Hammar Guard. Once inside we are sure to get caught by someone."

Locke's eyes lit up with a crazy idea that he did not bother explaining. He pulled the astromancer compass from under his shirt, holding it in his hand with a smirk.

"And just what do you plan to do with that?" Baryk asked.

"Get ready," Locke said, pressing his hand over the closed eye of the compass. He focused his mind on finding a room for keeping prisoners like Rowan, which activated the compass. The magical eye opened and the arcane iris rolled about, reading the stars through the clouds finding patterns hidden to normal sight, before pointing toward the castle interior.

"What are you doing?" Baryk growled, "They'll detect that!"

Locke smiled.

"That's the idea, brother."

Locke grabbed Baryk and ducked out of sight as a nearby mage hunter looked in their direction. "I think that was enough to get their attention," he said, unfocusing his mind and closing the compass as its magic went dormant again.

He quickly put the compass back under his shirt and leaned against a wall trying to stay out of sight. Locke peeked around the corner to see one of the Hammar Guard closing in on them, while staring intently at the bracer on their forearm. A small blue gem was still glowing faintly which had shimmered when the compass activated.

Locke whispered, "When he comes around the corner, we grab him and take him out." Baryk picked up a large piece of scrap wood to use as a club, and Locke readied himself as the sounds of clanking of armor stomping through the mud drew closer.

The mage hunter turned the corner but only saw an unattended cart and horse. Locke jumped out of the shadows from behind him, grabbing the guard's helmet and pulling it off his head. He shouted, "Now!" before ducking out of the way as Baryk swung the makeshift club with all his might. The swing connected with the guard's head making a loud crack and knocked him backwards into the mud.

The boys stood silently for a moment waiting to see if anyone heard or noticed anything, while they calmed their nerves. When they were satisfied that no one had heard the commotion, they went to work stripping the unconscious guard of his armor.

"Here, put this on," Baryk said, shoving the chestplate into Locke's arms.

"Why do I have to wear it?" he asked as Baryk pulled the undressed guard to the other side of the hut and dropped him under an overhang, out of sight of the thoroughfare.

"Because they are searching for me, not you. So, you, my dear brother, are going to play the part of the guard who brings the traitor Baryk Blackwood into custody."

Locke reluctantly donned the armor, "I don't like this plan."

"Well, this whole thing was your *idea*," Baryk said smugly, before pulling a jug of wine from the back of their cart and dumping it over the unconscious guard's face and chest. Finally, he put the empty wine container in the guard's arms, making it look as though he drank too much and passed out. "Okay, let's do this," Baryk said. Locke placed the heavy helm onto his head, completing his Hammar Guard disguise. He grabbed Baryk's arms, putting them behind his back and wrapping rope around his wrists to make them look bound.

Locke took a deep breath, "Alright, let's go get Rowan back."

Then he led Baryk toward the food cellar door with the singular guard posted there, who placed his hand on his weapon as they approached. "Stop there! What are you doing?" he shouted.

Locke swallowed hard, and with a gruff voice said, "I caught this mage sympathizer roaming the city. His father was taken into custody yesterday and this bastard was rooting around like a rat for him."

The guard smiled in a way that made Locke feel uneasy.

"Well, well, if it isn't the heir of Therred himself, Baryk Blackwood. How brave of you to come here, kingling."

He grabbed Baryk by the face, getting uncomfortably close to him, "I will enjoy watching when they try you in the square for all to see, you traitorous wretch. Gerod Hammond alone rules the kingdom of Therred and after you are dead; no one will question that again."

Baryk glared genuinely and reached out instinctively to strangle the guard, but Locke held him back.

"Calm down!" Locke said sternly in his gravely guard voice. The food store guard looked sideways at Locke with a distrustful glare, but slowly let go of Baryk's face.

"Take the prisoner inside and escort him directly to the dungeons, no detours!" he snapped. Locke nodded stiffly, pushing Baryk forward. The guard then pulled a keyring from his side, unlocking the door and opening the way for them.

As they walked past the guard, he noticed the mud caked across Locke's back and saw that Baryk's hands were not really bound as the rope hung loosely from around his wrists. He grabbed Locke by the arm, "Hey! What's going on here?"

Baryk spun around with his hands free and wrapped them around the guard's throat, throwing him against the wall. The guard reached for the sword at his side, but Locke drew his first. He brought the pommel down hard on top of the guard's helmet and he fell slack against the wall. Baryk quickly shut the door behind them and grabbed the keys from the unconscious guard.

"Take that off, quick! We don't have much time now."

"I just put it on, why am I taking it off?" Locke asked.

"Because it's loud and covered in mud!" Baryk said breathily while dragging the guard around the corner, hiding him as best he could. Baryk took the guard's sword while Locke doffed his armor grumpily mumbling in frustration. They dumped Locke's attempted disguise with the unconscious soldier, while Locke took the sword with him. Now that they were both armed and inside the castle walls, they actually had a chance to save Rowan; assuming they could find him. They went up a flight of stairs which led into a larger hallway connecting other parts of the castle. No guards were in sight, so they slipped through the doorway and down the hall.

Baryk's eyes were honed from many hunts through the woods behind the Blackwood Manor and he was a proficient tracker. But inside the castle his eyes were being led by dusty stone walls and worn carpet that had seen more traffic than the others. He figured the extra wear and tear was likely from the numerous prisoners dragged through the halls and across that floor. "This way," he whispered to Locke as he followed the worn carpet.

They remained on alert for any sight or sound that might warn them of approaching danger, but much to their surprise they made it deep into the castle without resistance of any kind. The quiet interior and lack of guards made them feel even more uncomfortable. The whole place felt uninviting, and the gloom that accompanied the darkness filling the long corridors made them both anxious. The pair rounded another corner, approaching a door which was partially open and had torch light peeking out of it. It sounded like a spirited conversation was going on inside and Locke leaned in closer, trying to overhear what was being said.

"Bring the prisoner to the pit. We're behind schedule and Gerod wants this thing operational by dawn's light."

The boys snuck into the room, passing metalworking tools and workbenches with large iron plates on them, and over to a large open space where wooden scaffolds were built around an enormous suit of armor. The armor looked like Therredan soldier gear, but impossible for a normal sized person to fit into. The top of its head nearly hit the ceiling in a room taller than the many ladders that occupied it.

The workers returned as the boys quickly hid behind a metal cart which was next to an incredibly hot furnace. They stared as the construct workers walked up to the giant iron suit of armor with tools in hand and started tinkering with it. Within minutes they had its chest plate pulled off and set to the side, exposing the hollow interior of the suit. One of them pulled open the door to the furnace next to the boys which spit strange blue flames out of it along with a small belch of smoke. The other man grabbed a set of iron tongs and especially carefully lifted a silvery ring from off of a table on the other side of the room.

"Don't drop that damn thing!" the man holding open the furnace shouted.

"I-I got it!" the worker with tongs stammered back as he slowly walked across the floor towards the furnace clumsily. The ring slid around in the tongs as he walked and as he tried to clamp down tighter on the object, it slid free from his grip. The boys saw both of the workers fumble while attempting to catch it as it bounced around a couple of times before the ring vanished in a flash of blue light. The ring transformed into a large silver shield with a red gryphon emblazoned upon it, which then hit the ground with a loud clang.

Baryk's eyes grew wide when he recognized the symbol of their former king, but for Locke this was the first time seeing the crest of Duren. "Pick it up already!" the incredibly frustrated man ordered while bending down to assist. Together they lifted the silver shield and hauled it over to the strange furnace, Locke and Baryk guessed what was going to happen next. Baryk started to get up but Locke held him back and shook his head. The boys stared in paralyzed outrage, watching helplessly as the workers tossed an artifact from their history into the flames.

A series of popping, hissing, and whistling noises came from the strange furnace before it spewed out a burst of blue sparks. Apparently, that meant it was finished because the workers grabbed shovels and scooped up piles of glowing dust from out of the furnace. They dumped the sparkling blue dust into the legs of the suit of armor, and tossed it all over the inner cavities. The strange glowing dust seemed to stick to the armor and coat its interior making a thin blue layer. When they finished the coating, they closed the strange furnace door and refastened the now glowing dust lined chest plate back onto the armor.

"Just need the special ingredient now," one of the men casually joked. The other worker tried to ignore it and walked to another door on the far side of the room and slammed his fist against it three times. From the hall they heard clinking chains and a muffled scream as the Hammar Guard entered the room, shoving an emaciated elderly man inside. He wore nothing but rags and a cloth sack over his head like the mage hunters had shoved over Rowan's face when he was hauled off.

"Fuel for the fire," one of the Hammar said to the iron suit technicians, "Bring our guest closer and let's get this over with."

The prisoner tried to plead with them through the gag in his mouth, but the guards ignored him, throwing him on the floor at the suit of armor's feet. They chained him in place over a drain in the floor, which Locke had not noticed when they entered the room. There were crudely carved symbols etched into the floor, which they both recognized as magical symbols used for spellcasting. The man shackled to the floor grabbed at the guards in desperation, but they stepped out of his reach without a word.

The door in the back of the room opened again and a man Locke only vaguely recognized entered. His hands and feet were also bound like the prisoners, but his head was uncovered. For a moment Locke tried to remember where he had seen his ghoulish face, then it hit him. He was that infamous warlock they believed was executed years ago for conducting magical experiments on the people of Therred. Baryk and Locke were only children when they heard the grisly tales about the man everyone called the Bone Keeper.

Locke could only imagine for what dark purpose Gerod would have kept a man so foul. The Hammar Guards in the room surrounded the warlock with weapons drawn, shouting, "Do it!" The gaunt man looked with empty eyes at the hooded prisoner, who struggled against his restraints. The warlock bent down and touched the sigil under the prisoner's feet, and it lit up with sparks of blood-red light.

"I am sorry," he said hollowly.

The warlock then breathed in deeply and started chanting in a strange language they had never heard before. The boys stared helplessly as crackling sanguine light lashed the prisoner's body, causing him excruciating pain. The blood light spilled out of the victim with each of his screams and it flowed into the giant suit of armor, which creaked as it started moved on its own. With a wave of the warlock's hand and a final scream from the prisoner, the light from the circle engulfed the man's body entirely.

It became so bright that Locke and Baryk had to look away until it faded moments later. When they looked again the prisoner was completely gone save for a pile of bones, rags, and chains. The warlock's head hung low in shame while the iron golem, glowing brightly with blood magic, stood up on its own. It knocked over the scaffolding built around it, pushing things over as it got up clumsily.

"Mandatu res golem, abulatum!" the Hammar Guards beckoned the iron golem forward with words of command, which it obeyed. It ducked and squeezed through the door as they walked it out of the room.

When the Hammar left, the technicians cleaned up the mess, unceremoniously sweeping up the bones and throwing them into a cart. The interior of which glittered with that strange sparkling dust, another byproduct of animating the iron golem. The iron suit workers pushed the cart out of the door and disappeared into the hall. After they left the golem assembly pit, Baryk went after them and Locke followed close behind. The technicians were too busy talking with one another to notice the boys trailing behind them. At the end of the hall was a large vault door stretching from floor to ceiling, which the boys hid behind as the techs stopped to argue.

The boys had hoped to wait there out of sight until it was safe to follow the cart again, but a mage hunter came around another corner and starting walking straight toward them. They climbed inside the vault and pulled the massive door shut behind them. After a tense few moments of holding their breath and hoping for the best, they heard the guard walking away at last. Baryk searched for a torch but it was completely dark inside the vault, making it difficult to navigate.

"Help me find the light," he said.

Locke chuckled, "I'm no priest, but I'll give it a shot."

Baryk tried not to laugh while groping around looking for a light source, "Just help me find a torch would ya?"

Locke searched and finally found a useable torch in a sconce hanging on the far wall, he pulled it down and lit it with a piece of flint from his pocket. The torch's orange glow reflected off of large piles of artifacts which filled the entire vault.

"Whoever threw these in here did so with as much concern as someone shoveling coal into a blast furnace," Locke commented on the chaos of the room. He was surprised that neither of them tripped over anything given how much stuff was strewn about.

"There is more here than the Hammar Guard could possibly have confiscated from our people alone," Baryk said ominously. "Look at this, this was not crafted by any Therredan, not even before the war."

Locke held up a puzzle box covered in glyphs, and examining the room more closely it was clear that large amounts of the artifacts were of Zierian origin. They bore the unmistakable craftsmanship of the eastern desert people, delicate designs covered with religious motifs in worship of a fire god. Locke was amazed to see relics that looked like they were pulled from the tales of the burning sands he read as a boy.

While searching, Locke thought he heard a woman start singing from the other side of the room. When he turned around however, there was no one there. As the singing continued, he realized the sound was originating from a red metal orb with gold trim which was segmented plates coiled into a ball. It resembled the small bugs Locke had found under rotting logs as a child. The strange orb floated above a stone pedestal which was related to the artifact only by virtue of holding it in place. A faint hum emanated from the strange relic, and when Locke got close to it, he felt a surge of heat as the entire thing unfurled before his eyes.

"What are you doing over there?" Baryk called out, but received no answer. Locke stared silently at the strange artifact opening before him.

"Locke?" Baryk called out, and again got no response. "HEY!" he shouted as Locke wordlessly reached out to touch the mysterious object, which now resembled a single arm of plate armor. Baryk, furious with Locke's fixation, crossed the room with the intent to put an end to his curiosity and get him back to their mission before the Hammar Guard discovered them.

"Locke! Let's go!" Baryk shouted, but he was too late. The moment Locke's finger made contact with the artifact it sprung like a trap, whipping like a scorpion's tail as it latched itself onto Locke's arm. Locke's curiosity wore off and he looked around alarmed, disoriented like a person recently woken from a dream.

The gauntlet covering his arm glowed red hot, like a sword out of the forge, and suddenly it felt like Locke had shoved his arm into a fire pit. The artifact ignited in blazing flames and Locke screamed in agony while the scorching hot metal seared his skin. Baryk was paralyzed with fear watching his brother shrieking and flailing wildly, trying to put out the fire engulfing his arm. Locke passed out from the pain, and the blaze went out as he fell over. Several objects clanged loudly as Locke inadvertently knocked them to the ground. Baryk ran to his side.

"Locke?" he said with a shaky voice. "Locke? Are you okay? Please be okay." Baryk tried to rouse him by shaking him and by gently slapping the side of his deathly pale face.

Heavy armor clanked outside the vault and Baryk panicked.

"Who's in there?" a Hammar Guard shouted from outside, but he chose not to respond to the question. The guard pounded on the door, "Open up or we'll break the door down." The tense moments of eerie silence which followed were shattered by a thunderous crash from the vault door buckling under a heavy battering. A hideous whine escaped the hinges holding up the doors as one of their iron golems tried to tear them down. Astonishingly, the large door held against the golem's first attacks, but it would not hold forever.

Baryk grabbed his unconscious brother, being careful not to touch the armor that burned Locke just moments before, fearing it might set him alight too. With great effort, Baryk dragged him to a nearby wall and scanned the room, desperate for a way out. Other than the vault door they came through, there were no other exits from the room. The walls were made of solid stone, but near the ceiling were a few windows for ventilation.

They were small and out of reach for anyone standing on the floor, but thankfully there was a pile of magical artifacts stacked against the wall which was high enough that Baryk thought there was a chance of reaching one of the windows from on top of it. Gripping his brother tightly, he climbed up the shifting pile. Another boom suddenly caught Baryk's attention as a portion of the wall around the door cracked, but thankfully the stubborn doors held still.

"This is your last chance, thieves, surrender! We will have you soon!" the guards shouted as they smashed their blades against the door. Baryk lifted Locke to the top of the heap, pulling them under the window. He looked outside to the ground below, and his stomach tightened from vertigo. Down below he saw the meandering cobblestone path which wrapped around the outside of the castle, and there he saw the horse and cart they rode into the city. The horse was standing aimlessly untethered just down the path.

"Thank the Allfather!" he said. Baryk placed his fingers into his mouth and whistled loudly to get her attention, and the old mare looked up at him, stamping her hooves.

"That's it old girl, come on!" he said excitedly, and he whistled again. The horse whinnied softly, tossing her mane and continuing to stamp about, but she did not come to him. "Oh, come on!" he exclaimed in frustration. He whistled again and shouted to her, "Get over here now!" She reluctantly trotted up the path toward him, stopping just under the castle window. Baryk's face turned purple from heaving the dead weight of his unconscious brother to the window sill.

With a final explosive boom, the hinges gave and the vault door clattered to the ground. Baryk scrambled to shove Locke out of the window, pushing with everything he had. The Hammar Guard hurried into the room, clambering their way up the pile toward Baryk as he pushed Locke out the window. He tried to jump through the window himself only to be pulled back down by a forceful grip on his ankle.

Locke's Exile

Locke tumbled through the air, falling almost two stories before landing in the back of the horse drawn cart with an awful crash. Terrified by the impact, the poor old horse bucked and ran off in a panic as the boy's body was being swallowed by the supplies in the cart. The horse barreled past the castle entrance, dragging the cart wildly behind her. Some soldiers tried to stand in the way of her in a feeble attempt to stop the panicked mare, but they ultimately dove for cover as she sped past them.

Everyone stood watching the frightened horse running for its life, and let it run past unimpeded, as they were afraid of being trampled. The terrified old horse ran out into the plaza of the inner city, stirring up quite the commotion as she kicked mud around and tossed wares form the cart through the streets as she went.

She eventually came to a stop near the north end of town, where some townsfolk managed to corral her and calm her down. They undocked the cart from her before taking the exhausted horse to a nearby stable where she could rest. Meanwhile Locke slowly regained consciousness in the back of the abandoned cart, shifting uncomfortably on top of the various goods holding him up. He was in a lot of pain, and extremely disoriented. "Baryk?" he called out but no one answered.

Locke sat up but found himself tangled in the tarp, with his contorted body sprawled out over broken boxes which were crushed beneath him. He groaned along with his bruised body as it complained with every movement he made as he rolled onto his side. He saw no one around, the crowds drawn by the horse having gone back about their business. Locke took the opportunity to crawl out of the cart while no one was looking. With a short tumble across the ground, he was back on his feet and running for cover. "Baryk?" he called out again, looking for his brother, but there was no sign of him anywhere.

He stayed out of sight, quickly realizing that he was not inside the castle anymore but somewhere else in the city entirely. It was difficult to see in the dark of the night but he saw guards running along the exterior walls of the city away from him and back toward the castle. People were running to hide in their homes, trying to avoid the chaos overtaking the city.

Locke looked around for his brother again, whispering out to him, "Baryk?" But still no answer. He searched the nearby buildings for his lost sibling, but he was nowhere to be found. "Baryk where are you?" he asked with panicked breath, and again got no response. A sinking, dreadful feeling set in as Locke realized that he was alone; Baryk was not with him.

He looked at his right arm which was covered by a strange red armor with gold trim over freshly burned skin. Locke tried to pull at the segments, cutting his fingers on the feather shaped metal armor. "Yavon's beard!" he exclaimed through gritted teeth. He found no latch or buckle or any other means by which to remove it. His nerves screamed in agony where his flesh was seared. It was tender, making it painful for him to pull at the artifact that was apparently fused to him.

Therredan soldiers started coming back from the castle, searching through buildings one by one as they went. Assuming they were looking for him, Locke ran in the opposite direction of them, seeking shelter inside someone's home. Locke spun around shutting the door behind him, he saw a woman huddled with her children. She noticed the panic on his face and the strange armor he wore, "You can't stay here!" the woman hissed, "Not with that... that thing on your arm. They'll hang us all if they find you here! Get out!"

She grabbed him and shoved him out the back door, bolting it shut behind her. Locke stumbled back for a moment, staring stupidly at the closed door and uncertain about what to do next. He was afraid to stay out in the open, so he searched for somewhere else to go and noticed that the woman had a storage shed in her backyard with an open door.

He snuck inside, taking a minute to catch his breath. There were heaps of metalwork inside and tools bearing the mark of the Hammar Guard on the bench. From the look of the equipment, Locke was sure the woman's husband was a blacksmith for the mage hunters. Locke noticed a long leather smithing sleeve hanging next to a pair of goggles. He grabbed the sleeve and slid it clumsily over his right arm. Fortunately, it covered the armor all the way up his shoulder where he fastened the straps. He briefly admired how well it hid the strange artifact from sight.

Locke put a brown leather vest over his shirt, which helped hide the straps and buckle of the sleeve. In the distance he heard a knock on the woman's front door and shouting from nearby houses. He knew guards would find him if he stayed too long so he left the shed, staying out of the light. He crept down a back-alley road quietly, looking over his shoulder to see a mage hunter break into the shed he left just a moment ago. His heart raced as he hugged the wall tightly, watching them from a stone's throw away.

Locke knew time was running out. It would not be long before they locked down the capital, trapping him inside the city. He would not be able to hide for much longer, even in a place this large. Luckily for him he found a horse tied up in front of a house that was ready to ride. But Locke had never stolen anything before and what he was doing did not sit well with him.

Like it or not, needs must and so he quietly untied the horse from its hitch. He grabbed the pilfered equine's reins and walked it further down the road and out of sight before climbing on top of it. The horse pulled against him hard as he settled into the saddle, but he took control quickly. With a snap of the reins, they rode off together, dashing toward Hammangard's northern gate.

Locke pressed the horse to run as fast as it could, gently kicking his heels into its sides and urging it forward more and more until it was running at full speed to get out of the city. The guards on the ramparts noticed him too late to close the outer gates in time, and he slipped through as they closed behind him. The archers let fly their arrows which whistled past his ear, landing in the dirt all around him as he fled.

Locke rode hard without slowing or stopping for hours to make sure he was not followed by the mage hunters before he finally slowed to a stop at sunrise by the last of the farms on the outskirts of the kingdom of Therred. He looked back across the rolling hills toward Hammangard and the rest of his homeland. It hurt deeply to see it from so far away, and it was starting to sink in that he might not be able to return. Their attempt to rescue Rowan failed, and he lost Baryk too. Locke barely escaped the city himself without being caught, and they would be hunting him now. There was nothing left for him to go back to now anyway.

Despite knowing that, he considered riding back anyway and turning himself in. He thought if his family was to going to be put to death then he should be with them. Locke shook with rage and fear, letting his emotions get the better of him. He wanted more than anything to throw his life away rather than dishonor himself and his family by running. But he remembered what Rowan always told him about fighting to survive against all odds, and he knew that his uncle would want him to go on. His future, if there was one for him now, was across the vast plains that stretched between him and the northern kingdom of Everund.

With a final look back at the only life he knew, he wished then that he could make himself hate it all; if only to ease the sorrow. But despite all he endured growing up in Therred, he could not bring himself to resent it. There were people there he never got to say goodbye to, people he cared deeply for. He thought of all the things he said that he wished he could take back, and everything he would have done differently if he had known that it would all end like this. Locke turned his horse to the north, turning his back on Therred, which was home no longer. He hung his head, accepting the weight of his failure, and vowed to himself to make it right someday.

The treacherous route through the plains of Arbereth were legendary to Therredan and Everunder alike, and neither kingdom ventured into those vast arid lands lightly. He had no choice now but to risk his life in the crossing. At least it was late autumn, the mildest and wettest season for the plains, which meant less chance for wildfires. While that gave him relative safety from fires, it also meant a greater chance of orc raids. Locke faced a perilous journey to a faraway kingdom he had only read about in the books he found in his uncle's study; he was unsure whether he was prepared for the test of his body's endurance.

Locke travelled light on gear but heavy in heart through the afternoon haze. The plains stretched endlessly before him in a dizzying monotonous blur which had become entirely disorienting after only a few hours of riding. If not for Ravendark's compass leading him north, it would have been easy for him to get lost, and out there in the middle of nowhere, that meant certain death. His hasty departure meant he had no supplies; he had no food with him or camping equipment; not even a canteen for water. He did find a sizable flask under the saddle, however, which helped him to sleep later that first lonely night in the plains.

~

Locke arose the next morning, confused, and feeling nauseous from the bottle-ache, the last laugh of the spirits he imbibed the night before. His mouth was dry as wood and his head felt like it was full of gnomes hammering away at the backs of his eyes. He groaned as he gathered his meager equipment and began saddling his horse once again. Locke petted the horse affectionately for comfort, "Are you ready for our journey? It's going to be a long ride to Everund; if we make it at all."

The horse only shook its mane, giving no answer. He smiled to himself, "Well, we are a full day's ride from Hammangard, so the last river we are bound to see for days shouldn't be far from here."

He hopped into the saddle, bemoaning the stiffness of his body already, while dreading the hard ride to come. He gripped the reins and took a furtive glance back toward Therred before forcing himself and his horse forward. As he predicted, after an hour's ride westward he came to the Coryn River, which flowed northward out of the Aldarlain mountains to the south. Unfortunately, he could not see any mountains from where he was, no forests either, in fact he saw nothing at all. This deep into the plains the only thing that changed the landscape was the river.

Locke carefully guided the horse into the water, which was fairly shallow, standing in its deepest parts the water did not reach the stirrups. Without letting go of the reins, he jumped off its back and into the river. "Ah see, this is nice, isn't it?" he said holding the horse still and calm. He splashed himself, getting his clothes and hair wet to cool himself off. Locke pulled out the flask and filled it with as much water as he could, it was not much. He did not drink from it however; he knew better than to drink straight from the river. He would boil the river water in the flask over a fire before he drank it. While resting Locke let time get away from him as he soaked his aching body in the refreshing water.

His arm still burned, though Locke worried it was less of a lingering sensation and instead a possible sign of infection. Nonetheless, the gentle flowing water seemed to relieve some of the discomfort. As he was busy enjoying the coolness of the river, he did not notice shadows on the horizon, the black silhouettes of the Hammar Guard that had been tracking him since he fled the capital. He did notice the flaming arrow that they shot into the sky however. "Yavon's beard!" he exclaimed as he sloshed through the river, pulling his horse to the other side as quickly as he could.

Locke was not the only one to see the flaming arrow that the mage hunters had used to signal to each other, hidden nearby a small band of orc raiders had seen it too. Locke scrambled to get back on his horse which was difficult while soaking wet, and by the time he made it back into the saddle, the Hammar Guard were shooting at him. He kicked the sides of the horse and snapped the reins with a shout as an arrow brushed his face and he could not tell if it was the wind from its passing or its fletching that touched his cheek.

Three Hammar Guard rode hard trying to catch him, slowing only to ford the river. Locke looked back as he pressed his horse onward, and saw what was coming only a moment before the Hammar did. A loud and strange horn sounded from the north as two enormous boars with orc riders on top charged the unsuspecting mage hunters as they were exiting the river. Long spears were thrust through the gaps of the soldiers' armor and they were dehorsed by the same attack. Blood sprayed into the air from the attacks and the orcs howled with their tusks bared as they rode down the last of the Hammar, and beheaded him with a stone axe.

The last thing Locke saw as he rode out of sight was a look of intense hatred and wrath in the golden eyes of a blood-soaked orc that watched him escape. The image of the orc holding the severed head of one of his countrymen while glaring at him was hard to shake. He could still see the orc's gaunt body in his mind, a body covered in the scars of battle. Locke managed to get enough distance between them that he could not see the orcs, the Hammar Guard, or the carnage that befell them at the Coryn River.

Despite the comfortable distance, Locke was far from comfortable with the idea of stopping, so he pushed himself and the horse through the night as well. Only when he saw no signs of being followed did he dare make camp and a fire to eat and drink what little that he had. The following days were a blur, passing in long lonely hours which left him too exhausted to complain. He slumped against his horse's back for support and to take some of the burden off of his weary arms and back. The days passing with no water and no food left Locke feeling foggy and weak. He became delirious from the isolation of the plains and the toll it took on his spirits.

After hours of riding in the hot sun, he stopped to rest and recoup under what little shade he could find. Despite the gnawing pains from his tight, aching stomach, he managed to make the most of his exhaustion by letting his consciousness slip away. He arose hours later from a dreamless sleep unsure of where he was. Once he remembered, he wished he could go back to delirium, that state of waking dreaming where he was still back in Dellow. Locke could not tell what felt worse, his body or his soul, as he forced himself back into the saddle once more. He drank the last sip of sun heated water from the bottom of the flask before continuing his journey to Everund.

Time flowed strangely for him as the monotony of travel and disorientation stripped him of any ability to comprehend what was or was not real. Locke was hallucinating, seeing and hearing people from his past. He tried to shake the visions from his mind for fear of losing what sanity he had left. It worked for a time, but after several hours of silence, he began hearing the voice of a woman singing to him from far away. The voice was too distant for him to make out the words but he felt like she was telling him to stop. So, after many long hours of travel he chose to camp for the night, hoping his mind would clear with sleep.

Locke lay restless until the stars came out. Staring into the dark he desperately tried to sleep, yet its numbing embrace eluded him. His mind would not be still or empty, dark feelings tormented him. How could I have let them down? he thought as he rolled onto his side, trying to breathe slow and shallow. You are a coward, he thought of himself. Locke was not sure where the words came from or why they stung so deeply. But they were not lies, he should have gone back to help Baryk. He should have rushed the guards, and fought his way back into the castle.

Locke felt he should have done something; he could have done *anything*! But he did not. He had done nothing at all. He let them take Baryk from him, just like he let them take Rowan. He got up and furiously kicked a pile of dirt, creating a feeble cloud of dust. He gave up on rest and with some effort, he got his horse up and started riding again. Locke was not sure he could make it to Everund before his body gave up, so he lashed himself to the saddle with rope and pressed on. The young man pushed himself and the horse as hard as he could all through the night.

The young Therredan was completely unconscious by the time his horse carried him to the border of Everund. The early morning sun rose over the lower plains beneath the great falls which fell from the city of Belcard, where several farms took advantage of the abundant river water winding its way westward away from the plains. The horse trotted gently through a farmer's field and over to the crops which were growing in it.

The famished beast drank deep from a puddle of water and then started chewing on the crops; having not eaten in many days the poor thing was starving. It was not long before one of the farmer's children spotted the horse eating their crops and moments later the farmer himself came running out from his home from the far end of the field.

The farmer got close enough to see the horse's rider had collapsed on top of it, the young man on the saddle hung limp over the side with his red hair blowing in the breeze. The farmer shouted pointlessly at the horse, trying to get it to stop eating his crops while it continued to chew on a juicy head of cabbage. The horse brayed, shaking its mane and stamping its hooves when the farmer got too close. "Whoa now, easy there. I'm not going to hurt you," he said. The horse pulled away from him when he reached for Locke. "Okay, okay! I'm not going to hurt your friend either. He doesn't look so good, if you let me get him down, I could help him."

The horse calmed as the farmer talked to it, he approached slowly with his hands in the air talking to the horse in a soothing tone, "That's it, good horse. Let's just get your friend off there and take a look-see what's wrong, hmm?" Locke was not moving the farmer noted, as the horse allowed him to get in close. The young man's skin was sallow where it was not red with sunburn, his lips were cracked, and his face looked sunken.

The farmer patted the horse on its side reassuringly while carefully undoing the rope that was holding Locke up. He slid right off of the horse and the farmer caught him heavily, lowering him to the ground gently. Several of the farmer's children came running up to see what was going on.

"Quickly go to the temple, and get a cleric. Tell them there's an injured man," the farmer said. His eldest nodded and ran back through the fields. "Stand back all of you," he said to the rest of his children. He examined Locke's body for wounds, and found no arrows, nor jagged sword cuts. It seemed he had not been attacked.

The farmer noticed redness in the veins along the side of Locke's neck, which disappeared under a long leather sleeve covering the arm where the discoloration was coming from. The farmer knelt beside him, unbuckling the smithing sleeve and exposing Locke's shoulder. He gasped when he saw the strange red and gold lined armor that wrapped around the boy's burned arm.

The wounds looked septic and the redness in his skin was from the infection that was spreading rapidly through Locke's body. The farmer was puzzled by the strange armor and the severe burns along the boy's arm, but covered it again out of respect. He brought his waterskin to Locke's chapped lips, pouring cool water down his parched throat.

The horse neighed and mouthed at Locke's fire colored hair tenderly. "Don't worry now, our friend here is going to be just fine," he reassured the horse while they waited for help to come. It was not too long before a cleric from the temple arrived.

"What is going on here?" exclaimed the breathless cleric.

"We need to get this man to the temple right away, he needs healing. I'm not sure how it happened but his arm was badly burned."

The farmer pulled back the sleeve to show the cleric.

"Let's get him to the healers," the cleric said quickly.

They lifted him up, shouldering his dead weight and carried him into the city.

~

Locke slowly opened his eyes to see wooden rafters in a vaulted ceiling, but his vision was blurry and he had to blink several times before he could see clearly. He sat up slowly, and realized he was on a white cot in a small room. He panicked slightly when he noticed that he was shirtless, fearing someone might see the artifact on his arm. Locke saw his clothes on a table across the room along with his other belongings, so he forced himself out of bed to grab them.

It was easier than he expected, in fact he was feeling stronger than he had in days. His burned arm had healed into wavy pinkish scars and the blood sickness spreading throughout his body was gone. He snuck over to the table, slipping his leather arm sheath on, buckling it over his shoulder and throwing his shirt over it. Locke shoved his feet into his boots hastily, hopping on one foot and nearly falling over.

After getting dressed Locke noticed a black leather-bound book resting on the bedside table among his things. Curious, he opened the blank cover to find that it was the holy doctrine of the Temple of Light. He closed it slowly and put it back on the table before sneaking over to the door. Locke pressed his ear against it, listening for sounds from outside, but heard nothing.

He pulled the door open cautiously, poking his head through. He saw a large open chamber filled with rows of wooden benches facing a central altar at the other end of the room. The chamber appeared empty and not far from him were two large doors which he assumed must be the entrance.

Locke stepped out into the chamber and reached for one of the exit doors. Just before he could grab a handle however, the doors swung open and a fair faced man wearing white robes with red trim entered. He was carrying a staff over his shoulders with large clay pots hanging from either end, which were full of water.

"Oh, you are awake, good!" he said, smiling warmly at Locke who smiled back awkwardly.

The cleric spoke again, "Do you mind?"

Locke looked around confused, before realizing he was blocking the door and preventing him entry.

"Sorry," Locke mumbled, stepping back out of the doorway. The cleric turned sideways to get the water pots through the door.

"Thank you very much," he said while setting the water down. The cleric pulled the staff through the handles of the pots and with a quick, effortless spin it came free. He pressed the staff to the floor and leaned against it.

"My name is Erdan. A cleric of Yavon and caretaker of this temple." He made a grandiose gesture; the long sleeves of his robes made it look dramatic. Locke took the moment to admire his surroundings instead of just checking to see if the room was empty. He saw the high arched vaulted ceiling, and enormous side windows with stained glass mosaics. It looked nothing like the humble temple he was accustomed to in Dellow.

"Where is this place?" Locke asked while keeping distance between them.

"You are safe in the hands of our creator and his faithful servants. The Allfather has smiled on you and has seen you safely to the city of Belcard."

Locke looked puzzled and relieved, "This is Everund?"

The cleric smiled, "So you *are* Therredan then?"

Locke nodded and held his right arm while tugging nervously at the leather sleeve concealing the artifact below.

Erdan took notice.

"We healed your burns while you were unconscious. You were frightfully weak when we found you. It takes a tremendous amount of courage to travel between Therred and Everund on your own. That journey is dangerous even without life threatening burn wounds. The old trade routes are abandoned territory, frequently raided by orcs and bandits. You are lucky to be alive."

Locke relaxed a bit, "So... you've seen it then?"

Erdan smiled gently, "Yes, I have seen it. We had to remove your shirt to heal your wounds. However, we were unable to remove the armor, which made treating the burns... difficult. Belcard is a trade city and has more than its fair share of thieves, but do not worry, I will tell no one what I've seen."

"Do you know what this is?" he asked, pulling back the sleeve to show off the red metalwork of the segmented plate armor.

"I am afraid not. I am just a cleric. I was trained to read ancient texts and to heal with holy words; I am no artificer. I do know this though: artifacts that cannot be removed or that cause harm to their wearers are usually the work of dark magic. A powerful curse may be upon you, Therredan. I am certain that someone in Belcard could be of help identifying it further, but be careful who you show that to outside of this temple."

Erdan paused.

"Before you go," he said, taking the bag he was carrying off his back and handing it to Locke. "Take this for your journey. While I was out getting water, I got you supplies. It's not much. Some dried meat and fresh fruit, but these rations should be enough for a few days. If you need more, the temple of Yavon will always receive you, brother."

Locke took the bag, slinging it over his shoulder.

"Thank you... for everything. I don't know how to repay you."

The cleric smiled.

"Don't worry, you don't need to, the Light provides. Be safe, Therredan."

Erdan bowed farewell and Locke left the temple. The cleric called after him, "Remember friend, those who seek refuge in the Allfather will always find it!"

Locke waved goodbye to the young cleric and ventured out into the bustling river-falls city.

The late afternoon sun blinded him as he stepped into the stone paved streets, but when his eyes adjusted, he saw that Belcard was enormous, several times larger than any city Locke had ever been to. He could fit his known world inside of it and have room to spare. Locke was in awe of it, and terrified by it. He was comforted somewhat knowing he had enough food to get him through a few days but by then it was imperative to have tracked down his parents or to have found a job. He thought about how he was going to survive now, something he never really had to consider before. The Blackwoods were never well off, despite a claim to the throne of Therred, but they always had enough. They grew what they could, and traded for the rest.

This was different, he was on his own now, without land to provide either food or trade. He was a dislocated foreigner in a story book kingdom. Locke had no idea where to start when it came to looking for his parents, as all he was ever told about them was that they lived in the kingdom of Everund. He never imagined the kingdom to the north could be so vast. It was entirely likely that his parents did not even live in Belcard; they could be in the farthest northern city of Arrincroft or even in the mountain capital, the fabled crystal city of Erendar. He had no clues to go on, no information to track down, no leads to follow, and not even a name to ask around for.

Locke pulled the astromancer compass from under his shirt and held it in his open palm while he concentrated on the desire to find the parents he never knew. "My parents left me with my uncle when I was just a baby, and I know almost nothing about them, but I do know they live in Everund. Please, show me where they are," he begged. But the lid of the magical eye remained closed. To make sure it still worked he tested it again, "Show me where Erendar is." The magical iris opened and rolled northward, pointing the way.

Maybe it would be better to look for work he thought, as inevitably he would be hungry sooner rather than later. He was hopeful that in a city as big as Belcard there would be opportunities for people like him to work, but he was not sure where to look. He put the compass back under his shirt and sat on a ledge of a stone bridge which spanned large man-made drains below it. The drains were meant to catch overflow during heavy rains to prevent flooding, but they often played the role of a babbling brook for young folk that lived in the city to enjoy. Being built on river waterfalls, Belcard had many clever ways of diverting water out of the city.

It was a marvelous town, to Locke it smelled of clean streams and he liked that its streets were paved with river stones. Smoke rose from thatched roofed houses and oil lanterns hung from the street corners to provide light at night. Locke remembered it being so dark at night in the village of Dellow that few left the safety of their homes after dusk. He dangled his legs over the empty stone drain below and listened to the commotion of the city. It hummed with a sort of energy you could feel.

Some kids walked past him carrying prizes, fried meats and breads, all while talking excitedly about a festival they had just been to. Locke spun around, interested. "Excuse me!" he called out to the young boy who was hugging a small plush doll made in the shape of a half eagle, half lion creature. "Where is this festival? I'm a traveler from afar and I'd very much like to see it."

The other boy pointed toward the city center, "It's in the park, you can't miss it!" but he warned, "Just don't play that one ring game, I think that sour man is cheating."

Locke smiled, "Thanks a lot, kid." He hopped down from the bridge and the kids took off giggling. He was unfamiliar with Everunder holidays and wondered if he had arrived in Belcard the same day as one of their special events. He walked to the city center, as the sounds and the smells of the festivities grew stronger. His stomach growled at the wafting scents of street cart food.

Closer to the park, more people were heading through the narrow streets winding through the river-falls city. His levels of excitement rose in anticipation the closer he got. The farmer festivals around Dellow had dancers, jugglers, and even games, but he could not imagine the spectacle a city like Belcard could put on.

Locke approached an elderly man sitting on a bench at the edges of the park, "Excuse me, sir?"

The man looked up at him, surprised to see him standing there.

"What is it boy?" he grunted.

"I was wondering if you could tell me, what the occasion is for this festival?"

The old man chewed on his answer before sharing.

"Prince Elisander has been throwing this damned debauchery for a whole week! Can't sleep a wink without passing out drunk first. These kids with their loud music and young women running around half-naked. Some prince! Thinks he's so special that his arrival warrants a whole festival."

Locke slowly backed away from the old man, though he could still hear him ranting in the distance as he found his way to the park at last.

A Mysterious Figure

Enormous tents occupied the town square plaza, while folk of all genders and ancestry from throughout the kingdom of Everund danced and sang with carefree delight. Massive crowds gathered around huge fires while the smell of smoked meats and fried foods filled the air and Locke wished he could eat it all. He passed people in the streets who performed demonstrations of physical ability or simple magical tricks and illusions. There was a man who ate fire, a girl who contorted her body into a ball, and a person wearing an oversized hat and long cloak who was levitating just above the ground.

Locke was swept up by the mesmerizing sights all around him. He saw an old woman sitting in front of a piece of looking glass and was enthralled by her youthful reflection in it. When she got up and walked away, he wondered what he would see in the reflection and tried to get a closer look. Instead, he ran straight into a dwarf that he clearly did not see, and nearly knocked the two of them over.

"Watch it bub!" the dwarf snarled with a deep gravelly voice, warning him with a hard stare. He shoved Locke off him and a glint of gold peeked out from under the boy's right sleeve, which caught the dwarf's shrewd eye.

The unfriendly dwarf walked away smiling with a dark look that made Locke uncomfortable, and he was not gone for long before Locke was approached by a man in ragged clothes that smelled strongly of unpleasant bodily functions. The vagrant got into his face, close enough that Locke saw that some of the man's teeth had gone black.

"Beware young man! Your mortal soul is in danger!" he cried with a wavering voice, "Guard your purity for the decadence of the world tempts you! Your flesh makes you weak with unclean desire, cleanse the stains upon your soul!"

Locke backed away from him awkwardly and disappeared into the crowd. He returned to the splendor of the celebration, wandering dreamily through waves of people who seemed to flow through the festival like a river runs through a forest. The air was filled with laughter and music, and the revelry was good for lifting his spirits. Over the din of the festivities, Locke heard even louder people who were gathering around a commotion on the other end of the park that was hidden from his sight by a wall of onlookers.

From the center of the masses came a piercing, inhuman shriek that was unlike anything he heard before. His curiosity got the better of him, as it tended to, and he ran to see what was going on all the while pushing his way through the crowd to get a closer look. Locke waded through the awestruck bystanders, but kept his right arm close to his body to make sure the cursed armor stayed hidden as best he was able. Sounds of a wild beast grew louder as he made it through the rabble to stand in front.

At the center of the circle of enthralled onlookers he saw the most majestic mythical creature, before him stood a wild gryphon, a creature of the fey lands, half lion and half eagle. Its feathers were a mix of light and dark brown, its talons black as pitch, and its golden eyes were filled with fear as it was being manhandled by shady looking beast tamers. Locke wanted to be excited about getting to see such a rare animal, but seeing it being treated so poorly made his heart sink.

The handlers struggled to control the gryphon, which clawed at them and swiped at the onlookers to their screams of terror and delight. The gryphon tore at the open air with its massive talons in a ferocious attack that narrowly missed the tamers, some of which let go of their ropes as they dove for cover. Without the handlers holding it down, the gryphon broke free and charged the crowd with startling speed. The gryphon became a blur of feathers and rage running straight toward Locke. His eyes went wide and he instinctively put his arm up for defense, but in the instant before it hit him, everything stopped. The multitudes of people fell entirely silent, they were all frozen in place around him.

The entire city was suddenly perfectly still, the abrupt hush was intense and unnerving. Even in the deadest hours of the night there was the sound of nature like rustling leaves, chirping birds, or noisy bugs, but the hum of life was suddenly gone as well. Locke found himself in a moment of surreal oddity, where there were no sounds at all and the world was unnaturally still.

Impossibly still, as if all things in the universe had stopped moving altogether. Everything, that is, except him. Strangely he could still move his body freely. He surveyed the bizarre scene of the temporal anomaly, witnessing impossible phenomena such as objects floating in midair, and ever-burning flames caught mid exhale from a fire breathing street performer.

It was truly an eerie sight to behold, even the frenzied gryphon in front of him was frozen mid-slash, which Locke thought looked like a statue or taxidermy. But the strangest of all sights in that time-locked moment was the sudden perception of movement out of the corner of his eye. Someone's shadow moved through the frozen sea of people, though its owner was hidden from his view by the throng of festival goers. The shadow crept closer, weaving through the motionless crowd, but Locke still was unable to see who or what was approaching.

When they finally came into view, stepping out into the open plaza, Locke saw that the stranger was cloaked in white feathers. They were wearing a thick, hooded cloak of humble construction and adorned heavily with white owl feathers, which covered them nearly head to toe. Their hood was drawn up over their head for concealment and Locke wondered if it was some kind of costume for the festival. He witnessed the mysterious figure stop abruptly, looking around the area for something. As the person turned to face him, Locke found himself staring into the nearly blank face of a simple barn owl mask.

The stranger stood nearly as still as the people frozen in time, yet Locke felt a piercing gaze from eyes unseen, hidden behind the white owl mask. His heart raced anxiously and a knot tightened in the pit of his stomach. He stared back at the disguised person watching him, with neither of them moving for several awkward moments. Suddenly Locke felt a weird lurch throughout his body, and a clamor of celebration came back to the world. In a whirl of feathers the white owl person vanished back into the sea of people, who were once again moving.

Unaware of his surroundings and distracted, Locke did not see the gryphon hurtling towards him as he was looking through the bustling mob for the white owl person. A loud screech pulled his attention back to the gryphon, which reared up before him and brought its claws down. Locke raised his arm instinctively to defend himself again as the razor-sharp talons tore through the thick leather of the blacksmithing sleeve like it was paper. The people watching gasped, as Locke fell to the ground after being mauled by the frenzied beast.

The handlers managed to gain temporary control over the great gryphon, by pinning it to the ground with ropes. The shreds of Locke's sleeve fell away revealing the ruby colored armor, edged in gold which glinted in the midday sun in front of everyone. Several people started talking among themselves and others were moving through the crowd toward him. Locke looked into the eyes of the gryphon and saw the same fear that he was now feeling as the mob of folk began surrounding him. The wild creature struggled against the restraints, the anchors to which were being hammered into the ground. Locke tried to stand but a Zierian traveler grabbed him roughly before he got off his knees.

"Where did you get that you thief?" he shouted, pointing a dagger at the armor on Locke's arm.

Things were getting dangerous quickly, he needed a way out, and fast. He rarely came up with good plans when his life depended on it, yet somehow, they usually worked. Either way, he had no choice but try one of his crazy ideas. He gripped some loose dirt from the ground and threw it into the guy's face. The man shouted and blindly swung at him, but Locke had already broken free and was running toward the gryphon. He rammed his shoulder into a guy who was about to hammer an anchor into the ground and sent him flying back into the crowd.

"What the hell are you doing?" yelled a man barely holding on to the gryphon's leash. Locke ignored him and punched through the ropes securing the gryphon, using the razor edges of the artifact to sever them. The armor had cut his own fingers when he tried to take it off the first time, and he was right to assume it was sharp enough to cut the beast loose. With the weakening of its constraints, the mighty gryphon heaved upward against the ropes, throwing the man gripping its leash into the air.

The gryphon let out a piercing shriek and swiped at the crowd again, while everyone was running in all directions away from its rampage. Locke slipped away in the confusion, covering his arm as best as he could as he disappeared among the people fleeing. He looked over his shoulder as the gryphon took to the skies behind him. Unfortunately for him however, he did not escape the gaze of unwanted attention, and of all the criminals that lurked in the dark corners of the river-falls city, none were as insidious as Bolgud.

The grimy dwarf had already gotten a close-up of Locke's artifact as they collided earlier, even before the leather sleeve covering it was torn to tatters by the gryphon's talons. Bolgud had an eye for antiquities and was a ruthless murderer who would not think twice about stabbing someone before dumping their body in the sewer over a pocket watch. Bolgud was especially good at taking advantage of vulnerable people, one of his many villainous talents.

And Locke was an easy target with a high value payout, just the kind of opportunity Bolgud was looking for.

Locke checked behind him to see if anyone was following him as he left the city center, but he saw only the gryphon flying over the rooftops in the distance. He kept running from the park and, bumping into revelers as he made his hasty retreat from the chaos of the festival. The number of people around him thinned considerably the further away from the park he made it, yet somehow, he felt even more vulnerable in the darker, and narrower alleys. However, he saw no signs of anyone following him so he stopped to catch his breath.

"Where you goin' kid?" the gruff voice from behind him made him jump. He spun around to see a one-eyed man with a broken grin leaning in towards him. Locke ran off back through some alleys between shops, trying to evade the stranger. Lost and frantic, Locke found himself cornered as a gang of ruffians appeared out of the shadows all around him.

They cut off his escape at both ends of the alleyway with goons blocking the narrow passageways. They brandished weapons while sneering at Locke and their wicked laughs echoed off the brick walls. He stepped backward into a puddle, which soaked a cat that hissed at him and ran off, knocking over waste bins as it went. His soaked foot searched for solid ground to hold as he got into a defensive fist fighting stance. There were five of them in total surrounding him. One of them was slowly swinging a chain with a spiked iron ball at his side, and a grizzled looking man tapped a short wooden bat into his open palm threateningly.

"That is quite the trinket you have there," spoke a voice which sounded like stones grinding, as the dwarf Locke nearly knocked over earlier appeared from behind two particularly large goons. Bolgud's face was covered in scars and he twirled a small curved blade in his palm. His thick black beard was braided with wrought iron bands that jangled about his waist as he stepped closer, "You're going to give it to me."

Locke backed away from him and backed into one of the bandits that had surrounded him.

"I would love to help you out..." he nervously joked, "... But the thing is, I can't do that."

Bolgud shook his head, "Now, now, now. Don't be like that. How about we make a fair trade? You give me that armor, and you can leave here with your organs intact."

The goon behind Locke grabbed him and he struggled but was unable to lift his arms or move.

"Hold on!" he shouted. The dwarf stepped closer, pressing the blade to Locke's belly.

"It's a deal then?"

"No. Listen, you don't understand! It doesn't come off! I can't give it to you because I can't take it off!"

The dwarf admired the craftsmanship of the armor with a lust that was terrifying.

"Cursed?" Bolgud mumbled to himself as he poked at it with the tip of his dagger, "Or, perhaps you think you are clever."

"I'm telling you the truth, it doesn't come off, trust me!" Locke pleaded.

Bolgud smiled wickedly, dragging the blade up Locke's arm.

"I guess we'll find out."

The dwarf motioned with a hand and the goons forced Locke to the ground, pinning him on his back. The dwarf started hacking into Locke's shoulder with his blade, determined to take the artifact from Locke by any means. Locke screamed as the blade disappeared deep into his shoulder.

The man holding him down pressed his hand over Locke's mouth, quieting him. The sadistic dwarf went in for another swing, when out from the shadows sprang the feather-cloaked figure with the owl mask. With a quick spin kick, the white owl person knocked Bolgud into a wall and scared the rest of the thieves away with a roar like a lion.

Locke saw the world tip over and the street rise to meet his head painfully. His flesh turned pale as blood poured out of the gash in his right shoulder. Locke saw the owl mask face staring down at him just before he lost consciousness.

~

The white owl person dragged Locke's limp body along, taking him through the back alleys of Belcard. Eventually he came to, and tried to get his feet under himself. Locke felt dizzy, like everything was spinning, it was making him queasy and weak on his feet. It did give the stranger a moment of reprieve from carrying him, they stepped back and the mysterious cloaked person pulled the owl mask off, revealing a young woman with raven-black hair.

The girl's enormous cloak had been designed to honor the barn owl, but the rest of her shabby outfit was hand-stitched together, and woven with random materials scavenged from the woods. She was certainly not from the river-falls city, honestly, she looked like she had never been in a city before. She seemed more at home in the wild. She had a pointed nose and kind gray eyes filled with concern.

"Come on, stay with me."

Delirious and faint, Locke stumbled on uneasy legs, forcing the raven-haired girl to catch him. "We need to get you out of here," she said walking him westward. Through the pain and blood loss, Locke could no longer tell where they were going and he barely noticed as they slipped out of the city and into the surrounding forests. When they were far enough away to be hidden from sight, the young woman set Locke down so he could rest.

He smiled weakly and said, "You should lighten up! We can clean the stables tomorrow! Rowan went to see the lady Roselyn about making you a new cloak." Locke was speaking incoherently, delirious from blood loss. It was not long before his head slumped back as he lost consciousness again.

She tried to wake him, "Oh, come on, don't die on me now." He was sickly pale and clammy with sweat breaking out across his body, which she knew was not a good sign. She took off her cloak and pressed it to his wound, trying to slow the blood loss. His condition was worsening by the minute and she realized that she could not wait to get to grove before getting him the help he needed, he would not survive the trip. His body grew colder with every shallow breath, and he would be in the Great Mother's welcoming embrace if she did not act fast.

The cloaked girl's mind raced, trying to remember her brief training with the healing arts before she had chosen a different path.

Her mind kept coming up blank, and she cursed that she did not pay more attention to her healing lessons. If she could not save him, she figured it would not be all that bad. After all, there was no strife or suffering in the presence of the Great Mother, so at least he would be at peace.

The more she thought about him dying though, the worse she felt. It was making her sick to her stomach. She witnessed him risk his life to free that wild gryphon, she could not leave him to die. But no matter how hard she tried, she could not remember the spells, so she did the only thing she knew how to do when she had no other options. She asked the Great Mother for help.

She knelt down beside Locke and spoke in a long-lost language not heard by civilized people since before the age of the modern world. Her words reached deep into the soil and out through the air, calling out for the Great Mother to come to her aid. The wind whispered back to her, calming her frayed nerves. She listened intently to the words whistling past her ears and the answer revealed itself to her. It was so simple, something she should have remembered from her childhood. She shot up with a smile.

"Thank you, Gaia!" she said before running into the woods, searching from tree to tree for one that had clothlike bark, whose sap was thick and full of rejuvenating powers. The bark and sap together would act as both a salve and seal for the wound. The tree she needed would be a short sapling with red-colored berries growing in bunches, and would smell of cinnamon.

However, there did not seem to be any nearby, and she unsure in which direction she should look for the plant she needed. She feared she might not find it in time to save the life of the young man, who she had risked the exposure of her kind in order to rescue. She darted across the forest floor, hoping to see a glimpse of it anywhere, when the hoot of an owl broke her focus. The cloaked girl spun her head around to find a hawk-owl perched high above her on the branches of a conifer. Most of her kin slept during the day, but luckily for her she found a diurnal cousin. She was relieved to see a relative of her order looking after her.

"Can you help me sister? I am looking for medicine to help someone who is badly injured. I need a certain tree with light bark that peels away in the summer and grows bright red berries in the spring. Have you seen one of those anywhere?"

The owl tilted her head as the cloaked girl spoke to her, and she gave a small whistle in reply before jumping from her perch and flying off into the woods. The girl ran after the owl, following through the light scrub brush while jumping over fallen trees. She struggled to keep up with the hawk-owl's speed and almost lost sight of it at one point. She heard a stream nearby and observed as the owl landed in the branches of the actual tree she was looking for. The owl let out a soft, happy hoot.

"Thank you, sister, you are a lifesaver!" she said emphatically as she ran up to the tree. With a quick prayer to the Great Mother and a thank you to the tree, she peeled away the outer bark, which came off in large strips covered in a thick sap on the underside. She carefully rolled up a few strips of the bark and smelled the distinct scent of cinnamon from them. She tied them around her waist and pulled out her water skin. She poured it around the base of the tree, in thanks for the gift. With a parting wave to her owl friend, she headed back to Locke.

The trees blurred past her as she ran back through the woods, while vaulting over obstacles like a doe bounding through a field. By the time she made it back to Locke, her heart was pounding and she was gulping for air. She knelt beside him and pulled his shirt off, which was soaked through with his blood. She undid the clasps of what remained of the tattered leather sleeve over his right arm and pulled it away. The gash in his shoulder was exposed, which had mostly stopped bleeding due to extreme loss of blood.

The girl was surprised to see that he wore some sort of strange red armor from his wrist up to his shoulder. Its segments were wrapped around skin that was scarred by fire. Ignoring the strange armor, she wiped away the caked blood from his wound and quickly unwound the bark she carried with her. The sap was unbelievably sticky, which she applied over the gash in his shoulder. She pressed the bark flat against his skin until the sap squeezed out from either side of it. She held it firmly in place until she was satisfied that it would stay on its own.

The raven-haired girl picked up another piece of bark and overlapped it across the previous piece. The girl continued the process until she was completely out of the bark. Afterward, she ripped the bottom of her shirt and tore it into strips, tying them together and wrapping them around his shoulder to hold the bark bandages in place. She waited at his side, praying to the Great Mother until color returned to his face and he looked stable enough to leave him alone for a while. She picked up her bloody owl-feather cloak and his blood-caked shirt and went back into the woods to find the creek she heard earlier so she could wash the blood from their clothes.

~

Locke awoke in the woods to the scent of fresh dirt and vegetation. He sat up and found his shoulder bandaged. Not long after, the white owl girl returned and upon seeing him awake, she bent down and checked his bandages. Locke looked confused but did not stop her.

"You are alive, that's good," she said.

"Did... did you save me back there?" he asked, really taking her in for the first time. He stared at her strange animal hide clothes, her feathered cloak, and the beads woven into braids across the side of her head. She nodded and offered him a water skin made from moose hide. He took a deep drink from it, wiping his mouth with his sleeve when finished.

"Who are you?" he asked.

She tied the skin back to her belt before responding.

"My name is Aeysha, of the Order of the White Owl."

He continued to look puzzled.

"Right, well, thank you for saving me. My name is Locke, from," he paused trying to think of how to tell her, "... well, it's complicated."

She waved her hand dismissively.

"We don't have time for you to explain, can you stand?" Aeysha asked.

"Yeah, I... I think so."

"Good, we cannot stay here," she said urgently.

"Where are we?"

"Just outside the river-falls city, but I cannot stay here any longer and, in your condition, it would be unwise for you to return to the city. Your wounds have stabilized but you require more healing, so you are going to have to come with me. If we can make it to the sacred grove before the meeting concludes, I am certain that my fellow druids can heal you."

Locke attempted to stand up on his trembling legs, and felt a sickening rush in his head. He lost his balance and stumbled but Aeysha caught him. She pulled his good arm over her shoulder to help carry his weight again.

"Careful, you lost a lot of blood," she said gently as she led them slowly through the woods, one deliberate step at a time. Locke was still disoriented, "Where are we going again?" he asked.

The Eternal Ring

Locke and Aeysha traveled northwest together for hours at a slow and steady pace, going deeper into the woods and heading toward the Eld Ridge Mountains. After listening to nothing but the sounds of leaves crunching and twigs snapping underfoot as evening was settling in, Locke started regaining some of his senses. "You know..." he said, breaking the silence between them, "I don't know how to thank you again for..."

"It was nothing, really," Aeysha said quickly.

Locke let it hang in the air for a moment before saying, "It wasn't nothing to me. I mean you kinda saved my life."

"The Great Mother Gaia teaches us to protect all life, even if they are towners."

"You really don't like people much do you?" he joked.

She looked at him sideways then wordlessly looked away.

Even in the fading light of day Locke could tell that the trees were getting closer together and the vegetation was growing denser as they walked and he saw the ominous Mountains of Eld through the treetops. The incline of their walk increased as they approached the foot of the Eld Ridge Mountains, and Locke hoped wherever they were going was not much further because he was getting really tired.

Eventually they came to a large stone structure in the forest, a primitive man-made arch which was covered in moss and had runes carved into it. When they passed through the ancient stone archway, they wound up in a massive clearing in the trees which had not been there before. In fact, looking at the trees, Locke was not sure if they were still in the same woods.

The dense canopy over the new clearing was blocking out the setting sun with branches that stretched like vines across the vast distances between the impossibly larger trees. The branches were intricately woven together in curling patterns of naturally made latticework; as if the trees grew that way.

Broken light filtered through the leaves around a large shaft of sun which beamed down on the center of the grove. The light fell perfectly halfway across an arrangement of upright stones as tall as a standing bear, all of which circled a glowing white tree. The tree and the inward face of the stones were lit as brightly as midday, but the rest of the clearing and the outward face of the standing stones were shadowed like night.

The grass in the clearing was damp and it soaked through Locke's boots as he walked through the hallowed grove. He stepped over toadstools which glowed softly from under their glacier blue colored caps. The mushrooms were growing in a perfect circle around the perimeter of the clearing, and their bioluminescence illuminated carvings on the backs of the stones. The tall, smooth stones which surrounded the luminous tree had primal runes carved into their outward faces that were barely visible in the faintly reflected azure mushroom glow. The rough carved shapes were a depiction of the moon, the lunar runes were representations of the different phases of it.

The inward face of the stones, lit by daylight, had different runes carved in them which Locke guessed must be related to solar phases since the back ones were about the moon.

"This place is sacred..." Aeysha whispered with reverence as she carefully walked across the soft moss that grew on the ground around the stones, "... my father used to tell me stories about the Grove of the Keepers." She looked reverently at a patch of brilliant yellow flowers shaped like bells which were blooming in the moss.

Locke was awed by the ethereal beauty of the sacred grove; the paradoxical place was enchanted by day and night at the same time. The colors were mesmerizing, the outer ring a bluish tint, the inner ring of sun yellow, and concentrated around the white tree's roots were a bunch of blood red crystals sticking out of the dirt. But before they could take another step into the grove, they heard noise coming from the trees around them.

From all around the clearing, strange-looking people suddenly came into sight. They were an odd assortment of hybrids; some of them had animal parts, like fur or antlers, and others were partly plant-like, looking like trees or mushrooms. There were nearly forty of them in total that Locke counted as they entered the grove, each one of them was unique and seemed to represent a different aspect of nature. They circled in on the intruders of their cherished thicket, staring at Locke in a way that made him feel entirely unwelcome.

"Why have you brought an outsider into our sacred grove, young one?" demanded a man who was half elk in appearance. His voice shook when he spoke, like the charms tied around his antlers did when he moved. Aeysha knew they would be upset, but hoped they would understand when she explained the situation.

"He saved a gryphon from captivity, and was attacked after. I couldn't leave him to die at the hands of a gang of murderous thieves."

Some of the druids gasped at her words.

"You went into a city?"

Aeysha could feel disappointment in their hushed whispers and in their exchanged looks.

"Yes, I-" she started but was interrupted.

"You risked the exposure of our people," said a woman whose hair was made of brambles and skin covered in patches of bark.

"You know we live out of sight; it is our place to maintain the Balance from afar. Not upset it by drawing attention to our kind. It was unwise to bring him here," scorned the elk-man. Locke started to feel faint, he turned pale again and was having difficulty standing. He was unsure if the half-animal, half-plant people he was seeing were really there or just a hallucination brought on by blood loss.

"Farashun, he is severely wounded! If Keeper Rianee could take a look at him, I know that he would be abundantly grateful! Grateful enough that he would not share any of what he has seen here," Aeysha pleaded.

The gathering of druids discussed in hushed tones what to do about the outsider in their midst, as the world spun wildly for Locke who looked on bewildered.

"I don't feel so good," he said as his legs gave out beneath him. Locke collapsed on the mossy ground, silencing the debate.

"Great Mother forgive me, but I will not wait for the council to decide his fate," said Keeper Rianee, a woman who was almost entirely made of flowers.

Many of her fellow druids looked on disapprovingly as the most knowledgeable healer among their order weaved fresh green shoots from the dirt beneath Locke. They grew into vines which gently coiled around his body, branching out and growing buds which blossomed into white, six-pointed star petaled flowers.

Keeper Rianee whispered to the flowers in an ancient language, far older than humanity itself, and as she did, a delicate green glow enveloped Locke. Rianee pleaded with the spirit of the world, "O' wise and ancient mother, embrace this wayward child with your boundless compassion and take his wracking pain. Heal his wounds, and open his heart."

She chanted more words in that ancient tongue which made nature stir at the sheer sound of it. More vegetation grew around the young man's wounded shoulder and the deep cut in his flesh closed beneath the dressing Aeysha put over it. After completing her magic, Rianee stood up while the magic continued to work on the gash in Locke's right shoulder until it healed completely.

"He will be fine. Gaia looked into his heart and has chosen to heal him. And if the Great Mother saw fit to help the outsider, then so should we," she ended by speaking to her fellow druids.

Farashun nodded, and his antler charms rattled.

"There will be no more discussion. Until we have concluded our meeting he may stay. But you, Aeysha, shall be responsible for him. Including making sure that he does not discuss what he has seen with anyone."

The raven-haired girl nodded in agreement.

"Of course. For the Balance."

Locke slowly came to, stirring beneath the roots and vines growing over him. His eyes popped open, and he pulled against the tendrils of nature wrapped around him. Rianee and Aeysha helped him remove the flora and got him back on his feet.

"What did you do?" he asked, touching his shoulder where the gash was, and feeling only his own skin. There was no scar marking where the dwarf cut him or where the wound had closed. "Amazing..." he said dumbfounded, "... thank you."

Rianee smiled softly.

"Do not thank me, young one, thank the Great Mother. She is the reason you are still alive, in more ways than one."

He smiled back uncomfortably before she walked away from him. Aeysha hugged Locke, which he returned hesitantly.

"I am glad that you are safe," she said.

Locke looked at the druids who still had their eyes on him.

"Yeah, me too."

Aeysha stepped into the center of the stones and under the glowing white tree and addressed the crowd.

"Keepers of the Balance, the real reason I have come here is not to save this towner, but to share with you ill news. My father, the Keeper of elemental air and also leader of the Eternal ring, is dead."

Mourning for this news enveloped the clearing as she continued, "He has been missing for some time, as you know, and I have been trying to track him down for weeks. When I finally caught up to him however, I found only his body. He was murdered."

Locke looked just as shocked as everyone else to hear that Aeysha's father had been killed.

"Without a Keeper to protect and guide the energy of air, the elements will fall out of equilibrium," the elk druid stated.

"Violent storms will ravage Averon if there is no one to control the Eternal Ring," said another druid, who appeared to be part rabbit and was of indeterminate gender.

"In order to prevent elemental chaos, we must promote a new leader, immediately!" a turtle-man shouted from the back.

"Leadership should pass to the next element in line! Vardoc should take control of the Eternal Ring," someone else stated.

"We should seek another Keeper to take the mantle of the Order of Four Winds!" the bramble woman shouted.

"We cannot wait to train a pledgeling to take on that burden in order to lead the Ring. It should pass to the next in line!" said another druid to raucous approval.

"The Keepers nominate Vardoc of the Feral Flame to serve, for the Balance," they all agreed. "Until a new druid of Air can be chosen and trained, the cycle changes hands."

Aeysha interrupted them.

"That will not be necessary. I intend to take my father's place."

The gathering of Keepers broke out into shock and derision, especially from Vardoc, who was personally insulted by her arrogance.

"You are already bound to service, youngling!" he spat.

"That is true, I am. But it is not written in the rings that one of the Keepers must be unbound. So therefore, I offer my life for the Balance. I will renounce my current Order, take my place among the

Eternal Ring, and I shall take my father's mantle as my own," Aeysha said firmly.

"Impossible!" Vardoc screamed, his rage no longer boiling under the surface but visibly burning across his skin as it started on fire. "This is unheard of! In all the ages of this world that we have protected the Balance, never has a druid broken their bond!"

"It has never been done. But it is not forbidden," Aeysha said coolly. She had come too far and been through too much for this moment, and she would not be told no. The Keepers reluctantly discussed the matter, reigniting the same argument as before. There was little that could be done to stop her, so ultimately, they decided to allow it. Gaza T'sann of the Wise Waters approached Aeysha, and in a comforting tone he spoke to her.

"Following the binding ceremony, you will lose your humanity forever. To be a Keeper is not an easy path and it is more trying than you know, youngling. Are you certain this is what you want?"

She nodded.

"Gaza, you have always been a kind friend to my father, and your wisdom is invaluable as ever, but this is what must be done. For the Balance," Aeysha spoke with the same confidence that her father had led the Eternal Ring with, which helped assuage some of the doubts from her fellow druids.

Vardoc fumed, crossing his arms over his bare chest, while the other Keepers gathered around the mound of earth which was drawn for the Eternal Ring. Aeysha followed after, stepping up to the rune on the ground marked for the element of air. Gaza T'sann of the Wise Waters slowly walked to his place in the binding circle and stood upon the rune for water.

Followed by a grunt, as a man of the stone hills walked up to the young woman. She was given an intimidating look from Thoran Nale of the Enduring Earth, whose stony face and gem-like eyes measured her carefully as he towered over her. She looked him straight in the face and did not falter. He smirked and then took his place within the binding circle, standing upon the rune of earth.

"This is an outrage!" Vardoc hissed as embers flitted from him, "You would allow this owlet to abandon her kin and deny me my right to rule?"

Locke saw mixed reactions to Vardoc's complaints upon the faces of the druids, at least on those who still looked human enough to have them.

Gaza said, "It is unusual Vardoc that is true, and many of us agree with your claim. However, the girl is determined and as she has pointed out, it is not against our rules."

Farashun, lord of elks, chimed in to offer his support.

"We have decided. Aeysha will take her father's place as Keeper of the Four Winds. For the Balance."

"If you choose not to honor our people's decision you would be opposing the will of the Great Mother," Gaza said calmly to the infuriated Keeper of fire, "Do not make enemies of family, brother."

Vardoc looked around the gathering, meeting the eyes of every druid around him, before allowing his arms to drop to his sides.

"Fine then."

He glared at Locke as he stepped up to the binding circle. Locke appeared confused and looked around to see if anyone else knew why he was being glared at, but no one else seemed to notice him. The fiery easterner, Vardoc of the Feral Flame, stepped onto the rune for the element of fire and with all of them gathered, Gaza began the binding ceremony.

Thoran, Gaza, Vardoc, and Aeysha all closed their eyes, chanting words in their primal language, while the runes beneath them glowed with power. The elements of nature reacted to their summons and the spirits of fire, water, and earth surrounded the three Keepers of the Eternal Ring. Whirling winds gathered in the center of the circle, forming clouds which darkened and crackled with blue lightning. They stopped chanting and the Keepers glowed with the primal power of early cosmos; from this point they could only observe the elements as they decided if the girl was worthy of them.

"Aeysha, step into the circle and be tested. If the element of air accepts you as we have, then you will be allowed to complete the binding ritual and join the Keepers," Gaza said reassuringly. She nodded and stepped off her rune and into the center of the ring.

The winds whipped around her body, and started violently pushing her around, but she stood her ground. Feathers flew off her cloak, torn away by the high winds, before the whole cloak itself was pulled from her shoulders. The charms and talismans she wore such as the white owl talons, the symbols of her Order, were stripped from her clothes one by one. The swirling tempest surrounded her and everyone took a step back as the young girl was battered by severe winds.

Aeysha remained still and calm at the center of the storm, and once her former attachments were gone, the elements started to calm as well. The wind's temperament seemed to change as they became playful, blowing her hair about and brushing against her body like a cat. The element of air lifted her arms from her sides and then lifted her whole body into the air while she giggled.

The clouds darkened as they swirled about her body, making her glow like the other Keepers. Lightning crackled off of her skin as she became one with the element to which she was now bound. She struggled to contain the wild energy, but she slowly starting to absorb the power of air into herself while ascending beyond her humanity and into a new state of being.

"Arise, Aeysha of the Wandering Wind, daughter of the sky!" said Farashun, leader of the Ring of Blood.

"Serve the Order of the Four Winds and lead the Eternal Ring!" spoke Rainee, leader of the Ring of Seasons. When Aeysha stepped forward, she walked upon the air rather than the earth, and her eyes were filled with lightning.

"Fellow Keepers, I will honor my father's legacy, and protect the element of air with my life. For the Balance!" Aeysha said, joining Farashun and Rainee as the leaders of the Three Rings.

"For the Balance," the druids all said in unison.

Locke stared in awe of the event, completely unable to comprehend what it was that he just witnessed. All he knew was that Aeysha looked changed after the binding ceremony, and not just physically either. There was a different air about the way she carried herself. Locke sat down and observed the druids as they embraced each other in celebration. He was utterly fascinated by them, their culture, their rituals, and their magic. The druids of Averon were a peculiar group made up of all the mortal beings on the planet. An entirely unique culture, ancient traditions passed down in secret.

They rejected the modern world, preferring a harmonious way of living with nature, a simpler way of life.

To learn that they were just people who decided to eschew the niceties of the developed world in order to live within the natural world, was a life altering experience indeed. The contrast between the light and shade of the grove, cast them in a peculiar way which made them look more surreal than they already did. Perhaps he was still lying unconscious in the streets of Belcard and the whole scene before him was an illusion crafted by his mind in some fever dream.

Despite Locke's struggle with the reality of their existence, they continued on, nearly forgetting that he was there. The gravity of being the sole witness to their enigmatic order was not lost upon him as he quietly and contently listened to their discussions. To be in their hallowed grove, to meet their reclusive members, to experience their amazing powers, and see their most sacred rituals was an honor to say the least. He knew this memory was going to be worth more to him than all the gold he could spend in a lifetime at the Old King's Glory, retelling this tale over and over again.

Farashun quieted them with a swift stomp of his hoof, "Keepers, now that our Order has been restored and the cycle preserved with the Eternal Ring back in balance by installing a new Keeper, we need to discuss the dark whispers in the forest."

He was referring to a growing restlessness and unease in the natural world from unnatural powers stirring in the mountains above them. "The Great Mother has called to each of you with a dire warning. A shadow is creeping over the world, and it poses a threat to Gaia. It is up to us to discover the source of this corruption and to shine light on the darkness that endangers the Balance."

The druids brought forth rocks, leaves, feathers, fishbones, and a dead crow, placing them on a flat stone altar. Each piece of nature that was offered was marked by the dark magic which was woven into the world.

"These signs are what you have seen, or what your Order companions have revealed to you. Let us see if we can learn what is behind this magic," Farashun concluded, "Nature, our gift from the Great Mother, has the infinite power of healing. Streams wash away filth, sands absorb poisons, winds carry away toxic fumes, and flames burn away rot. Nature has always cleansed this world of the decay that mortal beings weave into it."

He motioned to the gathering to move in closer. The druids huddled tightly around the bits of nature that were touched by the darkness in the mountains above.

"Together now," Farashun said, leading their chant in that strange ancient language that made trees dance. Locke felt the presence of an energy surrounding him that came from nowhere. It was an uncomfortable feeling, the kind of dread when something is right behind you. He heard a voice which did not come from the rising power in the grove looming over him. It originated from within his mind, he felt as though he 'heard' it coming from somewhere to his right. The female voice whispered warmly to him.

"Do not be afraid," was all she said.

It was so faint he could not be sure he had heard it at all. The presence within the grove seemed to be growing all around him, as if the whole forest was coming to life. It thrummed along with the druids' chants, and he wondered if they were calling their Great Mother. There was no way for him to know for sure but that was what it felt like. Shadows grew darker and the trees moaned as cold winds assailed them. A horrific shriek came from the altar, which ended the druids' chanting.

Their attention was drawn to the objects the druids had collected from the forest as the river stone sizzled and gave off acrid smoke before it melted. The leaves on the altar withered and became dust. The feathers burst into green flames before turning into ash. But most terrifying of all was the crow, whose corpse started moving on its own. Locke's mouth hung open, transfixed with terror, as the dead animal stood up from the altar, opened its beak and screamed. The sound which came from it was unlike anything he had ever heard before and it made all the hairs on the back of his neck stand up.

Farashun waved his arm over the altar quickly, which seemed to sever the spell they had evoked. The crow fell silent and fell back to the ground, stiffly. Aeysha looked shocked at what she just witnessed, for she had never seen dark magic before. Few had ever encountered so foul a blight upon nature as the curse they just revealed, but they at last understood why Gaia was crying out. Gaza T'sann was deeply concerned, but he was not frightened like they all were, it seemed familiar to him as though he had seen it before.

Farashun spoke aloud his thoughts.

"The Balance is in danger. All of Averon could succumb to this... this evil magic, whatever it is." Gaza closed his glacier-blue eyes slowly and crossed his arms. "It is death magic," he said, gaining everyone's attention.

"What do you know of this death magic?" Rianee asked, her voice heavy with concern. Gaza did not open his eyes, remaining calm and guarded as he spoke.

"I have seen it before. A memory of a dark past for my people, a cult who worshiped a man who controlled the dead. When I was a boy, they came to my village. They desecrated my ancestors' graves and raised an army from their corpses. Most of the living were killed before they were stopped."

Farashun ran two fingers through the tuft of fur growing from the bottom of his snout-like chin.

"If what Gaza says is true, then it is a magic from the towners. We have no known way of stopping this death magic."

Rianee offered optimistically, "We will find a way, the Great Mother will help us."

Vardoc scoffed, "What good are the Keepers if they can't deal with a curse? You brought us all here, wasted our time and all to discover you can do nothing?"

Gaza looked annoyed.

"We heal that which lives, and help return the dead to nature. This magic is beyond our understanding and violates the cycle. We can't fight what we don't understand."

Aeysha suddenly had an idea and looked up enthusiastically.

"No, we can't," she said, pointing to Locke, "but maybe he can." Suddenly all eyes were on the fire-haired man from Therred who was sitting at the edge of their gathering.

"What? Me?" Locke asked looking confused, and Aeysha smiled brightly back at him.

Farashun looked exasperated.

"And how exactly is he going to be able to help us fight death magic?"

Locke looked at Aeysha, wondering the same thing because he had never seen anything like it and had no idea how to fight it.

"He will help us gain an audience with the prince of Everund, who happens to be in the river-falls city, not far from here."

That idea did not go over well with the druids who grumbled to one another.

"Outsiders?"

Aeysha responded, "As was said before, we cannot fight this magic, but perhaps the outsiders can. Gaza told us it is magic from their world, so they must know a way to stop it. And *that* man can get them to listen to us. We will get the outsiders to fix the evil their magic has produced, purge it from our Great Mother, and restore the Balance."

Farashun nodded, the charms on his antlers clacking,

"Very well, Aeysha, but you will go with the outsider to find this prince of Everund. You will deliver the Great Mother's plea for help. The Balance now rests upon your shoulders."

Aeysha looked at all of them and said, "I will not fail."

Farashun gestured respectfully.

"Who else will go with the Keeper Aeysha?" he asked, and no one volunteered. After a long moment of silence, Gaza T'sann finally sighed deeply.

"I will watch over the youngling."

The Prince's Offer

Stepping out of the sacred grove of the druids was just as disorienting as going in was, it was like suddenly waking from a dream. Locke was pretty sure the sun was still out when he entered, but it was deep night by the time he left. They ventured back to the bustling trade city of Belcard with Aeysha and Gaza in tow, under the veil of the starry sky above. The young Therredan was eager to meet the prince of Everund, "I can't believe we're really going to try to gain audience with Everunder royalty!"

Aeysha did not share his enthusiasm.

"What if the prince won't listen to us? We druids keep to ourselves for a reason, you know. Most of these 'civilized' people look down on us like we are simpletons who live in the woods. They do not know they are the ones who are blind, they don't see how they mistreat nature. They are deaf to the cries of the Great Mother; they are callous and arrogant," she spoke with anger and hurt.

"How much do you know about the kingdom of Everund, Aeysha?" Locke asked earnestly.

"Not much. Though I'm sure it is no different than any other, concerned with its own power and wealth, and nothing else."

"This is the first time I've ever been to Everund myself, but I've read about it and I've heard lots of stories. It's nothing like where I grew up. The man who holds Therred hostage blamed the Magi and their magic for the losses we suffered in the war when our former capital, Durengard was destroyed by Duscar. His supporters spread propaganda about how it was the Magi who left Therred to burn after they provoked the wrath of the dragons, and how the new, 'illegitimate' kingdom of Everund was founded on their lies. I have no idea how much of what I heard growing up is true or not. I do not know if this king rules his kingdom with honor, but I do know Duscar and how they nearly destroyed the world. Our people still talk about the horror of dragons burning our lands to ash."

Aeysha's gray eyes met Locke's sympathetically as he continued, "I also know that Everund was founded after the war, and that it was created for a single purpose. To defend the realms should the dragons engulf this world in war again. They may not listen to nature, and they may not listen to me, but they will listen to threats of Duscar's return. If there is dark magic rising from the ruins of that place, then it is their duty to do something about it."

Gaza smiled at Aeysha.

"Keeper, this outsider you found is surprisingly wise."

Locke laughed awkwardly, unsure if he should be insulted or not. Aeysha seemed suddenly lost in thought and paid no attention to Locke's reaction, or to Gaza's words. A lot was resting on her shoulders at that moment and she was feeling uncertain about her decisions. It was her idea, after all, to trust an outsider to protect the Balance. An act which did not make her popular among the Keepers. There must be some reason the Great Mother revealed him to her in that crowd at the festival she reassured herself.

"But will it be enough?" She voiced her concerns aloud.

Locke pulled the astromancer compass from under his shirt.

"This was given to me by one of their esteemed magi, a Lord Ravendark."

Locke was pained somewhat when memories of Baryk and Rowan came back to him, he continued nonetheless, "Shortly before... before I fled Therred. It might get us the prince's attention, but we will still have to convince him ourselves. So, we just tell one of the most powerful men in Averon to commit knights and weapons to fight a death magic threat we don't fully understand, because it is definitely a danger to everyone, we think. Yeah, easy."

Aeysha appreciated Locke's candor but she was not convinced that the word of the wind and a necklace from one of their magi in the hands of a Therredan exile would be enough to gain the prince's favor. Their thoughts about the likelihood of the success of their mission aside, they made the trek through the woods toward Belcard without more discussion about it. Each of them secretly hoped their plea would be heard, but only time would tell what the prince would do. They walked through most of the night before stopping to make camp, deciding to get a couple hours of sleep before they finished the rest of their journey in the morning.

~

"Your highness, what happens when your father finds out about this? We should return to Erendar and report back to the king about the failed negotiations at once. Preferably before the supplies we were supposed to give to Therred are all used up," said the stoic female knight standing at the prince's side as she brushed some of her bouncy strands out of her face. The gallant prince Elisander's pouty lips curled into a scoundrel's grin.

"What is there to find out, captain? We are docked in Belcard to refuel, and you know how hard it is to come across enough brimstone for a ship. We, my good lady, are merely enjoying the festival these good townsfolk happen to be throwing on my behalf. You know these merchant class folks are always looking for an excuse to throw a party!" Kayara was not amused. She thought his hedonistic behavior to be beneath the prince.

"The knights are weary Kayara, soon enough we will have to bring bad news to our people. War with Therred seems inevitable. So, for now I want them to enjoy this peace, however long it lasts."

Their conversation was cut short as their attention was drawn to the revelers surrounding them who excitedly murmured at the sight of druids walking through the city, along with the young man with fire colored hair in their company. Locke, Aeysha, and Gaza strolled through hushed whispers and strange looks as they made their way to the heart of Belcard where a grand viewing platform was constructed for the prince to watch the festivities in luxury.

The dashing prince of Everund seemed unconcerned with the spectacle, instead hanging halfway out of his seating box, making his captain blush by flirting with her. Kayara chastised him for his behavior because it was entirely improper of him to be courting one of his own knights. She pushed the prince to the side while holding her head high. Her tight, springy curls framed her face while she pressed her lips inward expressing quiet frustration. The prince snickered and looked away, brushing his blonde bangs out of his face to literal gasps from the young women in the crowd.

Kayara's chestnut-colored irises, full of steely determination, carefully regarded Locke and the druids who were walking up to their seating box. Captain Kayara carried herself differently than the other knights, she commanded respect, earned by her honor. She was not about to let herself forget how hard she worked to become captain of her own airship and while a marriage to the future king of Everund would please her father, she wanted to earn her post, not be given it.

Elisander having given up trying to garner her affections finally turned his attention to the small band of travelers that were approaching him directly. He sized up the young man with red hair and sharp blue eyes and noticed he was wearing a piece of Zierian armor. Following behind him was a beautiful raven-haired girl in handstitched clothes whose distrustful gaze changed direction with the wind. Lastly there was an old man with a long beard from the southeastern islands region of Nagoda who appeared to be made of water.

Aeysha immediately caught the prince's eye; she wore pieces of jewelry carved from wood, decorated with glass beads, and owl feathers. Her thin lips pursed with a stern yet noble decorum. She was dressed like a wild woman from the northeastern hills, yet she carried herself with more grace than a lord's daughter.

"Well then, the bedtime stories my father would tell me are real," Elisander joked. He got up from his seat to greet the band of strange folk approaching him, "The mystical druids really do exist! And they've come to attend our party no doubt!" The knights around the prince tried their best to keep from laughing, but the crowd did so openly. Elisander quickly quieted them and shifted to a formal tone, he placed his right fist over his heart in greeting, while resting his offhand on the hilt of his sword.

"I am Prince Elisander, and I welcome you to Everund!"

Aeysha and Locke were reluctant to speak after being made a joke by the prince, but Gaza T'sann stepped up to greet the young prince with a smile. The wise old druid bent forward at the waist, bowing his head in a show of respect for the prince.

"Our kin have shared these bountiful lands with your people, and have lived in harmony for generations," he said softly, before slowly rising to meet Elisander's eye. "But we have not come to party. We come to you with a dire warning, and to ask for your assistance. Our meeting was the will of the Great Mother, for nature cries out in terror from a darkness that is poisoning the world. The ruins of Duscar overflow with a death blight that is seeping into the world."

The crowd broke out into spirited conversation as Gaza continued, "A terrible evil has awoken, a dark power that corrupts souls and creates abominations that violate the cycle. If left unchecked it will destroy the Balance." Elisander raised an eyebrow to Kayara, then to his advisors, all of whom looked as confused as he did.

"I am sorry, did you say Duscar?"

Aeysha stepped forward.

"That's right! The Great Mother has told us that evil is stirring in the Mountains of Eld."

One of Elisander's most trusted advisors inquired, "And you have seen this first hand? Do you have proof of this outrageous claim?"

Locke answered them.

"No, we do not. No proof that you would believe anyway. But I saw their divination ritual with my own eyes. I witnessed plants wither to ash, stones melt into black puddles, and I saw..." He paused remembering the disturbing scene in his mind.

"What did you see?" Elisander asked.

Locke looked up at him.

"I... I saw a dead crow stand up on its own and then it screamed horribly, unlike anything I have ever heard."

The prince's advisors laughed.

"You saw a bird wake up and heard scary noises, why should we be concerned?"

Locke shook his head.

"It wasn't alive. It was dead, exceedingly dead. And then it just starting moving around on its own somehow. Look, I know how it sounds, but I've seen dark magic before and I know what I saw."

Locke pulled on the chain of the astromancer compass he was wearing and held it out for Elisander to see.

"Did you pickpocket one of our magi too?" the prince jabbed, but Locke ignored his glibness.

"This was given to me by Lord Dilandau Ravendark, who showed up at my uncle's manor almost two weeks ago. I think he knew my uncle Rowan, and that was why he wound up there after doing *something* he said he deeply regretted. Something happened to him in the Mountains of Eld, and now a curse is spreading across the lands of Duscar. If it is not stopped, it could spread across all of Averon."

Murmurs of disbelief spread among the listeners as Locke went on, "You spoke of bedtime stories, well my uncle told me some about Everund, and why this kingdom was founded. You swore to defend the Great Kingdoms against destruction, and you should honor that duty. Investigate the source of this threat before something terrible happens."

Everyone stared at Locke in silence, but Elisander smirked at the punchline for a joke that only he seemed to get.

"That was a rather entertaining tale, I must admit. You nearly had me fooled. Clever to use the mage's trinket Therredan, but I'm not going to fall for this trick. You have proven an amusing distraction for an otherwise uneventful afternoon. I shall see that you and your troupe are paid for the theater you have performed here today, now go." Elisander motioned with his hand in a dismissive gesture shooing them away from him with a smug look. Aeysha frowned and glared at Locke as she stomped past him.

"I told you they would not listen! Kings are liars, and so are their rotten seed." Elisander motioned to the knights guarding his seating box to block her exit, which they did with drawn swords. Elisander stood up from his chair and walked over to Aeysha slowly, and with a finger he pushed the guard's swords out of her face.

"You call my father a liar, miss uhh... what did you say your name was?" Aeysha looked at Locke then back at the prince, whose eyes were filled with a friendliness that she was not accustomed to.

"I am Aeysha of the Wandering Wind, Keeper of the Balance of the Eternal Ring," she stated matter-of-factly refusing to return his charm.

The prince smiled.

"Well, Aeysha. My name is Elisander, son of Armon the king of Everund. He is many things, young druid, but a liar is not one of them. And neither am I. Now, I would ask what makes you feel like my kingdom is under the rule of charlatans."

Aeysha pointed to Locke.

"He told me that you would listen to the pleas of the Great Mother. He told me your kingdom would defend this world from evil. But instead, you mock us like a spoiled child." She turned her back to leave once more, adding, "We don't have time to waste on *you*. We will seek help from this world's true guardians." She began walking away with Gaza following grimly behind. Locke stood in front of Elisander, who looked upon him sourly.

"Here. Keep it." Locke said, slapping the astromancer compass into the prince's hand, and ran after Aeysha.

"Should we let them go, my lord?" one of the knights asked. Elisander looked deeply at the Ravendark family crest on the compass and thought about the secret mission he had overheard his father send the wizard on before he left on his doomed diplomatic mission to Therred.

"Wait!" the prince called out. "Do not leave. I will confer with my council on how Everund will deal with this situation." Aeysha and Locke turned back to the prince, who was more somber than he was moments ago, a sign perhaps that he was taking the situation seriously. "Come, we shall discuss the matter together," he proposed before gesturing to the diplomats, bureaucrats, and other delegates of his royal accompaniment.

Gaza T'sann smiled proudly at Aeysha before joining them inside, and she felt deeply relieved. Locke was hopeful that the

Everunders could be convinced to help the druids after all. Elisander stopped Locke on his way in and handed him back the astromancer's compass.

"I do not know why Dilandau would give you this, Therredan, but he did give it to you. You should keep it." Locke thanked him as Elisander sat casually across the arms of a chair instead of in its seat like normal. He picked up a chalice of wine, taking a long drink from it and earning a disapproving look from Kayara.

A lordly man draped in green silk, who wore gaudy rings on all of his fingers, gripped a large ruby which sat atop of his walking cane and spoke quietly in a tone of disbelief.

"Prince Elisander, surely you do not believe that this Therredan is speaking the truth. It seems obvious to me that this is some trick by Hammond to draw us out for an attack. This is a dirty ploy spoken by an assassin, who for all we know, murdered Lord Dilandau. How else could he be in possession of that compass?"

Locke stood up angrily.

"How dare you! I did no such thing; I am no assassin!"

Kayara reached for her sword but Elisander stayed her with a motion of his hand.

"Please, sit," the prince said calmly to Locke and the others. Locke reluctantly plopped back down while still fuming.

"That thought crossed my mind as well," Elisander said. Locke looked betrayed by the admission.

"But I do not believe the reclusive druids of myth would have come out of hiding in the support of lies from a Therredan assassin. No, something else is at work here. Strange coincidences which make me uneasy."

Another noble from Elisander's court who wore a dark leather vest over a pale blue shirt and whose dark hair only appeared in tufts just above his ears and round the back of his head, stood and spoke up.

"We're nearly a week late reporting to the king and now we are entertaining the idea of showing up in Erendar with a Therredan and a couple of primitives who wandered out of the woods? And on their word and their word alone, prepare for what exactly, war? Against Duscar, or some death magic, was it? We don't even know what we're up against, here."

Aeysha scowled.

"Perhaps if your ears were not plugged with hair, you could hear the voices all around you crying out. There are dark whispers in the world and Gaia's children have heard them."

Elisander stifled a chuckle before interjecting.

"I have not decided what shall be done on this matter. I have not said that I will commit our forces to anything yet."

The nobleman looked sour at the prince's words and could not resist another verbal jab at the absurdity of the situation.

"The king would not entertain such obvious deceit, and that is the benefit of experience. You will learn in time, young prince."

Elisander shot him a look that cut like a blade.

"Do not think me a fool, magister. I do not trust them any more than you do. However, these circumstances can't be ignored." He got up and started pacing before he continued, "My father sent Lord Ravendark on a mission, secret even from me and he has been missing for weeks. Then suddenly he turns up in a Therredan farmhouse of all places, this boy's home, and tells him that he has done something inexplicably terrible and disappears again. Yet, somehow that same Therredan arrives here before Ravendark returns? Then *druids* appear in our cities offering a dire warning for the realms. These events make me awfully uncomfortable; something is amiss."

A councilman from Arrincroft spoke for the first time.

"That is true, but it could still be a trap to lure out our forces, my prince. I do not doubt the convictions of these people, I think that they believe what they are saying is true, but that doesn't mean that they weren't set up. They may have themselves been deceived."

The prince turned to Locke.

"Then the key to understanding what motives are behind this plot lie with him." All eyes turned to Locke as the prince continued, "Why are you here, Therredan? Did you come all this way just to give us this message?" Locke shook his head no but did not immediately offer an explanation.

"See, he is withholding information from us," the sour-faced magister interjected, only to be silenced by the prince.

"Allow him to answer."

For a few minutes Locke wondered how to tell them what had happened to him, he chose instead to show them rather than speak. He pointed to his right arm, to the brilliant glint of the red metal shone, drawing attention to its extraordinary craftsmanship and elegant design.

"I fled my home because of this," was all he could think to say. Everyone was certainly intrigued by the armor, except the druids who had seen it before and could not fathom its worth.

"I was meaning to ask you how you came by it," Elisander asked, looking the armor over.

"You wouldn't believe me if I told you."

"Try me."

Locke shrugged then explained.

"My brother and I snuck into Gerod's castle fortress to free our father Rowan Blackwood after he was arrested for sheltering Lord Ravendark. Inside the castle we found a secret vault where they were hoarding magical items. I saw this artifact among them and I..." Locke trailed off without finishing his sentence, so Elisander did it for him.

"You touched it, didn't you?"

Locke nodded, embarrassed.

"Impossible!" the magister shouted, looking infuriated. "There is no way two farm boys could break into Hammangard, and what in all of Averon would a mage-hater like Gerod Hammond be doing with magical artifacts like that?"

Locke tried to describe what he had witnessed inside the castle.

"We saw them doing something with them, like breaking them apart. I don't understand exactly what they were doing, but it seemed to fuel some kind of terrible spellwork. We saw them infuse that artifact essence into huge suits of armor that could move on their own."

The advisors started talking animatedly among themselves while Elisander waved his captain over, whispering something imperceptible in her ear. She whispered back to him before the prince turned his attention back to Locke.

"For what it's worth Therredan, I believe you."

His advisors did not seem to agree with the prince on that, but it was really only Elisander who needed to be convinced. "You have brought us information that could be of great use to us. Would you consider sharing this information and more details about what you saw in Hammangard with the king?"

"I have told you what I have in order to convince you to do the right thing, and nothing more. I am only interested in defending this world from evil."

Elisander rubbed his chin.

"And if we investigate your claims, would you consider delivering what you know to the king? Including the castle layout, the number of troops Gerod has, and more details about this ritual that you have seen?"

Locke nodded, "I will."

Elisander stood up.

"Very well, we will discuss how to go about investigating the ruins of Duscar. Please be patient, and give me some time to deliberate with my advisors."

Locke, Aeysha, and Gaza stayed out of the conversation as the Everunders argued amongst themselves. After nearly an hour of debate, Elisander slapped his hand down on the armrest of the chair in which he was seated and the raucous rabble ceased at once.

"I have decided! Per the wishes of the council, I will not commit our military forces to this endeavor. As has been made abundantly clear, the king alone commands the armies of Everund."

His advisors seemed pleased with themselves.

"However," the prince continued, "I shall investigate the matter personally. I will take my airship, and only my royal guard who shall escort our guests to keep them safe, as well as honest."

The council of advisors' smiles faded once more, and they quickly started arguing again but Elisander had heard enough deliberation. He was sobering up and their blathering was exhausting him physically.

"I understand that the king alone can send our army to war, but the king has no say aboard my ship or command over what skies she soars."

Elisander emerged from the seat box, "It is settled, you three shall accompany me and my knights on an expedition into the Mountains of Eld."

Locke looked at Aeysha excitedly, but she looked surprised.

"They listened," she said incredulously.

He smirked.

"Never had a doubt."

Locke gave a look of gratitude to Elisander, and the prince nodded back to him in acknowledgement.

"Come Therredan, let me show you something truly spectacular!" Elisander was beaming. He laid his arm across Locke's shoulder, pulling him in close.

They were escorted by the knights of Everund through the busy streets of Belcard as people stared at the peculiar entourage. Cheers broke out for the prince, who graciously waved back to the throngs of Everunders. Locke noted that despite his obvious character flaws, the prince was highly regarded by his people. But as it was, Locke was more focused on the strange looks he, Aeysha, and Gaza were receiving than with how the people loved their prince.

The group certainly made for a strange sight all walking together, but even so the people of Belcard were excited to see their prince with Locke and the druids. After wading through cheers and handshakes, the group eventually arrived at the docks where several large river boats were anchored. But one of the ships among them stood out, for it was unlike all the others. The prince's personal transportation was an airship, a boat that could fly.

Elisander's airship was truly something to behold. It was slightly larger than the water bound transport ships it was docked alongside. Locke was amazed by its sleek design; even while resting peacefully, the ship produced an optical effect that made it look like it was soaring through open sky. It was decorated with elaborate filigree on every edge, trim, and railing; from tail tip to figurehead. The most striking feature of the craft is also what made it so special and different from regular ships: it had massive brimstone burning engines attached to the outside of the hull. These engineering marvels powered the massive blades which generated the necessary amount of lift to make it fly.

Elisander stepped in front of them, grinning like a fool, and with an elaborate arm gesture he presented his ship like a proud father.

"Here she is! The Nomad Sky! My father had it custom-built for me. He commissioned the best engineers in Averon and the brightest minds in the royal alchemist academy to create the fastest and lightest airship yet. It's based on an early prototype that the founders of Everund designed, but abandoned in favor of larger gunships due to the weight and thrust limitations of the engines of their day. My father made it happen though, they designed lighter more powerful engines and they modified the aft section into a tail to reduce the ship's weight. Even made the old bird fly with just four props."

Locke could not hide his boyish delight at the sight of such a marvelous craft.

"It's incredible! It seems impossible that, *that* can fly."

Elisander was bemused by Locke's interest.

"Look to your lucky star, Therredan, that you are my guest upon it. Remarkably few have been as fortunate as you to ride in my personal airship. Enjoy this moment, because if you have sent me on a fool's errand then I shall escort you back across your borders in it and turn you over to your mad king myself."

Locke scowled.

"Gerod is no king."

Before more sparks could fly a dwarf with gray hair tied back in tight braids and covered in soot walked up to them while they were admiring the ship.

"Elisander!" the dwarf shouted.

"Drovann!" said the prince while giving him a big hug.

Elisander looked back to Locke and the druids, "This is my chief engineer. He's the one who keeps my ship flying, no matter how hard I try to break it."

The dwarf smiled warmly at them all.

"Nice ta meet ya, if ye have any questions before we board, feel free to ask em."

Locke looked up at the ship, unable to contain his curiosity.

"How long did it take to build it?"

The old dwarf smiled from under his salt and pepper beard.

"I'm glad ya asked! It took us seven years to design and build the Nomad Sky in total, largely because of those engines. You see, they burn brimstone in sealed chambers to produce the power which turns the rotor blades. That process creates a lot of heat, which is why normally the engines are built larger in order to dissipate that heat. We couldna make the combustion chambers any smaller without risking a breach, so instead we rerouted the gas recycling pipes to the exterior of the turbine. A personal improvement of mine," he boasted.

The prince and Drovann continued to answer Locke's numerous questions while the ship was loaded and prepped for flight. Aeysha was less impressed by the technical jargon than the men were, but even she had to admit she was excited to fly in it. She had never flown before and as a devotee of the white owl, she always envied the gift of flight that Gaia had bestowed upon her avian kin.

With the ship finally made ready, everyone climbed on board. It was smaller inside than it seemed from the outside, the young Therredan noted. Locke looked out from the gem-shaped windows while the brimstone engines roared to life. He studied the rotors spinning and he felt an odd pull in the bottom of his stomach as the ship lifted into the air. With Elisander taking the helm, they were all set to travel off into the forbidden mountains.

"Onward," the prince said, pushing the throttle up, and the Nomad Sky shot out of the dock like an arrow. The river-falls city of Belcard faded quickly into the fields below as they ascended into the clouds.

The Fallen Kingdom

The Nomad Sky made quick work of the distance between Belcard and the Mountains of Eld. The ship itself was truly a marvel and Locke was living a dream, flying for the first time. He was not alone in that feeling, as Aeysha was also rejoicing about soaring through the sky. She whooped and hollered as they dove in and out of the clouds. Elisander smiled and indulged his guests with unnecessarily garish aerial maneuvers, to their delight and Kayara's disapproval. When they made it over the mountain peaks, they dropped through the clouds, which splashed the ship with rain which streaked along the windows from the high speeds. As the windows cleared, the ancient mountains came into view, and with them the ruins of Duscar.

The Nomad Sky came to a stop alongside the castle walls and hovered a safe distance away from the peaks, but still close enough for a breathtaking view. Cathedral-like spires framed the dragon-forged castle, whose eerie silhouette dominated the backdrop of the mountains. Icy winds whistled around the deck and bit into Locke's flesh as he stepped out of the cabin into the open air, determined to see it for himself. He wanted to experience with his own eyes the place where the old world had died and the world he knew began.

The silence and stillness of the mountain kingdom combined darkly with the aggressive architecture of the ruins; it was filling them all with a deep sense of dread. The view from the deck of the Nomad Sky was certainly unparalleled, but there was something wrong about Duscar that made him want to head back inside and insist that they turn back.

The whole castle city looked too impossible to be real; it was surprisingly artistically designed with delicate filigree and ornate dragon motifs throughout its architecture. Dragon wing shaped flying buttresses sprawled over the peaks of the Eld Ridge Mountains, holding up high walls of melted black stone. Between three separate mountain peaks, the walls of Duscar converged at a center point around a depression the size of a lake. The caldera was encircled by dragon-forged ramparts which stood guard along its rim. All of which surrounded a city of exceptional workmanship, grander in scale and flair than anything Locke had ever seen.

The city was defended by a labyrinth of nearly impassable terrain on all sides which wound all the way up to the fortified walls. The melted walls looked sturdy enough to take a full barrage of cannon fire from the Nomad Sky without failing. The castle seemed to have nearly impenetrable defenses and Locke could only guess as to how many thousands must have died trying to take Duscar during the Great Wyrm War.

Despite the foreboding look of the castle, it was pretty apparent that it was entirely deserted. They had expected to find little evidence that suggested danger from a fly-by alone, but Elisander was already getting cocky about it and he wanted to rub it in.

"Land in the ruins, let us walk over the dead and see if we can kick up a ghost," he said. The prince wanted to show them all what he already knew; that it was impossible for Duscar to pose a threat to anyone. Everund was founded to defend the world should the few dragons that survived the war ever return, but the humans of Duscar were definitely long gone. Only a fool would believe that they could come back from annihilation. The war was unbelievably brutal and no Duscan was left alive by the end of it.

"Locke, stay put," the prince said as the airship landed just outside the front gates.

"Excuse me?" he snapped back.

The prince addressed Locke while his knights disembarked.

"You, Therredan will stay here, under close watch. If this is a trap, I will not have you stab my people when their backs are turned. The vision, or prophecy, or whatever it was came from the druids, and it doesn't include you. The ruins of Duscar are no place for tourists, so you will remain here with our rear guard."

Without another word, Elisander then walked off the ship and into the snow flurries that everyone else had already disappeared into. Aeysha looked back to Locke with a sympathetic look before following after the prince.

Locke walked down the ramp into the chill mountain winds, discovering that its thin, freezing air was difficult to breathe in. The air was so thin that each breath did not give him all of the oxygen he needed. He had never been on the peak of a mountain before and found that every step he took felt like a hundred. The knight who was left to watch him glared at him with a look of pure spite, as Locke paced back and forth.

"The first time anyone has explored this place in over a hundred years, and instead of getting to see it, I get stuck watching you," he chided. The knight went back inside the ship to avoid the bitter chill, rather than joining the Therredan who was staring into the bleak desolation of the tomb-like ruins. "Don't go getting yourself lost now. It would be a *real* shame if we had to go back to Belcard without you," he called out. Locke scowled and glared from the bottom of the ramp as everyone disappeared.

It did not take long before he grew tired of waiting around, and with no one actively watching him, he figured it would be easy for him to slip away. Directly disobeying Elisander's order, he stomped through the large snow banks which crunched beneath his feet. He snuck around the exterior walls of the terrifying architecture of Duscar instead of following after the others, who had gone to the front gate. Locke touched the blackened walls with his bare fingers and felt the cold stone beneath them, wondering if the walls really were forged by dragon's fire. He had seen similar effects on the walls of Hammangard, the burn scars that the kingdom bore from the war.

Navigating the perilous mountain proved to be a slow and arduous task. To make matters worse, Locke was unsure what he was even looking for. All he knew was that he was walking in the opposite direction that Elisander and his troops went, wishing to avoid a confrontation with his royal *highness*, the prince. He edged his way around the exterior of the castle and noticed something strange about the mountainside. The slopes around him had been disturbed and there were many places where the snow was recently cleared, exposing large patches of soil from where something was dug up. Chills went down his spine, not from the biting winds, but from seeing what looked like unearthed, empty graves and remembering the dead crow screaming.

There were remnants of war all around him, evidence of magical explosions and vicious fighting, but strangely there were no bodies or weapons to be found. He started to think that maybe listening to Elisander was not such a bad idea and that perhaps he should return to the ship where it was safer. I really wish I had brought that knight with me; he thought as he continued exploring the ruins alone. Fortunately, he noticed an old storm drain with a broken grate sticking out of the castle city and figured he might be able to get inside through it.

"This is insane," Locke said aloud to himself, "What am I even doing here?"

Locke turned around, heading back to the ship but he only made it a few steps before stopping and chastising himself for being cowardly. He stuffed his hands into his armpits for warmth, staring back and forth between the path that was heading back to the ship and the one before him leading to the old drain.

He thought of going back and warming his hands on the recycling pipes from the ship's engines, but the image of Elisander's gloating smile came into his mind. Locke imagined the prince returning to the ship, having found no danger or evil magic and finding him huddled around a heat source. He scowled at the thought, staring at the drain before trudging through the snow towards it.

"Elisander may not find anything, but I will! I won't endure that pompous buffoon and his condescension unless I know for certain that nothing is here. Even if that means I have to search every corner of this damned place myself," he said pushing through the waist-deep snow to the barred drain. The thick metal bars sealed the drain normally, but they too had seen war, and in the lower left corner was a narrow gap where a blast of some kind had bent the bars open. Looking at it from up close, he was unsure he could fit through the hole. There were no other entrances on this side of the castle and no way to scale the walls, so like it or not it was his only way in.

Locke got down on his hands and knees, scraping away at the built-up snow which was packed in the front of the unused drain. Once clear, he laid on his back, and shimmied his way through the open hole in the metal gate. He was able to get his head through fine, but his shoulders were slightly too big to squeeze through comfortably, so he was forced to bend at an awkward angle to get one shoulder through at a time. He then had to pull his torso through the tiny gap, straining enough to make his face turn red as he struggled to pull himself through it.

His upper body made it through the gap with a relieving plop, as he fell back into a puddle on the floor of the drain.

"Lovely," he said, exasperated, before placing his palms on the sides of the drain for support. Locke lifted himself into a sitting position and started pulling his legs through the gate quickly out of impatience and discomfort. His left knee caught a sharp edge of the bent bars, which tore through his pants and cut into his skin. He fell backward, whispering profanity through gritted teeth, and Locke did his best to hold back a scream as the pain shot through his leg.

The deep cold made his skin extra sensitive and though the cut was superficial, it felt like his knee had just been ripped out with a red-hot hook. Locke bit down on his left sleeve to gag himself until the pain subsided enough for him to breathe normally again. He pulled back the torn cloth of his pants and examined the cut, wiping the blood away with his hand. He washed the blood off with some snow, pressing a handful of it to his knee. The snow was so cold it felt like it was burning his skin, making Locke wince, but he held it tight against the wound until the snow melted entirely.

Locke shook his head at his clumsiness before crawling the rest of the way up the drain and into the castle. When he reached the end of the massive pipe, he was able to stand up in a small room with a ladder. He climbed it carefully as it was in a state of disrepair and when he safely reached the top, he popped open a cover. Locke found himself in a closed corridor, with empty mounts in the walls where torches would have been placed to give light to the loathsome halls. It was incredibly dark inside and it only now occurred to him that he had no source of light other than the afternoon sun which only just peaked through the narrow windows of the castle.

He kept tightly to the walls as much as possible as he crept along and was painfully reminded about what had happened last time he snuck into a castle. Locke wondered about Baryk for the first time in more than a week and silently wished his brother was here with him now. The doubts plaguing his mind only got worse the more he thought about Baryk. Why was he screwing around, risking his life for this crazy wyvern chase when he ran away instead of going back for his family.

Locke took a deep breath trying to calm his mind, unfortunately the air inside the castle was stale and musty. But at least the slight chill of the lonely halls was not nearly so bad as being completely exposed to the harsh weather of the Eld Ridge Mountains outside. He gave himself a little time to appreciate warming up slightly now that he was finally out of the wind. Everything about where he was at that moment kept reminding Locke of the last time that he saw Baryk and he wondered where this bravery was when his brother needed him.

Locke thought maybe after this was over, after he proved himself to the prince, perhaps he could convince the king of Everund to liberate the people of Therred next. For now, though, he needed to find proof of dark magic incontrovertible enough to convince the skeptics. Locke thought about the strange course of events that brought him to this moment and wondered if he really believed that the world was in danger. Were the druids right about this curse? Could the kingdom of Duscar really rise from the dead? His murky thoughts concluded he was entirely sure that he was not entirely sure of anything, but *if* the curse that the dead raven was under could spread, then all of Averon was imperiled.

Locke pushed himself onward though he could barely see in the dingy halls, but if he ran into anyone in the forlorn Duscan castle at least they would be at the same disadvantage he mused. The deeper into the castle he explored, the more his hair seemed to stand on end. There was definitely something about the whole place that was creeping him out.

Everywhere he looked was barren, there were no signs of life within the castle walls, even the tapestries and furniture had rotted away over the century since their abandonment. Locke imagined it had never been a terribly warm or inviting place, even when it was occupied. Long, purple, dragon blood-colored banners hung from entryways that he passed, which displayed the iconography of Duscar, a black, downward-facing sword with dragon wings forming its cross guard.

The halls became significantly wider the further in he ventured, and the stone walls were scratched and scuffed up at heights higher than a human could reach. The scratches seemed to only be around the narrower parts of the castle and he wondered to himself if they were made by the scales of dragons slithering through the halls. He was one of few people to ever see the interior of Duscar, and he could not help but be impressed and momentarily enchanted by it. It was a place of such significance and he was lurking around inside of it like it was his neighbor's barn.

Locke quietly approached a heavily adorned archway, seemingly leading somewhere important, when suddenly he heard something moving through the castle other than himself. At that moment he was not sure what would be worse, getting caught sneaking around by the prince, or coming face to face with what he was really looking for. He held his breath while pressing against the wall, hiding in the shadows and trying not to move a muscle. He listened intently for the sound again, and his eyes went wide as he heard the clanking of armor in the distance.

He briefly thought of running back to the ship, but the sound was coming closer fast and he dared not move. Instead, Locke stayed quiet, listening to the sounds growing louder as they moved towards him. He tried not to panic but he was already losing control of his heart rate. Locke started hoping it was just Elisander and the knights of Everund, having circled around and made their way through the castle's interior. Perhaps they were heading back to the ship after making a full sweep of the castle grounds and had found their way here. Who was he kidding, he thought, he was never that lucky; it was far more likely that the proof the prince needed was shuffling round the corner any minute.

He took in a few slow breaths, hoping that the approaching clamor of shifting armor would cover up the sounds he made by taking in some much-needed air. As soon as he took a breath, however, he was met with a terrible smell. An oppressive odor washed over him which he managed to smell despite breathing through his mouth. Locke nearly vomited from the horrendous odor, but he clamped a hand over his mouth as his eyes started watering from the nauseating stench now filling the halls.

Whatever was coming closer was definitely not the host of Everund. He turned his feet sideways so that they would not stick out into the hall and his heart jumped as the clanging sounds came from just around the corner. Locke fought the urge to run, but as the shambling dead stepped into view, he froze completely.

His eyes fixated on the horror unfolding before him as a troop of soldiers bearing the dragon-wing blade symbol of Duscar on their corroded armor stepped into the hall before him. Their armor looked nothing like the iron plate worn by soldiers of Therred nor the higher quality steel armor worn by the knights of Everund. If he had to guess at what their armor was made out of, he would say dragon scale.

The warriors of Duscar were larger than most humans Locke had seen, each carrying a large spear or greatsword which were pock-marked from weathering. There were female warriors within their ranks as well, which surprised Locke, as he never heard that mentioned in the retelling of the war. Though, most of what he heard were the drunk epics of bards who spoke of Duscans like they were monsters. He had only ever imagined them in his nightmares and now here they stood before him like they had walked right out of one.

The reanimated were heavily decayed, many with bones exposed, with limbs entirely missing or held in place only by the magic that bound their tormented souls to their corpses. Because of the state of their bodies, they slumped, and shunted as they moved and their motions were jerky and stiff in a deeply unsettling way, yet Locke found that he could not look away from them.

The Duscan warriors stomped in unison, then struck their weapon against their chest, while spreading out. Clearly, they were making room for someone or something else to make its way through and it was then that Locke remembered the dragons. His thoughts raced faster than his heart pounding in his chest. If it was possible for the people of Duscar to return from the dead, then could it be possible that the dreaded fire-spitting lizards who had nearly burned the world to cinder could have, too? Locke's fear-addled mind was now entertaining any wild idea he could imagine.

He was so distracted that he barely heard the footsteps that were approaching now. They were definitely not the sound of a giant, scaled monstrosity. A thin Duscan man wearing blackened cloth armor emerged. The armor was adorned with dragon fangs and the bones of both humans and dragons alike. He wore a mask made of a human skull which was missing the lower jaw. It was attached to a helm with ram horns which curled down and around the face. The Duscan's corpse body was burned and only visible through the gaps of his armor. The Duscan turned sharply in Locke's direction and the young Therredan felt eyes upon him, though he could see none behind the mask, for there he saw only green fiery embers.

After what felt like an eternity to Locke, the robed Duscan looked away and walked down the hall away from him. It was then that Locke noticed a strange book chained to his waist as he disappeared into darkness. Locke jumped slightly as the warriors of Duscar bashed their weapons against their chests again. They stomped their feet, moving back into a single formation, and then marched down the hall after the robed man. Locke inhaled deeply as soon as the dead were out of earshot and not a moment too soon, as he was close to passing out. It took several moments of gasping to catch his breath and to get the stink of their rot out of his nose.

Despite being utterly terrified, Locke was relieved that he had not been discovered, because if they had seen him, it would have been the end for him. Locke now knew that the druids were right, death magic was at work in the Mountains of Eld. The only problem was that Elisander would never believe him. After all he was told to stay with the ship and he had snuck inside the castle instead. Though he felt validated by what he uncovered, he quickly realized that all he had was his word.

"Damnit," he said to himself, realizing he would need physical evidence to take back with him if he was ever going to convince that thick-headed prince. Reluctantly, he snuck down the hall chasing after the undead host of Duscar. He followed as closely as he could without risking being heard or seen. Their foul odor led him to a throne room which had to have been the seat of power for the former ruler of the dragon kingdom.

Locke watched the robed man with the skull mask sit upon the throne, and when he did, every undead warrior in the room kneeled before him. The Duscan pulled the strange book from his waist before opening it, and Locke was shocked when he heard a voice come from the book as if it was talking.

Ir'zane, your army is strong, but you have nearly burned away your soul, it said.

The sorcerer responded by sort of talking to himself.

"The elves hold the secret, I know it. They have stretched their worthless lives across thousands of years. They have the power to give life to the withered, a power which can be made to work for me. I will twist it to my will, use it to restore my mana, and then I will crush the Great Kingdoms before finally raising their dead into my service."

Locke did not like what he had already overheard, but Ir'zane continued speaking his evil thoughts out loud.

"The only problem is that Silthradel cannot be found, no one has seen it in a thousand years of searching. The elves have kept it hidden better than their darkest secrets, which is the only reason we never burned it to ash. So, how do we find what cannot be found?"

The book spoke.

Seek out the Eye of Orynos. It is a gift of the void, made ages ago to hunt Magi. With it, you can see all things, even that which is hidden by magic.

Ir'zane inquired, "Where would I find such a thing?" And again, came the voice from the pages of the grimoire.

It was taken by Eldric and sealed away. Ir'zane puzzled for a moment as he thought about what little information his old mentor had shared with him, when it suddenly came to him.

"The Isle of Knives."

Locke had never heard of such a place in all of Averon.

"Eldric spoke of an island far out in the western seas surrounded by rocks which stand out of the ocean like blades, a place which no ship could reach. There he made a tower with enchanted walls so steep and razor sharp that they could not be climbed. He called it the Isle of Knives, and that is where Eldric put things he could not destroy."

Armor rattled from behind Locke as a revenant on patrol found him leaning in the doorway while he was listening in. The undead warrior grabbed him painfully hard and pulled him out of hiding. He was shoved into the throne room and dragged in front of Ir'zane. The sorcerer stepped down from his throne and casually strolled over to his new prisoner. Ir'zane grabbed Locke around the throat and pushed him against the wall.

Ir'zane's spectral, burning green eyes glared ferociously into Locke's, his dead face screwed up into a vicious snarl as the shadowmancer's grip on Locke's windpipe tightened. Locke kicked wildly at Ir'zane while struggling to breathe, he tried to pry the fiend's hand from his throat, but was unsuccessful. He was lifted off the ground by Ir'zane with one arm, and Locke stared into the cruel, unholy glow of green fire burning in the empty eye sockets of the sorcerer's skull. As he started to lose consciousness, he heard the voice from the treasure vault of Gerod's castle again.

Normally it was so quiet he could hardly hear it at all, but this time it shouted his name, *Locke!* His eyes sprang open again as he heard, *let me help*. He felt like he was fighting to hold back his right arm, so he let whatever it was take control. As he let go, he felt the armor on his arm transform, the thin segmented plates sprang up into blades like the quills of a porcupine.

Locke swung the blades wildly, severing the skeletal hand which gripped him. Ir'zane screamed in rage as Locke ran out of the throne room as fast as he could. The blades on his arm settled back into armor as he ran back through the halls with undead Duscans in pursuit.

~

In the courtyard just outside the throne room, Elisander and Aeysha met up after finishing a perimeter sweep of the castle. The prince had seen enough, which was to say he had seen nothing at all and was ready to leave, when he suddenly heard Ir'zane's scream of anger and pain, which filled the courtyard with its unholy sound. Locke burst through large wooden doors and was met by the swords of Elisander and the knights of Everund.

"What are you doing here?"

Locke was nearly out of breath.

"I'll explain later! Run!" he shouted as undead Duscan warriors charged through the doors.

"Retreat! Everyone back to the ship!" Elisander commanded.

Ir'zane appeared in the courtyard with his hand reattached by magic, and saw that they were all standing over the almost entirely submerged corpse of a dragon. The sorcerer once again turned to the Book of Souls and used a dark ritual from it. The Everunders tried to run away but the ground beneath them shook as the earth split apart and reptilian claws upheaved the massive corpse from beneath their feet.

They all stared, paralyzed as a dead dragon with bones breaking through its decayed skin, slowly rose above them. Its head was missing teeth and some horns, its throat was also torn out but somehow it still managed to roar. The force of it was strong enough to nearly knock the Everunders over. The undead dragon stood tall with its head held high, its only remaining eye was white with decay yet still struck fear in whoever it rested its unholy gaze upon. Its four legs held up its massive body, the belly of which was so high off the ground Kayara wondered if her sword would even reach it. The dreadwyrm spread its torn wings, casting a gargantuan shadow over them, while Captain Kayara held high the crest of Alathor emblazoned upon her shield.

"Protect the prince, drive back this monster!" she shouted to the royal guard. At her command they rallied around Elisander forming a defensive perimeter. The monstrosity lunged forward, its hind claws tearing through the solid rock beneath its feet like it was dirt. The beast snapped at them with a crooked jaw filled with sword-length fangs. Its teeth crashed into Kayara's shield, and though the magically enchanted shield was not pierced by its teeth, the force of the bite knocked her to the ground. The dreadwrym clamped its jaws tightly on the shield and she let go of it just as the dragon ripped it away with a violent jerk which would have taken her arm with it.

Wispy threads of darkness coalesced in Ir'zane's palm, making a mournful sounding wail, and he cackled menacingly as he prepared to assault the royal guard with his shadow magic. With the knights pinned down by the dead dragon and surrounded by undead Duscan warriors, things were looking terribly grim. Locke had to act fast, a brave and stupid plan formed in his mind.

"Hey! Over here!" he shouted at Ir'zane, "Remember me? I'm the guy who cut off your hand!"

The sorcerer snarled at Locke.

"That's right, I did that! I bet that really hurt!"

Ir'zane commanded the revenant to kill Locke, "Destroy the boy!" Locke's gambit worked; all attention was on him but unfortunately, he had not planned for what to do once they were focused on him. "Yavon's beard," he said as he turned and ran.

Elisander gawked incredulously as Locke somehow drew their enemies away. "We have to get out of here, now!" the prince shouted, as the Everunders ran back to the ship. Meanwhile, Locke tried to outrun the hordes of Duscar and the dreadwyrm biting at his heels, which trampled several Duscan warriors as it thrashed around. Aeysha and Gaza used their powers to push the winds and snow at the undead, burying them with a huge blast of ice.

With Ir'zane and his dreadwyrm crawling free from the ice, Locke turned around and ran for the ship, catching up with the others beyond the front gate. The prince stopped at the door of the ship, helping them all onboard.

"Quickly, everyone inside!" he shouted as they clamored into the Nomad Sky.

"Drovann start the engines!" Kayara yelled, while helping Aeysha and Gaza inside. Locke was the last to arrive and he ran right past Elisander, who did not meet his eye. The prince was instead watching Duscar close in on them, but with everyone safely onboard, Elisander climbed into the ship and fastened the hatch behind him.

Kayara took the helm, pushing the Nomad Sky to take off, but as the ship was climbing into the air, so was the dreadwyrm that Ir'zane had sent after them. The ship turned sharply away from the ruins of Duscar but was grabbed by the undead dragon, which started tearing holes in the ship like arrows piercing armor. The monstrosity smashed one of the front engines, which burst into a blue fireball.

"Hold on to something!" Elisander shouted. The ship was released from the dragon's grip and it immediately spun out of control. The remaining front prop overheated and exploded, causing the ship to roll as it fell from the sky.

Through the Western Wood

The crew grabbed onto anything they could while holding on for dear life as the Nomad Sky spiraled toward the ground. Locke saw the world outside spin dizzyingly through the windows and wondered if his time had come. Smoke billowed from the front of the ship where the engines had been, while Kayara desperately tried to gain control of the ship. But without anything generating lift from the front of the craft, the damaged airship fell out of the sky like a maple seed. Beyond the Eld Ridge Mountains they fell, hurtling toward the western Feywilds.

Elisander and Kayara desperately pulled a stuck steering lever together, attempting to use the tail fins to slow their descent. Unfortunately, before it could do much good, they came to a violent stop as the front of the ship smashed into the ground. It skidded forward before crashing through the enormous trees of the forest of the Feywild, which shook the ship as it collided with them. When everything finally came to a rest, it became deathly quiet.

Locke came to and tried to sit up but found himself pinned; his right shoulder was caught under debris. He looked around the crash site but could not see anyone else around him, and he no longer recognized what part of the ship was he was in. He struggled trying to free himself for several minutes until he became too exhausted from the effort and chose lay back down.

"Just can't catch a break," he muttered, thinking through the surprisingly long list of injuries and mishaps he was experiencing lately. He laughed a bit, though he had no idea why. Perhaps it was because what had he been through was all too unreal to believe, or maybe it was because he was just relieved to be alive. As he pondered the preposterous predicament that he found himself in, an enormous shadow fell over him while he lay trapped by broken parts of the ship.

Locke looked up as the dreadwyrm that had attacked them in the ruins of Duscar flew overhead, flying to the southwest with Ir'zane on its shoulders. Urgently, Locke starting reaching into his shirt with his one free hand, and after a few fumbling moments he had the chain of Ravendark's compass around his fingers. With a quick tug, he pulled it free from under his shirt and into his open palm. He held the compass up as he viewed Ir'zane fade into the horizon.

"Show me where the Isle of Knives is."

The compass pointed southwest along the same path that the sorcerer had just flown.

"That's not good," he said.

Locke heard shouting as knights began searching the wreckage around him. "I'm in here!" he shouted, and within minutes one of the Everunders found him, digging through the pile of rubble to get to him.

"Are you alright?" the knight asked.

"Yeah, I think so, but my arm is pinned," Locke replied.

The knight pulled on the debris, and with great effort he finally hoisted the heavy wooden beam from Locke's shoulder, freeing him. The knight expected to see a mangled limb under the wreckage, but to his astonishment, he saw instead a shimmer of red light gleaming off the metal of the armor that was protecting the Therredan's arm. Locke took a look at the armor as well and thought maybe it wasn't so cursed after all. The knight helped Locke to his feet, and they worked together to help each other down the uneven rubble.

"You're Therredan right?" the Everunder knight asked. Locke nodded weakly before looking away, giving the knight the impression that he should not press the issue further.

"My name is Edmund."

"Locke," he replied, limping along.

The knight seemed a bit jittery and blurted out, "I've never been outside of Belcard before. I thought I would be posted outside the records hall, standing in the sun while giving lost travelers directions until I became an old man," Edmund laughed, but Locke's head was ringing and he was not terribly interested in small talk at the moment. He heard quivering in the knight's voice and thought Edmund must be shaken up from the crash, and was likely chatting to calm his nerves. Locke smiled weakly at him while they gathered with the other survivors.

Locke looked through the group, taking stock of who was there and trying to get a count of who made it. He took note of their conditions as well, and fortunately it seemed that most of them had sustained only minor injuries.

He found Gaza, and Kayara, but as he searched around, he still had not seen Aeysha anywhere. Panic welled up inside him, a sinking feeling that maybe one of the bodies which were laying around the crash site belonged to her. He found Elisander kneeling next to one of his knights who was gravely injured. Locke saw that parts of her armor were bent inward and blood was gushing from where they pierced her. Elisander held her hand in his.

"Stay with me now. Don't you give up yet, there are a lot more festivals ahead of us, okay? And you're gonna live to see them all." She was deathly pale, and her face contorted in pain as Elisander gripped her hand tighter. Locke and Edmund stood shoulder to shoulder watching helplessly, as a familiar raven-haired girl in primitively made clothes ran past them holding an armful of plants. Elisander gripped her arm as she knelt down.

"Please, druid, save her," he pleaded.

"I'll do what I can for her, but I cannot guarantee that she will survive these wounds," she replied. The knight groaned, and started coughing violently before spitting up blood. "We need to close her wounds, but we'll need to get this armor off, it's cutting into her body," Aeysha insisted.

Aeysha placed her hand on the suffering knight's forehead and whispered in that strange and ancient language of the Great Mother, and the enormous trees of the forest around them groaned while swaying back and forth. The injured woman calmed as a magically induced slumber put her under.

"Quick, while she is unconscious, let's get this armor off."

Elisander and Aeysha doffed the knight's armor as carefully as they could. Many pieces came away easily, but the chestguard and legplates were partially puncturing her flesh. They removed them delicately while knights handed them medical supplies recovered from the wreckage. Elisander pressed white cloth bandages soaked with medicine to the freshly exposed wounds as the last of her armor was removed.

Aeysha closed her eyes, placing her hands over the severely wounded woman and used the same healing spell that Locke recognized as the one that had closed the wound in his shoulder. The green magic danced from Aeysha's fingertips and flowers sprouted from the ground, wrapping themselves around the knight's body. The magic gently wove her rent flesh back together as much as it was able, managing to close most of the wounds at least. The glow faded from Aeysha's hands as her magic reached the limit of what it could do. The next several minutes were tensely spent tending to her remaining injuries and moving her to a safe place to rest.

"I think she will live," Aeysha said, breaking the silence. Elisander embraced her tightly in an honest spontaneous gesture of gratitude.

"Thank you, you have done a great service to Everund this day."

Aeysha blushed from being held so tightly by him. She said nothing however, but returned the hug in kind. Locke saw something in the prince of Everund for the first time, something which was truly worthy of his royal station. Though he was an irresponsible and sometimes arrogant man, Elisander genuinely cared for his people, and Locke gained some respect for the prince as he witnessed him fight to save one of his own.

Aeysha saw Locke, who was still being supported by Edmund, and ran over to him. Locke noticed the blood on her hands and arms.

"Are you alright?" he asked.

"Yeah, I'm fine, it's not mine. I mean, I'm not injured. You?"

Locke nodded.

"The crash took the wind out of me and Edmund here had to pull me out from under some debris, but yeah I'll be okay." Aeysha was relieved to see he was not gravely injured, but Elisander was not. The prince charged over to Locke and grabbed him roughly, pulling him away from the knight holding him.

"Hey what's your problem?" Locke asked.

Elisander pulled him close, looking him in the face.

"You are my problem, Therredan!" The prince shoved Locke and shouted, "This is your fault! People are dead, others might not make it, and their blood is on your hands!"

Edmund stepped forward, putting his hand on Elisander's shoulder, "Sir." The prince shot him a menacing look for daring to touch him, and Edmund immediately took his hand off him, "My lord, I understand you are upset, but our fight is not with Locke. We can't afford to fight amongst ourselves, we need everyone we can get right now." Captain Kayara had just returned from checking on the wounded to catch their conversation and to see Elisander ready to swing on Locke, but she grabbed the prince quickly.

"Let him go, Elisander. Edmund is right, Duscar is our enemy, not the boy."

Elisander released him roughly and they exchanged looks like they might still trade blows before Kayara stepped in again.

"My lord, we need to figure out what we're going to do about Duscar. We need to get word to your father, the king."

The prince walked away from Locke and Kayara gave him a sympathetic look before following Elisander. Aeysha stood by Locke as they left.

"Don't worry about the prince, he doesn't mean it," she

inspected his shoulder, "I don't think he's lost anyone before. He's not taking it well."

Locke scowled.

"Yeah, well taking it out on me isn't going to bring anyone back either. If he wants to blame someone he should stare into a looking glass. If he had listened to us in the first place we wouldn't be in this mess."

Aeysha discerned that his shoulder was bruised but left it alone.

"Well, at least they believe us."

Locke rolled his eyes.

"A lot of good that does us *now*. That undead lunatic is out there. The ruins right over our heads are crawling with hundreds of those... those, well whatever the hell they are. Without that airship we are stranded here with no way to warn the rest of the world that Duscar is coming for them."

Aeysha pulled some errant sticks from her hair.

"Do you think the dragons will come back now too?"

Locke shrugged.

"I don't know, but it seemed like Ir'zane wasn't ready to reveal his army. I think he was seeking something first, something he needs to do before he can cover this world in war once more."

Aeysha looked bewildered.

"Ir'zane? Who's that?"

"That Duscan sorcerer you saw back there, the weird robed guy with the skull mask who raised that dead dragon out of the dirt. Seems he is responsible for bringing back the dead of Duscar, with the death magic we saw back in the grove," Locke explained.

Aeysha was unnerved when she thought of the dead warriors

who had attacked them.

"The way they all followed his orders like puppets, was so creepy. Wait, how do you know that he is looking for something?"

Locke shook his head and half shrugged.

"Something I overheard in the throne room back in Duscar. There was this creepy voice speaking to Ir'zane which mentioned some object, an eye or something. I don't know what it was exactly. But I think he plans to use it to find a way to regenerate his body, which obviously can't be good for us."

Locke continued after a short pause, "The terrifying other voice mentioned a place too." He pulled out the astromancer compass and opened it again. "Show me the Isle of Knives," he spoke to the compass and the magical eye at the center rolled over looking to the west. "Whatever he's after is that way, beyond the forest. In the direction that Ir'zane went atop that flying corpse lizard."

Aeysha grabbed him by the wrist, dragging him back towards the circle of crash survivors.

"Come. We must tell the prince."

Locke pulled his arm back.

"Why should I tell him anything? He didn't believe us last time, he won't this time either. Not to mention he seems to think *this* whole mess is my fault."

Aeysha frowned, frustrated.

"At least come see what's being said, maybe we can help."

Locke was not a fan of the idea, but went along with her and the two of them joined the discussion anyway. Drovann, the dwarven engineer who was sporting a fresh black-eye, was pacing around furiously while listening to everyone talk. He looked like one of the pressurized gas recyclers from the Nomad Sky's engine compartment about to blow. Elisander sat upon the remains of one of the front engines, which was partially sticking out of the dirt.

The prince was frenetically proposing a plan, without a filter between what he thought and what he vocalized, "We need to repair the ship. We get it flying, we get back to Erendar and we tell the k-" A loud, metallic ringing burst out as a length of pipe went flying across the ground, kicked straight through the group.

"Get it flying? HA!" Drovann's voice sounded like black gunpowder charges going off, "The bow o' tha ship is smashed. Both o' yer front engines and props are scrap. This thing couldn'ta get ta flying if ye threw her off a cliff!"

But Elisander went on.

"We *will* repair the ship. Collect wood from the forest and use what tools we can scavenge from the wreckage. We start immediately, and we work through the night, in shifts."

Drovann managed to scowl even more than usual.

"Yer not listenin. I can fix tha rear engines. We can rebuild tha hull. But yer not gettin' her airborne. She was built ta fly with four props, and ye have two! I can't shite two engines outta nothin', there's not but scrap 'ere."

Elisander crossed his arms.

"That doesn't change the fact that we have to get it flying. I'm sure you'll come up with something. In the meantime, we rebuild the hull, and get the rear engines working. We start now."

Elisander turned to address all of them.

"Drovann will be the foreman, as I'm putting him in charge of repairs. I ask that you all work with him to gather supplies and so we can get the Nomad Sky airborne again. She's our only ride home, so let's get to work people!"

The crash survivors dispersed, breaking off into different and smaller groups. Aeysha pushed through the crowd to get to the prince, while she called out to him.

"Prince Elisander!"

He turned around to see her with Locke in tow.

"What can I do for you druid?" he asked politely.

She smiled at him.

"Locke was hoping to be of some help. He has information that could-" Elisander cut her off.

"If the Therredan wishes to be of use, he can go collect firewood. It's going to be dark in a few hours," his words were stern and definitive.

"Forget it Aeysha," Locke said, walking away.

Locke put the astromancer compass around his neck and walked away from the makeshift camp, heading toward the forest. He fumed as he stomped out of sight.

"I'll get your firewood, you spoiled child. I'll make a stupid campfire while you let the world burn for your ego."

Even his thoughts were angry as he reflected, *I only overheard the creepy dead guy's plans but sure, I'll go pick up sticks since you have an attitude problem.*

Locke stormed through the tall grass that was growing around the forest until he stood at the edge of the Western Wood. He craned his head back to see the canopy far above him, he steeled his nerves before taking determined steps into the ancient forest. Locke disappeared into the dense vegetation, yet having barely entered into the forest, the trees were already so thick that he could no longer see their makeshift camp behind him anymore.

The forests beyond the Mountains of Eld were ancient and wild, their trees grew unusually tall and wide. The Feywilds spanned the great valleys which stretched to the western coast, and he could tell this forest was not like the ones that Locke remembered growing around his small village of Dellow. These trees were living towers which had grown undisturbed by mankind for ages. Just to look upon them was awe-inspiring and Locke swore he could feel the antiquity of the place in the air.

The trees were so tall you could stand Elisander's airship upright, end to end, and it would not reach the canopy. It was surreal to be in the presence of such monstrous trees, and it made him feel a bit uneasy to be surrounded by the looming forest. Locke had read stories about the legendary Feywild and he knew enough to know it was a dangerous place for humans, for many who ventured within never returned.

Locke decided that he had gone far enough, afraid to venture too deep into the ancient woods. He started looking around for anything that would make suitable kindling, picking up twigs and branches as he went. While he was picking up a sizeable piece of firewood, he noticed what appeared to be a flower that was shaking strangely.

Upon investigating further, it took flight as if startled by him. He was able to get a better look at it as it flitted about. It was a forest sprite, or so he thought, noting its twig-like body and flower petal wings. Bewildered by it, Locke followed it with his eyes as it danced around him, spinning him in circles. It giggled at him with a strange voice that sounded like birds chirping.

Locke smiled.

"Alright little fellow, I need to get back to work now."

He went back to picking up sticks, but the sprite dove in his way, making him shift the bundle he carried in his arms awkwardly and he nearly dropped them all. Locke was starting to get annoyed, and when he went to grab a different stick, the sprite danced in his face as he tried to work. The playful fey kept getting in his way and giggling at him when he tried to shoo it away. Frustrated, he swatted at it furiously, dropping the load of firewood onto the ground as he did. Cursing, he started picking up the pile of sticks again while the sprite kept giggling at him. Before long Locke was met with another one as it flew around him curiously.

"Great, now there's two of you," he said exasperated.

They bounced like dandelion seeds in a light breeze across the pile as he struggled to pick it up. They even pretended to lift it from underneath, making serious faces and grunting noises. Locke was not amused, but they continued giggling as he angrily swatted at them again, dropping the wood once more.

"Alright! That's it!" he shouted and chased after them. He snatched one up in his hand and it wailed painfully while the other sprite grabbed the astromancer compass from around Locke's neck and flew away with it.

"Give that back!" he shouted. The captive sprite struggled against his grip and then bit Locke hard; who yelped as he let the little biter go. The sprite made a mean-spirited mocking face and flew off after the one who took off with the compass. He chased them both into deeper woods, which grew ever greener and wild.

As he ran after the sprites, Locke could hear water running from a stream nearby, before long he saw it rolling over humble waterfalls and cascading into a placid pool of the brightest, clearest water he had ever seen. The small river which fed the tranquil pool trailed back through the woods the way he came, but as he was admiring it, the forest sprites buzzed past his head giggling. Locke nearly grabbed the compass back from them, but they evaded him and flew backward over the tranquil pool. The sprites hovered over its gently rippling surface while dangling the compass above it.

He pleaded with them.

"Come on now little guys, don't do anything hasty. Let's talk about this! I've got some food with me; you want some food?"

They stared back at him with delight and he could see what mischief they intended; it was written all over their little faces. "Don't you da-" Plop. The astromancer compass dropped into the pool of water and the sprites flew away laughing with their bird-like chirping sounds.

Locke groaned and bent down to the water's edge, staring through the crystal-clear waters to the bottom of the pool where he could easily see the compass resting in the silt. He placed his hand in the water to find it pleasantly warm, but when he cupped it and brought it to his lips, it was cold as mountain run off in the thaw after winter. With a quick look around to see if anyone or anything was watching, he undressed and placed his clothes by the banks of the pool before jumping in.

Locke found that not only was the water warm, it was hot enough to be soothing. He felt his stiff muscles ease and his bruised shoulder healed beneath the red armor, which shone brightly in the waters of the pool. Locke took a deep breath and dove to the bottom, easily retrieving the compass from the silt. He came up for air with the compass and placed it back around his neck before deciding to enjoy the pools. He swam over to the modest waterfall, putting his head under it and he let the water wash over his face until the sound of it drowned out everything else.

While under the waterfall he noticed a tiny cove behind it which had a shelf-like rock where an assortment of ornate glass bottles in a variety of colors rested peacefully. Locke was bewildered by the sight of such finery in the middle of the forest and wondered if they were an illusion of the pond, or another trick being played on him by the sprites. He picked each of them up one at a time and unstoppered them to smell the enchanting sweet and flowery aromas that each contained.

Locke was so caught up smelling the bottles that he did not notice the elf woman who was watching him. She stood silently at the water's edge watching the red-haired man curiously smelling her perfumes. She silently unfastened her white gold dress, letting it slide off her body so quietly it fell like a whisper to the ground. Her toes entered the pool so delicately that she did not disturb the surface of the water as she stepped into it. She slipped into the pool unnoticed by Locke, who was distracted trying to pour some perfume out onto his finger.

She swam across the water, floating like a lily across the pond towards the falls. Locke placed the bottles back on the shelf, and passed back through the waterfall. He wiped the water from his eyes to see an elf woman swimming toward him and his heart stopped. Her long flowing hair was the color of starlight and splayed out across the surface of the pool, while somehow not getting wet. Her long ears pointed upright in curiosity, the tips of which just peeked over the top of her head. Her large eyes were the color of the flora around them, the colors and patterns within shifted with the motion of the leaves blowing in the breeze. He had never seen such perfection or beauty, and all other thoughts faded from his mind and were quickly forgotten.

But as she drifted closer to him, Locke became painfully aware of their nudity and he jumped back as though a snake had dropped into the pond in front of him. He splashed wildly as he swam away, but she calmly followed after him, pinning him against the rock and between her arms. His face turned the color of his hair and he swallowed hard, trying to find anywhere else for his eyes to look.

"You have entered my personal, usually *private* bathing pool," she said to him in a lecturing tone, with a voice as sweet as honey.

"I-I am very s-sorry, I didn't-" he stammered, but she interrupted him.

"An age has passed since men from the outside have entered these woods. You are far from home, traveler, where is it you have journeyed from?"

He replied, vaguely uncertain of what he was saying.

"Nowhere you have ever heard of, from a place so small even this wouldn't be able to find it," he joked, holding up the astromancer compass. Her eyes widened in curiosity.

"Such an unusual man I have discovered lurking in my private bath. A man who hails from the southern kingdom, wearing a mage compass of the northern kingdom, and wields the weapon of the eastern red desert. There are no more trinkets here in the Western

Wood for you to claim, Therredan. What is your name?"

"I am Locke," he replied slowly, as though it took some effort to remember. He clutched the armor on his right arm protectively, "What is your name, elf? And why are you holding me here?" Before she could answer, another voice shouted from the woods, "Princess! Princess Aerilynn!" An elvish ranger entered the clearing. When he noticed that she was naked he turned away quickly, hanging his head shamefully. "Apologies your highness-" But he also caught sight of Locke out of the corner of his eye, and in an instant, he knocked an arrow while drawing his bow.

"Stop!" the elf woman shouted. The look on the ranger's face was a mix of surprise and frustration, but he reluctantly lowered his weapon.

"Princess, why is there a human in one of our sacred pools?" he asked. She turned her back to Locke and addressed her elven kin.

"I should ask why you are inviting yourself into *my* sacred pool."

"Forgive me, your highness," he bowed low, "I came to tell you that our scouts have discovered the wreckage of an airship not far from here. It appears to be from Everund, my lady."

She turned around slowly to face Locke again.

"So, it is no coincidence that I should find you in my woods after all." Her lips curled into a playful smile, "Prepare an armed envoy to investigate this crash site. This man might be leverage, should we need it." She gave Locke a knowing look he did not like before she got out of the pond. As she stepped out of the tranquil pool, the water ran off her body so quickly that by the time she reached for her dress, her skin was already dry.

Locke however, was pulled out of the water abruptly by the

ranger and told to dress quickly, "Keep your eyes on your toes or I'll put an arrow through them," he threatened.

Locke barely got his dry clothes over his wet body when he was shoved along by the ranger. Soaking in his clothes, he was led away roughly through the forest. They were soon joined by a few elven soldiers wearing thin metal armor whose plates were shaped like leaves. Despite the situation, Locke was enjoying the moment in the mythical company of elves.

"Where are you taking me?" he asked, while getting shoved from behind by a stern-faced elf as reply.

Aerilynn looked over her shoulder with a pleasant smile.

"Back to your people, of course. I'd very much like to meet them," she said no more as they walked through the woods. His captors were so supernaturally quiet as they traveled that he wondered if they weighed anything at all, or if perhaps they were spectral beings. They walked in silence through the wild wood while he crunched along the forest floor clumsily.

The scenery was breathtaking, though Locke found it impossible to look away from the princess. Perhaps it was from some elven magic, a spell she had cast upon him, or something in that pool of water. He snapped back to reality, noticing disapproving glances from the elves on either side of him. Locke jumped because he had forgotten that they were there. Aerilynn looked back at him, her eyes were shining brightly, which filled him with an indescribable fire. The armed guards with her proved to be entirely unnecessary, as she needed only to ask and he would have followed her anywhere.

The All-Seeing Eye

Though he was technically their captive, Locke walked lightly and smiled brightly while strolling through the ancient woods. Yet he also felt the narrow glares and seething disapproval from the elves surrounding him. He wondered if it was because he was a human trespassing in their lands or if it was because he was caught naked in a private bath with their princess. He smiled sheepishly at them but that only seemed to make them grumpier.

The ranger who found him in the bath clearly did not like him being so cavalier about the situation and he shoved Locke so hard in the back with his bow, it knocked him to the ground. Locke coughed and sputtered, after landing face first in the dirt. The ranger stood over him threateningly.

"That will teach you to show respect," he growled.

Aerilynn stopped everyone.

"What is the meaning of this?"

She walked over and reached down, helping Locke to his feet. After assisting him back up, she scolded the ranger who shoved him, "It is not your place to say what it means to show respect."

Locke dusted himself off.

"Thank you," he stated, before adding, "Your highness."

Locke then bowed his head to her, and she smiled back at him before addressing the others.

"You will not administer unwarranted violence on unarmed prisoners. And since you seem to be concerned with respect, I'll have you remember my authority as princess. You will see to it that no further harm will come to this human."

She then smiled at Locke and said, "I am fond of him." Before she continued walking. Her guards followed behind silently, not wishing to be chastised further. Locke had a cocky smile on his face for the rest of the journey through the dense wood.

After a short hike they came upon a large field of tall grass, which Locke recognized as the edge of the forest. But this field was not the one he crossed to enter the wood, for this one had short trees in it. As they walked through the odd trees, Locke noticed something even stranger than how short they were; there were *faces* in the bark. It was common for people to see images in clouds and the like, but this was different. Where usually nature produced a facsimile which somewhat resembled a face in the abstract, these were unnervingly detailed. These trees looked like they had grown out of people, and their faces were all twisted in agony.

Locke went to one of the elves at his side to ask about it, but the smirk on the elf's face made him think twice.

"This is what happens to those who trespass in our woods, outlander," the elf offered.

Aerilynn looked over her shoulder to Locke.

"They came to hurt the forest, and our kin. But we are gracious hosts, so we shared our lands with them. They learned to respect the forest in the end."

A chill went down Locke's spine as she explained and he swallowed the hard lump in his throat. He was all too happy leaving that macabre scene behind, as they eventually came upon broken trees and torn up earth. They arrived at last at the crash site and wreckage of the Nomad Sky. The knights of Everund who were working on repairs were caught off guard by the elves' sudden appearance.

Elisander spun about sharply, placing his hand on the hilt of his sword as Aerilynn and her small band of elves walked into their camp with their own weapons at the ready.

"Relax young prince," the elven princess said.

"We have come to return something that belongs to you. We found him wandering around lost in our woods, and we're simply returning him."

Elisander looked puzzled, unable to work out who she was talking about. The elven princess motioned with her hand and one of her rangers grabbed Locke, pushing him into the open. Elisander was not enthused to see him, especially not as a captive of elves.

"I told you to make yourself useful, or leave. It seems you have done neither, instead choosing to wander into elven lands and getting yourself captured."

Locke scowled, but said nothing as Aerilynn concluded, "As I said, young prince, we are merely returning him to you."

She grabbed Locke by the arm and walked with him over to the prince. Elisander had his knights stand down, and the elven princess kissed Locke on the cheek before letting him go.

Locke walked back to the Nomad Sky's wreckage, looking at Aerilynn while touching his cheek.

"We thank you, my lady, for returning our... guest," Elisander said with as much decorum as he could muster. She nodded and addressed him directly.

"Now that the matter is settled, I suppose a formal introduction is called for. I am Princess Aerilynn Everdawn, caretaker of Lorlinden and the Western Wood, and I would like to know why you are here?"

The prince bowed again.

"Forgive me, my name is Elisander, son of Armon, and I am the prince of Everund. As you can see, our ship has crashed. We were investigating the ruins of Duscar and we were attacked."

Aerilynn appeared surprised by his statement.

"Attacked? In Duscar? By what?"

Elisander continued, "By a dragon, an undead one. And also, by warriors from Duscar, all risen as reanimated corpses. The dreadwyrm tore our engines off like it was plucking feathers from a bird."

Aerilynn looked serious.

"How can that be?"

"We believe that Ir'zane, the Dragonblood sorcerer, has been resurrected, and that he has raised the armies of Duscar."

Aerilynn looked deeply concerned.

"I have not heard that name since the exile of the last dragons."

Elisander sighed.

"We are still trying to understand how it happened, but for now we need to focus on stopping him before he gets what he is searching for. Currently, he is flying on the back of that monstrous dreadwyrm and heading west out over the ocean for some reason."

"I know where he's going... and what he's after," Locke said bluntly, shifting everyone's attention to him again. Prince Elisander looked annoyed and Princess Aerilynn looked bemused as they waited for him to elaborate. "I overheard Ir'zane speaking to someone in the throne room, who told him about something that would help him locate a power to regenerate his body."

Elisander crossed his arms.

"Who was he speaking with?"

Locke shook his head.

"I honestly don't know; I couldn't actually see them. I only heard them talking together, but Ir'zane was recalling information about this island in the western sea. He called it the Isle of Knives."

Elisander seemed to recognize the name.

"I know of it only from tales my grandfather would tell me. It's nothing more than a rock spire that rises from the ocean and is famous for sinking ships. Why would Ir'zane be going there?"

"He's after a magical artifact of some kind, it's hidden there," Locke answered.

Aerilynn asked, "Did you hear what it was? Do you know what they said they were after?"

Locke nodded slowly.

"The Eye of Orynos."

Elisander's brow furled.

"Orynos? Hmmm... I've never heard that name before. I'm not sure what this could mean, or what this Eye is, but I don't like the sound of it." Elisander looked to his dwarven engineering officer, who was grumbling to himself, and continued his thoughts, "All the more reason to get the Nomad Sky repaired, we'll need it if we have any chance of catching him."

Drovann grunted.

"I told ye' it's impossible."

Aerilynn inspected the wreckage of Elisander's downed airship.

"We may be able to help you with that. Our artisans can fix the hull and repair structural damage, though we cannot replace your engines. You will need to find another way to make it fly again."

"We would be grateful for your assistance, lady Aerilynn," Elisander said genuinely relieved. The princess ordered a runner to return to Lorlinden and to bring their best woodweavers at once.

"I will leave my rangers with you to provide extra labor and protection for my people. As for Duscar, I will fly to the Isle of Knives and stop Ir'zane myself."

Elisander objected.

"You are mad if you think you are going alone. Lend me a mount and allow me to assist you."

Aerilynn did not seem to like the idea initially, but decided debate was a more unfavorable outcome of such a protest and she was deeply troubled by the words of Locke. The human had mentioned Ir'zane wanting to regenerate his body, and she had a sinking feeling that meant he was seeking Silthradel.

"Very well, but we must leave now."

The elven ranger who had escorted Locke seemed to anticipate his princess' needs before she had to ask, and was already off securing them transportation. Elisander sensed they would be leaving shortly, so he delegated responsibility for overseeing the collaboration between the Everunders and the elves of Lorlinden to the only woman he trusted with his life.

"Kayara, I am putting you in charge. See that the repairs go smoothly, we need the Nomad Sky operational as soon as possible!"

She nodded solemnly, and though she tried to hide it, she also looked genuinely worried about Elisander.

"Don't worry, my prince, I'll make sure the ship is fully repaired by the time you return. Just make sure that you do return, okay?"

Elisander smiled before turning to his grumpy dwarf friend.

"Drovann, I need a miracle!"

His chief engineer huffed in acknowledgement, and Elisander left him to put his broken airship back together. The prince joined Aerilynn, who whistled loudly, and from the heart of the forest two white-feathered gryphons took to the skies. The ranger who had secured them insisted she reconsider.

"My lady, it is too dangerous, you cannot go."

The gryphons circled overhead waiting to be called again.

"I can, and I must. Watch over our kin, Caden, and stand guard over Lorlinden. Send word to Silthradel, warn my mother that should I fail to stop Ir'zane at the Isle of Knives, that they should prepare for an attack."

He looked incredulous.

"But my lady, you know we are forbidden to have contact with our homeland by order of the queen."

Aerilynn whistled sharply twice and the gryphons swooped down, landing next to her gracefully.

"Send the warning, Caden. I can only hope that it will be received." She turned to Elisander, "Come, we must go before this escalates further." She mounted one of the gryphons, handing the reins of the other to the prince, but before they took flight Locke called out to Aerilynn.

"Wait! Take this! It can help you find the Isle of Knives," he said as handed her Ravendark's astromancer compass. She hesitated before taking it from him.

"Thank you, I will make sure this gets returned to you."

Locke smiled and stepped to the side. Elisander climbed onto the creature's back as the gryphon's mighty talons tore into the dirt. The legendary creatures flapped their enormous wings and took flight. Locke was surprised at how fast they could fly, for they had no more than left the ground and already they were nothing more than specs on the horizon. He felt concerned for Aerilynn's wellbeing as she vanished beyond his view, and he hoped he would see her again.

~

The Isle of Knives rose from the ocean depths before Aerilynn's eyes, as she and the prince of Everund flew over rows upon rows of dagger-like rocks which reached above the crashing waves. The rock spikes all surrounded a tiny island with a tower of volcanic stone at its center that rose beyond the storm clouds which gathered overhead. The black obsidian shone in the fading sunlight peeking through the clouds as twilight was approaching. The sunbeams created thousands of tiny rainbows as they traveled through beads of water that the ocean was spraying into the air.

Aerilynn held tightly to the long feathers of her gryphon's mane, gripping its muscular body with her thighs in order to keep herself anchored to its back. While she flew elegantly with acrobatic grace, Elisander found controlling the half eagle, half lion creature much more difficult than riding a horse or piloting his airship. It was all he could do to keep from falling off the thing as they weaved through the sharp rocks around the island. Calling the Isle of Knives an island was a bit of an exaggeration, as it was little else besides the tower.

The peak of the obsidian tower was obscured from their view by the clouds of an enormous storm which raged around the top. Trying to avoid the sharp rocks everywhere made finding a spot to land difficult on the Isle, but with some careful maneuvering they managed to find just enough space to roost without being carved up by the blade-like stones. After searching the exterior of the tower, they found no doors or other ways in.

"The entrance seems to be hidden," said the prince, who was happy to feel solid ground beneath his feet again. Aerilynn looked up at the storm above them and noticed that the clouds were only directly above the island.

"I'm willing to bet that storm is an enchantment, and that means it's protecting the way in."

Elisander reached out and touched the wall of the tower to see if it was possible to climb it, but as he gripped the stone its sharp edges cut into his hand painfully.

"Looks like we'll have to fly to the top," he said while pulling his bleeding hand back quickly.

The two of them climbed back onto their gryphons, and flew up into the storm raging around the tower's peak. Lightning crashed around them as they entered the tempest. From inside the winds whipped around them furiously, threatening to throw them from their mounts and into the bladed sea below. Elisander fought to stay atop his gryphon while searching through the low visibility inside the storm. They heard a deep rumbling growl that was entirely distinct from the thunder just before Ir'zane's dreadwyrm ambushed them both by diving out of the shadows.

The gryphons instinctively pulled away from the undead dragon's gnashing teeth, using their superior agility to dodge its attacks. The dreadwyrm's massive size and decayed wings made it hard for the creature to catch the smaller and more agile gryphons. It flew past Aerilynn as she narrowly avoided its rot-ridden jaws, and Elisander was nearly unseated as he was hit with its tail. The prince drew his steel sword and struck one of the dreadwyrm's wings with his blade as it passed him again. The beast howled in an unholy fury, chasing him through the storm.

"Go!" he shouted to Aerilynn over the thunder, "I'll destroy this foul thing and strand Ir'zane here!" She nodded and pulled away from the fight. With the dreadwyrm chasing after the prince, Aerilynn slipped right past it, flying down into the dark of the tower to confront Ir'zane alone.

~

At home in the lightless reaches of the vaults which lay at the bottom of the tower, Ir'zane concentrated the shadow surrounding him into a singular point of light between his fingers, and a faint luminescent purple filled the room. It was not enough light for someone else to see their surroundings, but for the shadowmancer it looked like a cloudless night during the brightest moon of the year.

He pulled the book from his hip and held it out before him, releasing it from his grip as it floated in midair. With a gesture of his skeletal hand, the clasp unhooked and the book opened, revealing its pages of human flesh. The whispers of a thousand voices fell from between the pages as it levitated menacingly.

Each time Ir'zane used the book, a hideous aura assailed everything around it psychically, trying to destroy the consciousness of anyone unfortunate enough to be within range of its horrendous power. Ir'zane heard the voices within the book inside his mind, he felt them clawing at him, their screams like banshees' wailing. If he was not careful, it would obliterate his mind as it had done to the wizard who had resurrected him. With his magically empowered will he wrestled the souls of the damned into submission, and their raucous chattering quieted.

"Where is the Eye?" he asked, and from the book came a voice which was more distinct and malevolent than all the others.

Not far, it said with unnerving enthusiasm. Ir'zane knew it would be unwise to trust the book implicitly; it was clear it had its own motives. One thing he knew for sure was that there was one voice which stood out from the others and was in command of the dark power contained within the book's pages. *Through the tunnel of limitless night, you will find hidden chambers at the end of endless mazes.*

Ir'zane assumed he must be key to whatever wicked plot the book was weaving; after all, it had brought him back from the dead. It was most likely an alliance of convenience, a power struggle in which he currently had the upper hand, but was still at a disadvantage overall. The book seemed to know all his schemes and heart's desires, while he did not know what the book was after.

He headed through twisting corridors which led to a small chamber with three doorways, each passage revealing its own tunnel leading off into darkness. Ir'zane found the start of the labyrinth which his former mentor, Eldric, had built to keep people from plundering the vault of its forsaken secrets.

What you seek lies at the bottom. Ir'zane was certain the book would turn on him eventually, he was always wary of those who would use him to their own ends.

Ir'zane remembered the way his blood would boil inside his veins when the dragons were angry, and the feeling of his body betraying him. He would not allow himself to be a servant again. Ir'zane's paranoia and his vulnerability made him desperate for power. The knowledge in the book bound the dead to his will and ensured his absolute control over them. Once his body was renewed and brimming with mana again, no one would stop him from cursing everyone with undeath and bringing the world under his control.

He wound his way through seemingly endless passageways, guided by the direction of the book for what felt like hours in the dizzying monotony of the labyrinth.

It's not far now, I can feel it breathing... can you? The book laughed quietly and Ir'zane chose not to respond. He raised his shadow-light over his head so he could see farther as he entered a large room whose walls were too far away to reflect much of the purple light. He saw a large arch engraved with primordial runes and he reached out to touch one, brushing away millennia of dust from the carved stone. The symbols resembled warding enchantments, and he reasoned that they must protect the vault beyond the arch.

Ir'zane picked up a stone and tossed it through, watching closely to see what would happen. As it passed through the arch, the stone blazed with fire and became red hot, melting into a small blob of molten stone before splattering on the ground.

"An invisible wall of fire magic without mana would need a massive alternate power source to keep it active," he said aloud to himself as he examined the arch. He pressed his only remaining ear to it and heard a soft, flowing noise within. The tower itself was formed out of volcanic stone, so it made perfect sense for its spells to be powered by geomancy. No doubt if he had still been able to feel temperature, he would have felt the heat from within it as well.

"You were always so clever," he said, presumably to his former mentor. The sorcerer once again used his unique magic of umbramancy to create thick, sticky webs of pure shadow which latched onto the arch. He pulled on the strands of darkness until the archway cracked, and magma flowed out of it. The runes powered down and as they did, the spell defending the vault failed. Ir'zane walked safely through the archway, stepping into an open room with a stone dais floating in the middle of it. He saw no ceiling to the room, and looking down he saw no floor.

He looked around the room, but saw nothing besides the dais in the large pit. However, Ir'zane noticed that a black liquid was dripping from the dais into the abyss below. He never heard the sound of it hitting ground or water, as if it was still falling through endless dark.

The Eye is here.

Ir'zane found the thing resting atop the dais which hung from chains anchored into the walls of the chamber. A platform of stone was encrusted beneath the dais, which offered just enough room to stand on. Unfortunately for him it was floating farther away from him than he could jump.

Ir'zane stared greedily with glowing green flame eyes at the black blood dripping from the stone altar upon which the fleshy blasphemy bled eternally. He peered into the deep impenetrable darkness of the descent that the black blood dripped into, and a smile tore across his rotten face. Ir'zane raised his arms like he was pulling up roots and the darkness of the room clung to his fingers like spider webs. He gripped them in his hands and pulled up thick strands from the shadows.

The smoke-like tendrils formed a web which bridged the gap to the platform. His feet sunk into the shadow web slightly when he stepped on it, and the strands stuck to his feet. When he pulled up his foot to step forward, the strands snapped back into place. Ir'zane leaned over the dais, feeling power radiating from it, and he felt a sick need to possess the accursed artifact resting upon it.

His mind raced in a frenzy of twisted delight as he reached for the bleeding eye. The flames of his eyes danced wildly as his dead fingers closed around the Eye of Orynos with a squelching sound. Ir'zane watched the black blood from the eye fill his palm; it dripped down his forearm as he raised his prize to his face in order to admire it more closely.

Ir'zane uncoiled his gaunt fingers from the eye, mesmerized while watching it bleed, and for a moment he thought he saw it move. The eye indeed twitched, rocking back and forth for a moment in his palm before rolling over so that it was staring back at Ir'zane. The orb of flesh was grayish in tint, covered in engorged veins which pulsated. The iris was blood red and luminous, rimmed with ivory-colored protrusions which looked like quills, growing in rows around the iris in such a way that resembled lamprey teeth. These 'teeth' pressed against each other as the pupil shrank, like a mouth closing. It was a magnificent phenomenon to Ir'zane, and he took great delight in watching the thing 'breathe' as the pupil undulated.

The eye mouthed hungrily with its unblinking stare, which was fixed upon Ir'zane like an animal ready to pounce. Worm-like veins grew out of the back of the eye, and suddenly spread across his open palm. Within moments they tore painfully into his skin, boring their way through deep tissues, and wrapping around bones. His arm stiffened, curling upward awkwardly as though about to snap itself in half. He screamed as his vision blurred. Ir'zane swayed on his feet as his consciousness waned from the onslaught of physical agony. The pain flowing through him was so powerful that it brought him to his knees.

As the horrid eye finally came to a rest in Ir'zane's palm, the pain ceased, though he could still feel the odd sensation of it wriggling under his skin. The Eye of Orynos gave him vision which pierced through all things, allowing him to see through the solid stone walls. It showed him invisible things that were otherwise imperceptible to the naked eye such as the spellwork woven into the vault. With the All-Seeing Eye, Ir'zane was able to perceive more than he dreamed he could. It was as though the threads of the world were laid bare before him.

An unnerving grin spread across his face, reveling in the power he now held. He threw his head back and laughed with the maniacal cackle of a lunatic. The hideous sound of his laughter echoed through the dark corridors beneath the Isle of Knives, crawling its way through the obsidian tower. Ir'zane pointed the monstrous eye upwards, and saw straight through the labyrinth and into the chambers above.

Beyond that he saw the length of the tower as it reached into the storms above and to his surprise, someone was descending the tower. A woman, wearing a pale white dress which glowed like moonlight. She was an elf, likely a member of a royal line, he assumed by her outfit. If she was allowed to leave this place, she could warn her people that he was coming for them, and he would never allow that to happen. Ir'zane smiled evilly, keeping the Eye of Orynos in his palm fixated on her.

"I see you," he said darkly.

Dawnbreaker

The soft white glow of Aerilynn's elven dress reflected off the interior of the obsidian tower. The narrow path down through the tower meant that she and her gryphon had to avoid hitting the walls as they dove down toward the unknowable bottom. They flew through nearly total darkness, travelling below the ocean outside and into the lightless depths beneath. Her enchanted dress glowed brighter the darker her surroundings became, until her dress was shining with the light of a full moon. When they landed and her feet touched the ground, the light of her dress awoke an amber glow from deep within the volcanic glass. The walls were a frozen river of magma, left over from the tower's violent magical creation.

Aerilynn's starlight-colored hair was glowing as well, reflecting the light emanating from her enchanted gown. Her irises turned into a fiery mix of red and orange which matched the molten glass around her. She pulled a crystal from a pouch secured about her waist, in which she stored components that she could use to hasten or empower her spellcasting. As she opened her hand, the clear crystal levitated from her palm and floated before her face. She pressed her lips together and blew a deep breath over the crystal, which responded by glowing brightly like the embers of a fire.

Aerilynn released the crystal and it floated to the outer edge of the room, but the aura of light the crystal emitted ended before reaching back to her. She pulled out five more crystals and repeated the process until the room was half lit by magical light. The low light revealed the domed roof of the chamber and the tunnel in the ceiling that she had emerged from. It was an otherwise entirely unremarkable room with walls that were made from the same volcanic glass as the rest of the tower she had come down. She noticed a set of footprints in the dust at the far edge of the room, there a patch of unlit darkness indicated a passageway leading out of the central chamber that she was currently in.

She and her gryphon were having difficulty breathing in the stale subterranean air, but the noble beast calmed a little after the princess lit up the room. To conserve its energy, the gryphon laid down in the dust while panting. Aerilynn rested her hands upon its head stroking its feathers gently, and it squeaked in approval. She grabbed it by the beak and playfully shook its head before standing back up.

"Don't worry my friend, I won't be long. I'll stop Ir'zane, then you and I are out of this creepy place, okay?"

Aerilynn knew she currently had the advantage of surprise, but only if she stayed undetected until she managed to find him, and only if she moved quickly. She looked down the passageway out of the chamber which led into the unknown depths below. It would be a good idea to have a way back out in case she got lost in the dark, and Aerilynn knew a little translocation enchantment which would work perfectly.

However, she required something to anchor the spell to and there was nothing in the room to attach it to, let alone something unique enough to use for the recall. Aerilynn sighed, placing her hand over the pendant her mother had given her as a child. She closed her eyes in resignation as she would have preferred to use something less sentimental for the spell. At least it would be easy to cast the translocation recall on, due to its strong emotional and personal connection. Her fingers ran along the necklace chain to the spot where it had been repaired.

She undid the clasp and the pendant slipped into her palm. Aerilynn held it in front of her face, staring at the golden wings rising like daybreak with a sunstone at its heart, and it brought back painful memories for her. The pendant of the Everdawn, her family's crest, was more than a pretty heirloom; it was also all she had left of her home. Despite her complicated feelings about it, Aerilynn laid it on the floor, she hesitated a moment before casting the enchantment which created a link between herself and the pendant. A small circle of glowing blue sigils appeared and hovered above her palm as wisps of blue-white mana swirled between them. So long as Aerilynn held the spell it would anchor the recall to her heirloom, which she would leave behind.

Part of her mind would need to stay focused on maintaining the spell or it would be lost, but the princess was a gifted spellcaster who could hold spells such as this as easily as holding a torch. With her free hand she reached into a large pouch on her hip and pulled Locke's astromancer compass from it, opening the eye to activate it. She thought about Locke and his shy smile, replaying their parting scene in her memory. Remarking to herself about how he had the kindest eyes she had ever seen, and she found it was hard to stop picturing them. She ran her thumb across the compass absentmindedly before clearing her mind of distractions.

Of all the astromancy spells she knew, only one would be a help to her in this place, an augury which her people had once used to travel the stars by detecting nearby terrestrial objects. She cast the spell upon the compass, which glowed with a bluish-purple light, and the magical eye unlocked from the housing it was set in. The star-speckled eye floated just above the socket and projected a blue light against the walls, mapping the terrain of the caverns as opposed to identifying the size and velocity of asteroids.

"Now, where is Eldric's vault?" she asked, and the eye pointed forward through the passageway leading out of the chamber.

The princess ducked through the narrow hallway because the natural rock was not formed enough to walk through the passage comfortably. It felt like spelunking through an unexplored cave, as she wound her way through the cramped curving tunnels. She found herself in a room which had several other tunnel entrances around the outside and she could not tell which was the path she just came from. The floor was stone, which meant that there were no footprints to follow, and it also meant she would not easily find her way back out.

Aerilynn relied on the compass to guide her from there, she let it scan the room and its iris rolled around reading the various passageways before pointing down the tunnel to her right. She made a mental note to thank Locke again for the compass when she returned. She wound her way through confining tunnels that always came to puzzling crossroad chambers, and each time she consulted the astromancer compass to guide her through.

The deeper down she went the worse the air quality became. She was starting to feel lightheaded and her lungs burned from the exertion of her expedition. Aerilynn had no idea how far down she had gone or how many tunnels or turns she had taken since she had left the main chamber. The further down she went through the twisting dark, the tighter the princess held her translocation spell, and the more she considered using it to leave. After navigating through endless tunnels, she came at last to a wide doorway and a room larger than her dress could illuminate.

She slowed her breathing, trying to be silent and listening for noise coming from inside. She heard a faint sound like water dripping in the distance and nothing else. The dripping echoed through the stillness as she slowly stepped through the broken stone archway. Though she had made it this far without finding Ir'zane, she knew he was down there in the dark somewhere and sooner or later they were bound to run into one another. Aerilynn checked the astromancer compass again because the magical eye was still looking for the secret vault. The glowing white pupil pointed straight ahead of her, but to what, she could not see.

Aerilynn walked into the room and the source of the dripping water was revealed. It was coming from a stone dais which floated mid-air over a chasm, which was so deep that she could not see the bottom. She recoiled slightly when she realized that it was not water that she heard dripping, but blood which was black as the dead of night instead. The blood was pouring slowly out of a shallow basin at the top of a stone pedestal. She saw no sign of the artifact in the basin or on top of the pedestal. Aerilynn glanced down at the compass to see if its position changed but it was pointed toward the stone dais.

The princess stepped to the edge which hung over the chasm in order to get a closer look when she heard the sudden sound of whooshing despite there being no flow in the thick, stale air. She heard something above her in the darkness, then felt it fly past her. Ir'zane called out to her from the shadows, making her shiver.

"I see you, elf witch," he sneered as she spun around.

Stuffing the compass back into the pouch on her hip to store it away safely, Aerilynn took a defensive posture. She conjured a sphere of destruction which rolled around her fingertips but before she was able to launch her attack, Ir'zane used his umbramancy to animate shadows which lashed out at her. Tendrils of solid darkness wrapped around her wrist and pulled her hand back as she released the spell, resulting in it detonating against the wall in vibrant a prismatic explosion. Aerilynn caught a brief glimpse of Ir'zane's undead body in the illumination caused by the blast, the silhouette of his skeleton haunted her eyes for just a moment before the darkness closed around her once more.

"No one shall ever see you again," Ir'zane taunted, while his hideous mockery of laughter echoed through the stone halls as he escaped. More shadowy tendrils latched onto her and started pulling her toward the ground, throwing her off balance. Aerilynn slid into a wider stance for stability, but her foot nearly went over the edge. She caught herself before almost falling into the abyss below. Fighting against the shadow magic seemed to be a losing battle however, and whether or not she continued struggling she would eventually be dragged off the ledge to her death.

The princess remembered the translocation spell in her hand and she let the contained magic free, activating the spell just as she was pulled off the ledge by the shadow magic. Her body became enshrouded in a blue-white glow and then in an instant she vanished. The pendant of the Everdawn dynasty to which she had anchored the spell swapped places with her, and she with it. The darkness ate her heirloom hungrily, pulling the necklace into the depths beneath the Isle of Knives.

Aerilynn's body was hurled through time and space, up through the tunnels below the tower, before materializing in the first chamber where she left her heirloom pendant. Her gryphon squealed loudly in alarm as she reappeared, but she did not have time to comfort her feathered friend. Instead, she readied more spells for combat. She felt Ir'zane's dark presence approaching from the tunnel in front of her, Aerilynn knew she did not have long before he caught back up to her but she was still surprised at the speed by which he did.

Before she could react, more smoke-like shadow tendrils reached out from the dark parts of the room, grabbing her crystals and smothering the light they gave off. She heard them crack as they were broken one by one. The illumination of her dress was now the only light in the room.

In total darkness, the princess was at a disadvantage against Ir'zane's twisted magic. She needed to find a weakness if she had any chance of defeating him now. A mad cackle echoed around the room, but Aerilynn could tell precisely where it was coming from. Despite being unable to see him in the pitch black, her keen ears were able to hear the shadowmancer moving around making faint sounds like snakes slithering through grass.

"Step out from the shadows and I shall give you peace, sorcerer," she spat her words at him. A blinding green fire flared up in front of her, revealing Ir'zane's rotted body and lighting up what was left of his face.

"The shadows are my home, o' fair and ancient witch. Time has not been as kind to my body as it has been to your kin, but they shall taste its bitter sting soon," the devil grinned as he gloated before disappearing again.

Aerilynn listened intently, waiting for an opportunity to attack or for Ir'zane to strike first. Her practiced hand was ready to unleash a blast of cosmic energy, having already charged a spell with her mana. She would bury his bones in the walls of the chamber if she could land it.

"Death has been far less kind to you than time, Lightslayer. It has slowed your mind. I guard your only escape and I will not allow you to remove that blasphemy from this place!"

"Do you intend to take it from my hand?" Ir'zane laughed, holding his palm out where the hideous Eye of Orynos wriggled and dripped black blood. The All-Seeing Eye pierced through her soul drawing a long-forgotten memory out of her, and for a moment she saw herself as a small child on a different world. Aerilynn saw her father speaking with her mother, the queen was pleading with him not to go. She saw her father walk away, watching helplessly as he joined a large group of elves who stood at the edge of their fracturing world while they cast a spell together.

It was a cloudless night but there were no visible stars that she could see. Something larger than the planet itself was blocking them out, and as it opened its endless maw over the horizon she snapped out of her memory. Her eyes were wide with terror, and she felt more naked and unnerved than she had ever been before. Aerilynn hurled her spell at Ir'zane but her reckless attack proved easy to dodge, he vanished into the shadows and her spell struck the wall instead. The explosion created a flash bright as daylight for the briefest instant before everything faded to total darkness again. Aerilynn's gryphon was startled by the blast and screeched, flapping around the room erratically.

Her eyes darted across the pitch-black room searching for Ir'zane, with more spells at the ready. Aerilynn's ears pricked up and twitched about listening intently for him, but she was having a hard time hearing his nearly silent movements over her own panicked breath and her gryphon's fussing. She tried to calm her breathing but Ir'zane appeared in front of her in a blaze of green fire. Aerilynn jumped back, conjuring a lance made of plasma and throwing it at him. Ir'zane counterspelled it and the lance fizzled away midair with a hiss and crackle.

Aerilynn quickly drew more sigils and as she did a volley of unerring magical arrows of force shot at Ir'zane, who again reversed the motions and magically countered each arrow as they launched.

"I was taught offensive combat spells by the most powerful and knowledgeable Magi to ever walk this world," he taunted while unweaving her spells as she cast them. The bones of his hands cracked as he formed complicated gestures with them before throwing what looked like sand at Aerilynn. She recognized it as a petrification spell, and cast it in reverse as Ir'zane had done to her spells, and it faded to harmless smoke before it could touch her.

"Are we done playing around?" he sneered. She threw a ball of magically conjured fire at him, but he shifted into the shadows and disappeared. Ir'zane reappeared out of green fire directly behind her to taunt her some more.

"Your people will suffer as my people have, and you shall suffer as I have suffered! I will break you, and leave you to rot in the dark while every last one of your prideful kind are snuffed out. And you, princess, shall waste away here until all your pitiful screams fall silent!"

A tendril of shadow reached up from the dark and grabbed Aerilynn's wrist, leashing her to the floor with a forceful grip. She struggled against it while Ir'zane gathered necromantic fire from underneath his rib cage, working it between his hands to control it. Her legs trembled as she fought to keep herself from being pulled to the floor, and he delighted in the desperation on her face.

Ir'zane threw the orb of green fire at her, which she could not escape while tethered and thus could not dodge. As the soul-burning flame was about to hit the princess she overcharged her enchanted dress with her mana, which exploded around her in a nova of light that dissolved both the necrofire and the shadow tendrils like they were smoke in the wind. The force of the blast also threw Ir'zane against the wall, extinguishing the glow of his unholy fire.

Sweat was dripping down her face from the exertion of raw power that was unleashed. It consumed nearly all of her mana to overcharge her enchanted gown, but when the enchantment broke, it became a powerful anti-magic pulse. The magic in her dress was now completely spent, and absolute darkness filled the chamber.

Aerilynn whispered arcane words while the air around her grew colder. As she spoke the spell, a frigid wind came out of her mouth and formed solid ice where she blew. She breathed over her body, covering it in glimmering hoarfrost, which she wore like armor. As Ir'zane pulled himself back up, his necrofire reignited too which was the only light in the room, making it easy to see where he was. Aerilynn took out a small glass bottle from her bodice which glowed an electric blue color. She tossed the bottle at Ir'zane's feet and it shattered, causing lightning bolts to shoot out from the broken bottle like an upside-down thunderstorm.

The shadowmancer yelped in pain from the electricity coursing through him. When it looked like he had recovered from the excruciating electrocution, she used a powerful incantation which made the air around him shift like heat rising from desert sands, before ensnaring him with a spell of her own making. As it took effect, Ir'zane fell upward, hitting the ceiling with a crash as gravity reversed direction in the area of her spell.

After recovering from the fall, the undead sorcerer pressed his hands to the ceiling beneath him. He shouted words in draconic which even the wisest elves did not know, and a dragon blood-colored glyph appeared across the top of the chamber. The rock beneath the symbol became liquid before forming into large spikes which shot out of the rock puddle and stabbed into the ground below, like spears thrown with the force of falling boulders.

Aerilynn's concentration was broken as she dodged the spikes, and was unable to maintain the anti-gravity spell. With the spell effect ended, Ir'zane fell back to the ground. As soon as he landed, he started throwing bolts of shadow at her, which looked like screaming skulls. Aerilynn grabbed at a bracelet on her wrist made of large glass beads which looked like they were filled with galaxies, but before she could use it, she was forced to jump backwards again to avoid more spikes. The shadow skulls also continued to chase after her while she backpedaled. The princess plucked one of the beads from the bracelet and tossed it into the blood glyph on the ceiling, the resulting explosion was so strong it shook the entire tower.

The rune Ir'zane had affixed to the stone was shattered, cleared from the ceiling by the radiant blast. The rock spikes turned to dust which fell harmlessly from the cracked dome. She left herself open by dispelling the blood glyph however, and Aerilynn braced herself as the shadow skulls caught up with her. The force of the shadow bolts pummeled her but were partially absorbed by the magical ice instead of killing her outright as they would have without the armor.

After being pelted by enough of them to completely shatter her ice armor, she lost consciousness and fell to the ground with a heavy thud. Ir'zane struggled to get back to his feet after the galaxy bead explosion knocked him down, the green fire in his chest was barely an ember. He limped toward her intending to finish her off, but as he went for the coup de grace, her gryphon flew at him; swiping blindly. Despite its valiant attempt to defend the princess, the noble beast was easily dispatched with necrofire which burned its soul away, killing it abruptly.

Ir'zane turned back to Aerilynn, and her dress flickered with a faint glow. The book spoke to him.

We have the Eye. Leave before she wakes, take her wings. Let her rot!

The Duscan sorcerer grabbed the book from his hip and heard many voices speaking an incantation. Sickly-green sigils flew off the pages to encircle the dead gryphon. The magically-conjured symbols sank deep into its flesh, causing the corpse to twitch and convulse.

The unholy power infused the beast, and with a sickening jerk it rose to its feet, thrashing wildly. Ir'zane raised his undead hand to it and it calmed. He closed the book and deftly jumped onto the back of the newly risen gryphon. With a dark command, it flew back up the tower towards the pinhole of light at its peak, through which the Duscan sorcerer and his prize escaped.

~

Elisander's battle with the shadowmancer's undead dragon was not going well. Hot on his heels, the dreadwyrm snapped its jaws at him, nearly catching him in its teeth. He veered hard to avoid the attack and nearly slid off his mount. Pulling himself back up after almost being unseated from his gryphon, Elisander prepped for another attack when he was unpleasantly surprised to see Ir'zane emerging from the tower before Aerilynn. The prince had hoped the Duscan would not leave the tower at all. With the dreadwyrm keeping the prince occupied, Ir'zane was free to fly out of reach and soon disappeared on the horizon.

"We failed," Elisander said defeatedly, "... I hope the princess is still alive." He looked back at the dreadwyrm chasing him, and after fighting the abomination to no avail, Elisander hoped to lure the dreadwyrm over the knife-like stones surrounding the tower to use them to finish the damned thing off. He dove toward the razor rocks as fast as he could, with the dreadwyrm racing behind him. But right before crashing into them, Elisander pulled away at the last second. The dreadwyrm was heavier and moving faster, so when it banked to follow him, it crashed into the jagged rocks and impaled itself instead. Unable to pull itself free, with its body wrapped around the spikes, it roared feebly as Elisander flew away.

He hoped beyond hope that Aerilynn was still alive as he reached the tower's peak. The prince raced through the storm above, and the darkness within the tower. He called out for her, but all Elisander heard was his own echo bouncing off the cavernous walls. Landing in the darkened chamber he called out for her again, and again he heard nothing. While walking slowly around the room, he nearly tripped over someone lying on the floor. He knelt beside her and placed his hand over her head, praying to the Allfather for help. She woke with a start and Elisander caught her in his arms.

"It's alright, he's gone," he said.

Even through his comforting words, she discerned sadness in his tone.

"He got away, didn't he?" she asked weakly.

Elisander hung his head low.

"I am afraid so," he said, helping her to her feet.

"Then let us hope your dwarf friend has found that miracle, for your ship maybe the only hope we have of reaching Silthradel before Ir'zane does," Aerilynn said. They climbed onto the only remaining gryphon's back together and departed the tower in haste, back toward the crash site as swiftly as they could fly.

Of Birds and Stones

The crash site was bustling like a colony of worker ants as they hauled lumber from the woods to the worksite. Remarkably only a single tree from the Feywild was chopped down to rebuild the hull, as it alone produced more than they needed for the repairs. Drovann was running back and forth across camp on his short legs while shouting orders and teaching people how to use the tools he kept handing out from his engineer belt.

Aeysha and Locke huddled with the wounded and those not actively working on the ship, trying to come up ways they could help. There was a good deal of discussion among them, but few ideas of merit surfaced. Gaza T'sann grew tired of talking and stood up slowly, gripping a string of glass beads that were the color of the ocean.

"I will ask the Great Mother for guidance. Long is her memory, and vast is her wisdom. She will know how to make your ship fly again, master dwarf," he said to Drovann before strolling away from camp toward a nearby babbling brook. Many of the knights and elves exchanged confused looks as they debated investigating further, but only Aeysha and Locke got up to follow him.

Gaza stood at the edge of the camp on the bank of the brook, where he spoke in words of prayer to the Great Mother which sounded like the splashing of water to Locke's ear. When he finished the chant, he pulled out a staff with a top carved from a whale tooth and placed one end into the stream. Gaza leaned forward, placing his ear to the other end. The babbling brook flowed around the whale-tooth staff and the vibrations traveled up to his ear. Gaza spoke aloud the words he heard in the water.

"Follow the path that no man walks, to find the place with flying rocks."

Gaza pulled his head up and his staff out of the stream, satisfied with the answer he received.

Locke was less satisfied.

"That's it?" he asked sharply. No one answered him so he continued, "That was all you heard? No actual answer to the problem we're facing? Just a riddle?"

Aeysha interjected.

"Gaia is beyond our understanding and our concerns are beyond hers. It is not a simple thing to speak with her, and to hear anything back at all is truly a gift. She has given us the answer, and at the end of this puzzle lies what we seek. We just need the wisdom to figure out what it means and we will be airborne in no time!"

Gaza T'sann smiled at her.

"Well said, Aeysha of the Wandering Winds, you do the Keepers proud. Now go, solve Gaia's riddle and return to us with her gift of flight."

Aeysha nodded and ran off through the woods, with Locke chasing after her.

"Hey, wait up!"

Aeysha's hope was renewed by the quest given to her by the Great Mother, and with her Keeper powers she truly ran like the wind. Locke found it difficult to keep up with her.

"Aeysha, hang on!" he shouted after her. She did not slow down or pay any attention to him, and instead she spoke aloud to herself, trying to figure out the riddle.

"Follow the path that no man walks, to find the place with flying rocks."

The trees thinned as she climbed to the top of a hill to get a better take of their surroundings. "The path that no man walks," she pondered as Locke finally caught up to her, completely out of breath. It was several minutes before he was able to speak, yet Aeysha continued to think out loud.

"A path that no man walks... somewhere that people don't go."

"I'm coming with you, let me help," he finally managed.

She did not look amused.

"If you really want to help then help me solve the riddle. Where would people avoid traveling?"

Locke looked past her for a moment, seeing the Mountains of Eld looming behind her, and she turned around to see them too. Without another word, Aeysha started climbing up the hill towards the mountains with an exasperated Locke following after. They climbed for hours until they reached the foot of the mountains. By the time they had climbed high enough that the stones on the ground were larger than them, it was getting late in the day.

"We need to stop, Aeysha!" Locke pleaded, struggling with how much harder it was to breathe as they went. She agreed wordlessly, before finding a spot to plop down on the ground. He found a large mound of earth nearby to rest on but when he leaned against it for support, he noticed something sticking out of the soil at its base. It was a dark grey, metallic-looking toe. Against his better judgment, he reached down and touched it.

Locke's eyes opened wide in surprise as the ground below his feet trembled. He stepped away from the mound as a massive pile of black stone rose up from beneath it, its rocky skin was made of lustrous onyx-colored crystals of repeating octahedral geometric patterns throughout.

The metallic stone creature stretched upright and stood over Locke, who fell backward onto the ground stupefied. The young Therredan found himself at the feet of a humanoid creature made of stone who was emerging from the dirt, which was cascading off its shoulders and head as it stretched. The elemental threw the soil off of its body like it was a blanket that it was sleeping under. The simple features of its face appeared confused and agitated before it spoke slowly.

"Why awake?"

The ancient elemental asked while towering over Locke, and looking down at him. Bluish-white light crackled like lightning in its glowing eyes. Aeysha slowly backed away from the creature which had been nothing more than a sedentary pile of stone just moments ago. The placid features of his face stared curiously at the two young humans who stood uneasily at his feet. Aeysha took another step behind Locke as he got back to his feet.

"Talk to it!" she encouraged him.

Locke looked at the elemental as it locked eyes with him.

"Um greetings... uhhh... stone-man-person, thing," Locke began stammering out a weak, impromptu introduction.

"We are... uhhh, well we are rock friends!" he said.

The stone creature's eyes widened as he studied the young man. Locke made exaggerated arm motions toward himself and Aeysha, speaking in a forced manner while painfully overemphasizing his words.

"I. Am. Locke." -

Aeysha covered her flustered face with her hand.

- "This. Is. Aeysha," Locke coughed nervously when he saw that he was embarrassing himself and wondered what to do next.

The elemental placed a stony fist to his chest and spoke in a low gravelly voice, "I am Dyce. Now, why you wake me?"

Aeysha looked up from her palm, but Locke looked confused.

"Wake you? No, no, we didn't mean to wake you. We were just passing through and stopped to rest... on you, by accident," he explained poorly.

Dyce stared at Locke as though he had said nothing at all before repeating himself.

"Why you wake me? What you seek?"

Aeysha lit up, finally understanding and spoke aloud the riddle that Gaia gave to them.

"We need to find the place where no man walks, to find the place of flying rocks. We seek flying rocks!"

Dyce looked at the druid girl and spoke very plainly.

"Rocks no fly. Birds fly."

"Please, can you help us? O' kindred spirit of earth, by our love of Gaia can you help us find the flying rocks? Surely you would know where to find levitating stones," Aeysha implored.

Dyce repeated himself again.

"Rocks no fly. Birds fly."

The elemental then turned away and slid through the earth and up the impossibly steep hillside, pushing soil and stones aside as he went. Locke and Aeysha ran after him, climbing up the stony pathway with great difficulty. It took them a bit of hiking to reach the elemental, who had earth glided to the top and was waiting patiently for them to catch up.

They rested for a moment when they reached the top of the massive hill so they could catch their breath. Dyce stood silently, staring at the two of them and waiting for one of them to notice him. When they finally looked his way, they saw the elemental's arm outstretched, and one of his three massive fingers pointing to a series of cliffs north of them. The cliffs were covered in massive aeries that Locke mistook for brambles at first glance. The west-facing slope of the Eld Ridge Mountains was slightly concave, and many burrows dotted the mountainside.

Dyce muttered in a gravelly tone, "Birds."

Aeysha and Locke stared at him in utter confusion, and he said, "Birds, fly." They took a closer look and in some of the massive burrows, there were signs of creatures living within them. On the roofs of the caves, there was plant detritus which seemed to be arranged deliberately in circular depressions.

"Are those nests?" Locke asked, dumbfounded.

"I think so," Aeysha replied, "but they are on the ceilings of those caves... they are upside-down."

As they wondered how the enormous dwellings could be made in such a fashion, a distant roll of thunder from a far-off storm cracked overhead. The thunder reverberated off the mountainside and was immediately followed by the sound of whooshing winds as suddenly the cliffs started moving before their eyes.

"Do you see that? The mountain just rustled!" he exclaimed, and Aeysha finally understood.

"No. It's not the mountains themselves, those aren't moving. Look closer."

What he initially mistook for stone turned out to be giant birds with mountain-colored feathers, who were shaking their massive wings around. The giant birds were roosting against the mountain with their heads tucked into the burrows, covering the dwellings with their bodies.

Aeysha started talking to herself.

"Follow the path that no man walks, to find the place with flying rocks." She then pointed to the caves and explained, "This is it! Of course, how could I have missed it! It's not rock, it's roc! R-o-c," she spelled out. "They are giant birds, mythical creatures as old as the Feywild itself. They were spoken of in legends, where it was said they were so massive that they eclipsed the sun."

Thunder cracked again as a stormfront was growing overhead. The sound was followed by a sharp screech and rustling of enormous feathers as a roc fully opened its enormous stone-colored wings and revealed its true size: which was large enough to fit the Nomad Sky in its talons like a trout caught in an eagle's grip.

Dyce smiled and said, "Birds, fly."

With a single flap of its enormous wings, the majestic beast was airborne, and it looked like a massive gray cloud flying against the wind. They looked on as the giant stone-colored bird flew off into the distance, away from the edge of a storm forming over the wild wood of the west. Locke and Aeysha smiled at one another.

"Did you see that?" he said enthusiastically before joking, "that bird was bigger than my home town!"

"My friends in the Order of the White Owl would have loved to see this. Blessed spirits of air, thank you," Aeysha sighed relieved. As the roc disappeared into the horizon, they witnessed a single feather fall from the tip of one of its wings before the feather ascended into the sky and vanished. Locke and Aeysha both watched it in awe.

"That has to be why no one has ever found a roc feather, they float!" Aeysha pulled a talisman from under her vest and knelt to pray, muttering words which Locke could not understand. Whatever she was speaking, sounded more like whirling wind than words. She rose once more, returning the talisman to her chest and out of sight.

"We have the answer to Gaia's riddle, let us claim our prize!"

Locke was thinking the same thing: with enough of those feathers, they could get the Nomad Sky airborne again. Locke smiled at the thought of gloating that he was partly responsible for getting Elisander's precious ship flying again. He was eager to prove to the arrogant prince that he was not useless. However, he slowly realized they had no way of reaching the roc caves from where they were, which dampened his spirits some.

"How are we going to get over to their roosts to collect the feathers?" he wondered, and Aeysha shrugged.

"Can't you just use your wind powers or something to get us over there?" he asked.

She didn't directly respond to his ridiculous question, but the annoyed look on her face answered it all the same.

"We have to find a way to climb over," she said.

Locke was getting frustrated.

"If we could only fly right up to them, it would be as easy as stealing the hat off my sleeping uncle."

Aeysha looked confused by the expression.

"What does that mean?" she asked and he laughed.

"Sorry, it's a bit of an inside joke with my brother."

"I didn't know you had a brother," she said surprised.

"I likely don't anymore. I'm sure they've executed him for treason by now."

"I'm sorry Locke, I didn't know," she said.

"I never got the chance to say goodbye, you know. He was captured as I fled, and I had to leave him behind."

Aeysha looked at the talisman around her neck and said, "I didn't get to say goodbye to my father either. When he went missing, I went looking, but when I finally tracked him down it was too late, he was already gone."

"That must be really hard, I'm sorry."

"It is, but thankfully I have the Great Mother to watch over me. My father used to say that nature is our first home and our final rest, so in a way he's still here. I do miss him, though."

Dyce walked up behind them as they spoke and wrapped his arms around them, pulling them both into a great big hug. They wheezed uncomfortably as he squeezed them.

"Me help," he said in a low rumble.

"Okay! Okay! I think that's enough, thanks!" Aeysha said with a purple face. Dyce let them both go and they coughed and stretched their sides while laughing.

"Hey big guy. You got us this far, what do you think? Can you help us get some roc feathers?" Locke asked being unserious.

The elemental nodded slowly, picking a boulder off of the ground next to him and palming it in his big hands. He pulled his arm back before throwing the massive stone at the roosting rocs.

Locke shouted, while waving his arms.

"No, don't do that!"

But it was too late. Dyce hurled the stone like a trebuchet, which slammed into the mountain side. The resounding noise reverberated discordantly, irritating the rocs roosting against the cliffs. The two of them looked on helplessly as screeching came from the caves while the rocs stirred from their hollows. Dyce reached for another, even larger boulder.

"Put that down! Are you mad? You're going to scare th-"

Dyce wound up, and tossed another boulder while Locke was in the middle of scolding him. Aeysha and Locke braced for the hit, and they both winced when it smashed against the cliffs. Several rocs prepped for flight, stretching their massive wings and cawing angrily. When Dyce reached to collect a boulder a third time, he went for one that was considerably larger than the previous two. Locke and Aeysha both jumped in to stop him, holding onto the boulder and to his arms trying to weigh them down. Their combined efforts failed as Dyce easily lifted the boulder into the air, along with them.

They both let go and fell to the ground, knocking the wind out of them. Dyce held the boulder over his head, and wound up before throwing it at the cliffs a final time. The sound was so loud it sounded like an explosion, which shook the dwellings of the enormous birds. The rocs screeched angrily while taking flight, creating gusts so strong they nearly pushed Locke and Aeysha off the hill. They were forced to grab onto Dyce's legs to keep from blowing away. The flock of rocs darkened the skies above them as they circled menacingly overhead.

"This isn't good, I think he made them mad," Locke said.

The giant birds were now aggressively closing in on them instead of flying away like the first one had.

"I think we are in trouble," Aeysha said right before one of the rocs dove through the sky swooping at them and only narrowly missing. They clung tighter to Dyce as the force of its downdraft nearly tore them away from the ground. The elemental swung his stony fists at the roc, attempting to scare it away. The enraged bird bit back, but the roc's sharp beak had little effect on his stony skin. Dyce stood firmly against the attack, rooted to the earth beneath.

Furious squawking filled the air from the giant birds that kept swooping at Locke and Aeysha. The rocs clawed at them and pecked at their limbs that stuck out from under the elemental's body. Dyce shielded the two of them from the angry beaks and talons, fending off a flurry of particularly vicious attacks from an older roc who had a scar over a milky eye. When the enormous raptor became frustrated that it could not get to its prey, it flapped its wings hard to create winds so strong that neither of them could hold on any longer.

"Dyce!" Locke screamed as he flew into the air and over the edge of the hill. Aeysha was pushed back several feet also but she used her control over the element of air to redirect the violent winds to push her back to safety.

Locke however, was in total freefall, having been completely blown off the hillside. He felt like his stomach was suddenly in his throat as the world spun around him. He started to panic as massive talons wrapped themselves around his body and his fall came to a sudden halt. The abrupt stop hurt immensely and he nearly passed out from the force of it. He felt nauseated as the giant bird ascended pulling him into the clouds. He saw the cliffs where he was moments ago shrinking away as the scarred roc carried him away.

Before long another roc swooped at him, snapping at him and nearly taking his leg off. The scarred-eye bird carrying Locke pulled away too sharply as it accidentally released its grip and dropped him. Locke fell but not for long, for he landed on the back of the other roc. He gripped its feathers tightly, holding on as it screeched angrily and tried to buck him off. Locke barely held on as it rolled, trying again and again to throw him from its back.

Thunder cracked once more through the darkening sky while the roc, blind with anger, flew towards the storm. Locke saw bright flashes in the storm from the lightning that was arcing from cloud to cloud. He felt the temperature of the air drop around him as the furious bird continued head first into the approaching tempest.

Locke was dragged through the clouds, soaking him with condensation. The storm air chilled him to the bone but he also felt a warmth coming from the armor on his right arm. It was not the dangerous blast of intense heat he felt when he first touched the strange artifact; no this was something different, something comforting. He felt like someone else was riding alongside him, but saw only the gauntlet. While he was distracted the roc flailed, still trying to get Locke off its back. The giant bird dove in and out of clouds which were flickering dangerously with lightning bolts, that nearly struck him.

"Locke."

He heard his name spoken clearly in his mind, while the armor became hot enough that rain landing on it instantly evaporated into little bursts of steam as the droplets hit. Though it was hot enough to boil rain water on touch, the inside of the gauntlet was not hot enough to burn him. The parts touching his skin remained a comforting level of heat, like being next to a welcoming fireplace.

"You are in danger!" the voice called to him more clearly than he ever heard it before. The sound of her voice rang through his mind like temple bells echoing through a valley. He heard a bird's cry which was distinctly different from the roc he rode.

Who are you? he thought.

"You are in danger," she warned again, as another bolt of lightning arced toward him, narrowly missing his head. Locke leaned away to dodge it, nearly losing his grip on the roc's feathers in the process. The giant bird felt Locke's body weight shift and it veered sharply in the other direction. He held onto the base of the feathers and luckily for him, they did not come loose because he was otherwise entirely airborne. The roc snapped at his legs while he was floating midair, but Locke quickly pulled himself back against its body and kept his limbs away from its beak.

"You cannot keep this up, foolish boy!" the voice from the armor chastised him.

"You need to get off this thing before it kills you. Rocs are terrified of storms and normally they would not venture so close to the domain of the sylph, but this bird is particularly adamant about removing you from its back," she said.

Locke was confused.

"Wait, how do you know all that, can you speak to this thing? How are you speaking to me for that matter? What is a sylph? And seriously, who are you?" he blurted out.

"There's no time for that! If the roc doesn't throw you into the ocean, or tear you limb from limb, then the storm maidens will get you! Once the sylph realizes you're here, they will try to kill you. We need to get away from here!"

We? he thought, before realizing they were connected to one another.

"Well, I don't know if you had noticed or not, but I cannot fly! So, if you have any ideas about how to get off this crazed mountain pigeon, I'm listening!" he said in a sarcastic tone.

"Use the feathers! Cut them free and glide down with them."

Locke remembered watching the feather that came loose earlier and recalled how they drifted up into the sky instead of falling to the earth. He let go of the bird with his right hand, reaching for his boot knife but he fumbled trying to grab the wet grip of the blade. While pulling it free from its sheath, the roc rolled sharply away from sinister clouds which were twisting in ominous ways. Locke nearly went flying off of its back again, and in the furor, he accidentally dropped the knife. Locke desperately grabbed plumage to hold on to and cursed as the blade tumbled through the air.

"Now what?" he asked angrily, watching the strange clouds.

Within the swirling vortex of the storm, he saw something he thought was a trick of the eye, because he thought he saw a woman inside the clouds.

"We have to get off this bird now!" the voice in the armor implored him, sounding more desperate than before.

"Well in case you weren't watching just now, I dropped my damned blade. So, unless you have one lying around, there's nothing I can do short of pulling them out with my bare hands."

She snapped back at him, "Don't be ridiculous, you couldn't pry them free any more than you could pull a tree from the ground. The armor has an arm blade, use it!"

"Arm blade?" Locke repeated, puzzled. The roc dove low, trying to avoid the twisting clouds, and again he saw a woman made from the storm itself. She was shaping the clouds in front of her, creating the actual storm she that was flying inside of. He looked at her with astonishment, but she looked back at him with the fury of the tempest itself.

The storm maiden yelled ferociously with the sound of rolling thunder. She shook her fist angrily, and it crackled with electricity. With a simple flick of her wrist, she threw a blast of lightning at Locke. The bolt narrowly missed hitting him in the side of the head because he ducked at the last second. The roc however, was less fortunate as the lightning grazed the wing of the giant raptor. It veered away sharply, screaming in terror and pain from the powerful electric shock.

"I warned you that the sylph would try to kill you if they found you! Now quickly before we all get killed, use the weapon and get us free!"

Locke held on to the injured roc with everything he had while it reeled from the attack by the storm maiden.

"The artifact to which I am bound is more than just armor, it is a weapon too. Together we can open it," the voice within the armor implored him. With no real idea what he was doing, he reached out to her with his mind, and she did the same. For a brief second the world disappeared. He felt fire surrounding him. It was hot, beautifully hot. It felt incredible. He felt himself soaring through the open sky, darting playfully on updrafts and pockets of air.

Locke saw places he had never been to appear in his mind, like faraway deserts of red sands, and domed palaces made of gold. He realized they were more than just visions, they were memories, only not his own. He heard her name spoken with a tender admiration, *Alahi Niwe Talle Sorren.* Though he did not understand the language her name was spoken in, somehow, he knew what it meant, 'Fire that dances in the wind.' It was a perfect name for her.

After a moment he came back to his perception of reality, Locke found that not only could he now feel the armor, it felt as though it was a part of his body. He stretched out his arm, unfurling the weapon by opening his hand from a closed fist. The clasps of metal that once coiled around his arm released and flattened into blades which were shaped like phoenix feathers.

The whole segmented armor detached from his shoulder and fell away with the pull of gravity, leaving a bracer on Locke's forearm from which the chain of blades was attached. A metal cord ran down the length of what was once the armor plating and formed a sort of backbone for the bladed whip. Locke could hardly believe his eyes as the armor transformed into a beautifully deadly weapon with unparalleled majesty. Never in his life had he seen such an elegant weapon. Sorren reveled in his admiration.

While connected to her this way, he could move the weapon easily with his mind. He snapped the chain back, collapsing the phoenix-tail shaped whip down into a punching dagger.

"Let's fly the coop," he said, while pushing up a bunch of feathers from the roc's back and exposing the quills near the skin. With a swing of his arm, he brought the forearm blade down in a precise slash through the base of the feathers. The blade passed through the quills effortlessly, immediately severing them from the bird's back. Locke hugged them tightly with his whole body the moment they came free, and he floated away from the roc's back. He wrapped his legs and arms around the clump of feathers as he was blown about by gale force winds.

Locke was struggling to keep the feathers together, so he unfurled the punching dagger back into a bladed whip and wrapped the phoenix-tail around them tight like a bushel of hay. He sighed in relief from the momentary peace the change of circumstances had brought. But it was then that he saw his arm for the first time since the artifact had bonded to him. His flesh was scarred with twisted burns which permanently molded in effigy of the flames that created them.

Locke failed to notice that they were floating towards strange twisting clouds and were about to run right straight into a sylph who was busy weaving the storm.

"Uh oh. This is seriously bad," Locke muttered, leaning to one side hoping to steer clear of her, but the cyclonic winds of the storm pulled them in closer. He was getting way too close for comfort but from this distance, Locke got his best look yet at the stormborn. The sylph was dressed like a warrior with tightly-braided hair and light armor that was made entirely of storm. Her body was also made of clouds, all shaped in perfect lifelike semblance of a woman.

The stormweaver was startled by the sight of a human clinging to a bundle of feathers while floating through her skies. The turbulent gale of the tempest spun him around and Locke ended up hanging upside-down, waving awkwardly to her. Her face softened and she giggled before placing her hand to her mouth then blowing a kiss to the sky which calmed the winds around him. The sylph gently pushed him away from her with winds gusts created by her waving at him.

With a final farewell wink from the storm maiden the winds picked him up and carried him back towards the cliffs where Dyce and Aeysha were desperately calling out for him. Locke watched them running along the cliff's edge to where it looked like he was going to land. Aeysha started waving her hands and shouting something at him but he could not tell what. Without being propelled by the stronger winds of the storm or the blessings of a sylph, he started to float more erratically.

Locke was losing speed and altitude fast as he got closer to the cliffs. Seeing that he was in trouble, Aeysha touched a rune on her talisman summoning a powerful vortex around herself, which pulled both the winds and Locke towards her. When Locke and his bundle of roc feathers came close enough, Dyce reached out to catch him. Locke missed and smacked into the elemental's chest instead. Dyce quickly wrapped his massive arms around Locke and the roc feather bundle so they would not blow away. Aeysha dashed over to see if Locke was injured while Dyce set him down on the ground.

"Are you alright?" she asked.

He was a little dazed after crashing into the stone elemental but he smiled when he saw them both.

"Look what I found!"

The Siege of Erendar

While the crew of the Nomad Sky and the elven woodweavers of Lorlinden congratulated themselves on the repairs to the ship, the prince of Everund and the princess of Silthradel were flying back to the camp as swiftly as they could. In addition to managing the wild gryphon, Elisander also had to hold Aerilynn up while they rode because she was still recovering from her fight with Ir'zane. From the skies it was not hard to find the prince's downed ship even in the twilight, because it left a trail of destruction through the Western Wood which was clearly visible from above. Elisander commanded the gryphon down towards the crash site, landing to the cheers of the knights and elves who were gathered around.

Several elven handmaidens fluttered up to take the unconscious princess. Elisander was not able to see what they gave her, but Aerilynn awoke with a start and was alert again in seconds. The princess could see her people's concerned faces and she waved them away, "I am alright, but our people are in danger. I believe Ir'zane is going to attack Silthradel next." She stood on shaky legs, but refused assistance wanting to show that she could do it on her own. Elisander addressed the Everunders who were listening and watching, "We failed to stop Ir'zane from obtaining the object he was after, and with its power he poses a serious risk to the world. We need to get back to Erendar and warn the king."

Drovann rubbed his chin with a gloved hand before approaching Elisander, wondering to himself how he was going to deliver the bad news. He cleared his throat to get the prince's attention who was still mostly addressing the crowd, the look in Elisander's eyes was desperation, "Please tell me the ship repairs have been completed."

"The structural damage has been repaired, upgrades have been made ta lighten the ship further and I have engineered gliding fins out of scraps ta replace the front engines," Drovann explained.

Elisander seemed to unclench as his shoulders dropped and he breathed a sigh of relief, but the dwarven engineer's facial features hardened in turn, "But there is no way she can fly."

The prince's heart sank, and Drovann could already see Elisander trying to think of something they missed and he put up a hand as if to stop him, "Look, I told ye before, I cannot rebuild the engines from salvage, this ship was streamlined by me to run on fewer props than our warships, but it will not fly on jus' two. Ye have nothin' to pull the front of the ship up! My prince, she's patched and polished to a quality that I can personally attest is higher than I made her, with thanks to our friends here. But she will not fly."

Elisander stared at the ship as it was suspended by vines and held up by hastily constructed scaffolding, feeling powerless as he struggled to find a solution to their situation. The Nomad Sky looked as if it had never crashed in the first place, he noted while admiring it while it was slowly lowered from the makeshift loft. The elven wood weavers had put their impressive skills on display in quickly getting the ship not just back to working order, but better than new. Drovann had constructed what looked like fish fins for sails, attached to the spot where the front engines had been. They were made of dragon wing membrane which he had salvaged from parts of the dreadwyrm that had gotten lodged in the ship. It was a clever way of utilizing the wind that would be crashing over the hull and along the sides of the ship to add stability during flight.

"We've done all we can for her, for now. Unless we find somethin' for lift, she'll jus' flip over on launch," Drovann sounded utterly defeated despite the pride he took from the repairs.

The prince turned once more to Aerilynn and knelt beside her as she rested, "Princess Everdawn, I am already in your debt but you your wood weavers have put my ship back together with a craftsmanship unknown to my people, do you perchance know of a way to get my ship flying?"

Aerilynn's face softened, "If I did, I can assure you it would have already been done. Unfortunately, the only spells I know for levitation only work on smaller objects. Even if they could help, I do not have the strength to cast them now. What you ask for cannot be done with the resources and time that we have available to us. In the morning after I and the gryphons have rested, we will take as many capable people as we can and make for Silthradel, with luck if we ride hard, we can catch Ir'zane before he reaches it."

Elisander stood up defeated and sighed, "Fine, then we make camp for the night. I will pray to the Allfather that our wounded survive until we return."

A solemn silence fell on heavy hearts that night, no songs were sung and no laughter was heard beneath the twinkling stars.

~

No one was ready for what they saw coming down the hill the next morning at dawn. Floating off the ground, while clutching an armful of large feathers was the lodestone elemental Dyce, being pushed along by Locke.

"Gaza! We solved Gaia's riddle!" Aeysha called out while laughing from sleep deprivation.

Drovann looked over his crooked nose and furrowed his brow to get a better look at the massive elemental floating towards him. His mouth hung open in genuine surprise.

"By the Stonefather's beard, what sorcery is this?"

Gaza laughed, "This is not the parlor tricks of magi, my friend, the Great Mother has given us the gift of flight."

Locke put his hands on Dyce to stop him.

"Master engineer, I present to you... roc feathers."

"Roc feathers?" Drovann repeated, confused. The dwarf stared at the elemental, who was gripping the enormous feathers as they tried to fly away. Aeysha was beaming and looked proudly upon the floating elemental. Locke smiled brightly.

"These feathers are light enough to make even our stone friend here float. In fact, we had to help hold him down."

Dyce giggled as he slowly spun in the air.

"Rock, fly."

Drovann got excited.

"Ya know, I think these jus' might work. We could anchor em to the dragon wing sail struts ta offset the weight of the ship." Locke looked up at the newly repaired airship.

"Do you think it will be enough to get her flying?" he asked.

Drovann was already fumbling around for tools, "Only one way ta find out." With some exertion and some helping hands, Drovann was able to attach the feathers to the ship's frame, which miraculously pulled the nose of the ship off the ground. The dwarven engineer placed his meaty hand beneath the floating hull and waved it back and forth, demonstrating for everyone the effectiveness of the levitating feathers.

"These roc feathers are incredible!" he added with a chuckle.

Aerilynn got up when she heard that Locke returned.

"Are you alright?" he asked earnestly, walking over to her.

"I'll be fine, thank you," she responded weakly while standing. She took Locke's astromancer compass from around her neck and handed it back to him, "And thank you for this, without it I might have been truly lost."

He smiled, "I'm really glad it brought you back."

Prince Elisander looked over his ship eagerly.

"Is she flight worthy?" he asked excitedly.

Drovann smirked, "Aye, I believe she is. Thanks to those two."

He pointed at Locke and Aeysha with a big greasy thumb.

"My thanks to you both, but proper gratitudes must wait. We failed to stop Ir'zane from obtaining the Eye, and Aerilynn believes he is preparing an attack on Silthradel as we speak. We leave for Erendar at once, where we will rally the fleet and fly north with Aerilynn as our guide." The group whispered among themselves concernedly, but Elisander pressed on, "Load the injured on the ship, and get ready for takeoff."

Drovann looked surprised.

"You don't wan tay do a test flight first?"

The prince looked back at him.

"Every second we waste is lives lost. The sooner we get the wounded to the clerics in Erendar, the better their chances of survival."

Aerilynn turned to her guards to give them her orders.

"Head back to Lorlinden and arm our fastest gryphon riders, tell them to make for Silthradel at once."

Within minutes, the entire camp around the crash site was torn down and the supplies were loaded into the ship's cargo hold. The knights helped everyone into place, seating them in rows along the sides of the hold. One knight in particular was especially shocked when Dyce plopped down next to him and nearly broke the bench they sat upon. Aeysha started stepping onto the platform when Gaza grabbed her hand.

"Keeper, where are you going?" he asked.

She looked at him, confused.

"I am going to help our friends."

Gaza stroked his waterfall beard, splashing water about.

"Our part in this journey is done, youngling. It is time for us to return to our charges. War is not our way."

Her gray eyes were steely and resolute as she responded.

"Gaia summoned us to save her, she intervened to save Locke's life, and she gave flight to the towner's ship so that we could stop Ir'zane from poisoning our world with death magic. The winds of change are blowing, and I believe she chose me to fight on her behalf!"

Gaza sighed before smiling, bemused by her wild spirit.

"Very well then. May she guide you. I will inform the others and we will watch for your return."

Aeysha smiled back before climbing aboard the Nomad Sky.

Drovann climbed into the engineering bay and started the engines, which slowly rumbled to life. The props spun up quickly and Elisander took the wheel. They walked through some quick start-up checks, making sure the flaps and wing struts were working. The prince looked over his instruments to make sure they were accurate and checked the pressure readings from his gauges, readying the ship for takeoff. He shouted into a fluted brass megaphone, "How're the engines holding up?"

Drovann's voice grouched back from the engine room, "Running hotter than dragon's breath, but holding steady! Let's get her home!"

Elisander heard all he needed to hear.

"Here we go!" the prince shouted as he pushed forward on the throttle. Everyone was thrown back by the force of their departure. The lighter, rebuilt ship took off like a bolt of lightning, soaring through the sky once more. Drovann whooped triumphantly, his voice booming back through the brass megaphone. The knights of Everund cheered as the Nomad Sky chased the clouds and flew off north.

It was not long before the thrill of the takeoff and the joy wore off however, as the long flight to Erendar eventually steadied into monotony. Locke sat against a wall trying to stay out of everyone's way as they worked to keep the Nomad Sky in the air. The amount of effort and coordination between the crew was something to see, it was nearly as impressive as the ship itself. Elisander pulled the wheel and took a sharp turn encouraging the sun to shine in through the crystal windows, annoyingly though, it fell directly on Locke.

And I was just starting to get comfortable in this spot he thought before noticing the bright red glint shining off of his right arm and into his eye painfully. He rotated his arm enough to move the reflecting light out of his eyes before staring at the armor on his arm, and thinking about the being who was contained within it.

"Fire that dances in the wind," he said aloud while admiring the Zierian weapon.

"Ren, are you there?" Locke whispered to the spirit inside hoping no one would notice that he was talking to his arm.

"I don't think I've had a chance to properly thank you for helping me out before. I got to be a hero for a few minutes back there thanks to you."

Sorren felt a pang of guilt as he expressed gratitude toward her, knowing she permanently scarred him the first time they 'met' as punishment for touching her.

"You're welcome, I suppose," was all she could think to say.

Locke was happy she spoke back, "So, this armor thing really doesn't come off right, we're really stuck together?"

"I did try to warn you," Sorren said.

"Yeah, in another language or some kind of gibberish that I could barely hear. None of which sounded anything like, 'do not touch or you'll be burned to a crisp' by the way."

When she did not say more, Locke joked off handedly, "Well it's not so bad really, I mean the armor is beautiful and the weapon is useful. If only the company didn't suck," he grinned.

"I could have apologized sooner," Sorren admitted.

"You let me talk to myself for over a week," Locke said.

"It was less talking and more incoherent babbling."

They both laughed together and Locke tried to remember the last time his heart genuinely felt this at ease, "This is a great start to a wonderful friendship."

"I haven't connected with someone in ages," she said solemnly.

"That sounds lonely," he said.

"It was."

Locke looked out the window, watching the clouds passing beneath the Nomad Sky, "Well I guess we have that in common."

Sorren agreed, not that she needed to say it however, as she could feel everything inside his heart and knew exactly how much it all pained him, "You know, that armor thingy and its weapon? It's called a grappler. It is a masterpiece of Zierian magical crafting, and you are going to need more practice if you are going to wield it correctly."

"Now we're talking!" Locke exclaimed, "When do we start?"

~

It was nearing nightfall as the Nomad Sky dropped below the clouds over Lake Senacea but Locke had fallen asleep against Dyce and was missing the sights. Elisander gently roused Locke, "You're going to want to see this," he said before moving on to wake the others. Captain Kayara flew them over the enormous silver-blue lake in which the tiered crystal city was mirrored in its reflection while Elisander helped his guests out of the cramped cockpit and onto the deck outside.

An unparalleled view met them as they stepped out into the open air, as the city of Erendar rose before them. The capital of Everund was known to their kingdom as the shining crystal heart of the world, and it was easy to see why. Nestled in the Eld Ridge Mountains, the city and its light stretched out over the hills and fields that lay beyond them. Everyone on deck peered down from the rail guard into the hallowed valley that cradled Elisander's breathtaking home, Erendar, the crystal city.

Elisander spoke excitedly.

"If you look to your left, you can see the Grand Citadel built to protect the crystal heart of Erendar. Oh, and look over here, there's the Aasadar which was built in memorial to the clerics of Yavon who perished by dragon's fire in the Battle of Light's Fall!"

The angelic statue he referenced, held a sword with a feather shaped blade to the sky, while being engulfed from behind by wings of fire.

The Citadel itself was encircled by lavish buildings which were the living quarters of the noble district. The middle level of the city was built on the sides of the hill and had libraries and temples, as well as the mage academy. It was also where the Aasadar stood and was home for both the knights and the magi of Everund.

The lower portions of the city were at the foot of the mountains and laid out across the plains that led southeast. The lowest level was made up of mostly residential homes, small shops, and markets for the farmers and traders that filled the bustling streets of Erendar. As they crossed the lake, they saw the great Bulwark of Alathor which was built around the city to protect it from floods as well as invaders. The high walls of the Bulwark lied just beyond the farms and marked the edge of the city. Locke was in awe of the size and splendor of the crystal city of Erendar; it was beautiful and immaculate, the antithesis of Hammangard.

Horns blew from the Citadel in alarm while archers defended the outer wall from ramparts as the Nomad Sky approached the city. They all looked out the windows to see a large procession of troops headed for the Bulwark, but they were not Everunder. They watched as constructs made of slipshod metalwork clunked and jerked, marching with mechanical precision towards the city. The archers' arrows whistled through the sky, but collided with bodies of lifeless iron and bounced off without damage done to their targets. The magi came running from the inner courtyard in battle gear, wearing a sort of armor that was made from many layers of cloth pressed together into plates or pads that gave them partial protection from martial weaponry.

The battle-magi took their positions on the ramparts, reinforcing the front-line defenders overlooking the main gate to the city. The battle-mage commander directed them, unleashing a devastating barrage of spells at the iron golems below to no effect. The magi's spells shimmered and dazzled with color but their bolts of fire, ice, and other elements had little effect on the golems. Largely unaffected by the magical assault from the magi, the golems lumbered to the gate and smashed their heavy iron fists against it. The gate shuddered from their forceful impacts and held for a few strikes more, but as more golems made it to the gate, they overwhelmed it and eventually broke through.

"Fall back!" yelled the battle-mage commander over the din of the unrelenting iron army of Therred invading Erendar.

Gerod Hammond looked pleased as he surveyed the carnage, he unleashed on Everund's largest city. Its gates were torn open and his iron golems crashed through the city's defenses, opening the way for the human dragoons of Therred's army. Therredan foot soldiers charged through the Bulwark of Alathor, which had protected the great city of Erendar for a hundred years before now. With the gates of the city laid bare, only the knights stood between its people and the besieging Therredans.

Therred's iron dragoons ran through the city with their spears turned towards the Citadel where King Armon directed the defense of the city. The assault led by the Hammar Guard pierced through each defense that Everund had, and it was happening so fast that the city's defenders were finding it difficult to mount proper counter offensives against the iron tide that was washing through Erendar.

Elisander clenched his teeth angrily while looking at the battle raging below.

"Therred dares attack our home? We shall make them pay for every step they have taken on our land!"

He spun around and shouted to Kayara, "Set us down! Behind the outer gates." He turned to everyone else, "Ready for battle! We will use the Nomad Sky to cut off their advance forces and trap them within the city. We stop them at the gates or the whole Therredan army will march straight to the Citadel. Their assault will stall if we can hold them at the Bulwark!"

Aerilynn looked shocked.

"You cannot be serious! We have to continue on to Silthradel! You said we would stop for supplies here, not fight a war!"

Elisander's face filled with righteous fury.

"That was before I knew there was a war *here*! It is the duty of our knights to defend our kingdom, and mine to lead them. Your people will have to hold Ir'zane for now."

Aerilynn looked utterly betrayed.

"You will sacrifice my people and my homeland to brawl with Therred over old grudges?"

Elisander's eyes flashed dangerously toward her.

"My duty is to *my* people, not yours."

Locke was astonished too, but Elisander turned his attention back to Kayara, "Put my ship down. Now!" Captain Kayara obeyed the orders of her prince and turned the ship to intercept the Therredan forces. The Nomad Sky veered toward the front gates of Erendar through which the forces of Therred were pushing back retreating Everunders.

"Fire the cannons! Clear the landing zone and get ready to join the Therredan forces in battle!" Elisander ordered.

Locke gripped the rail tightly as the ship took a sharp turn, swooping down on the Bulwark. The starboard side of the ship opened fire on the gates. Stone and iron exploded in clouds of smoke, taking out several golems and Therredan soldiers.

The flow of troops into the city was briefly halted by the cannon fire, giving them just enough room and time to land the ship. The rear bay door opened like a castle drawbridge upon touchdown, and those on board who could fight filed into streets which were littered with bodies and scraps of golem. The gale winds coming off the props whipped at them as they headed to reinforce the gate.

"Kayara, hold the Bulwark, while I take the Nomad Sky to the Citadel to protect the king. Defend our home with honor."

She drew her sword saying, "Defend the king, at all costs."

The prince looked grave, but nodded. He climbed back into the ship as Aerilynn climbed out, visibly upset, while Aeysha and Locke followed close behind.

"Come on big guy, this is our stop!" Locke shouted back to Dyce while running after Aerilynn. Dyce stepped off the ship, which then rose slightly without his weight. Elisander pulled the doors shut behind them before he flew off.

Acacius Lordain, the battle-mage commander in charge of the front line, strode up to Captain Kayara with a military salute which she returned.

"What's the situation, Acacius?"

They shifted uncomfortably, nervously brushing some of their lavender-colored bangs out of their face.

"I am sorry to report that our initial defenses failed. The enemy appears to be equipped with iron armor that possesses strong anti-magic properties. It has rendered our magi useless against them, myself included."

Kayara smirked.

"If I know anything, it is that Acacius Lordain is far from useless. Not many magi can say they were handpicked by the king for leadership at your age."

Acacius looked defeated.

"But I couldn't-" they began, but Kayara cut them off.

"No one was prepared for this kind of assault, Acacius, our enemy knew our weaknesses and hit us hard when we least expected it. You did your best, and gathered vital intel. Now I want you to take the magi to the mid-level of the city and get creative. If anyone can find a way to use magic on something that can't be affected by magic, it's you."

Acacius smiled warmly before ordering the magi to follow them deeper into the city.

"Well come on then, the city's not going to save itself!" Kayara said to everyone else.

Aerilynn was furious, but joined Kayara in battle against the Therredan forces, because without her heirloom necklace she had no way to teleport to Silthradel. Her only hope to get back to her homeland now lay in liberating the city from Therredan control. She tried casting devastating blasts of cosmic energy at the iron golems but they had little effect on the lifeless constructs. Instead, it only resulted in her already weakened body losing mana rapidly.

Locke reached out in his mind to the gauntlet to reconnect with that presence he had felt on the back of the roc, and found her more easily this time. Sorren needed no convincing and willingly gave him control over the grappler weapon, which he then formed into a forearm blade. Together, he and Ren, attacked one of the golems with the weapon, and with a resounding clang Locke's right hook buried the blade into the empty body cavity of the animated suit of armor.

"Uh oh," he blurted out as the iron golem raised both of its fists over its head. With a flick of his wrist, he extended his hand, pushing the grappler straight out into its whip form which burst through the other side of the golem. Though it was impaled on the blades of the phoenix-tail, the lifeless construct seemed unphased by the damage it had taken and brought its heavy hands down on Locke. He rolled to the side, narrowly escaping and pulled his arm back in toward his body, forcing the grappler to retract the blades.

The blades caught on the iron as they passed through the golem's side, shredding it with a terrible sound of metal scratching against metal. It shuddered with each passing blade as they exited through its body, and by the time the grappler was fully retracted, the construct was torn nearly in half. It teetered uneasily, trying to regain its balance, but Dyce finished it off with a crushing slam which flattened the animated.

The hematite-colored colossus charged into battle, enraged at the sight of the Therredan-made iron golems. His furious punches dented them so deeply that they folded in on themselves, his attacks crumpled their metal bodies, and he tore them limb from limb. The Therredan foot soldiers tried to stab him with their spears, but they could not pierce his solid stone body and he batted them away like they were insects. Locke was both surprised and scared to see that Dyce had that kind of ferocity and power in him.

Using an invisible force, Dyce was able to pull metal weapons out of the hands of soldiers, as well as grab iron golems from several feet away. The elemental pulled the Therredan forces towards him, where he would promptly destroy them with a flurry of pummeling attacks. Locke had never seen such fury before, and was so amazed by watching Dyce make short work of the poorly made constructs that he did not see a dragoon lunge at him with a spear.

Locke barely brought the phoenix-tail grappler up to deflect the spear as it glanced past his head. The Therredan soldier glared through the slits in his iron helm, pulling the spear back for another attack. As the iron dragoon spun around with an arcing strike, Locke jumped back and tripped over rubble.

He rolled back to his feet as another lethal lunging strike nearly found his heart. Locke saw an opening in the missed strike and when the soldier pulled the spear back in the same manner as before, Locke charged him, jamming the forearm blade of the phoenix-tail into his neck through the gap between his helmet and breastplate.

The dragoon died instantly, dropping the spear he was swinging as Locke pulled the blade from the Therredan's neck. The man fell to the ground and his helmet rolled down the street. Locke looked into the face of one of his own people, and though he did not recognize him personally, there was a moment of connection between the two of them. Their fates had become linked as they had fought each other for their lives.

Though Locke had long ago accepted that killing some of his fellow Therredan was an inevitable outcome of trying to free them from the grip of Gerod Hammond, somehow this felt different. It felt wrong. He had every justification in the world for killing the dragoon. But as he stood over the Therredan, whose life he had just ended, he found that the act itself did not sit well with him. Was there really no other way to have stopped the man, he thought, was there no way to have saved him too? He felt sick to his stomach, and found he could not stop himself from vomiting into the streets, his head was spinning and he nearly passed out.

~

Elsewhere in the city, King Armon gathered the last of the royal guard to the inner keep, which was all that stood between their few forces and the onslaught of the Iron Tyrant's war machines.

"Darkness falls around us," Armon said somberly as he drew his crystal-bladed weapon, the kingsword Everund. He faced his loyal knights and continued, "but we are Everunder! We will defend our world or have our honor laid upon our tombs!"

The din of battle drew close and the clamor of iron rang through the Grand Citadel, shaking dust from the ceiling. The golems approached the gates, cracking the stone steps underfoot as they shambled toward the entrance of the Citadel. Their dominating size shut out the light of the sun, blanketing the courtyard with darkness. Armon raised his crystal blade, whose shining brilliant light glowed with a pure white luminescence.

"For Everund!" he shouted, lifting the spirits of the knights who bore witness to the shining symbol of their kingdom. The doors of the Citadel suddenly shattered as a golem threw itself through them, crashing face down onto the stone courtyard floor. It slowly stood back up as several more golems stepped through. "Attack!" shouted King Armon, and the emboldened knights with him charged the animated armor assaulting them. Unfortunately, their weapons did superficial damage to the unliving armor, which made the act of destroying one of them a monumental effort.

The golems' attacks however, were truly devastating, breaking enchanted shields and throwing knights around the room like children throw toys. Several of Therred's soldiers were now coming in through the broken doors and joining the knights of Everund and their king in battle. Spears clamored off of shields and swords pierced through flesh as chaos consumed the chamber. Armon's skill made him as lethal as all of the Everunder troops at his side combined, but no matter how hard they fought, in the end, Therred's numbers were slowly overwhelming them.

~

Elisander gripped the wheel anxiously as he flew the Nomad Sky to his father's defense.

"We're going for a fast drop," he said to his royal guard, while his voice trembled. When he saw the front gates of the Citadel torn open and Therredan troops climbing inside he shouted, "Be ready to cut our way to the king. If Kayara is successful we only have this rabble to deal with. We clear them out, we take back our home!"

The prince maneuvered the ship down toward the broken doors. He turned the Nomad Sky broadside, firing its cannons into the Therredan troops to weaken and disrupt them before landing. Harpoons launched out from the deck of the ship and anchored the ship down. While hovering with the rotors still spinning, the back of the prince's ship opened; Elisander and the remainder of his knights attacked the confused and scattered remnants of Therred's troops. Elisander fought his way into the castle but froze at the devastation he saw once inside.

A lone iron soldier ambushed Elisander with a spear, which he dodged before grabbing it from the dragoon. Pulling the weapon out of the soldier's hands and the prince spun it around in his own before thrusting it into the Therredan's chest. The soldier fell dead, adding to a massive pile of bodies and motionless constructs, in the middle of which was the broken body of the king.

The steel sword he held fell from Elisander's hand, clanging against the stonework as he was overcome with grief. He clutched his father tightly and pleaded in desperation.

"Yavon, please don't take him! Please don't take my father from me!" Elisander let his head fall on the king's shattered breastplate, wailing. The knights of his honor guard all knelt around Elisander and their deceased leader. They bowed their heads in silent mourning and respect. As his grief turned to anger, Elisander saw the kingsword Everund lying next to where his father fell and stood to claim it. He picked it up slowly, as though it were as heavy as the weight of leadership it represented.

Between his hands the prince balanced the sacred blade that formed the symbol of his great realm. His eyes drank in all of the detail, seeing it clearer than he had before. The translucent crystal glowed with a white light when held and the handle itself was wrapped in fine leather. The golden cross guard was the same sun cross symbol of the kingdom, with one of its arms longer to make up the handle. The rubies inlaid into the ends of the cross glittered in the light as he looked it over. Elisander had never seen it used in battle, it was a decoration for the king to wear. He always thought of it as a symbol of administrative power and nothing more.

Everund rested in his hands now and Elisander held the way it had been handed to his father when he took the throne. Just as it was handed down through each monarch since the sword was made by Alathor. Forged from a shard of the Crystallis, it was a material unlike any other, and blessed with otherworldly properties that made it both sharper and stronger than steel. The crystal blade glowed brighter as he gripped the handle tightly with renewed determination.

"Make contact with Captain Kayara at the Bulwark, tell her to evacuate the civilians near the edge of the city. Inform her that I intend to take the hangars back and undock the warships. Their heavy cannons can put an end to this siege," he ordered the knight that was closest to him, while looking up from the blade.

The knight nodded.

"Right away my king."

Elisander winced at the formal address which in its acknowledgement of the transfer of power, only highlighted the pain of his loss. He tried not to think about it further, as she took off running into the city; instead focusing on the situation at hand, speaking to the last knight that was with him in the Grand Citadel.

"Come with me, we need to get to the hangars quickly. If we can get even one of our warships airborne, we can push the Therredans out of the city."

Elisander looked back at his father once more before climbing back aboard the Nomad Sky. The new ruler of the kingdom closed the bay door behind him and climbed up into the cockpit. After grabbing the wheel and detaching the harpoon anchors, he pulled the ship up and flew toward the hangars at full speed. Elisander reached over and grabbed the knight, pulling him to the wheel.

"Hold this, and keep her straight."

The astonished man started to protest, but Elisander walked away, concerning himself instead with picking up a heavy cannonball and loading it into one of the port side cannons. He took back the wheel a moment later and brought the ship around to the unused side of the hangar; hovering in front of a locked metal door. "Fire that cannon!" Elisander commanded. The knight struck the charge and the barrel exploded with a blast that knocked the door clear off its hinges.

They stepped out of the ship and through the blast-scarred doorway, entering the upper hangar through a nearly unused maintenance hatch high up in the rafters. Elisander climbed onto the narrow scaffolding while whispering, "I used to sneak in here as a kid, back before they locked the door."

The knight followed him cautiously.

"And the king never caught you out here?"

Elisander's blue eyes lit up with amusement.

"He never figured out how I found my way in, but he knew I would come here to see the ships being built and to watch them disembark." Elisander motioned for quiet as they got further inside and within earshot of the occupying Therredan troops below. Slipping silently through the upper decks of the airship hangars they hid behind the bow of a warship called The Penitent.

The ships docked in the hangar were not at all like the Nomad Sky, these behemoths were three times the size, and each were equipped with ten prop engines to lift them. All generations of airships that Everund ever been designed were represented in the fleet, and despite each of them having mostly unique designs, they did share some features; such as deep hulls with rows of cannons, and cargo holds large enough to fit a small army.

"We will need to find the crews first, then open the hangar doors," Elisander spoke as quietly as possible.

The knight pointed to the lower level where a group of mechanics and pilots were being detained by only a few soldiers.

"There, my king!"

That was the second time he was called 'king,' and he did not like it any more than the first time he heard it.

"Let's go," he said before climbing down the metal ladders toward the captured airship crew.

~

Locke and the defenders at the outer wall were successfully holding the forces of Therred at the Bulwark of Alathor, but the tyrant of the scoured kingdom was as clever as he was cruel, and Gerod's secret weapon had yet to be revealed. Captain Kayara fought an iron golem, but it was starting to get the upper hand. Her new enchanted shield weathered the iron giant's fists but she was pushed down to a kneel.

Kayara attacked its side while she had an opening, thrusting her blade deeply into its metal body. Unphased, it swung at her with a backhand, which she ducked as its barrel-sized fist narrowly passed over her. The golem turned to face her and the animated suit of armor lifted its fists in the air threateningly. That's when she saw the black powder leaking from its side where she cut it.

The knights of Everund were finding some success by wielding the spears taken from Therredan dragoons to impale and immobilize the iron golems, but when they charged the gunpowder-filled construct that was about to crush Kayara, their spears tore off its helmet which set off the detonator. The explosion was visible from the top of Vigil Hill, a small watch post that was taken from Everunder control; which the Hammar Guard were using as their command center for the siege of the capital. Gerod Hammond looked on gleefully as his hidden bomb went off, before motioning to send in more explosive filled golems. From behind the reserve troops just outside the city gates, two more of Gerod's golem grenades ran through the Everunder defenses which had just been blown apart.

Kayara slowly came to as the golems ran past her, spilling small amounts of black powder onto the street as they went. The heavy clang of the construct's feet sounded muffled in the captain's ears, which were still ringing painfully from the explosion. She struggled to get back on her feet as a knight from the Citadel ran down to her, extending an offer to help. Kayara politely refused with a dismissive wave of her hand, preferring to stand on her own.

"Captain, I bring word from King Elisander!"

Kayara froze, hoping that she misheard through the ringing.

"King?" she asked.

The knight nodded grimly before she continued.

"Unfortunately, Armon fell defending the Crystallis. Elisander has Everund, and is headed to the hangars to free our warships."

Kayara looked mortified as her eyes followed the path of the iron golems that ran past.

"Those things are headed for the hangars. If the king is trying to free our ships he is going to be blown to pieces by those bombs! We need to stop them from reaching the hangar."

The knight protested.

"But captain, the king ordered you to hold the Bulwark!"

Kayara was already running for the hangars at full speed, she managed to catch up one of the gunpowder-filled constructs around the mid-level of the city where the magi were fighting. In the heat of battle, the warcasters barely noticed the golems running past them in the chaos, that was until they saw Kayara chasing them.

"Stop them!" she shouted.

A quick-witted magi used geomancy on the ground, causing the carved stone street to melt into thick mud, which one of the constructs fell into. As it was sinking into the mud and getting stuck, the second one escaped and continued stomping on toward the hangars.

Captain Kayara and the Citadel knight gave chase through the narrowing streets, having to fight the occasional Therredan dragoon as they went.

"This way!" Kayara shouted, diving down a side alley shortcut, and the knight following her barely made the turn at a full run. They hastily climbed up a ladder on the side of a building, running across the roof to the other side of the road leading to the hangars. While the construct followed the street going around the block, Kayara grabbed some rope before tossing one end to the knight.

"Tie it off fast!" she shouted as she jumped off the roof. The knight threw the rope around a chimney and wrapped it around her arm as Captain Kayara swung across the street. As the golem approached, she tied off the rope around the trunk of a tree on the other side of the street and pulled it taut with all her might. The construct ran straight into the tripwire, decapitating itself and setting off the explosives within.

The ensuing fireball filled the street in front of the hangar, startling the Therredan troops guarding it. At the same time, behind them enormous doors slid open and from out of the darkness of the hangar, the bow of a warship emerged. The Therredan troops panicked and ran away from the hangar doors. Kayara cheered at hearing the rumble of the airship's enormous engines. She recognized The Penitent as the ship hovered over the entire block. Kayara ran back across the street to meet up with the woman from the Citadel, while the warship cast its massive shadow over the scattering enemy troops.

"Inside, quick go!" she said, pushing them both inside a building. The numerous cannon bays opened on The Penitent's port side as it flew overhead, eclipsing the building they were huddled in.

The iron golems pounded their metal fists together as if wanting to brawl with the mighty warship, but the human soldiers were running for their lives. The Penitent had a clear shot and Elisander ordered the crew to fire, letting out a barrage of cannon fire so loud it shook the ground below. Captain Kayara and the knight from the Citadel ducked under a stairwell, while covering their ears as dust shook free from the ceiling. The heavy cannon fire tore apart the entire city block. White smoke and clouds of debris filled the air as row after row of cannons hammered the earth mercilessly.

There was a stoppage in the barrage as the cannons were drawn back into the ship to be reloaded for another volley. When the smoke cleared enough for them to see, only a few soldiers were crawling away from the destruction. The street below them was full of craters and a single iron golem that was still standing. Most of the constructs lay in pieces strewn about the streets, while others were blown in half but were still trying to move.

The few surviving Therredan soldiers ran for cover, straight toward the buildings still standing. Right where Kayara was.

"Oh hell!" she shouted as the cannons were reloaded and The Penitent turned towards them. Kayara covered them both with her shield as another volley shot from the side of the warship, spitting absolute destruction everywhere. In the middle of the barrage, a cannonball burst directly overhead, tearing off the roof and dropping debris on top of them. The windows shattered and bathed them in shards of glass while a massive cloud of dust enveloped the room.

They waited and listened to The Penitent's cannon fire which sounded further away as the ship chased the Therredan forces through the city. The sound of it reached all the way back to Vigil Hill, and to Gerod. He snarled while the Everunder warship decimated his forces inside the city, and he knew then that the battle was over. He saw that the warship must have escaped from the hangar, knowing his forces failed to keep the Everunders from getting to their ships, and which his bombs failed to destroy.

The Penitent continued to fire its cannons sporadically as it flew over the streets of Erendar, taking out pockets of Therredan soldiers or golems who were still fighting within the city. Captain Kayara slowly rose from the rubble, brushing the dust out of the Citadel woman's hair tenderly, before helping her walk over the debris as they climbed out. They both stood in the street, still holding on to one another and watching The Penitent fly toward the Bulwark. Their home was being freed from the grip of the Iron Tyrant, street by street as the ship went.

While the Therredan soldiers fled from Erendar, Gerod looked past them to the man standing on the deck of the single airship which had liberated the city. Elisander held aloft the crystal blade of Everund but Gerod smiled darkly, knowing that although he had failed to take the city, he succeeded at killing their fool king.

Gerod Hammond grabbed his iron helmet and pulled it off so he could be seen clearly by his nemesis. His pitch-colored hair was slick with sweat and clung to the right side of his face, which was covered by a burn scar. Gerod's scars which were formed by the touch of dragon's fire reached across his jaw and down the side of his neck. He was a homely man even without the scars, his face was wide and his mouth reminiscent of bottom feeding river fish.

"Pull our forces back to the river and make ready to cross the Plains of Arbereth," Gerod ordered his general.

"My lord, our forces have rallied at the Bulwark. My men marched for weeks to get here to take this city, I believe-"

"I will not risk the loss of our entire army against Everund's airships."

"Understood my lord, I will have the men move out as soon as they have finished burial duties."

"That won't be necessary, we leave for Therred immediately," Gerod said sternly before smiling cruelly, "Don't look so defeated general, Everund will fall in time. For now, take pride in knowing that we made a giant bleed."

The Shadow Reborn

The cold mountain winds whipped at the torn clothes that clung to Ir'zane's charred and decayed body as he flew, but he felt none of it. The evil eye in his palm was fixed on the imposing peak of Monnd Ubremol, and the eminent Duscan castle built upon it. The training pits were full of armed undead warriors honing their skills, shaking off the rust of their deaths, and finding their new limits as revenants.

Viranas, the fallen king of Duscar, was personally overseeing the conditioning of Ir'zane's loyal army. The former ruler of the Duscan people bowed low as his master landed in front of him. Ir'zane dismounted the gryphon and with a dismissive hand gesture to the former king, he addressed Viranas' presence. Ir'zane turned instead to the poor beast that his magic enslaved and he undid the spell that was animating the gryphon's corpse. The once noble creature collapsed in a blaze of green, necromantic fire.

"Dispose of it," Ir'zane ordered coldly as his warriors hauled the remains away.

The flames which burned in his rotten chest flickered and dimmed. His soul was weakened greatly from the battle with the beast's mistress. The flame which had brought him back from death was slowly burning away his soul like kindling in a bonfire, and eventually, only ash would remain. However, his body would soon be restored, and his rejuvenated mana would sustain the flame eternally. With limitless life and power and an army of unstoppable undead loyal to his darkest dreams, he would fear nothing.

Ir'zane placed his hand over the dark grimoire, absentmindedly stroking its cover while trying to think over the screams of the souls trapped within. The Eye of Orynos allowed him to see the dark spell craft which was woven through the Book of Souls, but curiously it would not reveal the dark presence within. Ir'zane was wary of the cursed tome though it continued to be useful to him. The truth was that Ir'zane longed to be free of the influence of others, to be unbound by oath or blood, and he would gladly do the unthinkable if it meant never being controlled again.

Ir'zane reasoned that since the dead felt no pain, they would not suffer, and with no will of their own, there would be no strife. The hordes of Duscar, once fierce and full of violence like their dragon masters, now only existed to see Ir'zane's will done. The crazed Duscan sorcerer intended to use the book to raise the dead who fell upon the blades of his army, just as he had used it to raise Duscar from the ashes. Surely it was a more merciful fate than the horrors that nature would have wrought for their lives.

Ir'zane was raised a warrior in the pits with his brothers and sisters, treated as playthings for the dragons to abuse. But he still remembered the jealousy from those who had cherished beating him in the pit the day the Magi took him away for training. Even Viranas, the mighty king of Duscar who had murdered his way to the throne and was revered by all Duscans, looked upon *him* with envy the day the Magi revealed that Ir'zane was born with magic potential.

Power was the entire way of life for Duscans, and Ir'zane was the first of his kin to be treated as an equal with dragons. The look of envy in the eyes of the king, who had fought so hard to gain the dragons' favor only to lose it to Ir'zane, was a memory most delicious. That day, bruised and bleeding, he stood before the throne of his proud people as they were made to bow before him. Ir'zane believed the people of Duscar understood their true place that day. For all their muscle and wrath, his people were weak. Magic was real power, and among Duscans, only he possessed it.

Even the mighty dragons, who threatened to burn the world to glass before being forced to bend to humanity, could not fight the control of his dark magic now. Death would be the ultimate gift he would give to the world, and everyone would be united under his power. He was drunk with the idea of it, and it filled him with so much excitement that his dead heart nearly beat. He turned his right palm up to see the bulging, lidless eye which was worming around within his decaying flesh, and thought about how sweet it was going to be watching the sanctimonious elves fall first.

"My lord, you did not return with Fayrnir, did he fall in battle?" Viranas asked a distracted Ir'zane, who looked surprised he was still standing there.

"Right. Yes, regretfully he did. I shall need a replacement. Did you find any other dragon corpses suitable for the ritual?"

"Only one, Gor'Gana. Though not a warrior in life, she was a cunning hunter..." the former king began, but Ir'zane interrupted him, "I hope that means she's fast."

Viranas did not finish his description. Instead, he made a summoning motion with his arm, and several Duscan warriors dragged over the unearthed body of a dragon who had fallen during the Great Wyrm War. They laid her at Ir'zane's feet as he unlatched the Book of Souls from his waist and raised it over her motionless frame. The revenant warriors stood back as Ir'zane read aloud the heretical incantations, filling the dragon's husk with dark magic. Though only the simplest of reanimation magic seemingly worked on dragons, their physicality alone made them formidable weapons and worth the effort of finding one to raise.

An earth-shattering roar came from the corpse, and the dreadwyrm stretched its rotten and torn wings as it rose back to its feet. Viranas knelt before the terrifying creature as she towered over them, followed by the rest of the Duscan warriors. Though Ir'zane did not join them, he allowed the others to express their reverence, if only to demonstrate to his people that even their gods obeyed his command.

"Ready my warriors, Viranas. When I pierce the elven defenses, I shall summon you to distract them."

The fallen king bowed his head.

"As you command my lord."

Ir'zane smugly latched the book back to his hip, and then climbed atop the newly risen dreadwyrm, flying off into skies which were painted blood-red by the fading sun.

The Eld Ridge Mountains that the sorcerer spent hours flying over had once been considered the symbol of the dragon's dominion over the world. Beyond them were rolling hills leading into the boreal forests of the northland. Further yet beyond the taiga, Ir'zane saw the end of the Winterwood in the distance and he briefly thought of the frozen wastes in the Forgotten Vale beyond.

The enhanced sight that the Eye granted him allowed him to see the magical ley lines which flowed through Averon in the ground below. He raised his right arm, pointing the Eye of Orynos toward a convergence of ley lines in the distance and revealed the hidden remnant of the elven home world of Silthradel. A massive chunk of planetary crust levitated like an island above the tundra, its rivers fell like waterfalls to Averon where they formed a small lake underneath the world fragment.

The lake and the river flowing north out from it were hidden under powerful concealment spells, and without the All-Seeing Eye, Ir'zane could only see barren tundra. However, with the sight granted by the dark artifact, he could see the edges of the magical barriers projected from the elven world. The spells emanating from the island in the sky surrounded it all in a protective shell which had kept their sacred sanctuary safe for a thousand years; until now.

There were elegant illusory spells which prevented one from seeing Silthradel, layered on top of more complex sensory spells which prevented things such as animals from smelling through the barrier, and even a disorientation charm which would make someone forget why they had crossed the barrier to begin with. The spells protecting the elven home world did far more than just cloak it from curious eyes, and more than Ir'zane had expected. It was the most intricate spellwork he had ever seen, and he could not help but admire its artistry.

Silthradel's defenses were, without a doubt, the most advanced magical protections in the world. The craftsmanship with which they were cast was stunning; even the mage city Aeris-Terran had not utilized such clever methods to repel invaders or unwanted guests. He forced the dreadwyrm to the ground, landing just outside the barrier's edge. No doubt if the elves had posted lookouts, they would have seen him by now, but the sight granted by the Eye of Orynos showed him that they had none. Millennia of peace afforded to them by their cleverness had made them lazy, and Ir'zane was amused that the noble civilization of elves would be brought to heel by their own hubris.

The sorcerer's hand filled with black smoke which fell from his fingertips like mist, the shadows grew until his hand could disappear inside them. Within the darkness he reached into the depths below the Isle of Knives, pulling a piece of jewelry out of the sticky shadow and into his palm: it was a golden chain with a pendant shaped like golden wings which rose from a horizon with a sunstone set in the center. Holding it in his decomposed fist, he extended his arm through the magical barrier around Silthradel, which opened harmlessly as the pendant passed through it.

Ir'zane walked right through the warding spells with the aid of Aerilynn's necklace, which he had cleverly collected from the lightless reaches beneath Eldric's vault. Though the guards of Silthradel had not seen him yet, he was not naive enough to believe that a patrol would not be along eventually. Ir'zane did not want to risk being exposed before he was able to summon the army of Duscar. So, in order to conceal his nefarious machinations, he created an obscuring dark shroud that surrounded him in a veil of shadow, which would hide him from sight in the fading twilight.

The portal to Duscar would take a significant amount of time to construct, but being hidden meant he could work uninterrupted. Ir'zane worked diligently to craft the spell, creating intricate sigils which formed a gate as the last motes of daylight shrank behind the horizon. Ir'zane drew the final symbol in the center of the gateway, the sigil for his homeland. He placed his charred hand on the sigil, activating the portal, and the arcane symbols lit up with power drawn from the ley lines below.

Halfway across the continent in the ruins of Duscar, the hordes of undead waited, ready for a fight. The people of Duscar were bred for war by dragons; designed to be the greatest warriors the world had ever known, and they were eager to spill blood for their new master. So, when a bright light appeared in the center of the courtyard in front of the Duscan warband, which expanded into a wide circle they became excited. In the center of the vortex of magic, they saw the floating island-like landmass of the ancient elven world of Silthradel.

Viranas stepped up to the portal.

"Lord Ir'zane has made way for us! Bring them fury! Bring them pain! Bring them oblivion! For death and glory! For Duscar!"

The Duscan warriors smashed their swords against their chest plates, and one by one they ran through the portal and onto the tundra beneath Silthradel. The sorcerer's undead army formed ranks around the dreadwyrm as it crawled through. Ir'zane stepped out from under the cover of the shadow veil and toward the nearest waterfall that was cascading down. The elves were not the only crafty spellcasters in the world and he knew a simple spell which would allow himself a way to climb into Silthradel. An icy light glowed from his fingertips as the spell formed in his hands, the extreme cold from it turned the water spray into ice crystals.

Ir'zane unleashed the spell which touched the falls and froze the flowing river solid instantly, forcing the falling water to spray around it. The spell effect crawled up the falls and into the city, freezing the water faster than it could fall. The entirety of the waterfall transformed into solid ice, creating a frozen wall connecting the floating island to the ground below.

"Now!" Ir'zane commanded, dropping the shadow veil which had guarded them against sight.

The revenant Duscans hurried past him, climbing the frozen ice wall as quickly as they could. The elves of Silthradel had not yet discovered the forces of Duscar ascending the river toward their home and were unaware of the evil that was nearly upon them. Ir'zane walked back to his dreadwyrm while the remainder of his army exited through the open portal from the ruins of Duscar.

"It is time for you to cause as much distraction as you can, my pet!" he said to the dreadwyrm, and at his command the undead dragon rose. With a mighty heave of its tattered wings, it was airborne and heading for the city. Ir'zane delighted in sadistic glee as he watched the dreadwyrm fly over Silthradel.

Elves carrying books and vegetables in their arms screamed in terror as the dreadwyrm's silhouette darkened the skies over them. Nearby guards ran as fast as they could toward the screams to witness a dragon corpse attacking their people. One of the elven guards scrambled to the citizens' aid, pushing them out of harm's way and trying to fight it off while another reached for a satyr horn at his side, before bringing it to his lips and blowing. The sound of the horn cut through the air and into every dwelling across all of Silthradel.

Conversations came to a halt mid-sentence, work was dropped, each elf stopped when they heard it.

Queen Ellandra Everdawn stood up at the sound of the guard's horn, and without hesitation turned to her royal guard.

"Silthradel is under attack! Protect our people!"

The queen's royal guard sealed the building and led the queen and her entourage out of the royal hall as another horn sounded from the west of the island from where the warriors of Duscar had ascended. A cold mist rose from the frozen river and from the bodies of the dead as they marched toward the shaken forces of Silthradel.

The shadowmancer cloaked himself in shadow magic and crept past the chaos and into the courtyard beyond. The pavilion contained the font of power which he so desperately craved, the life force which sustained the elves. The ancient elvish script carved into the stone beneath him was difficult to read, but it spoke of rites of passage related to and ritualistic worship of a great tree.

It was what he came for, what the elves called, Eldashira. Ir'zane's mind was so singularly focused on gaining access to its mana that he did not notice the pendant of the Everdawn slipping from his dead fingers onto the ground below. The light of the mana font beneath the great tree's roots filled the hollow sockets of his skull as he rematerialized out of the shadows. He bent down in front of the mana font and placed his dead hands upon the stone basin, completely transfixed by the raw magical power which flowed from it like water from a fountain.

The radiance of the sacred font was intensely bright in the shade from the great tree which enshrouded the mana pool. Ir'zane's fascination was drawing him to the liquid-like energy which flowed out from the heart of the elven realm. Its aura radiated immense power from the mana spring. Despite the intensity of the force it emanated, it was harmless. In fact, the closer he got to the font, the more energized and rejuvenated he felt. The rotten muscles in his body regrew, and the necrosis in his tissues healed.

He eagerly stepped into the mana spring but it had an immediate, volatile reaction to his presence. The energy within the sacred font assaulted him violently as if trying to eject an invader. He could feel the pool of power pushing back against him but Ir'zane could not be stopped, and he forced himself through the surge of energy washing over him. With each determined step, he felt the chaotic energies sputter and thrash over him. He could hardly believe its enormous power and with a rotten laugh of dark intent, he began consuming it all. Ir'zane channeled a powerful necromantic spell, allowing him to siphon the energy out of the sacred elven mana font in order to fully restore his body to life.

The spell turned into a gleaming emerald light which engulfed Ir'zane's body in a chain reaction, converting the mana of the font into dark regeneration. His tissues were imbued with the storming essence of the cosmos, the iridescent energy coursing through his body winding back his death. The pale, burned, and decayed flesh healed, taking on a bronze tone and the warmth of life. The geyser of primal power spewed green light which illuminated the area with its unholy glow.

The reaction created a vortex of energy which thrashed with emerald lightning, crashing into nearby trees and setting them ablaze. The spell rejuvenating his dead flesh was leeching the life force out of the planetary fragment Silthradel, catalyzing a gray malaise which spread through the vegetation as plants withered around the desecrated pools. The vile corruption seeped its way under the feet of the distraught masses of elves who looked on in horror as their lush and sacred paradise was consumed by creeping decay.

The violent energies swirling in and out of Ir'zane's body battered him repeatedly, tearing off his armor and throwing the pieces out of the vortex at high speeds. All of the power was slowly drained from the sacred elven font by the dark magic coursing through him. Silthradel wailed mournfully as it died while Ir'zane's regeneration consumed the last of its life. Everything fell silent as Ir'zane floated gently back to the ground, over the former abundantly flowing mana font, which was now completely barren.

Ir'zane's clawed toes, which were stained black as pitch, crushed the once pale blue blades of Longshadow grass while he walked away from the desecrated pools. His bright emerald eyes admired the glow of his dusky skin and long curly black hair. When he reached out to touch his hair, he noticed his hands and feet bore a visible corruption where the tips of his fingers and toes turned black and ended in claws. The blackened skin discoloration ran down his fingers and into his hands, turning his blood vessels black before continuing on to his forearms, where it faded to a light gray and disappeared.

Ir'zane looked over his body, using his clawed hands to tear open his robes so that he could see his chest. His organs were no longer visible and he could feel the light thump of his heartbeat behind his ribs. A wicked grin spread over his handsome face, the once burned and dead skin was completely restored to the youthful glow of his prime. But more importantly, he felt the intense surging of mana through his body again.

The rejuvenated sorcerer heard the din of battle not far off and he was eager to get back to his army, so Ir'zane tapped into his mana and used his signature umbramancy to shadowwalk to his desired destination. He felt the connections between shadows from one another like a web of darkness which stretched across the elven city. In an instant he disappeared and reappeared in the central courtyard before the cathedral, right in front of where Ellandra Everdawn stood fighting the forces of Duscar that were encircling her. She was holding her daughter's necklace in her hands but her eyes were pulled away from it, drawn to Ir'zane as though by his will alone.

The Queen's Tears

Queen Ellandra Everdawn's eyes faded to gray as the vegetation of her home world died around her. Though she had been watching fearfully as the malaise spread throughout Silthradel, she was no longer focused on it. Her eyes were locked with Ir'zane's and her heart sank seeing him fully revived instead of undead like the other Duscans defiling her home. The queen knew that he must be the source of the blight that was killing everything, which could only mean that the heart of the elven world had been entirely consumed. Ellandra turned away from him, as she could not bear to look upon that hideous smile any longer, becoming deeply enraged at the sight of his twisted revelry.

Ir'zane was enjoying himself immensely as he casually approached the queen, stopping just to stand over her. She glared into his bright green eyes as he raised a blackened, clawed finger to her face, gently brushing away a loose strand of her starlight hair. Her fingers were slipping into her dress to the handle of a hidden blade.

"Just kill me already and let me rest with my kin," she demanded.

He smiled devilishly.

"My dear, you are already dead."

Ir'zane then wiped away one of the queen's tears with his claw while laughing, before turning his back on her, "Viranas, pull our army back. Leave them to the crows."

Queen Ellandra pulled a yellow dagger with violet sigils on it from her waist and tried to stab Ir'zane in the back with it, but he vanished like smoke before it landed. The sorcerer reappeared at the far edge of the dying world fragment, becoming corporeal again after shadow walking. With a wave of his hand, the spell on the waterfalls ended and the river was suddenly no longer frozen. The water cascaded off the cliff again and Ir'zane followed, jumping with the flowing water into the lake below. The Duscan revenants fought their way back out of the city and followed their master over the edge away from the arrows and blasts of magic the elves were shooting at them.

A roar from behind the elves stopped them from pursuing the revenants, as the undead dragon they had forgotten about charged them with its claws and tail thrashing. Gor'Gana's wrath demanded the full attention of Silthradel's defenders, forcing them to abandon their pursuit of Ir'zane. The dreadwyrm slammed its tail into a large stone building, smashing through its walls, and sending innocent civilians fleeing for their lives.

Queen Ellandra cut her palm open before tossing aside the dagger she was holding. She scooped up some of the ash, which covered the ground, in her bleeding palm while chanting a curse in elvish. The elves around her looked shocked as their queen tapped into forbidden magic, yet they said nothing about it, instead focusing on the undead dragon attacking them. The city defender's shields split as the dragon's claws rent them to pieces, their swords and their arrows did next to nothing to damage the creature in return.

The dark powers Ellandra was summoning combined the ash in her palm with the blood dripping from it, turning it into a bright glowing purple ooze. With a vicious flick of her wrist the queen flung her curse-blood at the dreadwyrm, spraying it with the corrosive spell. The ooze bubbled and hissed as it melted away the flesh and bone beneath where it landed on the dreadwyrm. Gor'Gana shrieked as the curse-blood burned through her body as it spread, consuming large parts of the dreadwyrm in a boiling purple spell. The undead dragon flailed, its tail crashing through some homes before falling off as the devouring spell severed it from the rest of the body.

Queen Ellandra's furious eyes glowed in the same color as the curse-blood while she chanted through gritted teeth to keep the spell going. The dreadwyrm lunged toward the queen but the damage to its form was so severe that its body collapsed on itself as it tried. Instead, it fell to the side, directly on top of a few city defenders who were fighting it. Their screams were all that escaped from the melting glowing goo that the corrosive dark magic reduced them all to. The queen pulled her hand to her mouth in shock as the elves died, while ending the spell that was powering the curse-blood which had dissolved a depression into the ground.

A sorrowful hush fell over Silthradel, the battle was over, but their suffering had just begun. While the elves were still preoccupied, Ir'zane's troops reached the portal on the ground below, which was still active. Ir'zane pulled the sigil for Duscar out of the spell, which vanished after being discarded, and he quickly wrote another. Viranas looked on, confused.

"Are we not returning to Duscar?"

Ir'zane completed the new sigil without answering him, changing the destination of the spell before they departed. Through the portal, a strange set of twin cities was visible in the vortex of energy, one on the ground and the other upside-down in the sky above it.

"We are going to destroy our people's old nemesis, and with the power of their city we will wage war on all of Averon," Ir'zane said stepping through the gateway, followed after by Viranas and the warriors of Duscar. A few elven archers reached the edge of Silthradel and fired a futile volley of shots after them. The army of Duscar ignored them entirely, hit or miss, and continued through the portal until the last of them slipped through.

The elves were devastated. They stood speechless because the weight of Silthradel's destruction was impossible to bear. The elves had transported their world across the stars to save it from total annihilation and for thousands of years they had kept Silthradel hidden from all eyes. It had remained untouched through countless wars, disasters, and even from the dragons when the elves made their stand against Duscar.

Only one other time in Queen Ellandra's long years had she felt suffering as great as that which consumed her now as she witnessed the aftermath of Ir'zane's assault. She felt as if every star in the sky had gone out, her whole universe devoid of anything which held enough of Yavon's light to still be called beautiful.

The sight of her people suffering and the collective sound of their mournful voices crying out as their world died around them overwhelmed the queen. She closed her eyes tightly, embracing her despair while shining pearls of tears fell from her eyes. Millennia of culture and decorum bled out of her as she slumped onto the stone path and her pride fell around her like her gown.

~

The Nomad Sky descended through the cloudless night as it approached the now visible planetary fragment of the dying elven home world of Silthradel. With the magical barriers gone, the passengers could see the city on the floating island through the glass windows of Elisander's airship as they soared closer. King Elisander looked grave, seeing their vegetation dying off rapidly from some unknown blight. He scowled, fearing that they were too late to help.

"Set the ship down at the edge of the city and keep the engines running."

Drovann grunted.

"Expectin' a warm welcome are ye?"

Elisander looked at him sternly.

"Just be ready to leave as soon as we return," he said before issuing a command to Kayara, "Have your knights keep their weapons holstered, it looks like we missed the fight for the city and I do not wish to send the message that we have come looking for another."

She replied with a small head bow.

"As you wish my king."

The formality of her address took him by surprise.

He wondered if he would ever get accustomed to the change in the way he was addressed now. Elisander disliked the decorum of the court and preferred the casual, friendly relationship he had shared with his people when he was just a prince. While he mused, the ship docked at the edge of Silthradel and as the cargo gate was dropped, Aerilynn ran past them all, disappearing into the city.

"Aerilynn wait!" Locke called after her, stepping off the Nomad Sky and into the elven city. Elisander found Locke as he was stepping off the ramp.

"Stay close my friend, and let us hope that the princess' fondness of you has not diminished."

Locke was not at all sure what Elisander meant by that, but he did not appreciate it. Nonetheless he stood beside the king, letting his eyes wander over the alien architecture of the once-hidden realm of the elves. Deeper in the city, Aerilynn feared the worst while she ran through her ancestral homeland for the first time in many long years. She was heartbroken to see the damage the undead army of Duscar had inflicted upon the once beautiful and serene city. A malaise hung upon the remaining vegetation and the ground had become a pale gray; Silthradel was rotting.

The princess' eyes likewise faded to gray while she witnessed her world slowly dying, despair almost took her before remembering something her father always said, "No matter how long the night, the dawn always rises." Aerilynn allowed herself to hope that her mother still lived. She pressed on to the city center but she clapped her hand over her mouth in surprise at the number of bodies lying in the open. The survivors had likewise collapsed or were mumbling to themselves in shock, processing the loss of their world.

The guardians somberly tended to the many wounded and crestfallen elves, finding and helping survivors as they ran all over the city. In the wake of destruction, many scholars gathered their people's written heritage as well as the many books of incantations and scrolls of magical knowledge. But in the ensuing chaos, many artifacts and scrolls of knowledge were lost or destroyed, beyond the limited power that the council had to protect their history in the crumbling Everdawn dynasty.

Aerilynn searched desperately through the disillusioned and despondent in search of her mother, her eyes flitting between pained faces of people trying to pick up the pieces of their lives. Aerilynn finally found her mother sitting on the ground completely lying completely still, and as she strode up to the queen for the first time in an age, a vast emptiness filled her. Moonlight shone down from the heavens, casting the queen's shadow across the floor where it merged with Aerilynn's own.

"Mother," Aerilynn called out, but Ellandra did not stir. It seemed she had not heard her daughter calling out to her and for a moment, Aerilynn feared the queen might be dead. She hurried to her side and their eyes met when Ellandra felt her daughter's arms around her. The queen looked upon the young woman's face and smiled weakly.

"My daughter," she said softly. It was then that Aerilynn noticed that the queen was holding a familiar heirloom necklace in her hands, something she believed she had lost at the Isle of Knives.

~

"What happened here?" Locke asked Elisander, looking at the dying plants and nearly tripping over one of Ir'zane's undead.

"Duscan warriors assaulted the city, but it looks like they were unable to take it," Elisander replied. Captain Kayara bent to a knee and examined one of the Duscan corpses.

"Most of the damage was from behind, they were destroyed as they were attempting to flee."

The king surveyed the palace.

"Let us hope then that Ir'zane was repelled. For all our sake."

The stillness was unsettling, and Elisander gripped the handle of his sword tighter as they entered the plaza at the center of Silthradel. As soon as they stepped into the open, a group of elves sprang out of hiding with weapons drawn on the Everunders, who started reaching for their weapons until Elisander motioned for them to stand down. Queen Ellandra Everdawn appeared as if from nowhere, her face wrought with sorrow and her eyes were dangerously empty.

"Why did you come here, princeling? Have you come to forfeit your life?"

Elisander looked at Locke and Kayara, hiding his own concern while reading theirs. He took his hand off his sword, raising both hands in the air slowly.

"No, my lady, I have not. I have come to offer you the service and protection of *my* kingdom, as king," he said bowing low, but never breaking eye contact with the elven queen. Her countenance did not soften and her glare cut like daggers at Elisander's attempted diplomacy.

"We have no use for your filth here," she replied.

Elisander stood back up and the nicety left his face.

They stared at one another until Aerilynn appeared.

"I told you to stay inside or leave," Ellandra snapped at her. Aerilynn looked discomforted, she ignored her mother's reprimand and addressed Elisander.

"It's all over, Ir'zane is gone," she said.

Ellandra grabbed her daughter by the arm.

"Do not speak to these *humans* about matters of our people!"

"Mother, they mean us no harm! Elisander is only here because I requested his help to warn you, and he offered to lend his knights to aid in the battle," the princess fired back while pulling away from her mother's furious grip. Ellandra dismissively released Aerilynn while glaring at Elisander, and without command elven bow strings were pulled taut with arrows nocked.

"So, you knew that the Lightslayer returned from the dead, and was leading an army to my home. You knew what was coming for us and you showed up here conveniently after *my* world was destroyed?"

Elisander hung his head.

"I am sorry, Queen Everdawn, I have failed you and your people. What your daughter says is true. We tried to stop Ir'zane from obtaining an artifact called the Eye of Orynos, which apparently gave him the ability to find Silthradel. The princess fought valiantly, but I was not there to aid her in her time of need, and he uhhh..."

Elisander trailed off without finishing his thought, instead hanging his head.

The queen scowled at Aerilynn.

"Alone? Are you moonstruck? You are lucky to be alive."

Aerilynn's ears drooped shamefully. The sting of her failure at the Isle of Knives had not completely faded. She bore the guilt of her devastated homeland as if she had done it herself.

"The elves of Lorlinden aided us in repairing my airship and for that, I offered my assistance to you and your people. I see many elves still standing, you must have succeeded where I and the princess have failed."

The elven queen narrowed her eyes.

"Elven sight is keener than it is among your kind, but surely even *you* can see that our land is dead. Ir'zane did not come here for my people, nor did he want to take my city. When our world was destroyed millennia ago our ancestors transported this remnant of our planet here to Averon, along with as many of our people as they could. But most importantly of all, they saved the mana of our world from being devoured by darkness."

Aerilynn looked surprised that her mother was sharing elven history with humans. Elisander continued to hold his arms in the air and never took his eyes off of the queen as she continued.

"A great well of power lies at the heart of every world throughout the Infinite, it is the light the Allfather breathed into it at the dawn of creation; we know it as mana. It is primordial energy used to power spellcasting, but it is also the literal life force of a world. For thousands of years, my people have drawn from this well to extend our lives. When drawn slowly, the mana will replenish over time. We have lived in a cycle of using its regenerative energies and tending its pools to nourish us for generations. This is how we have survived since our world was destroyed, and it was this well that Ir'zane came for."

Elisander's eyes widened at the revelation of the dark sorcerer's true intentions.

"But that means…"

Ellandra's expression softened for the first time.

"It means that he has consumed the heart of my world, and without it, my people will eventually die."

Elisander looked deeply concerned.

"And with the All-Seeing Eye and that tome of necromancy, he now wields tremendous power. It's all my fault, forgive me I… I gravely misjudged the danger that he posed. I should have let my people handle Therred on their own and I should have stopped that wretch before he set one foot here."

Ellandra's ears perked up.

"You were attacked too?" she asked.

The king let his arms fall to his sides.

"Yes, Gerod Hammond chose to end our long years of tenuous peace with a cowardly attack upon Erendar. Though his assault failed, he dealt Everund a devastating blow. My father Armon was slain defending the Crystallis."

The queen observed her troops, motioning for them to withdraw from their positions and to put away their weapons.

"And now you, young prince, have become king."

Locke watched as Elisander knelt before the elven queen.

"We have both lost much today, but our fight is not over. Now more than ever we need to work together to end this threat."

Ellandra seemed unmoved by Elisander's gesture and spoke flatly in turn.

"My world is dead, young king, there is nothing left for us to defend. We will not die fighting the ghosts of *your* past."

Elisander looked up, shocked.

"Averon is now your home as well! Ir'zane will not stop after he has destroyed my kingdom or any other. He will spread his madness to every corner of this world. Surely, you must see that."

The queen motioned to her guards, who stood alongside Elisander as he pleaded with her.

"I will let you live, despite trespassing on our sacred ground. That is the only gift that I give to you this day. Guards, please escort the king of Everund back to his ship," the queen ordered coldly.

Elisander stood, giving only a brief nod and gestured to the knights to go back to the ship as the queen had suggested.

"Mother please, we need to work together to stop Ir'zane, if not for their sake, then at least to avenge our home!" Aerilynn implored. Ellandra ignored the pleas of her daughter, choosing instead to watch the host of Everund leave. Only when they were heading back to their ship did the queen finally turn to Aerilynn, speaking venomously.

"Our home? Do you forget your place? Did you think we would accept you back after the shame you brought upon us? Do you not see what your foolish idealism has wrought? All of your love for their misbegotten kind, and what have they given you in return but misery and death? No. We shall not falter in our convictions, nor our belief that humans cannot and should not be trusted, and I think that you will find that you have fewer sympathizers for your *cause* after today."

Aerilynn looked into the empty eyes of her fellow elves and saw the contempt for her on their faces. With the Everunders readying for takeoff, the elves of Silthradel collected their belongings, and were preparing to leave the ruins of their home as well. The queen looked unfavorably upon her daughter with tears flowing from her eyes.

"This is our home no longer, but wherever we go now, know that you and other human sympathizers are still unwelcome. You should have never come back here."

The queen placed the Everdawn pendant in her daughter's hands with a look that let Aerilynn know that the queen knew Ir'zane got passed their defenses with it because of her. Without another word, Ellandra Everdawn turned her back on the princess and walked away from her daughter.

Aerilynn hung her head low, her ears drooping as she sulked away from her people for the second time. She followed Locke and Elisander, who said nothing as she climbed aboard the Nomad Sky as it left. The ship took off while she stared down on the dead world of Silthradel knowing she would likely never see it again. She wiped away her tears and tried to focus on the greater threat to Averon, which her mother refused to confront.

Battle for Earth and Sky

A dark mood hung over everyone aboard the Nomad Sky as it approached the abandoned twin cities of Aeris-Terran. Even the warmth of the rising sun could not lift their spirits as they flew past the sunken Harromere. Following behind the king's personal ship was the entire fleet of Everund, the massive airships were noticeably less elegant in design than the rebuilt Nomad Sky which led them. Their wide sides were filled with rows of cannons and their monstrous engines belched clouds of steam. Each ship carried over two hundred knights as well as a full crew to operate them.

The six warships of the Everund fleet were mobile fortresses, each with enough firepower to occupy a city. King Elisander commanded the fleet into ready position and they formed a defensive line behind the Nomad Sky. While waiting inside the cargo hold of Elisander's flagship, Locke was less ready for the battle to come. He could hardly believe that less than a month ago he was lying in his bed at the Blackwood Manor, staring at a magical compass and wondering what Everund was like. Now, he was flying on one of their airships to fight alongside of them as they tried to save the world.

While he was no stranger to fighting, war was something he knew nothing about. His stomach felt tight and he feared he might get sick, so he held onto the phoenix-tail grappler. Sorren tried to comfort him with the warmth of her soul, and to help calm his mind she shared her first memory with him. He saw a nest of phoenix chicks huddled together, and Locke could not help but smile at the sight of them.

The fleet kept in tight formation as they approached the oldest and greatest marvel of magically constructed architecture in all of Averon. The twin cities of Aeris-Terran were aptly named after the earth and sky, having been made with powerful geomancy and aeromancy. The city of Terran was dug into the ground and surrounded with high walls, while in the sky directly above it, floated the upside-down city of Aeris. The architecture was antiquated in its artistic attributes, resembling early human designs, yet it was also incredibly advanced in its engineering. Created through techniques so precise and efficient that it was hard to believe it was built nearly a thousand years ago.

The cities themselves were circular and identical in design, each building, road, and tower was mirrored and paired with its counterpart in the opposite city. There was also an impressive network sprawling across the cities of magic foci, large white crystals reminiscent of the ones that lit up the city of Erendar and Locke wondered if they were in fact the same. The white stone of the cities was accented by bright blue tiled roofs which filled the space between the cities. Locke tried to imagine the thousands of people who used to live there as they went about their lives, entirely dedicated to the pursuit of understanding magic.

The Everunder magi were talking excitedly amongst themselves about the abandoned cities while the warships slowly crossed into the fields just outside of them. Elisander ordered the fleet to stop before getting any closer. While hovering at the edge of the ancient cities, they saw no sign of Ir'zane or the forces of Duscar, and it seemed for a moment that they were alone. But then, the sound of stamping and dragging feet arose from the dead silence of the mage cities as a foul mist creeped out of the dirt. Enormous glowing geoglyphs lit up across the walls as a gateway into Terran magically appeared.

Sounds of shifting armor came next and then the dark shapes of undead warriors emerged from the gates, forming a defensive perimeter around the cities. They were clad in blackened armor forged by hellfire spat by their brutal dragon masters, and which bore the unmistakable emblem of Duscar. The black, downward facing great sword with the dragonwing cross guard symbol which was also emblazoned on their torn purple banners, just like the ones which still hung in the empty halls of the fallen kingdom.

Ir'zane monitored his army of revenants and the forces of Everund squaring up with a cold and calculating stare from the balcony of a tower overlooking the gate. He scoffed at their futility, at how absurd it was that a boy king thought his armored peasants and flying toys could stand against the might of Duscar. They were worse than fools! Let them spill their blood pointlessly, he thought. The Book of Souls was in his control, the All-Seeing Eye in the palm of his hand, his mana and body was restored, and the power of the mage cities was behind him; there was no one who could rival his power now.

Across the field, aboard the Nomad Sky, Elisander activated a resonating crystal device which transmitted his voice to other identical crystals which were installed in each warship so that the captains could communicate with one another during battle. The king spoke into a metal horn attached to the device.

"Captain Benthe of the Divine Edict and Captain Anora of the Resultant Verdict, move your ships to the front line and show Duscar the might of our Scalebane cannons!"

At his command, the massive warships broke formation and approached Aeris-Terran's gate. Ir'zane's undead warriors stood in the shadows of the airships stomping their feet and smashing their weapons against their armor. The Everund ships turned broadside revealing two rows of eight cannons each, all ready to fire.

"Now!" Elisander shouted, and the cannoneers aboard both ships lit the cannon's fuses, unleashing a barrage of deadly projectiles. Ir'zane waved his hand, activating Aeris-Terran's shield projectors while the cannons went off, and the shots exploded against the barrier uselessly. Both ships began reloading as Ir'zane fired back, lobbing bolts of necromantic fire at the Divine Edict. The blasts rocked the ship, throwing the crew across the deck. The green flames seemed to seek out people instead of wood or other combustibles and when they found their hapless victims, they were engulfed in magical fire that nothing would put out.

Locke heard the screams even from within the Nomad Sky, and he imagined the horror that was unfolding as the knights trapped within the Divine Edict burned alive. Elisander stared in shock as the ship veered toward the ground before smashing into the fields below and exploding. The Resultant Verdict pulled away as it took a bolt of fire in the side. While others in the cabin slid from the sudden shift in gravity, Captain Anora held the wheel preventing further instability. Elisander grimly studied the downed ship, hoping to see survivors before grabbing the metal horn and shouting into it, "Get back! Get out of range!"

Ir'zane threw another necrofire blast, but The Resultant Verdict turned hard and narrowly avoided another hit while it withdrew to join the rest of the fleet.

"We cannot take them from the air so long as that magical barrier stands, so we'll need to take them on foot. Get our ships down and our knights on that battlefield!" Elisander shouted. At the king's command, every warship in the fleet descended. The ships spun around as they set down to open their drawbridge-style cargo bay doors toward the cities.

While the knights of Everund disembarked, the voice from the Book of Souls whispered in Ir'zane's ear, *Crowns and blood... drowned in mud... never to reign again.* He found their nonsensical rambling disturbing, but he needed their help once more. Ir'zane pulled the book from his waist and started reading from it while it floated on its own in front of him.

"Now is the time for me to strike, before they can take the field. I will give you my blood, and you will give form to my wrath!"

The sorcerer cut his hand with a claw from the other and purplish blood trickled onto the pages of the book. The droplets sizzled and smoked as the runes written on the page consumed the blood, while glowing intensely.

On the other side of the battlefield the Nomad Sky touched down while the other airships were still unloading the hundreds of knights within their holds. Sunlight shone into the cargo bay as the door opened, blinding Locke temporarily as the knights in front of him started shuffling out of the ship. He ran onto the battlefield and his eyes adjusted to the brightness just in time to witness Ir'zane unleash a spell empowered by the magical amplification from the cities of Aeris-Terran.

The sorcerer's body flared up in a wall of green flames and plumes of black smoke, which formed into the shape of a huge dragon. Wings of green flame propelled the magical monstrosity into the air, and Ir'zane flew straight for the knights of Everund. Elisander's face hardened as the king faced down the dragon of necroflame that was diving toward them.

"Get our knights on the ground and our fleet back in the sky!"

The king turned to Locke, and the look in Elisander's eyes reminded the young Therredan of the way Baryk would look at him, "Hang back and protect our friends."

Locke nodded, taking the request like a loyal knight, despite not actually being one. Elisander drew the crystal blade of Everund from his side and the light within shone like bright moonlight. They stepped forward into the crowded battlefield but went separate ways. The army of Everund stood at the ready, the knights on the ground rallied behind the king, with the magi were stationed behind them. Once the ships were airborne again, they would all be covered by the warships flying overhead.

The undead legions of Duscar stared back at the Everunder ships whose cannons glared down at them. The Duscans starting stomping their feet and chanting in Draconic. The din of their fury hammered across the fields, shaking the ground below everyone's feet. The Duscan warriors screamed through decayed vocal cords while repeatedly striking their dragon-wing swords against their dragonforged plate armor.

Elisander climbed atop a warhorse and rode out in front of his troops with the few mounted knights that they had following him, each of them wielding glaives designed to fight from horseback. He raised Everund into the sky, before drawing it down with a slashing motion and shouting so loudly that his horse reared up.

"Destroy them! Burn their bodies! Leave nothing but ash!"

Ir'zane flew over Elisander's army with an ear-splitting roar, and the vengeful dead of the fallen kingdom charged the field. The knights of Everund ran toward them, raising their weapons and shouting, "By the sword we live and die!"

The two armies then crashed into each other and violence flared up from the trading of blows and blades. Shields rang like bells when struck, swords clashed with metal shrieks, and bones cracked beneath warhammers. Blood sprayed into the air as Duscan warriors cleaved through the enchanted armor that the knights of Everund wore and down to their flesh beneath. Locke took a moment trying to find the courage to overcome the fear that was paralyzing him. But as the battle waged on before him, his legs remained stuck while he watched the carnage rising.

Aerilynn commanded the elves of Lorlinden as they loosed fire-enchanted arrowheads which set their targets ablaze, but unfortunately that did not immediately stop the revenants. The warriors of Duscar continued cutting her people down even as their undead bodies burned. The princess drew on her strained mana supply once more, casting blasts of energy to push back the dead.

Ir'zane flew overhead again, this time belching accursed necrofire onto the battle, which set the elves and their souls alight. The dragon of necromantic flame landed on top of some of Everund's horseback riders and pulverizing them before spitting soul-burning flames up the hold of an airship onto knights that were still disembarking. Behind him, the Vagrant Destiny took to the skies again as Ir'zane's tail smashed into its hull, tearing out a few cannons and some of the crew.

The warship tried to climb high enough to escape Ir'zane, but he jumped into the air following after. With fiery claws, the transmogrified sorcerer ripped into the belly of the former king Armon's ship, but before he could pull the Vagrant Destiny from the sky, a barrage of cannonballs exploded in Ir'zane's side. He screeched in pain as the blasts tore through the smoke and flames of his dragon form.

Captain Fior of The Reverent ordered her crew to reload the cannons they had just emptied into the sorcerer, but it was too late. Ir'zane dove straight through the hull of The Reverent, which detonated in an inferno of green and blue flames. The debris of The Reverent rained onto the battlefield, crushing Everunder and Duscan alike. Aeysha, along with Acacius and the other warcasters used their magic to shield the clerics of Yavon from the falling debris, while they were searching for wounded.

The Nomad Sky used its superior agility to catch the sorcerer off guard, the ship swooped down at Ir'zane, attempting to ram him. Intending to use the ship itself like a spear, Captain Kayara flew straight into Ir'zane shouting to the crew, "Brace for impact!"

However, the transformed beast pulled back enough to avoid a direct hit and the bow glanced off his shadow hide. The crew held tightly to whatever they could as they were tossed around from the impact. Kayara barely kept control of the helm as the shock went through the entire ship, "Come on baby, keep it together," she pleaded with the Nomad Sky as she regained her footing.

The airship veered to the side putting Ir'zane in range of the harpoons lining the bow of the ship, which were normally used to anchor into cliff walls while hovering to prevent drifting. Seeing them gave Kayara an idea. "Riz, Bayard, and Guzdah, I need you on those harpoons now!"

Two of the knights she ordered immediately ran to the harpoon launchers and prepared to fire but one of them refused to move, continuing to cling to the railing for support. "Riz, get up there now and get on that weapon!" Kayara ordered again. But he just shook his head no. Furious Captain Kayara shouted to the others, "Fire!"

They pulled the triggers and white smoke blasted from the launchers as large metal harpoons shot through the air. The magical dragon of smoke and flame tried unsuccessfully to dodge them but they embedded themselves painfully into his body. Kayara shouted into a metal horn to the side of the wheel, "Give me full power now!"

Drovann shouted back, "Aye!" while he flipped a bunch of switches and pulled a lever which regulated the engine pressure. The whole ship shot forward pulling them back as the props whirred loudly, within seconds the slack from the cables on the harpoons were pulled taut. Kayara spun the wheel hard making the Nomad Sky bank to the left, pulling Ir'zane with them. She gripped the wheel with all her strength as she, the ship, and the cables all strained to pull the shadowmancer away from the rest of the fleet.

"It's working!" Bayard said as he and Guzdah crawled back inside the cabin. Ir'zane screeched in pain and rage before twisting his dragon body around, and with the same motion, he smashed his tail onto the bow of the ship which tore out the launchers that were tethering him to it.

The Nomad Sky snapped away from Ir'zane and started to flip upside down. Kayara killed the engines quick and used her entire body weight to pull the wheel in the opposite direction, managing to roll out of it. The sorcerer broke free from them and headed back toward the fleet, biting the harpoons out of his sides as he flew away. Kayara held on as the weight of the ship settled from its maneuver, her curls stuck to her face, which was dripping sweat, as she yelled, "Riz! Next time I give an order, I expect it to be obeyed!"

He looked taken aback, "It was reckless and dangerous..."

"Tell me who is the captain of this ship?"

"You, but Elisander would never have risked his ship like that!"

The captain calmly reignited the engines before righting the ship again and said, "Yeah, well I'm not him and right now he is not in command of this ship, I am. And my name is Kayara."

~

Locke saw Elisander vanish in the blur of combat and it felt like his knees nearly gave out. He closed his eyes and took a deep breath, trying to steady his body. With a whisper in his mind, he reached out to Sorren.

"Ren, it's time."

Her warmth filled him and the plates of the phoenix-tail grappler separated as she replied, "We fight together this time!"

He felt her touch his mind and a connection was made. The armor segments fell down into a whip as the feather blades of the phoenix-tail slid out from beneath.

Locke's heart beat so fast it felt like it would break through his ribs and fly out of his chest. The volatile mix of fear and adrenaline coursed through him and propelled his body forward. Locke had not spent his entire life preparing for war like the knights of Everund, and he had never faced a foe as dangerous as the army of Duscar. If not for the adrenaline, he wasn't sure he'd be able to move at all.

He felt Sorren's memories of battle, how the conflicts between the warring states of her former homeland had honed her into a weapon long before being bound to the grappler. With her companionship and guidance Locke felt ready to take on the world. So long as he had Sorren by his side, he assured himself that he would never turn back, not even from certain death.

The knights protecting Locke were engaged in combat with the fiercest warriors he had ever seen, and they were losing ground. The battle was starting to close all around him, it was time he entered the fight. An unusually tall Duscan revenant wielding a great sword cut down two of the knights in front of Locke with a single sweeping strike. Locke assaulted the warrior as the knights fell, swinging the bladed whip at the rotting Duscan's head. Moving faster than Locke could have imagined, the Duscan spun his sword up along his body and brought it up to block Locke's attack just in time.

Locke adjusted, wrapping the whip of the phoenix-tail around the brute's sword and with a pull from his shoulder, he ripped the sword from the Duscan's grip. He flung the sword backwards, throwing it through the air and away from the battle. The unarmed Duscan shoulder-charged Locke and tackled him into the ground. He saw little flecks of light in his vision from hitting the ground, but even still he could see the decay of the warrior's body from the long years of its rest in the ruins of Duscar.

The Duscan warrior screamed in Locke's face and his foul corpse breath made him instantly nauseous. Locke grimaced, turning his head to the side to avoid the smell. He planted his boot in the warrior's hip and kicked with all his might, throwing the Duscan off him.

Locke rolled onto his feet and as the undead warrior was getting up, he and Ren pulled the phoenix-tail grappler across the ground before snapping it up between the warrior's legs, cleaving his leg and arm off. Locke drew the blades back in, collapsing them back into the forearm blade and then punched it straight through the skull of the Duscan. The fierce warrior twitched before dropping to the ground, the young Therredan stood over his first kill of the battle, breathing heavily.

"We did it!" he said excitedly.

Locke then looked through the storm of blades for the next fight, letting his adrenaline guide him through the battle. He noticed a knight who was fighting off two Duscan warriors at once. Locke attacked the closest warrior, who was forced to step back as the grappler's whip snapped past them, severing the arm of the other.

The Everunder used the opening made by Locke's attack to make a daring piercing strike, shoving his sword through the neck of the revenant. Pulling the blade back, he separated its head from its body, which then rolled across the battlefield. Another snap of Locke's arm brought the bladed grappler back, sawing through the midsection of the remaining Duscan making its upper body fall backward over itself.

~

The armies of Lorlinden and Everund closed in around Ir'zane, who was still breathing fire on them from above while Elisander commanded the remaining ships of the fleet through a crystal box linked to the Nomad Sky's communication systems to take aim at the transmogrified sorcerer. At the same time, Aerilynn enchanted the arrows of her archers with the power of a supernova, making them glow intensely bright. Acacius and the warcasters of Everund's magi also combined their destructive flame spells to empower them, weaving them into an enormous firestorm.

Aeysha summoned storm lightning which immediately struck the Duscan warriors, knocking them backward and setting them on fire with the arcing plasma. Dyce picked up massive pieces of Everunder ship metal and levitated them over his head before throwing them at high speed toward Ir'zane.

The dragon of green flames and black smoke swatted some of the debris away yet other pieces crashed directly into Ir'zane's magically altered form. He flinched from the damage before shifting focus on Dyce just as arrows bright as starlight pierced his body and exploded.

The spell which had transformed Ir'zane wavered from the force of the explosions, and did so again when hit by the empowered fire tornado launched by the warcasters. It faltered yet again when Acacius cast a prismatic beam of disintegration through the magical smoke and fire. The destructive magic annihilated everything it touched for the brief second it was active as it tore through Ir'zane with a high-pitched whistle.

Aeysha shouted as powerful winds lifted her into the sky, "I am your anger and your pain, Great Mother, and by your will I am your wild vengeance!"

The Keeper channeled the tempest into a single massive surge of lightning which trapped Ir'zane and burned him at the same time. While incapacitated by Aeysha's lightning, Elisander ordered his warships to fire and the sky darkened with cannon blasts. The airships of Everund unloaded on the sorcerer, the cannonballs hitting him with tremendous force before exploding and then pelting him with shrapnel.

The damage proved to be more than Ir'zane could take and his focus on the transformation slipped. The blaze of necrofire died down as the Duscan sorcerer reverted back to his normal form. Ir'zane panted heavily, soaked in sweat and injured, before realizing he was surrounded by enemies.

"Quickly, get him!" Elisander shouted, but the shadowmancer was already dissipating into a wispy cloud of shadow. The sorcerer cackled madly as he soared over the battlefield and back to the safety of the towers of Terran. Elisander shouted, "Press the attack, push them to the walls of the city!" He commanded the warships to take position behind him, using the cannons firing from their broadsides to clear the way for the knights to follow.

Elisander rode deep into the fray pushing his horse through the hordes of undead, his sword made quick work of the Duscan warriors as the crystal blade turned their rotten flesh and bone to ash. Its brilliant glowing light gleamed through the air as Elisander swung it overhead, cleaving Ir'zane's army in two. The knights following him skewered, hacked, and kicked their way through the swaths of reanimated warriors which were attacking them from all sides. Eventually, when he felt he made it far enough into the Duscan army, Elisander raised his blade straight into the air, then motioned with his free hand to the airships to move around for an attack.

The Penitent and Vagrant Destiny moved from the rearguard position, flying to the left and right of the battlefield, flanking the entire army. With most of the Duscans' attention focused on Elisander and the knights of Everund, few noticed the airships moving in behind them. The hordes of the dead fought to get to the king of Everund, scrambling over one another for the glory of taking his head for Ir'zane. They got their chance as a Duscan managed to drive a spear through the gaps in the warhorse's armor, stopping Elisander mid-charge while his steed reared in pain. The young king struggled to stay on the horse as it screamed and kicked, yet was still able to cut the head off one of the Duscan warriors approaching him.

Elisander gripped the reins tightly, trying to get the horse to move but it fell, its legs buckled and the king was thrown off of its back as the horse collapsed onto the battlefield. Elisander rolled across the ground and stood back up, tossing aside the cloak which had gotten wrapped around him during his tumble.

Weathered blades and spears emerged from the dust as several Duscan warriors threw themselves at him, all vying for a killing blow. He lifted his shield, absorbing as many attacks as he could, and used the sword of Everund to parry the others. The king found himself momentarily alone, fending off attacks from all sides before his knights could catch up to him.

The Vigilant and Vagrant Destiny turned slowly overhead while aiming their cannons towards the unsuspecting army of the dead that they were flanking.

"Hold the line!" Elisander shouted to the mounted knights who caught up to him.

"Form a protective circle around the king!" commanded one of the knights as she leapt from her horse. She grabbed the reins and handed them to Elisander, while the mounted knights circled the two of them, fighting back the vengeful dead assailing them.

From Locke's position, he saw Elisander fall from his horse, then disappear into the silhouettes of the Duscan warriors surrounding him. While he stared at the spot where Elisander vanished, a knight of Everund was killed directly in front of the young Therredan by way of a blackened spear through his chestplate, spraying blood all over Locke. Forming the grappler into the forearm blade, Locke jumped forward while the warrior was pulling her spear back and he punched the blade into her chest.

She dropped her spear but was still squirming, and she grabbed Locke's arm and tried to pull the blade from her body. Sorren spread the feather shaped blades out, which tore through the warrior's rotten sinew and flesh. Locke pulled his hand back, and with a quick motion of his arm the grappler lashed back out into a whip, which then shredded the Duscan warrior's upper body and threw pieces of her into the air. He wiped the blood from his face, smearing it mostly as he looked up at the Everunder ships taking aim at the horde of revenants.

Ir'zane's sadistic bloodlust overtook him as he spread his necromantic fire across the battle, and he was so enthralled in the violence that he did not notice the airships flanking his warriors. By the time he caught sight of them in the corners of his eyes they were already behind his forces. He was watching his whole army close in around the king, just as Elisander motioned for the airships to attack. From out of both ships row after row of cannon bay doors flew open, barrels poked out as the cannons rolled into place. Ir'zane commanded his warriors to evade, but with their attention on the king of Everund, most of them did not hear his orders.

Clouds of white smoke rose from the sides of the warships, hurling thunder across the battlefield as heavy cannonballs hit solid earth and exploded. The knights of Everund raised their shields to protect themselves as a wall of exploding metal flew up from the ground as the cannon fire tore through the Duscans. With their attention diverted, the knights and king Elisander drove their blades into the distracted warriors, killing many of them. The earth shook violently from the relentless barrage of cannon fire obliterating any revenant unlucky enough to be caught in the blasts.

The warcasters on board the ships took to the decks and lobbed bolts of fire and ice, throwing blasts of raw power and raining unstable energies of primordial chaos which blew apart the bodies of the reanimated they hit. Bombardiers and archers fought alongside the magi, adding their own devastating attacks to the assault. A hailstorm of arrows pierced their legs and feet, nailing the undead to the ground so that they could not escape from the grenades of stone, filled with volatile alchemy which fell on top of them and scattered their smoldering remains across the battlefield.

Ir'zane opened a hand filled with green necrotic fire, and he threw it towards the gunship closest to him. One of the magi saw it heading for them and tried to counterspell the attack, attempting to undo the magic that wove it together, but found it could not be undone.

"Take cover!" he shouted as the blast sprayed across the deck, consuming them in its rampage. Those that were burned found the dark magic latched onto their life force, burning their mana like fuel. They erupted in a blaze of green flames no matter how little of the original blast touched them.

Ir'zane threw another bolt of green fire into the hull of The Vigilant, which was shelling the revenants near the front the gate to the city of Terran. The Vigilant's hull shuddered from the blast and the warship careened, almost colliding with another ship. The fire on the deck spread rapidly from person to person, but did little structural damage to the ship. People jumped from the deck while screaming in agony as they ignited.

Without a crew to control it, the ship slowly drifted toward the ground where it crashed like metal thunder onto the warring armies below. As the smoke and dust cleared, the warriors of Duscar crawled from under the wreckage and bent their broken bones back into place as though nothing had happened.

The battle was so intense that Locke completely lost himself in it as he and Sorren cut through seemingly endless waves of the undead. The screams of cannonballs, the dying, and the Duscan revenants filled the air as mist of blood stained the grass. Locke took a moment to collect himself, and he realized that what few knights still remained with him were quickly being overrun. The Everunders on the front lines were weary, fatigue was a weakness not shared by the tireless revenants of Duscar.

The Duscans not only had superior fighting experience, but their greatest advantage was in just how difficult the revenants proved to destroy. The dragon blood warriors' rotten flesh was less limber than it had been in life, but it gave them an unholy resilience to damage. They were able to take several lethal attacks and continue to fight, they could lose limbs and be hardly affected, they could be pierced by dozens of arrows, or have their bones crushed and still not come to a final rest.

Locke had to fend off attacks from multiple enemies as the knights around him fell. Not far and just as encircled by the dead, Elisander got back onto a horse, and continued fighting off the undead while waiting for the airships that were still operational to finish reloading. When they did, the Penitent rained destruction on the revenants with their heavy cannons, providing relief to the beleaguered knights on the front line. The king's strategy was paying off; the wall of Duscan warriors once as thick and dense as the forests of the Western Wood were now thinned out by the flanking ships.

As the fighting around them intensified, Locke and Sorren danced through combat together, but the blades of the phoenix-tail grappler were simply not enough to drive back the army of Duscar.

Locke's lungs ached with each breath, his muscles burned with every movement, and his sweat evaporated off of his skin as steam.

Locke was pushing himself to his limit, but the connection he had with Sorren never felt stronger, and as they fought with increasing desperation it unleashed her true power, igniting the grappler weapon with magical fire. They whirled like an inferno, spinning through the multitudes of undead while the red-hot weapon sliced through their armor and lit them on fire. Embers rose into the sky as the army of Duscar fell back to the gates of Aeris-Terran.

From behind the barrier, Ir'zane continued to throw bolts of green fire into the Everunder army despite it becoming clear that his forces on the ground were losing. The Penitent flew toward the tower from which the Duscan sorcerer was attacking everyone and unleashed a barrage of cannons at him, but unfortunately once again Aeris-Terran's magic shield absorbed the blasts. Mage commander Acacius Lordain looked on dismayed as yet another attack failed to get the shadowmancer before they sought the assistance of princess Aerilynn.

"If we don't deal with that barrier, we're not taking the cities."

Aerilynn looked at the tower, and then the wall.

"You're right, but those spells are powered by the cities themselves, which are currently being protected by that barrier. Ir'zane is sealed safely inside."

That's when inspiration struck, she looked at the ground while a plan began forming in her mind.

"You can't catch a spider with a chipped cup," she said.

Acacius seemed a bit puzzled by her statement, but they followed her eyes to the ground.

"Ley lines!" Acacius shouted as they figured it out.

Aeysha and Dyce looked at each other and shrugged in confusion, as neither of them had a clue as to what the magi were talking about.

"Aeris-Terran is a powerful locus, a place where ley lines converge. That's what powers the defenses of the cities," Acacius explained.

"And if we can sever that connection, we could take out a portion of the barrier!" Aerilynn continued.

"A chip in the cup," Acacius said, smiling brightly.

Aerilynn nodded excitedly.

"Precisely," she concluded.

"And how do we do that?" Aeysha grumbled, obviously annoyed that she did not get what they were referring to.

Acacius looked at Aerilynn.

"The big guy?" they asked, and Aerilynn grinned before confirming, "The big guy."

Dyce smiled as he realized they were talking about him.

"I'm big," he said, pointing to himself.

Acacius patted the elemental on the arm, "Yes, you are."

Aerilynn led their small team around the edge of the battlefield, blasting the undead warriors in their way with her magic. Aeysha empowered Dyce by charging him with lightning while he covered their rear using the power of his magnetite body to pull armored Duscan warriors into his devastating punches which buried their broken bodies in the dirt.

Acacius waved a hand in front of their own face while casting a spell which made their eyes glow intensely blue. With the spell active, it gave them the ability to see the rivers of mana flowing deep beneath the crust of Averon.

"There's a major ley line directly below us that runs under the wall, I believe it's what is feeding the barrier around the gate."

Aerilynn swept away her matted hair, as sweat ran down her face, looking visibly exhausted.

"Take Aeysha and Dyce to the convergence point and sever the ley line's connection. I will hold the dead of Duscar here," she said.

Acacius made a gesture to protest leaving her unguarded, but was immediately interrupted by Aerilynn.

"There's no time to argue, get it done or we are all lost."

They nodded sternly.

"I will see it done, my lady."

They hoped that those would not be the last words the two of them exchanged as Acacius left her side.

With their eyes illuminated by magical sight, Acacius led them to where the ley line met Terran's outer walls while the princess fought off the revenants with starbursts whose brilliant light burned and blinded the Duscans. Acacius groped along the stone wall, looking frantically for the exact point where the ley line ran beneath the wall.

While they were busy searching for the place to sever the convergence, Ir'zane finally took notice of them sneaking around his forces. The crazed shadowmancer threw a blast of necromantic fire at Acacius, but Dyce stepped in front of them to take the blast himself. The green fire splashed across the elemental's stone skin and fizzled away harmlessly.

"Many thanks, friend," Acacius said, relieved.

Aeysha's body shifted ephemerally into tempest winds as she focused her power as Keeper, and with the fury of storm in hand she fired lightning bolts back at Ir'zane.

Predictably the Duscan sorcerer again blocked the attacks against him with the magical barrier protecting Aeris-Terran, but Acacius was determined to make it the last time that he could.

"Big guy!" they shouted, and Dyce looked at them quizzically. Acacius marked the weak spot on the wall with a hasty rune and yelled, "Tear it down!"

The lodestone elemental charged the outer wall, rock-sliding as fast as he could, passing through the magical shield and throwing his shoulder into the stone, shattering it. Rubble flew through the air as an enormous crack appeared in the wall, splitting the whole thing in two. When the outer wall broke, it severed the connection from the gate to the ley lines below. Starved of its energy source, the barrier it fueled powered down.

The knights of Everund cheered as they stormed the gates of Terran, while Ir'zane looked on with growing fear as his undead legions were pushed back against the city walls. Gleaming swords cleaved through dead flesh and the knights broke through the Duscan ranks under the command of their young king.

Elisander pressed his knights forward and coordinated devastating aerial strikes from his fleet of airships from the thick of combat. Cannonball blasts sent clouds of dust into the air, hurling massive chunks of stone into the sky. The dead wailed in impotent rage as they fell at the feet of the knights, as they were unable to slow Everund's righteous advance.

Ir'zane's closed fist lit up with fire, ready to throw another deadly bolt, when out of the corner of his eye he saw an airship close in on him. Before he could throw his conjured flame, the ground below his feet fell away. The Penitent's heavy cannons hit support pillars, smashing in the ground level of the tower Ir'zane was standing on, and as it collapsed, he was flung backwards with the debris. The ball of energy he held tightly in his hand slid out between his fingers and exploded at his side, the flare of the blast lashing out at his exposed skin.

"Frashaat!" he cursed in Draconic while falling toward the ground. The sorcerer's body was enveloped in a shroud of black smoke, dark as night, and Ir'zane slithered away from the damage while the tower crashed onto the vacant streets below. The din of battle faded into the distance as the shadowmancer escaped through the alleyways of the deserted mage city.

Even in neglect, however, the cities retained their beauty; hidden mystery and majesty seemed to be built into the landscape of it. It was a shame there was no one now to look upon their splendor, as it was abandoned to its repose. Ir'zane flew away from the outer walls of Terran, silent as a whisper, and slid back down to the ground when he reached a safe distance from the battle that was inevitably closing in on him.

Falling Stars

Ir'zane's blackened, clawed toes clacked against clay stones as he ran through the muraled streets of Terran. Blood dripped from a wound on his forehead which he wiped away with the back of his hand, smearing it across his face and matting his hair. Ir'zane escaped to the city center, stepping into a park with a long since dried up fountain at its nexus. All around it pebbles and dust levitated while swirling in the air like silt in murky water. The blood-shot eye embedded in his right palm quivered as he reached for the fountain.

He traced a sigil carved into it and a low buzz of energy emanated from the ground beneath his feet. A bright blue light enveloped him as he flew upwards, heading towards the spires which hung above him like stalactites in a cave. For the briefest moment he was suspended in midair, floating over Terran, then came the abrupt pull of gravity from above him and his ankles were pulled over his head.

He deftly spun through the air, and fell upward to the streets of the floating city of Aeris. He landed crouched, absorbing the shock gracefully just as he had when he called the city home. As soon as he stood up, he felt the back of his mind licked by familiar voices from the Book of Souls, which hung open at his waist. *Tear at its soul! Make it crawl, take its legs and make it crawl!* Hearing the eerie sound of so many voices at once was disquieting, even to a mind as twisted as Ir'zane's.

The void awaits you, shadow master. It hungers, ready to reclaim your soul for your failure. The presence within the book was taunting him, but it was quickly silenced by the back of Ir'zane's hand as he slapped it off his hip and onto the ground.

"My failure? It is your useless gifts and spells that have failed me!" the deranged shadowmancer said as he stormed away, heading for Eldric's sanctuary which was at the top of the tallest tower in the floating city. *Traitor! Kill it!* The voices screamed after him. He moved with haste towards the door of Eldric's tower, shouting, "I am no one's puppet!"

With a furtive glance 'upwards' to the battle raging on the ground below, Ir'zane knew it would not be long before his enemies caught up to him. Gripping the doors to the Tower of the Ascended with magical force, Ir'zane tore them off of their hinges. The splinters spewed onto the ground, while in the city of Terran below, the battle-worn Everunders filled the streets.

The remaining ships of the fleet surrounded the floating sanctuary as the shields were deactivated. Cobblestones shot into the air around Ir'zane from exploding cannon fire as he slipped through the doorway and up the stone steps inside the sanctuary. The tower shook and waterfalls of dust slid from cracks in the stone, cascading down onto Ir'zane as he climbed the stairs.

A screeching cloud of debris took out a chunk out of the stairwell in front of him as well as the outer wall of the tower, revealing a patch of blue sky through which Ir'zane looked up and saw hundreds of knights running through the city below. He jumped across the gap, continuing his climb toward the top where he could reach his former mentor's sanctuary. When he finally made it to the sealed chamber, his claws scratched in desperation at the sigils transcribed on the border of the magical seal, to no avail. His disheveled black hair stuck to his sweaty face, and his green eyes shimmered with fear in the dim light.

Ir'zane traced the symbols and read the incantations in as many combinations as he could remember, going faster and making more errors in his fervor. A loud slap echoed from the empty chamber below, and he paused. When he looked down the spiraling staircase, he saw the shadows of tentacles appear in the basin of sunlight resting at the base of the tower. Exhausted and nearly out of breath as he was, he could not tap into his mana. It took a calm and focused mind to use it and a rested body to draw it from. He tried to force open the seal on Eldric's chamber with his umbramancy, but again it would not give.

"Open, damn it!" Ir'zane screamed as he pounded his fists on the unmoved door.

Ir'zane heard the whispers of innumerable disembodied voices mocking him and threatening him. *Agony awaits your eternal embrace! Feed your soul to the damned, false herald!*

Ir'zane sneered and spat his words in reply.

"So long as I draw breath, no one will rule me!"

He tried once more to focus his mind on opening the sealed sanctuary while ignoring the hateful sounds assailing him, but the pain from resisting the screams of the damned blurred his sight and scattered his thoughts. Black tentacles groped out from the binding between the pages of the Book of Souls, while the heavy book dragged itself through the dust like some strange mollusk, leaving a trail of purple-colored fluid which bubbled intensely as the accursed grimoire followed Ir'zane up the stairs of the tower.

His hands trembled as he cradled his head, and he fell to his knees as the book crawled toward him. Ir'zane was no longer aware of any individual voice; they all became indistinguishable, discordant noise. The book pulled itself awkwardly up the stairs as a nauseating aura overtook the Duscan sorcerer, and this time the voices he heard came from his own people.

They grew louder as the book crawled closer, filling his mind with terrible pain and terrifying visions of his people tearing him apart. He fell to the stairs, shaking and shrieking as the voices chanted something in unison amidst their rambling agony. Ir'zane tried not to listen to them, covering his ears with his hands, but the words were inside his mind. It seemed the more he tried to block them out, the louder the voices grew and the more recognizable the maddening gibberish became.

Perhaps to escape the misery of his head feeling like it was being torn to shreds, his consciousness started to latch onto sounds repeating in the storm of screaming, disconnected sounds which combined into a word; a word he had never heard before. The word hidden in their chanting was 'Uruzel,' and as soon as he knew it, his eyes went white and rolled back in his head. He shook violently and knew no more as the revelation tore at his soul, for his sanity completely abandoned him upon knowing that dark and terrible word.

The tentacles crawled out from the book, wrapping themselves around his slack face and shoving themselves into his mouth, which was frozen open in terror. They coiled tightly around his head and the book pressed itself to Ir'zane's face, filling his body with liquid darkness. His body could not contain the immense evil presence now crawling its way into him and it spewed its hateful form all around, filling the room.

The darkness coalesced into a mass of shadow-like smoke with Ir'zane's limp body at its dark heart. The shapeless darkness quickly filled the confines of the small tower, its bulk pressed against the stone walls which strained before giving way under the force of its expansive growth.

~

Elisander's vengeful glare looked upward, seeking any sign of the cowardly shadowmancer. While he was searching for Ir'zane, the Tower of the Ascended shattered before his eyes as the horror trapped within broke free. The top of the tower fell away from the spells which held it down to Aeris, dropping it toward Terran through the gap of sky between the cities. Shadows of falling stones appeared over Elisander and his knights, who ducked out of the way of cascading debris from the collapsing sanctuary chamber.

The ground trembled from the impact, knocking many off their feet. As the dust settled, weapons were drawn again and all stood ready to face whatever might emerge out of the rubble. Smoke rose as if from some unseen inferno and it coalesced into an enormous shapeless mass the color of deepest night, darker still than the expanses of the Infinite between stars.

Shadows of hideous limbs and tentacles appeared from the malevolent darkness, before reabsorbing themselves into the entropic mass surrounding its host. The knights encircled the thing with caution as their courage waned. They stared wide-eyed and with bated breath at the indescribable monstrosity looming over them as it thrashed and shrieked with primal malevolence.

Elisander was already unnerved by the unknowable, flailing thing even before the aura of pure dread emanated from the shadow of Uruzel which filled their minds with horrific visions. Their greatest fears manifested before their eyes: one knight saw a giant queen spider rising from the rubble, covered in thousands of her young that crawled over everyone.

Another knight saw a cyclops rampaging out of the shadows, ripping people in half with its bare hands and yet another saw themselves being set on fire by a cackle of imps. Each of them heard screaming from unnumbered voices, which were so loud it caused them excruciating pain. Paralyzed by fear and agony, the knights grabbed their heads, adding their screams to the cacophony of madness. The knights of Everund slashed frantically at the thing, but their blades passed through it like they were cutting smoke, and arrows loosed by deadeye archers passed through its body as if it was not truly there.

Captain Kayara finally caught up to the king, only to become trapped by the psychic horror of the shadow of Uruzel. She was paralyzed, fighting against the terror coursing through her body. Kayara stood before the rising abomination, carving into its ephemeral body with a series of futile attacks. Above her, shadowy tendrils morphed into scythe-tipped, multi-jointed insectoid arms which were poised to strike. The Archmage Geryn saw the imminent attack and charged her as the captain swung her sword, desperately trying to damage the thrashing horror. Geryn dove for her, shoving her out of the way just in time as the looming extremities came down where Kayara had been. The shadows passed right through Geryn, but caused no physical damage; there was only a bright white flash, and then the Archmage's eyes went blank, with his body falling under its own weight.

Kayara looked on in terror and screamed with grief as Archmage Geryn lay motionless upon the ground. The entropic horror's limbs were absorbed by the writhing mass, only to be replaced with newly-formed and even more hideous appendages. Kayara picked herself back up as the shadow of Uruzel grew over Geryn's body, its size now filling the street.

The captain started to pull the Archmage's body out by his pauldrons, but the darkness threatened to consume her too if she stayed there any longer. She let go of him tearfully and stumbled backward as his corpse was covered by the growing darkness. Elisander hurried to her side pulling her away from the entropic horror before it consumed her as well.

"Retreat!" he shouted to the others, while Kayara looked up at him, her eyes mixed with grief and fear.

"Fall back! Out of the city! Regroup in the fields! We'll lure this thing into the open and hit it with everything we've got."

The knights withdrew from the shadow of Uruzel and its frenetic attacks, and Elisander helped carry Kayara as they hurried out of the city. When they were far enough away from the blasphemous thing which Ir'zane had unknowingly unleashed upon the world, the screaming in their minds ceased. Elisander looked back and saw the hideous thing flailing aimlessly as it crawled slowly after them. Arriving at Terran's gates they were met by Locke and Aerilynn, who had just cut through the last revenants still fighting there.

"Get back! There's no time to explain! We have to get away from the city!" Elisander's voice was commanding and filled with urgency.

Locke did not wait for a glimpse of whatever it was that drove back the brave host of Everund, a feat that even the undead armies of Duscar had not managed. Aerilynn, however, looked past the knights as they fled, standing at the gate and staring into Terran. Elisander looked over his shoulder to see her lingering and handed Kayara off to another Everunder.

"Take her to safety and get all of our people back away from the cities," he said.

The knight nodded and took the captain away. Kayara was shaken so badly she did not notice that she was handed off and mumbled to the knight like she was still talking to the king. Elisander approached Aerilynn and gently grabbed her arm.

"We have to get out of here. It's coming," he said.

But she was frozen, Aerilynn's eyes were transfixed on the end of the street, and she continued staring without acknowledging him. She saw strange shadows cast upon the ground which contorted and writhed as the shapeless thing slid into view. Her eyes widened in terror as they fell upon its chaos.

"Aerilynn please, get back! We must fall back!" Elisander implored, but after seeing it, she turned to the elves of Lorlinden.

"Quickly! Take our people and fall back with the Everunders."

She faced Elisander, "We will follow you."

The king of Everund let go of her and went after his knights, but one of Aerilynn's advisors protested as the princess started to follow them away from the cities.

"Our magic is more powerful than that of these humans, I'm certain we can stop whatever the shadowmancer has summoned."

The princess shook her head.

"What I saw was no dark spell or conjured beast. You think the few of us here can hope to stop what our ancestors could not?"

His eyes widened and his mouth fell open.

"It cannot be," he said.

"Go now," she said firmly, looking back at the approaching darkness. Aerilynn dug symbols into the dirt at the edges of the city and drew them in a large arc through the fields.

"So, you have found us at last, world-eater," she muttered to herself while she carved intricate sigils in the earth, preparing a complicated spell. "Too bad for you that you've come too late to kill my world. Silthradel is already dead!" she said under her breath.

The circle of symbols she drew expanded until it nearly filled the field in which she stood. The princess said through gritted teeth, "This world, Averon, is all that remains now, and I will not allow it to fall!"

Instead of moving back to a safer distance with the rest of the elves, Aerilynn was making a final stand, despite telling her own people to get away. She hastily finished the massive ring of sigils before taking her place at its center.

"For the countless cries of help you silenced, I will answer. For taking my father, I will bring the very stars down upon you. This I do for all worlds and the lives that you have consumed. For my family, and for all of elven kind!"

She tapped into her mana and channeled it into the ring of symbols around her as the shade of Uruzel crawled through the shattered gate of the city, its writhing chaos creeping toward the princess. She slowed her breathing, closed her eyes and entered a state of deep focus which felt like dropping into the ocean of her mind.

Aerilynn raised her arms into the sky and as she did, glowing silver sigils used for astromancy appeared above her as if drawn by unseen hands. Tremors shook the ground beneath everyone's feet as her meta-sigil was completed. She tapped into the ley lines below with the sigils on the ground, and used them to amplify her magic with the same source that powered the mage cities. She reached out with her consciousness, letting her mind drift through the Infinite, into the abyss of empty space beyond the world of Averon.

Princess Aerilynn's mind was nearly torn apart from the effort of her spell reaching through such vast distances, but as the magic strained her consciousness, she finally happened upon an ideal asteroid near the edge of the solar system. It was just the right size; too small and it would break up in the atmosphere, too large and the planet would not recover from the impact.

Her mind warped the space around the asteroid, gently pulling the massive chunk of stone towards Averon. Trying to get the speed, and the aim right for an object traveling so fast and so far, was a nearly impossible shot, but if she did not succeed, she was certain the entropic horror would consume them all.

"Where is Aerilynn?" Locke asked as the elves of Lorlinden rallied to the new defense point. An elf lord pointed solemnly back towards Aeris-Terran.

"She is there."

Locke looked over his shoulder and saw the princess standing alone in the field as another wave of tremors rippled beneath their feet. Locke made to go after her, but the lord grabbed him.

"You cannot interrupt her!"

Locke struggled against him.

"Get off of me!" he shouted back.

"You don't understand, Therredan. She is channeling an unbelievably powerful spell. She must not be interrupted!"

Locke grabbed the elves' arms and struggled to break his grip.

"I said let go!"

The ground shook again much stronger, this time nearly knocking them off their feet.

"Those sigils are full of her mana, if you stop her, she will lose control of it - it could kill her!"

Locke watched helplessly while the crawling madness spread into the fields outside of Terran. Aerilynn backed up slowly, luring the shade of Uruzel toward the center of her spell. The princess harnessed the rivers of mana flowing through the planet from the ley lines below, the raw power reached from her fingertips out into space in the direction of the asteroid.

Aerilynn's mana turned her spellwork into a brilliant shade of magenta as her life essence bled from her and into the sigils which drew the asteroid. Aerilynn felt the hideous aura from the shade of Uruzel hitting her, and heard whispers of voices unnumbered screaming inside her mind. Everyone else heard an explosion louder than thunder, which could be heard from halfway around the world. The sound drew their attention upward as a massive ball of fire appeared in the sky.

"She's gonna get us all killed!" Elisander shouted as the asteroid smashed into Averon's atmosphere.

"My king!"

Elisander spun around to see Acacius Lordain approach him.

"I think I know a way we could contain the blast, but it might be a little bit dangerous," they said.

The king looked at the meteor engulfing the sky.

"That thing could create an endless winter from which the planet may never recover. I'd say a little danger can't hurt."

Acacius smiled gently.

"I think if enough magi work together, we could craft a spell matrix that might be large enough to contain the blast with a null barrier."

Elisander frowned.

"That's not dangerous Acacius, that's suicidal. The amount of force that thing is carrying would kill you all."

They nodded.

"Most likely. But better us than the whole world."

The king did not want to admit it, but Acacius was right.

"The fate of our world is in your hands. I pray they are strong enough." Elisander placed his hand on Acacius' shoulder as a farewell gesture. They nodded and ran off, grabbing every mage crazy enough to attempt their plan and hastened the brave casters to the elven princess' side.

"What are you doing? Stay back!" Aerilynn shouted, her eyes glowing with magenta fire from the strain of her spell.

"Naturally, we are here to save the world," Acacius smirked, and the other magi lined up on either side of Aerilynn. The princess nearly broke her concentration trying to warn them, "Seriously... get back! It's too dangerous, you need to get everyone as far from here as you can!"

The magi began drawing their null barrier sigils while Acacius turned to Aerilynn.

"We're going to need you too, I'm afraid," they said.

She looked stunned by their brazenness, but when she recognized the spell, they were casting, she understood.

"We'll have but the blink of an eye!" Acacius said as they and the other magi spread out into position. "We're only going to get one shot at this, so breathe as one, move as one, and we can contain the blast!" they shouted.

The shade of Uruzel was nearly upon them, assaulting all of their minds as the magi attempted to complete the spell. The spellcasters struggled through pain and insanity to keep their focus on the barrier. Aerilynn let go of the meteor astromancy with one of her hands so she could cast the null barrier spell along with the other magi. She struggled to hold the massive projectile on its trajectory using only one hand for channeling and with her attention split between the two spells.

"Everyone ready!" Acacius shouted, and the magi of Everund who were positioned in a hexagram formation around the outside of

Aerilynn's meteor sigil readied their spells. The shade of Uruzel writhed wildly in all directions as if it was trying to move toward each of them simultaneously. Aerilynn was drawing her sigil single-handed, unlike the other magi, who were able to use both of their hands to construct the complicated magical symbols.

"Like putting out a fire with a pot lid," Acacius said unconvincingly as they braced for the impact.

Aerilynn had seconds left to finish the spell for the null barrier, as the raging meteor flew towards the ground at speeds that she could not imagine. When she completed the final sigil, the meteor hit the planet, smashing into the entropic abomination with a violent explosion. The magi combined their sigils, casting the spell as one and created a magical barrier which enclosed the entire blast wave. The princess held onto the sigils projecting the barrier with both hands as she struggled to contain the explosive forces within it. Her hands burned from holding onto the sigils which were glowing brightly with overwhelming power. The magic symbols became blinding balls of light beneath her fingers while the ground beneath her shook from the force of the impact.

Aerilynn held their spell together despite the pain, while the barrier emitted sounds like chimes from the magic straining to its breaking point. At the points of greatest stress, the threads of the spellwork were visible to the naked eye, appearing as golden strands of gossamer light, woven in a delicate lattice which was slowly ripping apart from the pressure. Onlookers held each other, trying not to fall as the last of the shockwave escaped the barrier.

The Heart of Darkness

Acacius Lordain's gambit paid off for the most part, though the effort of containing the meteor blast seemed to have claimed the lives of a couple of magi. Acacius themself fought to stay on their feet as their muscles were shaking, and their fingers burned from holding the overcharged barrier sigils. The spell had completely drained Acacius and they collapsed from fatigue. A quiet fell over the survivors as the fallout from the meteor settled, and a sigh of relief escaped from everyone as the tension which had held their breath finally released. No one moved or said anything, they just stood frozen in awe of what just transpired. As the dust from the impact settled, a weakened Acacius' stared into the crater when their eyes widened in terror.

"That's impossible..." they said as Ir'zane's crushed body, which was sticking up out of the ground at the bottom of the crater, began twitching. Darkness started flowing from out of his broken form as his body slowly levitated into the sky above the crater. Everyone stared in horror and dismay as the blob of darkness rose again, twisting into endless terrifying mockeries of life once more. They heard animal sounds of an uncountable number of species that were howling, shrieking, and chattering coming from within the umbral monstrosity as it swelled back out to its full size.

Through the haze of swirling darkness, Elisander saw Ir'zane's crushed body at the core of its shapeless mass. Ir'zane's empty eyes stared back into Elisander's own, making the king's stomach tighten uncomfortably while watching the chaotic shadowy thing undulating and whipping its malformed grotesqueries about.

Elisander muttered to himself, "It cannot be stopped... death itself is upon us."

The terrible swirling darkness morphed into hideous shapes of innumerable alien extremities while it climbed out of the crater. The thing's vulgar putrescence overcame the horrified witnesses, choking the air from their lungs with a noxious odor that made them hack and cough. It bubbled and thrashed, throwing itself around in random directions while Acacius started to crawl away. The other magi who survived were struggling to get away from the monstrosity too while nearly blinded from the rotting corpse smell which emanated from it.

One of the magi closest to the hideous thing, narrowly dodged the unholy violence of its phantom extremities lashing out at them as they ran away. Acacius was still so drained that when they tried to stand again, they fell backward, and narrowly avoided getting hit by a tentacle. The mage standing next to them was not so lucky; the shadowy tentacle missed Acacius and crashed through him instead.

The mage put up his arms to defend himself in a futile gesture of self-preservation, but the shadow passed right through his body. A flash of white light burst from the young man as his soul was torn out of him, and his body crumpled to the ground. Acacius tried crawling toward Aerilynn, who collapsed at the edge of the crater, but they lost consciousness from the effort.

The hideous shadow thing thrashed ferociously, and several of Everund's magi were caught up in its furor. The casters fought for their lives against the shadow reaching for them, but their spells were rendered completely useless against its ethereal form. Before long they were consumed by the swelling darkness washing over them like a flood which devoured their souls. The bodies piled up around the swelling mass of entropic darkness, and it seemed to be growing larger with each kill, as well as more unstable.

Locke ran past everyone trying to hold him back, sprinting across the fields while jumping over bodies and shields laying in the battlefield, he ran through arrows sticking out of the ground in numbers as plentiful as the grass. Sorren was startled by his reckless action and touched his mind.

"Do you know what you are doing?" she asked apprehensively.

"I have to save my friends!" he said, but Sorren heard the uncertainty in him.

"Do you think we can save them both?"

Locke did not answer, afraid to say what he really thought, because he was pretty sure that he could get one of them to safety in time and definitely sure there was not time for both. Desperation and adrenaline were flowing through his veins like the steam pressure through the engines of an Everunder airship as he ran towards imminent death. The shadow of Uruzel was growing so close to his friends that he could not see them around the hideous thing. As Locke ducked beneath a flurry of its grotesque limbs, he found the defenseless mage commander first, without hesitation he grabbed them under their arms and dragged Acacius to a safe distance.

As Aerilynn was slowly regaining consciousness, Locke handed Acacius off to a cleric of Yavon, who had just caught up to the young Therredan. The cleric carried the mage commander away and without a word Locke went back for Aerilynn. The princess was attempting to stand, but was so weak she could only get to her knees, able to do little else to get away from the shade of Uruzel.

"Aerilynn!" Locke yelled, reaching for her as she finally stood up shakily, he watched as the entropic horror grew over her. A tentacle from the shade of Uruzel wound up to strike the princess but Locke jump tackled her, hoping to shove her out of the way of it. Aerilynn desperately tried to grab onto him, but only got the astromancer compass from around his neck instead.

While they were tangled up together, Locke tucked the blades of the phoenix-tail grappler away as much as he could and pushed her out of the reach of the attack by extending the whip blade outward. The chain of the compass around Locke's neck snapped as she tumbled backward. Aerilynn was thrown to the ground hard, which knocked the wind out of her. The princess was unaware she was bleeding from a scrape on her arm while she got up slowly from the fall. Aerilynn was spellbound by the nightmare scene occurring in front of her.

The monstrous tentacle, having narrowly missed the princess as she was just out of reach, had pierced Locke through the heart. Caught in the shade of Uruzel's terrible grip, the wail of dead voices from countless worlds pierced his mind as his soul was torn out. He screamed in fear as his body became cold, numb, and empty. To Locke's eyes the world disappeared, fading into total darkness.

Aerilynn screamed breathlessly, reaching out for Locke as the cleric picked her up off the ground and pulled her away.

~

Locke felt himself floating weightlessly in a space which was entirely too dark to see within. He could feel the void gnaw at him hungrily as his soul bled from his body. Locke thrashed in a panic, trying to keep from being swallowed by the endless dark but the shadow clung to him heavily. He felt the malevolent darkness seething all around him, but as his eyes searched the lightless abyss for an escape, a warm orange glow drifted playfully toward him.

Locke's eyes adjusted to its light and he saw that it was a single feather of phoenix down. He grabbed onto it, and it immediately started pulling him upward, but to where it was taking him Locke could not tell. He held onto the feather tightly, but Locke felt the mindless will of the void try to drag him down into it.

The power of the phoenix down was stronger than the force of the abyss, however, and slowly it pulled him out of the void and back toward his body. His soul emerged from out the shapeless mass of the shade of Uruzel and he saw a blazing phoenix flying over his body. Sorren's garnet eyes lit up when she saw his soul being pulled free of the entropic horror.

"Locke! Thank the stars!" she said glowingly. He seemed to have returned to the exact moment he was attacked, as his body was still frozen in terror with a shadow tentacle piercing his chest. But his attention was drawn to the grappler on his arm, which was incandescent, dazzling in a vibrant crimson hue, the same aura which radiated from Sorren's plumage.

"Ren? What's happening to me?" he said, trying to pull away from the sticky strands of the void still clinging to his soul.

"You may have died a little."

"What?!" he shouted, nearly losing his grip on the phoenix down. She ruffled her feathers, squawking in alarm.

"Don't let go! Remain calm!"

Locke struggled to keep his grip on the tiny feather as the last strands of darkness strained to maintain their hold on him as well.

"Remain calm? You just said I died!"

Sorren landed on top of the grappler, wrapping her lengthy tail plumage around the arm of his body.

"A little! I said you died a little!"

The strands of darkness snapped, releasing his soul from the hold of the shade of Uruzel, and it flew toward his body rapidly. Locke tried to hold onto the phoenix down as his soul hurtled toward his body, but it slipped from his fingers and disappeared.

Something happened then that Locke could not explain, without the phoenix down, his soul was unable to attach itself to his body correctly. While Locke tried to put his soul back into his body, he somehow put his body into his soul instead. Even so, the nightmare of his near death ended and the world snapped back to him. That moment of eternity which stretched between life and death was finally over. When Locke's soul touched his body it reconnected to his mana, which fueled a sort of pure white flame that began radiating from him.

The survivors of the Battle of Earth and Sky witnessed the shade of Uruzel strike the boy, followed by a flash of light, but instead of being snuffed out in an instant like the all others, somehow that light wrapped around Locke's body instead. The bystanders shielded their eyes from the intensity of light emanating from him, and the umbral horror shrieked in its innumerable voices as its body desperately shrank away from him.

They stood in awe, seeing the monstrosity react as if in pain, the first sign of the fight turning in their favor. The blinding light of Locke's soul dimmed to an aura of pure white light which coalesced around his silhouette. People uncovered their eyes and witnessed a phenomenon which would remain a mystery to them for the rest of their lives. The young man's fire-colored hair turned white and was flowing upward as though he were underwater. Locke himself hovered over the crater; the phoenix-tail grappler he wore started glowing with an otherworldly white illumination which had also ignited in his eyes.

Locke felt like he had the protection of armor on, yet it was entirely weightless and it did not restrict his movement. Sorren felt the power of it too, and she was just as surprised to feel what was happening. The shade of Uruzel flailed at Locke, but it could no longer touch him, nor affect his mind with its insane screaming and terrifying hallucinations. Locke saw it lash out uselessly as it tried to avoid him and attack him at the same time.

Though the void monstrosity could sever souls from the body, it seemed that it could not touch his directly anymore. And Locke's soul fire surrounded him, shielding him from the unholy thing's madness and violence. Locke discovered that he could float by his willpower alone, which seemed sufficient enough to move his body physically through space as well. He drifted toward the umbral horror, which shrank away from him, slithering back into the crater.

"Ren, let's end this," Locke said, readying the grappler. "Let's send that thing back to the abyss from which it crawled!"

Locke unfurled the grappler and the segments of bladed armor flew open. Together they drew out the grappler's true power again, but this time instead of the red-orange fire of the phoenix, an ethereal white flame made of Locke's mana-infused soul coated the weapon.

With a wide arcing attack, Locke brought the flaming bladed whip down and through the shapeless chaos that was the shade of Uruzel. The soulfire around the grappler changed the thing's ephemeral body, transforming it into something more solid akin to ash. The blades were then able to cut through its body, damaging the entropic horror for the first time. The attack from the soul-infused grappler scattered its black ash all around the crater, and nearly cleaved the writhing monstrosity in half.

The shade of Uruzel thrashed at him but its limbs shattered as they collided with his mana-infused soul armor before dissipating into wisps of black mist. Locke swung his arm and the grappler blades slashed through its body once more, and it turned to dust as the white flames tore through it. Locke flew forward, hacking its shadowy limbs off like he was clearing brush, and each strike got him closer to Ir'zane, who was the epicenter from which the endless darkness seeped.

Locke tore away the shapeless chaos surrounding the Duscan sorcerer until his broken body was revealed. His mouth was frozen open in horror while black smoke spewed from it, and his green eyes had rolled all the way back in his head. Locke looked at him with a small measure of pity; Sorren, however, was repulsed.

"Destroy Ir'zane's body and end this!" she said. At the same time, the shade of Uruzel was attempting to reform its body around Locke, closing like a bear trap. He and Sorren spun in a circle, using the flaming whip to shred it to pieces to keep it from snapping shut on them.

"If it could be destroyed that way then Aerilynn's meteor would have been more than enough," Locke mused as he puzzled something over in his mind. The umbral horror fought to keep Ir'zane away from Locke, pulling the sorcerer's body around violently and enveloping it back into its shapeless mass. It formed several new appendages in an effort to attack Locke from the side, but he cut them down too, removing the darkness covering the Duscan sorcerer with ease.

"You should put him out of his misery," Sorren said.

"Misery?" Locke repeated as though it was a question, before something dawned on him, "Misery, suffering, and guilt, they are all personal." Locke calmly carved through the shadows as they tried to attack him.

"You need to end this!" Sorren insisted.

"Only he can do that," he replied.

Locke cut away the darkness around Ir'zane.

"I don't understand," she said.

Locke reached out and touched Ir'zane's forehead with his palm, while closing his own eyes.

"You will."

When Locke opened his eyes again, he found himself in a castle with black stone walls and purple dragon blood tapestries hanging over massive roaring fire pits. He appeared to be dressed in finer clothes than anything he ever owned, with Sorren the living phoenix perched on his right forearm while her elegant tail plumage draped to the floor.

There was an enormous gathering of well-dressed Duscans dancing and playing music around a dragon who was curled up, sleeping on massive cushions in the center of the room. The dragon lay peacefully with its legs against its body and tail wrapped around them, it snoozed gently as wisps of white smoke rose from its nostrils. Massive horns grew from behind its eyes and out of the back of its head, and its leathery wings lay folded over its bulky shoulders and across its spike-covered spine. Its black scales shimmered entrancingly in the firelight, while the revelers danced around the enormous slumbering beast.

At the far edge of the room, stood a man with long, curly black hair and sharp emerald eyes who looked bewildered at his surroundings. The Duscan sorcerer, Ir'zane looked at his talon-less, flesh-toned fingers, before he noticed Locke standing there. Ir'zane looked unnerved to see him.

"What's going on here?" Ir'zane asked walking up to Locke.

"I think these are your memories. From before the war, before you let it turn you into a monster. This is who you could be again."

Their dream-like surroundings faded and swirled into a storm of Ir'zane's memories. Locke and Sorren saw him as a scrawny boy being brutally beaten by other children in fighting pits, while dragons looked on with sadistic glee. Ir'zane flinched and shouted, "No! Not again!"

Everything shifted once more and they saw a lonely young man spending long days in the dark interiors of the mage city Aeris' libraries, ostracized by his peers because of the dragon blood in his veins. Another sudden change of scene showed a man broken by a nightmarish war, his hands were covered in the blood of his mentor, as he struggled with the consequences of his actions.

"No. This, this is who I am. It's all I've ever been allowed to be," Ir'zane confessed as he showed them his lowest moments.

Locke shook his head.

"You seek strength in hating those who made your life difficult, but I see a refusal to let go of what was done to you. Where you seek the power to control others, I see shame for selfish actions. You are more than what you've endured. You don't have to keep choosing pain just because it is all you knew. You had dreams of your own, and you knew love onc-"

Ir'zane snarled, cutting Locke off.

"That man is *dead*!"

"Not yet," Locke replied, while shaking his head again. He placed a hand on Ir'zane's shoulder, and the Duscan's memories shifted around once more. This time showing them Ir'zane in the floating ruins of Aeris, defying the dark master of the Book of Souls while proclaiming, "I am no one's puppet!"

Locke went on, "You can change the ending to your story. But if you choose to hold onto your rage and pain forever then you will remain the puppet of darkness incarnate..."

The illusion of Ir'zane's memories faded, bringing them back to the present moment. Ir'zane's broken body was suspended by plumes of entropic shadows and Locke was glowing with a pure white aura of flame.

"... or you can let go of your need for vengeance, and do what this world's mightiest heroes could not, by sending that damned thing back to the abyss where it belongs!"

The memory scene changed a final time to the terrace of a dormitory overlooking the fields of Aeris-Terran back in the days before the Great Wyrm War. Ir'zane turned his back to Locke and Sorren, putting his hands on the railing while watching a blood red sun setting on the kingdom of Duscar on the horizon.

"For many years I watched the sun set on my homeland from afar, wondering if *she* was looking back at me, and even though I knew they would never let us be together, I wanted to return to her anyway. By the time the war brought me back to Duscar, she was already gone," Ir'zane reminisced.

"Your people are at peace, you should be too," Locke said while walking away, leaving the Duscan sorcerer to contemplate. Ir'zane let out a deep sigh, looking at his home one last time. When he was ready, he closed his eyes and smiled gently before letting go of his pain, as he did all of his memories faded to dust and disappeared.

~

Elisander stood with his crystal sword pointed to the ground, his hand barely hanging on to it while he observed the fight between Locke and the shade of Uruzel in bewilderment. No one else spoke, no one dared move, every eye was transfixed on Locke as he cut away the writhing chaos and with no more than a touch to the sorcerer's head, somehow, he ended the threat of what Ir'zane had unleashed. The entropic horror was no longer flowing out of Ir'zane, cut off from its source, the hideous blasphemy fell apart, and as it did it screamed a hideous death wail.

Everyone clapped their hands to their heads in pain as their minds were assaulted, even the dead rose to mimic the agony of the living. The shadow completely disintegrated as the link between Averon and the void was severed. The screams faded, and the corpses of the deceased fell still again as the remnant of Ir'zane's body turned to ash and fell to the bottom of the crater.

Locke had paid no attention to his body since his soul had turned inside out, so he was unaware how drained it was from the effort. When he focused on it, an intense exhaustion beyond anything he had felt before overwhelmed him as he descended from the sky. He felt the strain of each move he made while empowered, motions which had depleted his life force entirely. While slowly floating back to the ground the bright aura around Locke faded and his hair turned back to its normal fire color.

Locke's overtired muscles shuddered trying to hold up his impossibly heavy body as his feet touched the bottom of the crater. His once glowing eyes returned to their natural blue as his legs gave out under him. Locke's body collapsed under its own weight, falling face first in the soil, and his improperly attached soul could hold on no longer and slipped away.

Sorren stirred inside the phoenix-tail grappler, cold and alone. Her soul was still bound to the magical weapon that was fused to

Locke's body, but she could no longer feel him with her. Sorren felt a loss unlike anything since the Phoenix King was taken from her. Azar's death was a scar that had never healed, and a guilt she could not shake. She felt the emptiness of Locke's body and did not wish to bear another long slumber trapped inside of the grappler weapon, only to repeat the cycle again.

She began overcharging the weapon, and the magic used to trap her inside strained from the overwhelming power. The grappler burst into magical flames so intense that everyone saw its orange light suddenly shining over the edge of the crater. Sorren spoke to Locke, though he could not hear her.

"I am so sorry for burning you when we met, I was still grieving and I didn't want to open up to you. I am sorry for being distant with you, and leaving you to deal with the harshness of the world when you were grieving your family. Most of all, I am sorry you will have to go alone from now on because I won't be there to help you."

The grappler armor broke away from Locke's arm, as Sorren used her remaining power to escape the bindings. The flames erupting from the shattered grappler formed into the shape of a phoenix whose wings stretched across the sky. Sorren's effigy flew over him, with pieces of the grappler at the heart. Locke's body was raised into the air by an unseen force, lifting him off the ground.

Sorren then sang a song so beautiful and bittersweet which no one listening could understand, yet none would ever forget. They felt her sorrow in her cry and were overwhelmed by emotion. From the knights and magi of Everund, to the elven fighters from Lorlinden, none were unmoved. While she sang, a bright white light beamed out of Locke's eyes and mouth, as his limbs twitched.

~

Locke opened his eyes and found himself lying face down in a strange bright place, one that was pure white and completely indistinct. There were no features, no landscapes, and no visual markers of any kind for as far as the eye could see. He got to his feet and looked at the ground, it was the same vast white abstraction as everything else, and which was indistinguishable from the sky or the horizon. He called out into the haze, which echoed around him, over and over, quieter and quieter, until it was gone. Nothing reacted or called back; everything remained calm and still.

Locke slowly recalled the battle of the mage cities, and his fight against the shade of Uruzel, and his soul drifting away from his body afterward. He looked for signs of anything which could help him understand where he was, but everywhere he looked it was all the same vagueness stretching into endless liminal space. Locke started walking around in no particular direction, hoping to find something over the horizon beyond his sight. There was no way to tell how many hours passed or how far he walked, but he went the entire time without seeing anything other than the white wastes of vagary.

The more that time passed, if there was such a thing anymore, the more certain he became that he was dead or trapped somewhere between life and death. His mind was full of questions which had no answers. What was happening to him, he thought? Was this going to last forever? Would he be trapped here in this place for all eternity, or only until he went completely mad?

He sat down, feeling disoriented from the lack of visual distinctions anywhere in sight. Locke closed his eyes to find that instead of the comfort of shade from his own eyelids, he continued to see only bright white. Just as when he thought he was going to snap, Locke heard something out of the silence. It was faint at first and he was unsure he actually heard something or was hallucinating, but a moment later a sharp tone tickled his ear which grew louder as he listened for it. He heard the distinct sound of birdsong, and it was coming from nearby.

"Ren?" he wondered, as he got up and ran in the direction of her singing. When he arrived at the spot where the sound was the loudest, he found a glowing red rune on the ground which was calling to him. Locke stepped onto the symbol and then felt intense heat radiating through his body as a ring of fire encircled him.

As Sorren sang, Locke's life force found its way back to his body, which was now brimming with overflowing mana. His soul's radiant light spilled out of him as it returned from the Beyond. Locke inhaled deeply as though he had only been holding his breath, and his eyes opened briefly to see fire in the sky above him which rapidly faded as he came back to life.

Sorren's fire dwindled as the last of her light was dying. Locke drifted back down to Averon while falling unconscious with his heart beating steadily once more. With one final dulcet note, the wondrous phoenix sang no more as the fire of her soul went out and vanished from the world forever.

Out of the Ashes

Locke laid motionless at the bottom of the meteor crater for a long time before he finally opened his eyes. He rolled over lazily, like he was waking from a long rest on a morning where he was not needed for chores. He ran a hand through his hair and rubbed the sleep from his eyes. The world came back into focus, and then the memory of all that happened snapped back to him. He was suddenly painfully aware of his surroundings, he bolted upright and looked around to see corpses of magi in the crater. Thankfully, there was nothing left of either the shadow of Uruzel, or Ir'zane, but the carnage from their battle was unmistakably real.

He saw an unusual fragment of debris sticking out of the disturbed soil that was familiar in a way that made his heart sink. Locke recognized the metalwork of the shattered grappler, and he looked to his right arm. His scarred skin was entirely exposed to the air, which felt unbearably cold. He grabbed his flame-scarred arm and held it against his chest for warmth. Locke's eyes filled with sorrow, no longer able to feel Sorren's presence with him. The pain of the loss hit him hard, he hung his head heavily and gripped his arm tighter for comfort. She was gone, he knew in his heart it was true.

All that remained of the phoenix-tail grappler were bits of metal scattered around him in the ashes. Locke hoped beyond hope for a miracle hidden in the black ash, and even imagined the scenario as if it were real. He would see something strange on the ground, an odd lump in a pile of ash that had a unique, egg-like shape. Locke would reach into the pile of ashes and wiping it clean to reveal something just beneath. Uncovering an egg of reddish gold color, about the size of an apple, and warm to the touch.

Locke pictured himself picking it up, and cupping it with both hands, finding it almost too hot to hold. He would gently rock the phoenix egg between his hands to keep it from burning his skin before placing it gently on the ground between his legs. "I thought I lost you Ren," he would say. And he would wait as long as it took until she hatched and he could see her again.

That was what he hoped would happen when he dug through the immolated remains. But alas, beneath the pile of ash there was no egg. He did however pull out a gem the size of a shirt button, which resembled red glass, and he wiped it clean with his fingers. It was similar to a ruby in color, the gem was hollow but broken open. It was slightly warm to his touch, as though it was once filled with her fire.

"Ren," Locke whispered, searching his mind for her again, but he did not find her there, nor could he recall her memories either. Like Sorren herself, they too were gone. He stared into the clear skies overhead, trying not to let his emotions overwhelm him. Locke imagined seeing Ren soaring above him, flying free like in her memories. He envisioned her bright red plumage and long elegant tail feathers edged with gold fanning out across the sky.

He thought of her bright topaz-colored eyes shining with an inner light which danced like fire. He daydreamed streaks of flame left in her wake as she flew through the sky, setting it ablaze. That was all he had left of her now, a recollection in his mind that he needed his imagination to see. Tears formed in the corners of his eyes before streaming down his face as his fingers closed around the broken gem in his hand. He wept for Sorren, he wept for the fallen Everunders, he wept for Silthradel, he wept for everything he went through since he left Dellow, and he wept for the Blackwoods too.

Locke closed his eyes, shutting out the entire world, and he let the emptiness consume him. In his mourning he did not see Elisander running to the top of the crater, nor did he hear the king shouting down to him.

"Locke!" Elisander called to him, but Locke was lost in his grief. "You're alive!" the king exclaimed, but the Therredan could not hear him, nor could he see the smile all over the young king's face. Elisander jumped down the slope of the crater, sliding down the loose soil of its depression. He nearly lost his balance when he came to an abrupt stop at the bottom, stumbling over the body of one of his magi. Elisander looked gravely into the faces of his people.

The king solemnly turned his attention back to Locke who had not moved or seemed to notice him at all for that matter. He saw the streaks on Locke's face from tears and for a moment Elisander let himself feel some of the weight that Locke's heart held. At that moment, Elisander looked upon Locke differently than before.

When they first met in Belcard, he had looked down upon Locke as unworthy, lowly even. Elisander had looked at him with contempt for his impetuousness and lack of respect shown to authority, especially when Locke had disobeyed him in the ruins of Duscar. He had looked at him with genuine gratitude at the edges of the Feywild for getting his ship flying again, and with admiration for his part in defending the very heart of the kingdom of Everund. Elisander had looked to him as a brother-in-arms during the battle for control of the mage cities, and with reverence as Locke had battled the entropic horror seeping out of Ir'zane and when he achieved a victory where no other had.

Elisander stood at Locke's side as he wept uncontrollably, and really saw him for the first time. He saw his youthful face, his messy hair, and his innocent heart torn wide open. The king reached down, placing his hand gently on Locke's shoulder as comfortingly as he could. Locke opened his eyes, his vision blurred with tears, and looked up thinking he would see Rowan standing over him.

"Come brother."

Locke heard Elisander's voice as he blinked away his tears. Locke said nothing but nodded gently, and Elisander helped him to his feet, "All of Averon owes you a great debt my friend, and I owe you an apology. So, I ask you for forgiveness."

Locke looked confused.

"For what?" he asked.

"I was entirely wrong about you. I've judged you harshly and treated you worse. But at the end of all things, it was you who saved us all."

Locke saw the dead around the crater and he hung his head shamefully.

"... I couldn't save them."

Locke then held out his fist and opened his hand to reveal the broken fire heart gem, "Or her. I screwed up and Ren traded her life for mine. *She* saved *me*."

Elisander held Locke tighter.

"I was always taught that sacrifice was an act of love."

Locke was not used to Elisander sounding so wise.

"Come. Let's get you out of here," the king said warmly.

"Wait," Locke said before frantically digging around in the dirt.

"Locke what are you-?" Elisander stopped talking as the young Therredan pulled out a piece of the armor which had once been fused to his arm.

"I won't leave her here!" Locke shouted, frantically picking up the remaining pieces until he had an armful of all that was left of the grappler. Elisander then put his arm around Locke once more and the two of them walked out of the crater together. The survivors gathered around as Elisander and Locke approached, cheering for their return from the crater.

The clerics were busy tending to the wounded, sorting those who might live from those already gone. The knights of Everund were digging graves and laying their friends to rest. Locke heard the prayers of the clerics as they blessed the dead and he felt fortunate he was not among them, but also guilty for not being among the fallen. Acacius and Kayara paused talking with one another as Elisander returned with Locke. Dyce and Aeysha were waiting with Aerilynn, who was still recovering from the ordeal. Aeysha hugged Locke, her increasingly ephemeral body caused winds to swirl around him.

"The Great Mother must truly be fond of you for you to come back in one piece after that!" she exclaimed. He laughed as she let him go, only to be bear-hugged by Dyce the instant Aeysha released him. Locke's face turned as red as his hair before Acacius patted the elemental on the arm to stop.

"I think that's enough, big guy."

Dyce giggled and let him go and Locke took a deep breath before laughing uncomfortably.

"It has been a privilege," Acacius said, extending their arm for a formal greeting. Locke returned the gesture and the two grabbed each other's forearms with a firm and friendly shake.

Captain Kayara saluted Locke heartily.

"It's been an honor to fight alongside you."

He smiled back at her and then they kindly hugged.

"Thank you, captain," he said respectfully. "It's good to see you made it too," he said looking around at the smiling faces of his friends. Locke wished that he could revel in the moment with them, but his mind was still with Ren and the pain of her sacrifice. Everything felt muted, the laughter of the crowd was background noise, the smiles on everyone's faces felt painted on and nothing felt like it was supposed to. He should be happy; after all, the battle was over, they won.

Aeysha turned to Dyce, then back to Locke with a look of apprehension and disappointment. He knew it meant she was leaving. Now that he thought about it, there was no reason for any of them to be here together.

"I must return to the other Keepers, and tell them what transpired here. I do not know if we'll meet again, but I pray the Great Mother will watch over you."

Locke smiled softly.

"Thank you, Aeysha, for everything," he said.

He spoke to the towering stone elemental, "Take care of her for me, yeah?"

Dyce hoisted Aeysha onto his shoulders and nodded.

"Rock and bird must fly, bye-bye."

The druid and the elemental waved goodbye to everyone as Dyce began rock sliding back toward the Eld Ridge Mountains.

Elisander was still helping hold Locke up and could tell he was struggling to contain his sorrow.

"I think we'll have to save the rest of our goodbyes for later. I need to get Locke back to a ship and have our friend checked out by the healers. Plus... he's getting kinda heavy."

The king laughed, and Aerilynn smiled.

"Okay then, I will see you off shortly," she said sweetly.

The king bowed his head, and Kayara also helped carry Locke, while Acacius bid farewell to Princess Everdawn with a deep bow.

"Princess, what will we do now?" one of her attendants inquired of her, while the knights of Everund readied their ships for departure. When she said nothing, he continued, "Ir'zane destroyed Silthradel, and with it, our dream of ever returning home."

Aerilynn was still weakened and recovering but her eyes had lost none of their intensity.

"It is true that Ir'zane destroyed our home, but he has not destroyed our people. Our future lies within each of us. We will need to heal the wounds of our divided people, and cooperate with humanity if we are to survive." Though she was not rallying her troops to battle, she nonetheless commanded the respect of every elven ear.

"We shall shape a new destiny," she concluded. "We leave at once for Lorlinden. Send messengers to the Winterwood, ask the queen to meet us there, I'm hopeful we can work together to find a new future for our people."

To prep for departure, her kin performed funeral rites for the elves of Lorlinden who fell in battle, each of which Aerilynn presided over personally. She spoke kind words about each of them, reciting stories or memories they shared, before using sacred magic to turn their bodies into mana which they released into the planet. The princess rested for a while after they finished the laborious task, calming herself emotionally, and recovering physically before they made the long journey back to the Feywild.

Eventually, Aerilynn stood again and addressed her attendant, "Before we depart, there is someone I need to speak with."

"I can assist you if you-"

The princess waved her hand dismissively, "That won't be necessary, please instead see that the gryphons are well fed before our flight, and scratch behind their ears, they really like that."

She then crossed the makeshift camp as the small band of elves made ready to travel. The princess walked slowly because of her stiff muscles, yet she ignored their protestation. Princess Aerilynn passed by Everunders, who were busy packing their remaining ships with supplies and their wounded. Elisander stood at the center commanding his people as diligently as a foreman, stopping only as the young elven princess reached him.

"Lady Everdawn," he said, bowing. "Thank you, and the elves of Lorlinden for your support in battle. It was an honor to fight alongside you and I am grateful that you came to our aid... even though I was not able to come to yours."

Aerilynn bowed her head in return.

"King Elisander, thank you for kind words, but we did not come to aid Everund. We fought as you did, for all of Averon. The honor belongs to both of us, my lord."

Elisander smiled gratefully.

"Well said," he mused.

"Where is Locke? I wish to thank him, personally," she spoke directly and the king looked somewhat taken aback.

"Of course," he said, grabbing one of his personal guards. "Please escort Princess Everdawn to the Nomad Sky so she may extend her gratitude to our honored guest."

The guard nodded enthusiastically.

"This way my lady," he said leading her to the Nomad Sky, which was finishing up loading the last of Everund's forces. Aerilynn's eyes darted around, searching through all of the Everunders around the transport bay in search of the Therredan boy's familiar fire-colored hair sticking out among the knights and magi who were readying to leave.

She found him sitting on a crate with a few healers tending to him, seemingly unconvinced that he was not wounded and did not require further treatment. Despite their prodding, the only thing that really hurt was his heart, and there was no medicine that could restore *that* wound. They scattered as Aerilynn approached them, but Locke's head hung low and he did not look up to see her. Aerilynn stood in front of him, quietly looking down at him and waited for him to say something. She had the distinct feeling that he would eventually say something if she did not, and it was not long before she was proven correct.

"I can't shake this feeling..." he said, still not looking up.

"It's so strange, but it doesn't feel real. I know she's gone. I know it, but I can't accept it. Because if I accept it, then it makes it real. I don't know, maybe I shouldn't be so upset. After all, I didn't know her long even if we shared memories and experiences. We were total strangers when we met, but after we connected, it felt like I had known her my entire life."

Aerilynn took Locke's hand.

"It's normal to mourn loved ones that we lose."

He looked up as she spoke, and closed his hand around hers.

"What about you? What will your people do now?"

Aerilynn looked off into the distance.

"We were not welcome in Silthradel. The truth is, we lost our home a long time ago. The only thing taken from us today was the false hope that we could go back someday."

Locke stared into her eyes, in which shades of yellow and green grasses swayed while she looked across the plains. He saw them brimming with a deep sadness that she otherwise did not express.

"I'm sorry for asking this but, why were you exiled in the first place? What could you possibly have done to deserve that?"

She faced him, and smiled softly.

"For believing that we should be able to love whom we choose. For not banishing our kin for having relationships with humans. I was exiled for *this*," she said and raised their clasped hands to illustrate her point.

"I'm so sorry," he said tenderly.

"I guess even though we stopped Ir'zane, there is still a lot of evil out there."

"Do not lose hope. What you have done here will be remembered until the end of days, when all memory passes into a history that only the last stars of our universe will recall. It is no small thing to have risked death and to bare your soul as you have," Aerilynn spoke with genuine admiration. Locke never heard anyone speak like her before.

"Do... do you know what happened to me?" he asked, hoping she had even more insight, but she shook her head no.

"Whatever happened to you was something I doubt anyone else has ever experienced."

Locke looked away.

"I don't understand what happened, but I'm sure it was only possible because of Ren. She's the real hero, and yet everyone wants to thank me."

Aerilynn smiled at him softly.

"You are very unusual for a human, Locke. Really quite remarkable."

Her eyes were gleaming as they looked deeply into his, and his heart raced. She leaned in closer to him as if inviting him in, he leaned in as well until they were nearly touching. He hoped he was guessing right as he took a chance on the moment.

"May I...?" he started to ask, but she did not wait for him to finish his question.

"Yes," she said tenderly.

Locke reached out and touched her cheek gently, before sliding his fingers behind her head. He pressed his lips to hers, and they closed their eyes, embracing one another.

The princess' advisor ran into them before he realized how private the moment was.

"I am sorry to interrupt you, your highness, but we are ready to leave whenever you wish."

She nodded to him, and he bowed and left them alone. Aerilynn looked into Locke's bright blue eyes and sighed gently.

"Unfortunately, I must go, but I hope that our paths will cross again in the future."

He smiled back at her.

"I hope so too, princess."

She stood to leave before pulling out the astromancer compass which Dilandau Ravendark had given to Locke and placed it back in his hands.

"Maybe this will help you find your way back to me."

Locke watched her leave while absentmindedly running his fingers over the compass with the broken chain. He considered going after her, but he knew that she had unfinished business calling her home and he did not want his personal desires to come before the good of her people. Elisander came back to get Locke, for they too would be leaving soon.

"It is good to see you smile," the king said happily. "The ships are prepped, the wounded are onboard, and the last of our supplies are loaded. It is time to go, my friend."

Locke agreed and Elisander helped him to his feet. The two of them walked side by side through the cargo bay while the crew scrambled to get secured for takeoff. Before today, Locke never would have imagined walking arm in arm with a king, but in that moment, they were just friends. Elisander was not some mythical figure from a foreign kingdom, and Locke was not just a farm boy from a tiny village in the middle of nowhere. Having overcome their grievances with one another and having fought alongside one another, they had each gained a newfound respect for each other.

The cargo bay doors were shut behind them as they made their way to the upper deck of the ship and toward the cockpit. Each person Locke passed on the way looked at him differently, some with admiration, others fear. He saw them all differently as well; he no longer saw them as background characters in the narrative of his own personal life story. Touched by tragedy, Locke realized how precious life was, having seen it ripped away so easily from too many. Bravery, valor, nor power could thwart the thieving hand of death.

As King Elisander entered the cockpit, his crew stood at attention, including Captain Kayara who stepped down from the helm for the king.

"Fire up the engines and let's get this thing in the air," he said, and the crew scattered to their posts, responding, "Yes, my king!" Elisander stepped up to the ship's wheel and he felt the finely crafted wooden handle in his hands. The Nomad Sky's engines started up, and the airship shook, sending vibrations along the hull of the ship. The loud whir of the props filled the command deck and through the open windows one could smell the two other ships of the fleet fire up their engines as well. They were waiting for the king to take the lead, and Elisander turned to his engineering chief.

"Give me full power as soon as we're airborne, I'm taking us home."

Drovann saluted the king and ran out of the room. Elisander pushed the throttle up, increasing the rotation of the props to flight speed, and the ship lifted off, beginning its ascent. Elisander felt at ease again behind the wheel of his ship, taking command felt natural to him here, and it helped him to take his mind off of the weight of the losses they had sustained.

Locke stared out the window quietly, enjoying the relative peace he felt from the view. He looked down on the battlefield below them, at the broken cities of Aeris-Terran, and the meteor crater where he had nearly lost his life. Soon they would climb high enough into the sky that the only thing beneath them would be clouds, obscuring the land below from his sight. Locke wished his mind could be as free as it felt to fly, but even the distance they put between them and that battlefield did not dull his aching heart.

He clutched his scarred arm again and found himself thinking about the hearth in the Blackwood Manor. Locke was faced with discomforting thoughts, and a growing unease. Elisander, Kayara, and Acacius were on their way back to Erendar to rebuild. Aerilynn was heading back to Lorlinden to find a new future for the elves. Aeysha was heading back to the wilds and Dyce was wandering back to the other side of the Eld Ridge Mountains. He realized they were all going home, everyone except for him.

A Knight of Honor

The streets of Erendar were filled with celebration on the day of Elisander's coronation. The occasion was even more joyous, for a hard-won peace had returned to their wounded kingdom. Only a week had passed since services for the dead were held, and the people of Everund rejoiced in their honor, in order to make the most of their sacrifice. Despite the damage to the capital wrought by the Therredan invasion, the people of Erendar dressed the city in decorations; hanging large white and gold banners bearing the crest of Everund from the city walls and from their homes. Torches and braziers were lit and the streets were filled with people from all corners of the kingdom.

The knights of Everund were regarded highly by all people of the kingdom, no position was more revered for one of their citizens to serve. Farmers from humble villages and lords of the great cities all came together for the remembrance ceremonies and the crowning celebration to come. Many had attended services all morning for the fallen, as their memorials in the catacombs beneath the city were still open to the public. Many more waited just outside, unable to fit into the crowded temples.

People came in droves from all three cities of Everund to pay their respects to those who died in service of crown and duty.

Families noble and common alike grieved for their dead, whose sacrifice was honored by all, and in the hours before Elisander's coronation, thousands of Everunders would visit the graves of their beloved knights and former king.

Locke sat squat with his legs dangling from a window on the upper levels of the Grand Citadel. He spent the early morning hours looking out over the crystal city, memorizing each street, shop, park, and monument while he waited to be called into the Great Hall. His mind was still reeling from everything that happened over the past month; from his strange spiritual transformation, the battle for the fate of the world, meeting the elven princess, even his adventure with the enigmatic druids, and the long, lonely journey through the plains of Arbereth.

Now that things had settled for the first time in a long time, he found himself thinking of Therred, and the little village of Dellow. He noticed a flock of geese flying over Erendar, and pictured the chair on the porch of the Blackwood Manor where he would sit and read while watching clouds drift by. Locke traced the rippled burn scars on his right arm with his fingers while he thought of Castle Hammangard and the Iron Tyrant who still ruled it, and of his family's fate back in Therred.

To think that they were likely dead, and that he may never see them again, was a thought too painful to bear. Locke pulled out one of the metal feathers from the broken grappler and rolled it between his fingers, wishing that he could speak to Sorren again. He thought about staying in Erendar, of making a new life for himself among the Everunders. Maybe he could even find his parents someday. Surely, the kingdom of Everund was not so vast that it could conceal them forever. Yet it was not his parents that he was unable to take his mind off of; his mind was stuck on his brother, and his uncle. Locke's eyes filled with tears as the pain and guilt welled up inside him again.

Locke wiped the tears from his eyes and looked again at the people below, crowding the streets in celebration. He leaned out into direct sunlight and let it bathe him in its glow, enjoying its warmth on his skin. For the briefest of moments, the sadness in his heart abated, focusing on the warmth of the sun brought him a small measure of comfort. He felt so small sitting in that window, so insignificant to the universe at large.

Locke entertained the idea of walking away from everything, to leave with no plan, and with nowhere to go. He thought of going so far away that he would disappear entirely. The longer he sat, the more his mind tormented him. He hated being stuck in the Great Hall waiting to be called. Locke was flattered that Everund's new king wished to include him in the coronation ceremony and all, but truthfully, he felt undeserving of it.

He wondered if he would be missed if he left — after all, Locke had already waited so long that it was possible they had completely forgotten he was there. Maybe the ceremony was already underway and they had left him alone to wander the halls like a vagrant. He got up and started pacing, mostly to get circulation flowing in his legs again. Locke pulled his hair back from his face and sighed, boredom was becoming a serious concern for him.

Boredom meant dwelling on his loneliness again, and he did not want to wallow in his sorrow any longer. Thankfully he was rescued moments later when one of the large doors opened and an usher emerged looking flustered.

"All of the nobles have been seated, and we are ready for you to enter. If you follow me, I will escort you to your seat now."

The chambers of the crystal cathedral were packed with finely-dressed nobles from all corners of the kingdom of Everund, including those who traveled from its most distant corners to see Elisander officially crowned king. There was a lot of excitement surrounding the coronation and the historic significance of the moment was not lost on the assembly.

The High Cleric Baldric quieted the congregation before he commanded, "All rise for His Eminence, His Royal Highness."

They stood silently waiting for the ceremony to begin, as Elisander stood outside the main doors fiddling with his formal suit nervously.

"It will be over soon," he reassured himself quietly, "it's just a few steps, a few words, and a crown."

Surely a formal ceremony was nothing to be afraid of, so why was he more scared now than he was when fighting against the undead legions of Duscar? Though he had successfully led his people through the conflict against Ir'zane, it was not so long ago that he had been a carefree, rule breaking, roguish prince.

Now he felt the weight of responsibility which came with being the ruler of an entire kingdom. Perhaps that was why he had always evaded his administrative duties, ignored his etiquette training, and always snuck away from the endless squabbling of the nobles. Elisander chose to run away from the responsibilities of royal life because deep down he knew that this day would come, and when it did, he would not be ready for it.

The first bronze bell rang from the nearby temple, taking Elisander out of his thoughts and back to the present moment. The royal guards snapped to attention, turning toward him quickly and putting their backs to the doors behind them. The second bell rang and Captain Kayara walked up to him and put a reassuring hand on his shoulder.

"It's time," she said.

The soon to be official king nodded back, thankful he did not need to speak at that moment, for he was unsure that he could.

The third bell sounded and Elisander stepped up to the doors with Kayara following close behind him. His heart was pounding in his chest, and he was sweating anxiously. Elisander wrapped his hand around the handle of Everund tightly. The fourth bronze bell rang through the Great Hall as his royal guard pulled open the doors from the other side. Inside the cathedral, eager eyes looked upon Elisander as he stood silent under the arch of the grandiose doors. He stared straight across the hall, trying not to catch anyone's eyes, he was focused solely on the goal of reaching the other side of the room. Elisander's legs refused to move, however, and for an awkward moment he simply stood there.

The echo of the fourth bell was still ringing through the hall while the nobles beheld their would-be king standing stiffly in the doorway. They remarked about him to each other in hushed whispers, which only made him more anxious. By the sounding of the fifth and final bell, he summoned enough willpower to force a single foot forward, stepping into the hall and silencing everyone once more.

Step by step he crossed the room, reaching the stage by the time the bell fell silent. Kayara closed the doors behind Elisander, sealing the Great Hall once more. Elisander passed the High Cleric, who gave him a reassuring smile, before he walked up to the pedestal from which he was to give his speech. Elisander looked at the assembled crowd and tried not to think about his trembling legs as he cleared his throat to speak.

"Difficult times do not wait for you to be ready for them. They do not knock politely, or wait to be asked in. They come to us when we are at our weakest, our most vulnerable. We may not have been ready for the attack on Erendar, or for the loss of my father Armon Erenson, but we fought back and reclaimed our city!"

There was stomping and whooping from the crowd and Elisander paused briefly before continuing, "Our knights and our magi fought bravely to end the threat of Duscar, who tried and failed to crush our spirits. They could not destroy our hope! We were tested again at the ruins of Aeris-Terran, where we stood against death itself and prevailed." The knights in the chamber cheered, which was followed by raucous applause from everyone else.

"As you all know, eighty-seven years ago my great-grandfather Alathor discovered the Crystallis as well as the shard of it he forged into the sword Everund, with which he created a kingdom. My grandmother Eren, the first queen of Everund, who built the great flood wall to protect our capital, and secured the river trade in Belcard which helped us prosper. My father who fought together with Arrincroft many years later to defend its lands, and formally accepted their unification into our kingdom. Every one of them has given everything to expand our prosperity. They lived and died in service of Everund, and that legacy will remain unbroken!"

Elisander drew the king's sword, *his* sword, from the scabbard hanging at his waist. Everund's crystal blade was shining brightly as he held it aloft.

"I vow to you as your king, to protect our realm and live up to the ideals upon which our kingdom was founded. Under my rule, Everund will endure!"

The people rose from their seats, their eyes brimming with pride, each of them felt filled with a renewed sense of hope. The crowd clapped and cheered as Elisander held the blade above him with its light shining down upon them. He looked into the cheering faces of adoring subjects, and his anxiety slowly bled out of him. Elisander was starting to feel like he might be ready to be king after all. And after the speech he gave, the people of Everund were ready to receive him as their king as well.

Elisander stepped out from behind the podium to face the members of the royal court and the delegates from the three cities which comprised his kingdom. He knelt before them, turning the blade of Everund toward the floor. A crown bearer walked down the aisle toward the kneeling king, while carrying a white silk pillow in their arms, upon which the crown sat.

The crown itself was a thick golden circlet with three crests shaped like crystals adorning it. The center crest stood taller and wider, and rested above the wearer's eyes. There were no jewels in it, and it was not as lavish as Locke had expected it to be. Despite it being made of gold and fit for a king, its design was simple, almost humble.

The High Cleric from the Temple of Yavon stood over the kneeling king, as the crown bearer brought him the symbol of rule to be bestowed upon Elisander. Baldric picked up the crown gently from the pillow, and the crown bearer bowed before stepping out of sight. Baldric then raised the crown over the young king's head.

"By the light of the Allfather, and by the will of our people, I proclaim you Elisander Armonson, king of Everund!"

More cheers and applause from the gathered as the High Cleric lowered the crown onto Elisander's head. Baldric stepped back and out of sight as Elisander slowly rose to his feet. The newly crowned king respectfully bowed before the crowd and waited for it to quiet down before addressing them once more.

"Before we empty this hall and fill our cups, I'd like to give thanks to the man whose courage saved us all!"

The king leaned over to the guard on his left and whispered something to him. A guard maneuvered through the crowd and over to where Locke was sitting.

"The king has summoned you. Follow me."

Locke rose from his seat, mortified and confused but followed the guard, who formally presented him to the king. Elisander faced Locke and addressed the crowded hall.

"My first act as your king will be to bestow our highest mark of honor upon the man who defied all expectations, hereby granting him knighthood for his role in defending our world from evil."

Locke's eyes went wide, and he panicked as suddenly all eyes were on him as Elisander continued talking.

"Step forth, Locke of Therred, receive this blessing and join our people as an honorary knight of Everund!"

The chamber filled with cheers for Locke, who stared dumbfounded, before slowly walking towards Elisander. Locke stood before the king, who smiled and gave him a reassuring nod.

"Kneel, my friend."

Elisander then placed his hand on Locke's shoulder. Locke let his body guide him to a kneeling position, and he tried not to show his abashment. He kept his eyes on Elisander, since thinking about how being gawked at was making him uncomfortable. Locke had never earned an award or received an accolade for anything in his life before. He appreciated the gesture but would have preferred to sit anonymously in the back and just bear witness to the historic occasion, rather than be a part of it. Elisander raised the king's blade over Locke's head.

"For your service to my kingdom, and to me. I knight you, Locke of Therred."

Elisander withdrew the crystal blade and sheathed it as Acacius Lordain handed Elisander a steel sword and scabbard, identical to what the knights of Everund wore into battle.

"Take this sword as gift and reminder, it is the symbol of your duty as a defender of this world."

Locke reached up and took the sword from him.

"Rise, knight of Everund!" King Elisander declared.

Locke rose to his feet and faced the crowd while holding his knight sword and scabbard. Everyone applauded and cheered again, but this time, just for Locke.

Elisander put his arm around Locke and they stood side by side while everyone continued cheering for the two of them. Several members of the royal court surrounded them and Elisander grinned like a fool, having enjoyed making his friend share in his humiliation. He motioned to Locke with a nod of his head that he was free to disappear back into the crowd. Locke looked relieved to get away from all the attention, yet he shot an irritated glance back at Elisander, who rolled his eyes in return at the whole situation, which made them laugh under their breath.

The courtesans walked towards the balcony on the other side of the Great Hall which overlooked the city. The multitudes of people who gathered around the castle waited eagerly for the royal coronation to conclude and for the newly crowned King Elisander to step out onto the balcony to address the people directly. The king took his place at the end of the balcony and raised a hand to wave to the streets filled with people, and the entire city of Erendar cheered for him.

The High Cleric Baldric stepped up and stood next to the king, who continued to wave to his subjects. Elisander leaned over the balcony to watch as the Nomad Sky flew overhead with Captain Kayara at the helm. The ship made several passes in front of the castle, showing off its maneuverability and speed with death-defying aerial stunts which impressed the onlookers.

Eventually the Nomad Sky hovered over the crowds with its cannon bays opened, while firing streamers and bits of confetti from the barrels. The colored paper rained down on the Everunders below, while fireworks were shot from the bow of the ship and into the sky. People in the streets danced and reveled, as all across the city music rose above the rabble. More explosions burst across the sky as the denizens of Erendar shot off their own fireworks to honor their new king.

Though the festivities continued on for several hours after the coronation ceremony, Locke found it difficult to appreciate them. The music was wonderful, truly moving, and the dancing was unlike anything he had seen. The food was delicious, and the company was some of the best he had ever known.

Despite all of that, it did not feel right to be celebrating when the Blackwoods could still be out there. Locke allowed the revelry to fade away as he mulled over a difficult decision. Maybe the new friendships made him realize how lonely he really was, or maybe it was the way his right arm always felt so cold now. No matter the reason, Locke needed to get away from the crowds.

Locke slipped out of the enormous dining hall and away from the loud drunken singing, hoping that no one would notice he was gone. Finally, alone with his thoughts, Locke was able to find some clarity and with it, it was not long before he made up his mind. If there was any chance at all that Baryk or Rowan may still be alive, he could not live with himself if he did not at least *try* to rescue them.

He already traveled halfway around the world, rode giant birds through storms, fought in battles against an undead army, was burned by a magical artifact, nearly chopped up by thieves, and nearly died crossing the plains. Locke risked losing his soul fighting against an embodiment of darkness itself and he even died temporarily. It was time to go home, to face the threats he had not been able to before, to find out what happened to his family, and to make things right.

King Elisander found Locke sitting alone in the halls.

"Are you coming back to the party? You have to see this bard from Arrincroft who can play a lute with his... well, you have to see it for yourself, it's hilarious!"

Locke looked him in the eyes seriously.

"I'm sorry but I can't."

The king looked disappointed.

"You're leaving, aren't you?"

Locke only nodded in reply.

Elisander smiled gently and sighed.

"I will help you of course, but as your friend I have to know, what drives you away so soon?"

Locke stared at the southern horizon.

"I'm going to find my brother and my uncle."

"To Therred then?" Elisander shook his head, "That is not a wise move my friend."

He placed his hand on Locke's shoulder.

"Gerod will have you executed if he catches you."

Locke absentmindedly rubbed his scars before looking at his friend again.

"Then I won't get caught," he said brazenly.

Elisander smirked but got close and lowered his voice.

"My advisors are requesting that I convene a war council to deal with Gerod, and with the threat of Therred. They are bloodthirsty for vengeance, but I have convinced them to wait for spring. To instead spend the coming months recouping our losses. I cannot buy you more time than that to find your family before war comes to Therred."

It was not what Locke was expecting to hear but it changed very little about his decision.

"I understand. Maybe if I can find Baryk, we can deal with Gerod ourselves and avoid war altogether."

Elisander walked with Locke through the empty halls of the Citadel toward the stables.

"I like the sound of that."

After outfitting Locke with a horse and traveling supplies fit for a king, Elisander reluctantly said, "Farewell, my friend."

Locke placed his hand on Elisander's shoulder.

"Until we meet again."

Locke then climbed into the saddle while gripping the horse's reins tightly in his hands. He gave them a snap and he was off, riding through the city with the wind flowing through his hair. He looked over his shoulder as he rode out of Erendar, waving farewell to Elisander and the glowing crystal city. By the time he made it to the Bulwark of Alathor and the farmsteads beyond, he was already wondering if he made the right call. He pressed on anyway, riding through the fields before Lake Senacea.

Locke pet his horse comfortingly as they rode the ferry across the placid lake which laid out before Erendar. The view of the crystal city looked different from the ground than it did from the air, and Locke was surprised by how far the glow of its light traveled. Even from across the vast lake it glimmered beautifully, and when he started to ride south to Belcard, he was sad to see Erendar vanish on the horizon. He had little trouble following the river down to the merchant town built on its falls. The city of Belcard somehow always smelled of rain, and was lit by lamps with dull orange glows; it looked a lot more welcoming than it truly was.

Having experienced the dangers posed by the shady underbelly of the river-falls city firsthand, Locke knew he needed to be careful as he rode through. He rested his hand on the grip of the steel sword he was given and rode with purpose to the other side of town. There he found the Temple of Yavon where he was healed the first time when he crossed the plains of Arbereth after barely surviving the journey. Locke dismounted his horse and brought it around back to the meager stable where he was greeted by a familiar face; the cleric Erdan who came out to greet him.

"Welcome back, brother."

The cleric noticed that Locke's burn scars were no longer covered, and he wore the scabbard of a knight on his hip. "It looks like you have broken the curse on you," he said.

Locke smiled briefly in response.

"I have been traveling all day, and I could use a safe place to stay for the night."

"Of course."

Erdan led him inside and served him a small dinner of bread and soup before leaving him to rest.

Locke spent a few uneventful hours listening to the buzzing of insects before he finally fell asleep. When morning came, Locke was already partially awake before the sun hit him. The warmth of the dawn's light nearly put him back to sleep, but he fought against it. He dressed and gathered his things, then wandered out to the stable and into the chill air to feed his horse. It would be several days of hard riding through the plains, so he needed to make sure his steed was well fed before they left.

Locke went back inside to warm up and eat his own breakfast after feeding the horse. When he was ready, he bid farewell to the cleric and to the river-falls city of Belcard. He pulled the astromancer compass from around his neck, which hung from a newly repaired chain, and focused his thoughts on the Blackwood Manor.

"Take me home," he said to the compass that was resting in the palm of his hand. The magical eye opened slowly before pointing across the plains of Arbereth, back to where his journey began.

T.J. Harmoning was born in northwest Minnesota, and has lived all along the front range of Colorado. She fell in love with reading fantastical tales of adventure and mystery as a child and has been writing her own stories ever since. She enjoys drawing, cooking, hiking, going to the movies, and playing games with friends. She currently resides in North Carolina with the love of her life.